Up the Hill and Over

by

Isabel Ecclestone Mackay

Up the Hill and Over
by Isabel Ecclestone Mackay

ISBN: 978-93-68090-27-4

Published by

DOUBLE 9 BOOKS

2/13-B, Ansari Road
Daryaganj, New Delhi – 110002
info@double9books.com
www.double9books.com
Tel. 011-40042856

ABOUT THE AUTHOR

Isabel Ecclestone Mackay (1875–1928) was a Canadian poet and novelist recognized for her lyrical and introspective writing. Born in Ontario, she became known for her exploration of themes such as nature, love, and the complexities of the human spirit. Mackay's poetry often reflects a deep appreciation for the natural world, skillfully weaving emotional depth into her verses.

Her notable works include "The House of Windows" (1912), which offers a vivid exploration of personal and societal themes, and "Up the Hill and Over" (1917), a collection of poems that captures the beauty of life's journey. Another significant work, "Mist of Morning" (1919), further showcases her ability to evoke emotion and contemplation through her writing. In addition to her literary contributions, she was involved in social issues of her time, advocating for women's rights and education. Despite her relatively short life, Mackay's work continues to resonate, making her an important figure in early 20th-century Canadian literature.

CONTENTS

The road runs back and the road runs on,
But the air has a scent of clover.
And another day brings another dawn,
When we're up the hill and over.

CHAPTER I

"From Wimbleton to Wombleton is fifteen miles,
From Wombleton to Wimbleton is fifteen miles,
From Wombleton to Wimbleton,
From Wombleton to Wombleton,
From Wombleton—to Wimbleton—is fif—teen miles!"

The cheery singing ended abruptly with the collapse of the singer upon a particularly inviting slope of grass. He was very dusty. He was very hot. The way from Wimbleton to Wombleton seemed suddenly extraordinarily long and tiresome. The slope was green and cool. Just below it slept a cool, green pool, deep, delicious—a swimming pool such as dreams are made of.

If there were no one about—but there was some one about. Further down the slope, and stretched at full length upon it, lay a small boy. Near the small boy lay a packet of school books.

The wayfarer's lips relaxed in an appreciative smile.

"Little boy," he called, somewhat hoarsely on account of the dust in his throat, "little boy, can you tell me how far it is from here to Wimbleton?"

Apparently the little boy was deaf.

The questioner raised his voice, "or if you can oblige me with the exact distance to Wombleton," he went on earnestly, "that will do quite as well."

No answer, civil or otherwise, from the youth by the pool. Only a convulsive wiggle intended to cover the undefended position of the school books.

The traveller's smile broadened but he made no further effort toward sociability. Neither did he go away. To the dismayed eyes, watching through the cover of some long grass, he was clearly a person devoid of all fine feeling. Or perhaps he had never been taught not to stay where he wasn't wanted. Mebby he didn't even know that he *wasn't* wanted.

In order to remove all doubt as to the latter point, the small boy's head shot up suddenly out of the covering grass.

"What d'ye want?" he asked forbiddingly.

"Little boy," said the stranger, "I thank you. I want for nothing."

The head collapsed, but quickly came up again.

"Ain't yeh goin' anywhere?" asked a despairing voice.

"I was going, little boy, but I have stopped."

This was so true that the small boy sat up and scowled.

"I judge," went on the other, "that I am now midway between Arden, otherwise, Wimbleton, and Arcady, sometime known as Wombleton. The question is, which way and how? A simple sum in arithmetic will—little boy, do not frown like that! The wind may change. Smile nicely, and I'll tell you something."

Urged by necessity, the badgered one attempted to look pleasant.

"That's better! Now, my cheerful child, what I really want to know is 'how many miles to Babylon?'"

A reluctant grin showed that the small boy's early education had not been utterly neglected. "Aw, what yeh givin' us?" he protested sheepishly, "if it's Coombe you're lookin' for, it's 'bout a mile and a half down the next holler."

"Holler?" the stranger's tone was faintly questioning. "Oh, I see. You mean 'hollow,' which being interpreted means 'valley,' which means, I fear, another hill. Little boy, do you want to carry a knapsack?"

"Nope."

"No? Strange that nobody seems to want to carry a knapsack. I least of all. Well," lifting the object with disfavour, "good-day to you. I perceive that you grow impatient for those aquatic pleasures for which you have temporarily abjured the more severe delights of scholarship. Little boy, I wish you a very good swim."

"Gee," muttered the small boy, "gee, ain't he the word-slinger!"

He returned to the pool but something of its charm was dissipated. Vague thoughts of school inspectors and retribution troubled its waters. Not that he was at all afraid of school inspectors, or that he really suspected the stranger of being one. Still, discretion is a wise thing and word-slinging is undoubtedly a form of art much used in high scholastic circles. Also there had been a remark about a simple sum in arithmetic which was, to say the least, disquieting. With a bursting sigh, the small sinner scrambled to his feet, reached for the hated books, and disappeared rapidly in the direction of the halls of learning.

Meanwhile the stranger, unconscious of the moral awakening behind him, plodded wearily up the steep and sunny hill. As he is our hero we shall not describe him. There is no hurry, and there will be other occasions upon which he will appear to better advantage. At present let us be content with knowing that there was no reason for the hat and suit he wore save a mistaken idea of artistic suitability. "If I am going to be a tramp," he had said, "I want to look like a tramp." He didn't, but his hat and coat did.

He felt like a tramp, though, if to feel like a tramp is to feel hot and sticky and hungry. Perhaps real tramps do not feel like this. Perhaps they enjoy walking. At any rate they do not carry knapsacks, but betray a touching faith in Providence in the matter of clean linen and tooth brushes.

Before the top of the hill was reached, Dr. Callandar wished devoutly that in this last respect he had behaved like the real thing. In setting out to lead the simple life the ultimate is to be recommended—and knapsacks are not the ultimate. They are heavy things with the property of growing heavier, and prove of little use save to sit upon in damp places. The doctor's feelings in regard to his were intensified by an utter lack of dampness anywhere. The top of the hill was a sun-crowned eminence, blazingly, blisteringly, suffocatingly hot. The valley, spread out beneath him, was soaked in sunshine, a haze of heat quivered visibly above the roofs of the pretty town it cradled. There was a river and there were woods, but the trees hung motionless, and the river wound like a snake of brass among them.

The doctor regarded both the knapsack and the prospect resentfully. He had hoped for a breeze upon the hill-top, and there was no breeze. Raising his hand to remove his hat, he noticed that the hand was trembling, and swore softly. The hand continued to tremble, and holding it out before him he watched it, interestedly, until a powerful will brought the quivering nerves into subjection.

"Jove!" he muttered. "Not a moment too soon—this holiday!"

Then, hat in hand, he started down the hill.

It was a long hill, very long, much longer than it had any need or right to be. It had a twist in its nature which would not allow it to run straight. It meandered; it hesitated; it never knew its own mind, but twisted and turned and thought better of it a dozen times in half a mile. It was a hill with short cuts favourably known to small boys and to tramps with a distaste for highways; but this tramp, not being a real one, knew none of them, and was compelled to do exactly as the hill did. The result was, that when at last it slipped into the cool shade of a row of beeches at its base, its victim was as exhausted as itself.

He was thirsty, too, and, worse still, he knew from a certain dizzy blindness that one of his bad headaches was coming on—and there still lay another mile between him and the town. Pressing his hand against his eyes to restore for the moment their normal clearness of vision, he saw, a short way down the road, a gate; and through the gate and behind some trees, the white gleam of a building. But better than all, he saw, between the gate and the building, a red pump! Then the blindness and pain descended again, and he stumbled on more by faith than by sight; blundering through the half-open gate, his precarious course directed wholly by the pump's exceeding redness, which shone like a beacon fire ahead.

Fortunately, it was a real pump with real water and a sucker in good standing, warranted to need no priming. At the stroke of the red handle the good, cool water gurgled and arose with a delightful "plop!" It splashed from the spout freely upon the face and hands of the victim of the long hill— delicious, life-giving! The delight it brought seemed compensation almost for heat and pain and weariness. Callandar felt that if he could only let its sweetness stream indefinitely over his closed eyes it would wash away the blindness and the ache. Perhaps—

"I am afraid I cannot allow you to use this pump!" said a crisp voice primly. "This is not," with capital letters, "a Public Pump!"

Callandar wiped the surplus water from his face and looked up. There, beside him in the yellow haze of his semi-blindness, stood the owner of the voice. She appeared to be clothed in white, tall and commanding. Surrounded by the luminous mist, her appearance was not unlike that of a cool and capable avenging angel.

"This pump," went on the angel with nice precision, "is not for the use of pedestrians."

"Ah!" said the pedestrian.

"If you will continue down the road," the voice went on, "you will find, when you reach the town, a public pump. You may use that."

The pedestrian, feeling dizzier than ever, sat down upon the pump platform. It was wet and cool.

"The objection to that," he said wisely, "is simple. I cannot continue down the road."

"I should like you to go at once," patiently. "There is a pump—"

The pedestrian raised a deprecating hand.

"Let us admit the pump! Doubtless the pump is there, but there is a pump here also, and a pump in the hand is worth two pumps, an ice-box and a John Collins in town. You doubtless know the situation created by Mahomet and the mountain? This is the same, with a difference. In this case the pump will not come to me and I cannot go to the pump. Therefore we both remain *in statu quo*. Do I make myself plain?"

Apparently he did, for there was no answer. Logic, he concluded, had achieved its usual triumph. The avenging angel had withdrawn. Blissfully he stooped again, closing his eyes to the cool drip of the water, but scarcely had they felt its chill relief when a sharp bark caused them to fly open with disconcerting suddenness—the avenging angel had returned, and with her was an avenging dog! Seen through the mist, the dog appeared to be a bull pup of ferocious aspect.

"I am sorry," the cool voice had no ruth in it, "but it is my duty not to allow tramps upon these grounds. If you will not go, I must ask the dog—"

"ASK the dog!" In spite of his aching head the tramp (now no longer pedestrian) laughed weakly.

"Oh, please don't ask him!" he entreated. "He looks too awfully willing! Besides, I begin to perceive that my presence is not desired. Naturally I scorn to remain."

Very slowly he raised himself from the damp pump platform by means of the red pump-handle. In this manner he achieved an upright position without much difficulty and all might have gone well had he behaved like a proper tramp. But forgetting himself, under the tyranny of training and instinct, he attempted, in deference to the sex of the angel, to raise his hat (which was not on his head anyway). In so doing he released the red pump-handle, lost his balance, struggled wildly to regain it, and then collapsed with a terrible sense of failure and ignominy, right into the open jaws, as it were, of the avenging dog!

CHAPTER II

He had a fancy that something cool and kind was licking his hand....

It felt like the tongue of a friendly dog. He seemed to have been dreaming about dogs. Something soft and cold lay on his head. It felt like a wet handkerchief ... the pain had dulled to a slow throbbing ... if he opened his eyes he would know who licked his hand and what it was that lay upon his head ... on the other hand, opening his eyes might bring back the pain. It seemed hardly worth the risk ... still, he would very much like to know—

Without being able to decide the question, he fell asleep.

When he awoke, his head was clear and the pain was gone. He felt no longer unbearably tired, but only comfortably weary, deliciously drowsy. Had he been at home in his own bed he would have turned over and gone cheerfully to sleep again. As it was, he opened his eyes with a zestful sense of curiosity.

He was lying, very easily, upon soft grass. Above him spread the thick greenery of a giant maple; his head rested upon a cushion and close beside him, with comforting nose thrust into his open palm, lay a ferocious-looking bull pup. The pup grinned with delight at his tentative pat; barked fiercely, and then grinned again as if to say, "Don't mind me, it's only my fun!"

There was a noise somewhere, a loud, cheerful noise—the noise of children playing. Not one child, nor two, but children—lots of them! This was perplexing; and another perplexing thing was the nearness of a white stoop which led up to the door of a white building; neither stoop nor building had he ever seen before. Again the dog barked, loudly, and as if in answer to the bark, the door above the stoop opened and a young girl came out. She cast a casual glance at him as he lay under the tree, and, settling herself daintily upon the white steps, opened a small basket and took from it a serviceable square of white damask and a lettuce sandwich. He could see the lettuce, crisp and green, peeping out at the edges.

At the sight, he was conscious of a strange sensation; an almost forgotten feeling to which, for the moment, he could put no name.

And then, as the girl bit into the sandwich, illumination came. He was *hungry*! But what an unkind, inconsiderate girl!—Another bite and the sandwich would be gone—

"I am awake," he suggested meekly.

"So Buster said." The girl smiled approvingly at the dog. "Good Buster! You may come off guard, sir. Run away and get your lunch."

With a delighted bark for thanks the bull pup trotted away. Callandar's sense of injury deepened. The girl had begun upon a second sandwich. Perhaps there were only two!

"Are you hungry, Mr. Tramp?" asked the girl innocently.

"I think," he said, pausing in order to give his words full weight, "I am starving!" Then, as the blissful meaning of this first feeling of healthy hunger dawned upon him, he added solemnly: "Thank the Lord!"

"Yes?" There was a cool edge of surprise in the girl's voice. She proceeded thoughtfully with the second sandwich.

"Yes. Hunger is a beautiful thing, a priceless possession. Money cannot buy it, skill cannot command it. The price of hunger is far above rubies."

The girl looked down upon him and smiled. It was such a dear little smile that for a moment its recipient forgot about the disappearing sandwich.

"I am so glad," she said warmly, "that you feel like that!"

There was a slight pause. "Because," she went on, finishing the last bite of the second sandwich, "until now I had always thought that hunger wasn't a bit nice. Unless, of course, one has the power to gratify it."

"Fortunately," said Callandar a little stiffly, "I have that power."

The girl raised her eyebrows. They were long and straight and black, and she raised them charmingly. But she was a most unkind and heartless girl, for all that. Never while he lived would he ask her for a sandwich. With a comfortable feeling of security his hand felt for his well-filled pocketbook. It was gone!

"By Jove!"

Stronger ejaculation seemed forbidden by the Presence on the steps. He tapped all his pockets carefully. The pocketbook was in none of them—and he had used the last cent of loose change for a glass of milk for breakfast.

"I suppose," the girl had apparently not noticed his sudden discomfiture, "that you mean you have money? But the nearest place where money would be of use is Coombe, and Coombe is a full mile away. It is a pity that my principles, and the principles of the school-board, should be all against the feeding of tramps. Otherwise I might offer you a sandwich."

"You might," bitterly, "but I doubt it!"

"Even now, putting the school-board aside, I might offer you one if you were to ask prettily and to apologise to me for making rather a fool of me this morning over there by the pump!"

The pump! Why, of course, the pump! It all came back to him now— the pump, the avenging angel! (Had this been the avenging angel?) The avenging dog!—Oh, heaven, was *that* the avenging dog?

He burst into a boyish shout of laughter.

"There are only two sandwiches left," she warned him. The doctor stopped laughing.

"Oh, please!" he said.

There was something very pleasant about him when he used that tone; a persuasive charm, a trace of command. The girl liked it—and passed a sandwich.

"Anyway it was you who took for granted that I was a tramp," he smiled at her. "If I remember rightly I was hardly in a condition to contradict you. Not but that it was a natural conclusion. I am curious to know why you changed your mind."

"Oh! as soon as you fainted I knew. Tramps don't faint!"

"Not ever?"

"Well—hardly ever! And besides—look at your hands!"

The doctor looked, and blushed.

"Dirty?" he ventured.

"Not half dirty enough! And it wasn't only your hands. I noticed—oh! lots of things!" For no perceptible reason a tiny blush fluttered across the whiteness of her face like a roseleaf chased by the wind. The pleasure of watching it made the doctor forget to answer, and the girl went on:

"I know lots more about you than that you aren't a tramp. I know what you are. You are a doctor!" triumphantly.

"A Daniel come to judgment!"

"Yes, a Daniel! Only I wouldn't have been quite so sure if you hadn't dropped this out of your pocket." With a gleeful laugh she held up a clinical thermometer.

The doctor laughed also. "Men have been hanged on less evidence than that," he admitted. "All the same I don't know where it came from. Some one must have judged me capable of wanting to take my own temperature. Anything else?"

"Only general deductions. You are a doctor, you are going to Coombe—deduction, you are the doctor who is going to buy out Dr. Simmonds's practice."

Callandar scrambled up from his pillow with a look of delighted surprise on his face.

"Why—so I am!" he exclaimed.

"You say that as if you had just found it out."

"Well, er—you see I had forgotten it—temporarily. My head, you know."

The suspicion in the girl's eyes melted into sympathy. "I suppose you know," she said with quite a motherly air, "that old Doc. Simmonds hasn't really any practice to sell?"

"No? That's bad. Hasn't he even a little one? You see" (the sympathy had been so pleasant that he felt he could do with a little more of it), "I could hardly manage a big one just now. As you may have noticed, my health is rather rocky. Got to lay up and all that—so it's just as well that old Simpkins' practice is on the ragged edge."

"The name is Simmonds, not Simpkins," coldly.

"Well, I didn't buy the name with the practice. My own name is Callandar. Much nicer, don't you think?"

"I don't know. A well-known name is rather a handicap."

This time the doctor was genuinely surprised.

"A handicap? What do you mean?"

"People will be sure to compare you with your famous namesake, Dr. Callandar, of Montreal. Everyone you meet," with a mischievous smile, "will say, 'Callandar—ah! no relation to Dr. Henry Callandar of Montreal, I suppose?' And then they will look sympathetic and you will want to slap them."

"Dear me! I never thought of that! I had no idea that the Montreal man would be known up here. In the cities, perhaps, but not here."

The girl raised her straight black brows in a way which expressed displeasure at his slighting tone.

"You are mistaken," she said briefly. "I must go now. It is time to ring the bell. The children are running wild."

For the first time the doctor began to take an intelligent interest in his surroundings, and saw that the tree, the white stoop and the small white building were situated in a little, quiet oasis separated by a low fence from the desert of a large yard containing the red pump. On the other side of the fence was pandemonium!

"Why, it's a school!" he exclaimed.

The school-mistress arose, daintily flicking the crumbs from her white piqué skirt.

"District No. 15. The largest attendance of any in the county. I really must ring the bell." She flicked another invisible crumb. "I hope," she added slowly, "that I haven't discouraged you."

"Oh, no! not at all. Quite the contrary. It seems unfortunate about the name, but perhaps I can live it down. It isn't as if I were just out of college, you know.—In fact," as if the thought had just come to him, "do I not seem to you to be a little old for—to be making a fresh start?"

The girl's eyes looked at him very kindly. It was quite evident that she thought she understood the situation perfectly. "I shouldn't worry about that, if I were you," she said. "Young doctors are often no use at all. A great many people *prefer* doctors to be older! I know, you see, for my father was a doctor. He was Dr. Coombe; for many years he was the only doctor here, the only doctor that counted," with a pretty air of pride. "The town was named after his father-I am Esther Coombe."

The doctor acknowledged the introduction with a bow and a quick smile of gratitude.

"You are really very kind, Miss Coombe," he said. "If—if I should take Dr. Spifkin's practice, I hope I may see you sometimes. It is not far from here, is it, to the town—pump?"

Esther laughed. "No, but I do not live out here. I only teach here. We live in town, or almost in. You will pass the house on the way to the hotel. But before you go—" with a gleeful smile she handed him his lost pocketbook—"this fell out of your coat when I pull—helped you under the tree. I should have given it to you before, but I wanted you to understand just how far the blessing of hunger depends upon one's power to gratify it."

They laughed together with a splendid sense of comradeship; then with a startled "I really must ring the bell!" she turned and ran up the steps.

Smilingly he watched her disappear, waiting musingly until a sudden furious ringing told him that school was called.

CHAPTER III

Two sandwiches, an apple, and a glass of water may save a man from starvation, but they do not go far towards satisfying the reviving appetite of a convalescent. Walking with brisk step down the road, Callandar began to imagine the kind of meal he would order—a clear soup, broiled steak, crisp potatoes—a few little simple things like that! He fingered his pocketbook lovingly, glad that, for the first time in some months, he actually wanted something that money could buy.

Now that noon was past, the intense heat of the morning was tempered by a breeze. It was still hot and his footsteps raised little cyclones of dust which flew along the road before him, but the oppression in the air was gone, and walking had ceased to be a weariness. The mile which separated him from Coombe appeared no longer endless, yet so insistent were the demands of his inner man that when a town-going farmer hailed him with the usual offer of a "lift," he accepted the invitation with alacrity.

"Better," he murmured to himself, "the delights of rustic conversation with a good meal at the end thereof than lordly solitude and emptiness withal."

But contrary to expectation the rustic declined to converse. He was a melancholy-looking man with a long jaw and eyes so deep-set that the observer took them on faith, and a nose which alone would have been sufficient to identify him. Beyond the first request to "step up," he vouchsafed no word and, save for an inarticulate gurgle to his horse, seemed lost in an ageless calm. His gaze was fixed upon some indefinite portion of the horse's back and he drove leaning forward in an attitude of complete bodily and mental relaxation. If his guest wished conversation it was apparent that he must set it going himself.

"Very warm day!" said Callandar tentatively.

"So-so." The farmer slapped the reins over the horse's flank, jerked them abruptly and murmured a hoarse "Giddap!" It was his method of encouraging the onward motion of the animal.

"Is it always as warm as this hereabouts?"

"No. Sometimes we get it a little cooler 'bout Christmas."

The doctor flushed with annoyance and then laughed.

"You see," he explained, "I'm new to this part of the country. But I always thought you had it cooler up here."

The manner of the rustic grew more genial.

"Mostly we do," he admitted; "but this here is a hot spell." Another long pause and then he volunteered suddenly: "You can mostly tell by Alviry. When she gets a sunstroke it's purty hot. I'm going for the doctor now."

"Going for the doctor?" Callandar's gaze swept the peaceful figure with incredulous amusement. "Great Scott, man! Why don't you hurry? Can't the horse go any faster?"

"Maybe," resignedly, "but he won't."

"Make him, then! A sunstroke may be a very serious business. Your wife may be dead before you get back."

The deep-set eyes turned to him slowly. There seemed something like a distant sparkle in their depths.

"Don't get to worrying, stranger. It'll take more 'an a sunstroke to polish off Alviry."

"Was she unconscious?"

"Not so as you could notice."

"But if it were a sunstroke—look here, I'll go with you myself. I am a doctor."

"Kind of thought you might be," he responded genially. "Thinking of taking on old Doc. Simmonds's practice?"

"I don't know. But if your wife—"

The rustic shook his head. "No. You wouldn't do for Alviry. She said to get Doc. Parker, and a sunstroke ain't going to change her none. But if she likes your looks she'll probably try you next time. Tumble fond of experiments is Alviry—hi! giddap!" He slapped his horse more forcibly with the loose reins and settled into, mournful silence.

"Going to put up at the Imperial?" he asked after a long and peaceful pause.

"I want to put up somewhere where I can get a good meal and get it quickly."

The mournful Jehu shook his head gloomily.

"You won't get that at the Imperial."

"Where had I better go?"

"There ain't any other place to go—not to speak of."

The doctor let fall a fiery exclamation.

"What say?"

"I said that it must be a queer town."

"I'm a little hard of hearing, now and agin. But I gather you're not a church-going man. It's a great church-going place, is Coombe. Old Doc. Simmonds was a Methody. We were kind of hoping the next one might be a change. There's two churches of Presbyterians and they're tumble folk for hanging together."

The doctor laughed. "Thanks for the tip. I'll remember. Coombe is considered a healthy place, isn't it?"

"Danged healthy."

The commiseration in the other's tone lent to the simple question such an obvious meaning that the doctor hardly knew whether to be amused or annoyed.

"Heavens, man! I'm not an undertaker. I asked because I'm rather rocky myself. That is, partly, why I'm here."

The mournful one nodded. "Good a reason as any," he assented sadly.

"By the way—er—there used to be a Dr. Coombe here, didn't there? Didn't he live somewhere hereabouts?"

The sad one turned his meditative eyes from their focus upon the horse's back and rested them upon the open and guileleas face by his side. Then from deep down in his brawny throat came a sudden sound. It was unmistakably a chuckle. Without the slightest trace of an accompanying smile, the sound was startling.

"What's the matter?" asked the doctor irritably.

"Nothing. Only when anybody's seen Esther, they always start asking about old Doc. Coombe. It gives them a kind of opening. Yes, that's the old Coombe place—over there. The one with the fir trees and the big elm by the gate."

"A pleasant house," said Callandar in a detached voice.

"So-so. The old Doc. uster putter around considerable. But they say his widow isn't doing much to keep it up. Tumble flighty woman, so they say. Young, you know, just about young enough to be the old Doc.'s daughter—"

"But—"

"Oh! Esther ain't her child. Esther's ma died when she was a baby. There is a child, though, Jane they call her, a pindling little thing. But p'r'aps you've met Jane too?"

"I did not say—"

"No, but I thought likely if you'd met one, you'd have met the other. Jane's nearly always hanging around Esther 'cept in school hours. Awful fond of Esther she is. Folks say that Esther's more of a mother to Jane than her own ma. But I dunno. Alviry says it's a shame the way Esther's put upon; all the cares of the house when she had ought to be playing with her dolls. Stepmother with 'bout as much sense as a fly. Old Aunt Amy, nice sort of soul but—" he touched his head significantly and heaved the heaviest sigh yet.

"Do you mean to say that there is an aunt who isn't quite sane?" asked Callandar, surprised.

"*I* don't say so. Some folks does. Alviry says she's a whole lot wiser than some of the rest of us."

From the tone of this remark it was evident that Alviry's observation had been intended personally. Callandar choked back a laugh.

"What say?" asked the other suspiciously.

"I said, rather hard luck for a young girl."

The mournful one nodded and relapsed into melancholy. The doctor turned his attention to the house which a flicker of the whip had pointed out. It was long and low, with wide verandas and a somewhat neglected-looking lawn. At one side an avenue of lilacs curved, and on the other stood a stiff line of fir trees. The front of the house was well shaded by maples and near the gate stood a giant elm-tree, around the trunk of which ran a circular seat. It all looked cool, green and inviting. As the old horse walked sedately past, a woman's figure came out of one of the long windows and flung itself lightly, yet, even at that distance, with a certain suggestion of impatience, into one of the veranda chairs.

"That'll be Mrs. Coombe now," volunteered his informant. "Tumble saucy way she has of flinging herself around—jes' like a young girl! Mebby you can see what sort of dress she's got on. Alviry'll be int'rested to know."

"It's too far off," said Callandar, amused. "All I can see is that the lady is wearing something white."

"Went out of weeds right on the dot, she did! It's not much over a year since the old Doc. died. Esther's still wearing some of her black, but jes' to wear them out, not as symbols. Mrs. Coombe's got a whole new outfit, Alviry says. Turrible extravagant! Folks says it takes Esther all her time paying for them with her school money. But I dunno. What say?"

"I didn't say anything. But, since you ask, do you think all this is any of my business?"

"Well, since you ask, it ain't. 'Tisn't my business either; but it kind of passes the time. Giddap!"

Perhaps the old horse knew he was getting near the end of his journey for, contrary to expectation, he did "giddap" with a jerk which nearly unseated the doctor and caused a flicker of mild surprise to flit across the sad one's face.

"Turrible fast horse, this," he confided, "all you got to do is to get him going."

"Don't let me take you out of your way. If you'll tell me the direction—"

"Sit still, stranger. I'm going right past the Imperial. Hardly any place in Coombe you can go without going past the Imperial. It's what you call a kind of newclus."

As he spoke, the horse, now going at a fairly respectable rate, turned into the main street of the town; a main street, thriftily prosperous but now somewhat a-doze in the sun. Half-way down, the intelligent animal stopped with another jerk for which the doctor was equally ill-prepared. Before them stood a modest red brick building, three stories in height, with a narrow veranda running across the lowest story just one step up from the pavement. On the veranda were green chairs and in the chairs reclined such portion of the male Coombers as could do so without fear and without reproach. Along the top of the veranda was a large sign displaying the words, "HOTEL IMPERIAL."

Callandar alighted nimbly from the democrat, that being the name of the light spring wagon in which he had travelled, and shook his good Samaritan by the hand. "Thank you very much," he said, "and I sincerely hope that the sunstroke will not have terminated fatally by the time you reach home."

The deep-set eyes turned to him slowly and again he fancied a twinkle in their mournfulness. "If it does," said the sad one tranquilly, "it will be the first time it ever has—giddap!"

As no one came forth to take his knapsack, Callandar slung it over his shoulder and entered the hotel. The parting remark of his conductor had left a smile upon his lips, which smile still lingered as he asked the sleepy-looking clerk for a room, and intimated that he would like lunch immediately.

"Dining room closed," said that individual shortly.

"What do you mean?"

"Dining room closes at two; supper at six."

"Do you mean to say that you serve nothing between the hours of two and six?"

"Serve you a drink, if you like," with an understanding grin at his questioner's dusty knapsack.

Forgetting that he had become a Presbyterian, the doctor made a few remarks, and from his manner of making them the clerk awoke to the fact that knapsacks do not a hobo make nor dusty coats a tramp. Now in Canada no one is the superior of any one else, but that did not make a bit of difference in the startling change of demeanour which overtook the clerk. He straightened up. He removed his toothpick. He arranged the register in his best manner and chose another nib for his pen. When Callandar had registered, the clerk was very sorry indeed that the hotel arrangements were rather arbitrary in the matter of meal hours. He was afraid that the kitchen fires were down and everything cold. Still if the gentleman would go to his room, he would see what could be done—

The gentleman went to his room; but in no enviable frame of mind. So wretched was his plight that he was not above valuing the covert sympathy of the small bell-boy who preceded him up the oilclothed stairs. He was a very round boy: round legs, round cheeks, round head and eyes so round that they must have been special eyes made on purpose. There was also a haunting resemblance to some other boy! Callandar taxed his memory, and there stole into it a vision of a pool with willows. He chuckled.

"Boy," he said, "have you a little brother who is very fond of going to school?"

"Nope," said the boy. (It seemed to be a family word.) "I've got a brother, but he don't sound like that."

"You ought to be in school yourself, boy. What's your name?"

"Zerubbabel Burk."

"Is that all?"

"Yep. Bubble for short."

"Have you ever known what it is to be hungry?"

"Three times a day, before meals!"

"Well, I'm starving. Do you belong to the Boy Scouts?"

"Betyerlife."

"Well, look here. I am an army in distress. Commissariat cut off, extinction imminent! Now you go and bring in the provisions. And, as we believe in honourable warfare, pay for everything you get, but take no refusals—see?" He pressed a bill into the boy's ready hand and watched the light of understanding leap into the round eyes with pleasurable anticipation.

"I get you, Mister! Here's your room, number fourteen."

The boy disappeared while still the key with its long tin label was jingling in the lock. The doctor opened the door of room number fourteen and went in.

Rooms, we contend, like people, should be considered in relation to that state in which it has pleased Providence to place them. To consider number fourteen in any environment save its own would be manifestly unfair since, in relation to all the other rooms at the Imperial, number fourteen was a good room, perhaps the very best. A description tempts us, but perhaps its best description is to be found in its effect upon Dr. Callandar. That effect was an immediate determination to depart by the next train, provided the next train did not leave before he had had something to eat.

He was aroused from gloomy musings by a discreet tap announcing the return of the scouting party. The scouting party was piled with parcels up to its round eyes and from the parcels issued an odour so delicious that the doctor's depression vanished.

"Good hunting, eh?"

"Prime, sir. 'Tisn't store stuff, either! As soon as I see that look in your eye I remembered 'bout the tea-fight over at Knox's Church last night and how they'd be sure to be selling off what's left, for the benefit of the heathen." The boy gave the roundest wink Callandar had ever seen and deposited his parcels upon the bed. "They always have 'bout forty times as much's they can use. Course I didn't get you any *broken* vittles," he added, noticing the alarm upon the doctor's face. "It's all as good as the best. Wait till you see!"

He began to clear the wash-stand in a businesslike manner, talking all the time. "This here towel will do for a cloth. It's bran' clean—cross my heart! I borrowed a dish or two offen the church. They know me.... We'll put the chicken in the middle and the ham along at this end and the pie over there where it can't slip off—"

"I don't like pie, boy."

"I do. Pie's good for you. We'll put the beet salad by the chicken and the cabbage salad by the ham and the chow-chow betwixt 'em. Then the choc'late cake can go by the pie—"

"Boy, I don't like chocolate cake."

"Honest? Ah, you're kiddin' me! Really? Choc'late cake's awful good for you. I love chocolate cake. This here cake was made by Esther Coombe's Aunt Amy—it's a sure winner! Say, Mister, what do you like anyway?"

"Ever so many more things than I did yesterday. By Jove, that chicken looks good!"

"Yep. That's Mrs. Hallard's chicken. I thought you'd want the best. She ris' it herself. And made the stuffin' too."

"Did she 'ris' the ham also?"

"Nope. It's Miss Taylor's ham. Home cured. The minister thinks a whole lot of Miss Taylor's curin'. Ma thinks that if Miss Taylor wasn't quite so hombly, minister might ask her jest on account of the ham. You try it— wait a jiffy till I sneak some knives!"

Callandar looked at the decorated wash-stand and felt better. He had forgotten all about the room, and when the knives came, in even less than the promised jiffy, he forgot everything but the varied excellences of the food before him. The chicken was a chicken such as one dreams of. The salads were delicious, the homemade bread and butter fresh and sweet; the ham might well cause feelings of a tender nature towards its curer! The chocolate cake? He thought he might try a small piece and, having tried, was willing to make the attempt on a larger scale. The boy was a most efficient waiter, discerning one's desires before they were expressed. But when they got to the pie, the doctor drew up another chair at the pie side of the table and waved the waiter into it.

There was no false modesty about the boy; neither did he hold malice. If he had felt slightly aggrieved at not having been invited earlier, he forgot it after the first mouthful and for a time there was no further conversation in number fourteen. The doctor had temporarily discarded his theory that it is better to rise from the table feeling slightly hungry. The boy had never had so foolish a theory to discard. The chicken, the ham, the pie, disappeared as if conjured away. The boy grew rounder.

"Boy," said the doctor at last, "hadn't you better stop? You are 'swelling wisibly afore my werry eyes!'"

The boy shook his head, but presently he began to have intervals when he was able to speak.

"Better plant all you can," he advised. "Ma says the grub here would kill a cat. I eat at home. Ma wouldn't risk my stomach here. It's fierce."

"But I'll have to eat, boy. Isn't there another hotel?"

"Yep; two. But you couldn't go to them. This here's the only decent one. Gave you a nice room anyway." He looked around admiringly. "Going to stay long?"

"No—that is, yes—I don't know! How can I stay if I can't eat?"

The boy picked his round white teeth thoughtfully with a pin.

"You might get board somewheres."

This was a new idea.

"Why—so I might! Does Mrs. Hallard who raises chickens or Miss What's-her-name who cures ham, keep boarders?"

"Nope. But they're not the only oysters in the soup—There's the bell!" They never give a man a minute's peace. Say, if you don't really like that pie, don't waste it—see? Tell you about boarding-houses later."

Callandar had to clear the table himself. This he did by the simple expedient of putting everything on top of everything else. But he did not waste anything, a precaution whose value he realised that night upon returning from the dining room where he had spent some time in looking at that repast known to the Imperial as supper. Bubble, the bell boy, found him with his mind made up.

"Boy," he said, "you have saved my life. But I fear I can sojourn no longer in your delightful town. Find me the first train out in the morning.".

The boy's face fell.

"Ain't you going to stay? Why, it's all over town that you're the new doctor come to take old Doc. Simmonds's practice. Mournful Mark, that you drove up with, told it. He said he shouldn't wonder if you're real clever. Says he suspects you're an old friend of Doc. Coombe's folks—went to college with the doctor, mebby. Says that likely Alviry will have you next time she gets a stroke."

"Tempting as the prospect is, boy, I fear ..."

"Oh, dang it! There's the bell again."

He darted out, bumped down the sounding stairs and, while the doctor was still considering the words of his ultimatum, appeared again at the door, this time decorously on duty.

"A call for you, sir," said Bubble primly.

"A—what?"

"A call, sir. Mrs. Sykes wants to know if the new doctor will call 'round first thing in the morning to see Mrs. Sykes's Ann. She dunno, but she thinks it's smallpox."

"Quit your fooling, boy."

"Cross my heart, doctor!"

"Smallpox?"

"Oh!" cheerfully, "I don't cross my heart to that. Mrs. Sykes always thinks things is smallpox. Ann's had smallpox several times now. But the rest is on the level. What message, sir?"

Callandar hesitated. (And while he hesitated the Fateful Sisters manipulated a great many threads very swiftly.) "What train ..." he began. (The Fateful Sisters slipped a bobbin through and tied a cunning knot.) Without knowing why, Callandar decided to stay. He laughed. Bubble stood eagerly expectant.

"Tell Mrs. Sykes I'll come, and ..." but Bubble did not wait for the end of the message.

CHAPTER IV

Coombe is a pretty place. It has broad streets, quiet and tree-lined. It has sunny, empty lots where children play. No one is crowded or shut in. The houses stand in their own green lawns, and are comfortable and even picturesque. The Swiss chalet style has not yet come to Coombe, so the architecture, though plain, is not productive of nightmare. The roads are like country roads, soft and yellowish; green grass grows along the sides of many of them, and board sidewalks are still to be found, springy and easy to the tread. There is a main street with macadamised roadway and stone pavements, real flat stone, for they were laid before the appearance of the all-conquering cement. There is a postoffice with a tower and a clock, a courthouse with a fountain and a cannon, a park with a bandstand and a baseball diamond, a townhall with a belfry and no bell, an exhaustive array of churches, the Imperial Hotel, and the market. We mention the market last (as we were taught at school) because on account of its importance it ought to come first.

When Dr. Callandar, having been efficiently valeted by Bubble, set out to pay his first professional call, he drew in deep breaths of the pleasant air with a feeling of well-being to which he had long been a stranger. He had slept. In spite of the room, in spite of the chocolate cake, in spite of the pie, he had slept. And that alone was enough to make the whole world over. It was still hot but with a heat different from the heat of yesterday. A little shower had fallen during the night. There was a sense of the north in the air, a light freshness, very invigorating. He liked the quiet shaded streets; the cannon by the courthouse amused him; the number of church steeples left him amazed. He felt as if he had stumbled into a dream-town and must walk carefully lest he stumble out.

Bubble had given him very complete directions, indeed so minute were they that we will omit them lest some day you find the way yourself and drop in on Mrs. Sykes when she is not expecting company. But Dr. Callandar in his amused absorption had forgotten that he was going to Mrs. Sykes at all, when he was recalled to a sense of duty by a sharp hail from the corner house of a street he had just passed. Looking back, he saw, half-way down the road, a tall, red woman leaning over a gate, who, upon attracting his attention, began waving her arms frantically, after the manner of an old-fashioned signalman inviting a train to "Come on." Callandar's step quickened in spite of himself and he forgot his idle musings.

"Land sakes! I thought you'd never get here!" exclaimed the red woman fervently. "I suppose that imp of a boy didn't direct you right. Lucky I knew you as soon as you passed the corner. Mark Morrison may be as useless as they make 'em, but he's got a fine gift for description. Come right in. I'm dreadful anxious about Ann. It don't seem like measles, and she's had chicken-pox twice, and if she's sickening for anything worse I want to know it. I ain't one of them optimists that won't believe they're sick till they're dead. Callandar's your name, Mark says—any chance of your being a cousin to Dr. Callandar of Montreal that cured Mrs. Sowerby?"

"No, I am not that Dr. Callandar's cousin."

"I told Mark 'twasn't likely—or you wouldn't be here. Not if he'd any family feeling. I'm a great believer in a man making his own stepping-stones anyway," she went on with a friendly smile; "we ought to rise up on ourselves, like the poet says, and not on our cousins."

"A noble sentiment," said Callandar gravely, as he followed her up the walk, across a veranda so clean that one hesitated to step on it, and into a small hall, bare and spotless, where he was invited to hang up his hat.

"You're younger than I expected," went on Mrs. Sykes kindly. "I hope you ain't entirely dependent on your practice in Coombe?"

The amazed doctor was understood to murmur something about "private means."

"That's good. You'd starve if you hadn't. Coombe's a terrible healthy place and poor Doc. Simmonds didn't pay a call a week. I just felt like some one ought to warn you. I despise folks who hold back from telling things because they ain't quite pleasant. Know the worst, I always say; it's better in the end. Of course, as Mark says, your being a Presbyterian will make considerable diff'rence. Some folks thought Doc. Simmonds was pretty nigh an infiddle!"

Too overcome by his feelings to answer, Callandar followed her up the narrow stair and into a clean bright room with green-tinted walls and yellow matting on the floor.

Mrs. Sykes waved a deprecatory hand, at once exhibiting and apologising for so much splendour.

"This is the spare-room," she explained. "And there," pointing to the high, old-fashioned bed, "is Ann."

Callandar crossed the immaculate matting gingerly, taking Ann on faith, as it were, for, from the door, no; Ann was visible, only a very small dent in the big whiteness of the bed.

"Ann! Here's the doctor!"

A small black head and a pair of frightened black eyes appeared for a moment as if by conjuration, and instantly vanished.

"Ann!" said Mrs. Sykes more sternly.

There was a squirming somewhere under the bedclothes, but nothing happened.

"Great Scott!" exclaimed the doctor, "you've got the child in a feather-bed!"

Mrs. Sykes beamed complacently.

"Yes, I have. It may seem like taking a lot of trouble for nothing, but you never can tell. I ain't one of them that never prepares for anything. Jest as soon as Ann gets sick I move her right into the spare-room and put her into the best feathers. Then if she should be took sudden I wouldn't have anything to regret. The minister and the doctor can come in here any hour and find things as I could wish.... Ann! what do you mean by wiggling down like that? Ann—come up at once! The doctor wants to see your tongue."

This time the note of command was effective. The black head came to the surface, again followed by the frightened eyes and plump little cheeks stained with feverish red.

"Some cool water, if you please," ordered the doctor in his best professional manner. Mrs. Sykes opened her lips to ask why, but something caused her to shut them without asking.

When she had left the room, Callandar leaned suddenly over and lifted Ann bodily out of the dent and placed her firmly upon a pillow. It was a very plump pillow, evidently filled with the "best feathers," but compared with the bed it was as a rock in an ocean.

"Now," he said gravely, "you are safe, for the present. You are on an island; but be very careful not to slide off for if you do I may never be able to look at your tongue."

The child's hands grasped the island convulsively.

"Don't hold on like that," he warned. "You might tip." He leaned close so that she might see the smile in his eyes, "And if you tipped ..."

The child gave a sudden delighted giggle. "I'd go right in over my head, wouldn't I?"

"Yes. And next time you were rescued you might feel more inclined to tell your aunt what you had been eating before you became ill."

Ann stopped giggling.

"You don't need to tell *me*," went on the doctor, "because I know!"

"How d'ye know?"

"Magic. Be careful—you were nearly off that time! Does your aunt know anything about those things you ate?"

"No."

"Very well. But you must promise not to eat those particular things again. Not even when you get the chance." Then as he saw the woe upon her face, "At least, not in quantities!"

"Cross my heart!" said Ann, relieved.

"Here's the water," said Mrs. Sykes, returning. "Ann, get right back into bed. Do you want to get your death? Haven't I told you till I'm tired to keep your hands in? Is it measles, Doctor? She's subject to measles. Perhaps it's the beginning of scarlet fever. But if it's smallpox I want to know. No good ever comes of smoothing things over."

The doctor smiled at Ann.

"It isn't smallpox this time, Mrs. Sykes."

"Did you look at them spots on the back of her neck?"

"Yes. A little rash caused by indigestion. I wouldn't worry."

"Don't mind me. I'm used to worrying. I don't dodge my troubles like some I know. Indigestion? It looks more like eczema. Eczema is a terrible trying thing. But if the child's got it I don't want it called indigestion to spare my feelings."

"But it's not eczema! It's indigestion—and prickly heat. I'm afraid Ann's stomach has been giving trouble. It has been hotter than is usual here, I understand. Heat often upsets children. While I write out a prescription, you might bathe her face and hands."

Mrs. Sykes gazed doubtfully at the water. "She was done once last night and once this morning just before you came in," she remarked in an injured tone. "But if you think she needs it again, this sort of water's no good. Nothing's ever any good for Ann except hot water and soap."

The doctor looked up from his writing in surprise. Then as the meaning of the thing dawned upon him, he laughed heartily.

"Oh, Ann's as clean as the veranda floor!" he explained. "This is just to cool her off. Let me show you—doesn't that feel nice, Ann?"

"Lovely!" blissfully.

Mrs. Sykes sniffed.

"I suppose that's some new-fangled notion? I never heard before of cooling people off when they've got a fever. In my time, the hotter you were, the hotter you were made to be, till you got cool naturally. I suppose," with half-interested sarcasm, "that you'd give her cold water to drink if she asked for it?"

"Certainly."

"Well, I expect she knows better than to ask for it!"

Feeling Ann's imploring gaze, Callandar resorted to diplomacy.

"The fact is, Mrs. Sykes," he said pleasantly, "there really isn't very much wrong with Ann. You have been letting your forethought and your natural anxiety run away with you. There is not the slightest occasion for alarm. If there were, I should not dream of hiding it from one so well-prepared as yourself. As it is, you have taken a lot of needless trouble—this beautiful feather-bed, for example! I feel sure that Ann would do very well in her own bed."

The victim of the feathers gave a relieved gasp which her aunt mistook for a sigh of regret.

"Her own bed's well enough for anything ordinary," she admitted in a mollified tone. "Even if it is a store mattress."

"Quite good enough. Many a little girl would be glad of it." The doctor's tone was virtuous. "If you will allow me, I shall carry her in now. You see, she is cooler already. By to-morrow, if she takes her medicine, she ought to be as well as ever."

Ann's own room turned out to be on the shady side, and though not so grand as the spare-room, it was pleasantly cool. The little bed with the hard mattress and the snowy counterpane was infinitely to be preferred to the ocean of feathers, and the rescued maiden lay back on her smaller pillows with a sigh of gratitude.

"Sure you won't tell?" she whispered as he laid her down.

"Honour bright. Cross my heart! But you must take the medicine. It's nasty, but not too nasty, and you mustn't squeal—or it will be the spare-room again. Red cheeks and prickly heat are consequences, but feather-beds and medicine are retribution."

"That's right, Doctor," said Mrs. Sykes, who had heard the last words. "There's nothing like a word about retribution when a person's sick. It helps 'em to realise their state. I don't hold with the light-minded that want to get away from retribution. Depend upon it, they're the very folks that's got it coming to them. Yes. No one needs to go around denying that there's a hell, if their feet are planted upon a rock and they know they're never going there. It's years now since I've looked hell in the face and turned my feet the other way. But I do say that if I'd decided to go straight ahead in the broad and easy path, I wouldn't try to shut my eyes to the end of it, like some folks! Are you putting up at the Imperial, Doctor?"

"'Putting up' exactly expresses my condition."

"Well, you may as well know at once that a doctor in a hotel will never get any forwarder in Coombe. You'll have to get boarding somewhere. Have you looked around yet?"

"No. I—"

"Then I don't mind telling you that the spare-room is to let and the little room down below that has a door of its own and seems made exactly for a doctor's office. I shouldn't mind letting you have them if you feel sure that the smells wouldn't get loose all through the house and in the cooking. There's a barn where you could keep your horse."

"I haven't got a horse," protested Callandar feebly.

"But of course you'll be getting one. A doctor has to have a horse. If you can't pay for it down, Mark knows some one who'd let you have a good one on time. You can trust Mark, if he *is* mournful. Of course I don't say that these rooms are the only rooms to let in Coombe, but I do think they're about as good as you can get—being so near to Dr. Coombe's old house. People get used to coming for a doctor down this street."

"But that was, over a year ago."

"It takes more 'an a year for Coombe folks to change their ways. Only this day week I saw Bill Brooks tearing down this way on account of Mrs. Brooks' being took kind of unexpected, and Bill losing his head and forgetting all about Dr. Coombe being dead and Dr. Parker living on the other side of the town."

"And you think that if I'd been here he would have 'tore' in here?"

"If he hadn't I'd just have called out to him as he went by. He was that wild he'd have taken anybody."

"I see," with humility. "I lost a good chance there!"

"Well, if you live here you'll get others. Why, from the spare-room windows you can see the corner window down at the Coombe place. I could make out to let you have your meals, too. Only I'd expect you to be as reg'lar as Providence permitted. I know a doctor is bound to be more aggravating in that way than other folks, but if you'd be as regular as lay in you, I'd put up with it. 'Tisn't as if I wasn't always prepared. When will you want to move in?"

"Really, I—I don't know—" The bewildered Callandar glanced for help to Ann, but met only clasped hands and an imploring stare. "I'll—I'll let you know," he faltered.

Thinking it over afterwards, he could never understand why he did not promptly refuse to be coerced, but at the time surrender seemed the only natural thing. Besides, he couldn't stay another day at the Imperial. He had to go somewhere. Perhaps it was his destiny to secure Ann against further feather-beds. Anyway, he accepted it.

"Oh, goody!" cried Ann, clapping her hands.

"Ann! put your hands under those clothes. How often must I tell you that you'll get your death? If you like, Doctor, there's nothing to prevent your moving in to-morrow. I'll need a day to air the feather-tick and make some pie."

The doctor was at last roused to action.

"There are conditions," he said hastily. "If I come here, there is to be no feather-tick and no pie!"

"No feather-bed?" in amazement.

"No pie?" Ann's voice was a sorrowful whisper.

"You see," Callandar explained, "I am here partly for my health. My health cannot lie on feather-beds nor eat pie—well, perhaps," with a glance at Ann, "an occasional pie may do no harm. But I shall send down some springs and a mattress. I have to use a special kind," hastily.

"Oh! it's spinal trouble, is it?" Mrs. Sykes surveyed him commiseratingly. "You look straight enough. But land! You never can tell. Them spinal troubles are most deceiving. Terrible things they are, but they don't shorten life as quickly as some others. Not that that's a blessing! Mostly, folks as has them would be glad to go long before they are took. Still, it gives them some time to be prepared. I remember—"

"I must go now, Mrs. Sykes. Give Ann some of the medicine as soon as it comes. It isn't exactly spinal trouble that is the matter with me, you know, but—er—I'll send down the kind of mattress I like. In fact, I shall probably wish to furnish my rooms myself. You won't mind, I'm sure."

"Land sakes, no, I don't mind! Most doctors are finicky. Don't worry about the medicine. I'll see that Ann takes it."

She watched him go with a glance in which satisfaction and foreboding mingled. "Poor young feller!" she mused. "He didn't like what I said about his spine a mite. Back troubles makes folks terrible touchy."

CHAPTER V

Two days after the installation of what Mrs. Sykes persisted in calling the "spinal mattress," Esther Coombe was late in getting home from school. As was usually the case when this happened, Jane, designated by mournful Mark as "the Pindling One," was sitting on the gatepost gazing disconsolately down the road. There were traces of tears upon her thin little face and the warmth of the hug which returned her sister's greeting was evidence of an unusually disturbed mind.

"Why aren't you playing with the other children, Jane?"

"I don't want to play, Esther. Timothy's dead."

"Yes, I know, dear. But Fred has promised you a new puppy—"

"I don't want a new puppy. I want Timothy."

"But Timothy is so much happier, Jane. He was old, you know. In the Happy Hunting Grounds, he will be able to frisk about just like other dogs. Wouldn't you like an apple?"

Jane considered this a moment and decided favourably. But her tale of woe was not yet complete. "Mother's ill again," she announced gloomily. "I mustn't play band or nail the slats on the rabbits' hutch. Aunt Amy gave me my dinner on the back porch. I liked that. I wouldn't go in the house, not till you came, Esther."

The straight brows of the elder sister came together in a worried frown.

"You know that is being silly, Jane."

"I don't care."

"You must learn to care. Run now and get the apple and ask Aunt Amy to wash your face."

Jane tripped away obediently, her griefs assuaged by the mere telling of them, and Esther passed into the house by way of the veranda. It was a charming veranda, long and low, opening through French windows directly into the living room which, like itself, was long and low, and charming. There is a charm in rooms which can be felt but not described. It exists apart from the furnishings and even the occupants; it is an essence, haunting, intangible—the soul of the room! only there are many rooms which have no soul.

Through the living room at the Elms vagrant breezes entered, loitered, and drifted out again, leaving behind them scents of sun-warmed flowers. The light there was soft and green. The comfortable chairs invited rest; the polished rosewood table, the bright piano shining in the brightest corner, the smooth old floor in whose rug the colours had long ceased to trouble, the general air of much used comfort, satisfied and refreshed.

Esther loved the room. Her first childish memory was of the rosewood table shining like a pool in the lamplight and of her own wondering face reflected in it, with her father's laughing eyes behind. In every way it was associated with the beginnings of things. The magic of all music began for her in the sweet, thin notes of the old square piano; the key to fairy land lay hidden somewhere in that shelf of well-worn books.

Yet to-night she entered with a hesitating step. It was obvious that she felt no pleasure in the cool greenness. The room was the same room but it was as if the expression on a well-known face had unaccountably changed and become forbidding. The girl sighed as she flung her hat upon a chair.

"Esther," Jane's voice, somewhat obscured by the eating of the promised apple, came through the open window, "are you sure about Timothy being in the Happy Hunting Grounds?"

"Of course, dear."

"But he wasn't what you would call a Christian, Esther?"

"He was a good dog."

"Can Timothy chase chickens there?"

"Probably."

"And cats?"

"Certainly cats."

"Is that what happens to bad cats when they die?"

Esther viewed this logical picture of everlastingly pursued cats with some dismay.

"N-o. I don't suppose it would be real cats."

"But Tim wouldn't chase anything but real cats."

"Jane, I wish you wouldn't talk with your mouth full."

Being thus reduced to giving up the argument or the apple, Jane abandoned the former. It was clear that Esther was not in the mood for argument. The child's quick observation had not failed to note the lagging step, nor the quick sigh. She nodded her head as if in answer to some spoken word.

"Yes, I know. I feel like that, too. That's why I didn't come in before; that's why I'm not really in yet. It catches you by the throat and makes you breathe funny. What is it, Esther?"

"Why—I don't know, Jane. It's loneliness I think—missing Dad."

The child shook her head. But whatever her objection might have been it was beyond her power of expression. She slid off the veranda step and wandered back into the garden. There was another apple in the pocket of her apron, and apples are great comforters.

Left alone, Esther with a resolutely cheerful air took down a blue bowl and proceeded to arrange therein the day's floral offerings. A sweet and crushed mixture they were, pansies, clove-pinks, mignonette, bleeding hearts, bachelors' buttons, all short stemmed and minus any saving touch of green, but true love offerings for all that. Wordless gifts most of them, prim little bunches, hot from tight clasping in chubby hands, shyly and swiftly deposited on "Teacher's desk" when the back of that divinity was turned. The blue bowl took kindly to them all, and as the girl's clever fingers settled and arranged the glowing chaos it seemed that with their crushed fragrance something of the lost spirit of the room came back. Just so had she arranged hundreds of times the sweet smelling miscellanies which had been her father's constant tribute from grateful patients.

She had almost finished when the door opened to admit a little, grey wisp of a woman with a mild white face and large faded eyes which might once have been beautiful. She was dressed entirely in lavender, a fondness for this colour being one of the many harmless fancies born of a brain not quite normal. The rather expressionless face brightened at sight of the girl by the table.

"Why, Esther—I didn't hear you come in. Have you put a mat under the bowl? See now! You have marked the table."

Esther good humouredly reached for a table-mat, for the polish of this particular article of furniture was the pride of Aunt Amy's life. "It's all right, Auntie. It's not really a mark. Look, aren't they sweet? It is like one of father's posies. Is mother any better?"

"The children must think a lot of you, Esther!"

"Yes, although I think they would bring flowers to any one, bless 'em! Is mother—"

"Your mother hasn't been down all day. I went up with her dinner but she didn't take any. She wouldn't answer."

"Auntie, don't you think she ought to do something about these headaches?"

"I don't know, Esther. She'll be all right to-morrow. She always is."

"Yes. But they are getting more frequent, and you know—she is so different. She can't be well. Haven't you noticed it?"

"No," vaguely.

"Well, Jane has. So it can't just be imagination. She ought to consult a doctor."

"She won't."

"But it's absurd! What shall we do if she goes on like this? If there were only some one who would talk to her! She won't listen to me because she is older and married and—all that. All the same she doesn't seem older when she acts like this—like a child!"

"Well, you know, Esther, there isn't any doctor here that your mother just fancies."

The girl stooped lower over the blue bowl, perhaps to hide the little smile which crinkled up the corner of her mouth. The faint colour on her cheek may have been a reflection from the flowers.

"Yes, but haven't you heard? There is a new doctor. He seems quite different—I mean they say he is awfully nice. Mrs. Sykes' Ann was telling me all about him. He is going to board with Mrs. Sykes. The child just worships him already. Perhaps mother might see him."

"I shouldn't worry," said Aunt Amy placidly. "This pepper-grass will be very nice for tea. Did you tell Jane she might have two apples, Esther?"

"No. I told her she might have one. But I don't suppose two will hurt her." Esther was used to Aunt Amy's inconsequences which made impossible the discussion of any subjects save the most trivial. But she sighed a little as she realised anew that there was no help here.

"Jane is feeling badly about Timothy," she explained. "Don't you think we might have tea in here, Auntie? It is so cool."

Aunt Amy, who had been anxiously rubbing an imaginary spot on the table, looked up with a startled air. "Oh, Esther!" she said, in the voice of a frightened child. Then with a child's obvious effort to control rising tears, "Of course, if you say so, Esther. But—but do you feel like risking the round table? Couldn't we have it on the little table in the corner?"

The girl settled the last of her flowers and pushed back her hair with a worried gesture. A pang of mingled irritation and anxiety lent an edge of sharpness to her soft voice.

"Auntie dear! I thought you had quite forgotten that fancy. You know it is only a fancy. Round tables are just like other tables. And you promised me—"

"Yes, I know, but—"

"Well, then, be sensible, dear. We shall have tea in here." Then seeing the real distress on the timid old face, the girl's mood softened. "No, we shan't," she declared gaily. "We'll have it as usual in the dining room. You will fix the pepper-grass and I shall set the table."

But the end of Aunt Amy's vagaries was not yet. She hesitated, flushed and more timidly, yet as one who is compelled, begged for the task of setting the table herself. "For you know, Esther, the sprigged tea-set is so hurt if any one but me arranges it. Yes, of course, it is only a fancy, I know that. But the sprigged tea-set does feel so badly if I neglect it. All the pink in it fades quite out. You must have noticed it, Esther?"

The girl sighed and gave in. Usually Aunt Amy's vagaries troubled her little. Disconcerting at first, they had quickly become a commonplace, for the coming of Aunt Amy to the doctor's household had been too great a blessing to invite criticism. Esther had soon learned to express no surprise when told that the sprigged china had a heart of extreme sensitiveness, and that the third step on the front stair disliked to be trodden upon, and that it was dangerous to sit with one's back to a window facing the east. All these and numberless other strange facts were part of Aunt Amy's twilight world. To her they were immensely important, but to the family the really important thing seemed that, with trifling exceptions, the new inmate of the household was gentle and kind; her housekeeping a miracle and her cooking a dream. In the years she had lived with them there had been but one serious thrill of anxiety, and that came when Dr. Coombe had discovered her endeavouring to infect Jane with her delusions. This had been strictly forbidden and the child's mind, duly warned, was soon safeguarded by her own growing comprehension. Jane quickly understood that it was foolish to shut the garden gate three times every time she came through it, and that no one save Aunt Amy thought it necessary to count all the boards in the sidewalk or to touch all the little posts under the balustrade as one came down stairs. Some of the prettier, more elusive fancies she may have retained, but, if so, they did her no harm.

As for Aunt Amy herself, she lived her shadow-haunted life not unhappily. Dr. Coombe she had worshipped, yet his death had not affected her as much as might have been feared. Perhaps it was one of her compensations that death to her was not quite what it is to the more normal consciousness. It was noticeable that she always spoke of the doctor as if he were in the next room. Her devotion to him had been caused by his success in partially relieving her of the most distressing burden of her disordered brain—the delusion of persecution. Aunt Amy knew that somewhere there existed a mysterious power known vaguely as "They" who sought unceasingly to injure her. Of course it was only once in a while that "They" got a chance, for Aunt Amy was very clever in providing no opportunities. More than once had she outwitted "Them." Still, one must be always upon one's guard! From this harrowing delusion the doctor had done much to deliver her, indeed she had become more normal in every way under his care. It was only now, a year after his death, that Esther imagined sometimes that there was a slipping back—

The ill effects of sitting at a round table, for instance? It was a long time since this particular fancy had been spoken of and Esther had considered it gone altogether. Yet here it was, cropping out again and just at a time when other problems threatened. Things seemed determined to be difficult to-day.

The fact was that Esther was suffering from the need of a confidant. Really worried as she felt about her step-mother's health, the burden of taking any determined action against the wishes of the patient herself was a serious one for a young girl. Yet in whom could she confide? Girl friends she had in plenty but not one whose judgment she could trust before her own. Had the minister been an older man or a man of different calibre she might have gone to him, but the idea of appealing to Mr. Macnair was distasteful. Neither among her father's friends was there one to whom she cared to go for advice concerning her father's widow. They had one and all disapproved, she knew, of the sudden second marriage and Dr. Coombe had never quite forgiven their disapproval.

Often she felt like refusing the responsibility altogether. After all, her step-mother was a woman quite old enough to manage her own affairs. If she wished to foolishly imperil her health why need Esther care? Why indeed? But this train of reasoning never lasted long. Always there came a counter-question, "If you do not care, who will?" And the dearth of any answer settled the burden more firmly upon her rebellious shoulders. For one thing there was always the inner knowledge that Mary Coombe was weak and that she, Esther, was strong. She had always known this. Even when her father had brought home his pretty bride and Esther, a shy, silent child of eleven, had welcomed her, she had known that the newcomer was the weaker spirit. The bride had known it too. She had never attempted to control Esther, leaving the child entirely to her father—a bit of unwitting wisdom which did much to smooth daily life at the Elms. If the doctor saw his wife's weakness of character it is probable that it did not interfere with his love for her. Why need she be strong while he was strong enough for two? But he had forgotten one thing—the day when she would have to be strong alone!

The realisation came to him upon his death-bed. Esther was sure of this. He could not speak, but she had read the message of his eyes, the appeal to the strength in her to help the other's weakness. No getting away from the solemn charge of that entreating look!

Esther was thinking of that look now, as she sat alone in the dusk of the veranda. Tea was over and Aunt Amy was putting Jane to bed. From her mother she had had no word. Blank silence had met her when she had taken the tea tray upstairs and called softly through the closed door. Mrs. Coombe was probably asleep. She would be better to-morrow; but before long she would be ill again, and the interval between the attacks was becoming shorter.

There was anger as well as anxiety in the girl's mind. Her healthy and straightforward youth had little patience with her step-mother's unreasonable caprices. For her illness she had every sympathy, but for the morbid nervousness which seemed to accompany it, none at all. These constant headaches, the increasing nervous irritability from which Mrs. Coombe suffered lay like a shadow over the house. Yet the sufferer refused to take the obvious way of relief and persisted in her refusal with a stubbornness of which no one would have dreamed her light nature capable. Still, willing or unwilling, something must be done. Aunt Amy, too, was becoming more of an anxiety. Once or twice lately she had spoken of "Them," a sign of mental distress which Dr. Coombe had always treated with the utmost seriousness. Perhaps if a doctor were called in for Aunt Amy, Mrs. Coombe would lose her foolish dread of doctors and allow him to prescribe for her also. And if the new doctor were half as clever as Mrs. Sykes said he was—Esther's heart began to warm a little as her fancy pictured such a pleasant solution of all her problems. The little smile curved her lips again as she thought of the maple by the schoolhouse steps, and the lettuce sandwiches and—and everything. She closed her eyes and tried to recall his face as he had looked up at her. Instinctively she knew it for a good face, strong, humorous, kindly, but strong above all. And it was strength that Esther needed. When she went to bed that night her burden seemed a little lighter.

I believe he can help me, she thought, and it isn't as if he were quite a stranger. After all, we had lunch together once!

CHAPTER VI

Undoubtedly Esther slept better that night for the thought of the new doctor. It cannot be said that the doctor slept better because of her. In fact he lay awake thinking of her. He did not want to think of her; he wanted to go to sleep. Twice only had he seen her. Once upon the occasion of the red pump and once when casually passing her on the main street. There was no reason why her white-rose face with its strange blue eyes and its smile-curved lips should float about in the darkness of Mrs. Sykes' best room. Yet there it was. It was the eyes, perhaps. The doctor admitted that they were peculiar eyes, startlingly blue. Dark blue in the shade of the lashes, flashing out light blue fire when the lashes lifted. But Mrs. Sykes' boarder did not want to think about eyes. He wanted to go to sleep. He did not want to think about hair either. Although Miss Coombe had very nice hair—cloudy hair, with little ways of growing about the temple and at the curve of the neck which a blind man could not help noticing. In the peaceful shadows of the room it seemed a still softer shadow framing the vivid girlish face.

Still, on the whole, sleep would have been better company and when at last he did drop off he did not relish being wakened by the voice of Ann at his door.

"Doc-ter, doc-ter! Are you awake? Can I come in?"

"I am not awake. Go away."

Ann's giggle came clearly through the keyhole.

"You've got a visitor," she whispered piercingly through the same medium. "A man. A well man, not a sick one. He came on the train. He came on the milk train—"

"You may come in, Ann." The doctor slipped on his dressing gown with a resigned sigh. "What man and why milk?"

"I don't know. Aunt Sykes kept him on the veranda till she was sure he wasn't an agent. Now he's in the parlour. Aunt hopes you'll hurry, for you never can tell. He may be different from what he looks."

"What does he look?"

Ann's small hands made an expressive gesture which seemed to envisage something long and lean.

"Queer—like that. He's not old, but he's bald. His eyes screw into you. His nose," another formative gesture, "is like that. A nawful big nose. He didn't tell his name."

"If he looks like that, perhaps he hasn't any name. Perhaps he is a button-moulder. In fact I'm almost certain he is—other name Willits. Occupation, professor."

"But if he is a button-maker, he can't be a professor," said Ann shrewdly.

"Oh, yes he can. Button-moulding is what he professes. His line is a specialty in spoiled buttons. He makes them over."

"Second-hand?"

"Better than new."

Ann fidgeted idly with the doctor's cuff-links and then with a flash of her odd childish comprehension, "You love him a lot, don't you?" she said jealously.

The doctor adjusted a collar button.

"England expects that every man shall deny the charge of loving another," he said, "but between you and me, I do rather like old Willits. You see I was rather a worn-out button once and he made me over. Where did you say he was?"

"In the parlour—there's Aunt! She said I wasn't to stay. I'll get it."

Indeed the voice of Mrs. Sykes could be heard on the stairs.

"Ann! Where's that child? Doctor, you'd think that child had never been taught no manners. You'll have to take a firm stand with Ann, Doctor. Land Sakes, I don't want to make her out worse'n she is, but you might as well know that your life won't be worth living if you don't set on Ann."

"All right, Mrs. Sykes. Painful as it may be, I shall do it. Are you sure it's safe to leave a stranger in the parlour?"

Mrs. Sykes looked worried. "I hope to goodness it's all right, Doctor. He's been in the parlour half an hour. I don't think he's an agent, hasn't got a case or a book anywhere. But agents are getting cuter every day. Naturally I didn't like to go so far as to ask his name. And I'm not asking it now. Curiosity was never a fault of mine though I do say it. Still a woman does like to know who's setting in her front parlour."

"And you shall," declared Callandar kindly. "Just hang on a few moments longer, dear Mrs. Sykes, and your non-existent but very justifiable curiosity shall be satisfied."

The parlour at Mrs. Sykes opened to the right of the narrow hall. Its two windows, distinguished by eternally half-drawn blinds of yellow, looked out upon the veranda, permitting a decorous gloom to envelop the sacred precincts. Mrs. Sykes was too careful a housekeeper to take risks with her carpet and too proud of her possessions to care to hide their glories altogether; hence the blinds were never wholly drawn and never raised more than half way. In the yellow gloom, one might feast one's eyes at leisure upon the centre table, draped in red damask, mystic, wonderful, and on its wealth of mathematically arranged books, the Bible, the "Indian Mutiny" and "Water Babies" in blue and gold. This last had been a gift to Ann and was considered by Mrs. Sykes to be the height of foolishness. Still, a book is a book, especially when bound in blue and gold.

Upon the gaily papered walls hung a framed silver name-plate and two pictures. One a gorgeously coloured print of the lamented Queen Victoria in a deep gold frame, and the other a representation of an entrancing allegorical theme entitled "The Two Paths," illustrating the ascent of the saint into heaven and the descent of the sinner into hell. At the top of this picture was the legend, "Which will you choose?"—implying a possible but regrettable lack of taste on the part of the chooser.

Into this abode of the arts and muses came Callandar, alert and smiling. It was hardly his fault that he stumbled over the visitor who, whether in awe or fear of these unveiled splendours, had retreated as far as possible toward the door.

"Don't mind me!" said the visitor meekly.

"Willits! by Jove, I thought it would be you! Say, would you mind not sitting on that chair? It's just glued!"

The visitor arose with conspicuous alacrity. He was a tall man with a domelike head, piercing eyes and formidable nose. Ann's description had been terribly accurate. He observed the tail of his coat carefully and finding no damage, seemed relieved.

"Sit here," said Callandar affably. "And don't expect me to make you welcome, because you aren't. What misfortunate chance has brought you to Coombe?"

"Neither fortune nor chance had anything at all to do with it," declared the visitor. "I followed your luggage. I wanted to see you."

"Well, take a good look."

"I think you can guess why."

"Yes," with a sigh. "I was always a good guesser. And, frankly, Willits, I wish you hadn't."

"I do not doubt it. But, first, is there any other place where we can talk?"

"Don't you like this?" innocently.

The Button-Moulder's look of surprised anguish was sufficient answer. Callandar laughed.

"You always were a bit narrow in your views, Willits. How often have I impressed upon you that beauty depends upon understanding? I don't suppose you have even tried to understand this room? No? Will it help any if I tell you that Mrs. Sykes went without a spring bonnet that she might purchase the deep gold frame which enshrines Victoria the Good, or if I explain that Joseph Sykes, deceased, whose name you see yonder upon that engraved plate, was the most worthless rogue unhung. Yet the silver which displays—"

"Not in the least," interrupted the other hastily. "The place is a nightmare. Nothing can excuse it! And you—how you stand it I cannot see."

"My dear man, I don't stand it. I am not allowed to. It's only upon special occasions that any one is allowed to stand this room. You are a special occasion. But as you seem so unappreciative we can adjourn to my office if you wish."

"You have an office?"

"Certainly. A doctor has to have an office. This way."

Callandar strode across the room and opened a door in the opposite wall. It led into another room, smaller, with no veranda in front of it, yet with a window looking toward the road and two side windows through which the after flush of sunrise streamed. Its door opened upon a small stone stoop set in the grass of the front lawn. The furniture of the room was plain, not to say severe. Cool matting covered the painted floor, hemstitched curtains of linen scrim hung at the windows. There was a businesslike desk, a couch, a reclining chair, a stool by the door; another chair, straight and uncompromising, behind the desk. That was all.

Willits looked around him in a kind of dazed surprise. "Office!" he kept murmuring. "*Office!*"

"All rather plain, you see," said Callandar regretfully. "But for a beginner with his way to make, not so bad. My patients, three up to date, quite understand and conceal their commiseration with perfect good breeding. Also, the room has natural advantages, it is in the nature of an annex, you see, with a door of its own. Quite cut off from the rest of the house save-for the door by which we entered, the parlour door, which Mrs.

Sykes informs me I may lock if I choose although she feels sure that I know her too well to imagine any undue liberties being taken!"

The Button-Moulder with a gesture of despair made as if to sit down upon the nearest chair, but was prevented with kindly firmness by his host.

"Not that chair, please. It may not be quite dry. I glued—"

The voice of the visitor suddenly returned. It was a very dry voice; threadlike, but determined.

"Then if you will kindly find me a chair which you have not glued I shall sit down and dispose of a few burning thoughts. Callandar, as soon as you have finished playing the fool—"

"Consider it finished, old man."

"Then what does this, all this"—with a sweeping hand wave—"mean? You cannot seriously intend to stay here?"

"Why not?"

"Your question is absurd."

"No, it isn't. Let it sink in. Why should I not stay here? Examine the facts. I am ordered change, rest, interest, good air—a year at least must elapse before I take up my life again. I must spend that year somewhere. Why not here? It is healthy, high, piney, quiet. I had become utterly tired of my tramping tour. All the good I can get from it I have got. Chance, or whatever you like to call it, leads me to this place. A place which needs a doctor and which this particular doctor needs. There is nothing absurd about it."

The tall man observed his friend in interested silence. Apparently he required time to adjust his mind to the fact that Callandar was in earnest. The badinage he brushed aside.

"Then you really intend—but how about this office? If it is not a torn-fool office, where does the necessary rest come in?"

"Rest doesn't mean idleness. I should die of loafing. As a matter of fact since coming here I have rested as I have not rested for a year. Look at me! Can't you see it? Or is the renovation not yet visible to the naked eye? Great Scott! I don't need to vegetate in order to rest, do I?"

"No." Another pause ensued during which the gimlet eyes of the professor were busy. Then he seemed suddenly to leap to the heart of the matter.

"And—Lorna?" He asked crisply.

It was the other's turn to be silent. He flushed, looked embarrassed, and drummed with his fingers upon the table.

"Of course I have no right to ask," added Willits primly.

"Yes, you have, old man. Every right. But I knew you had come to ask that question and I didn't like it. The answer is not a flattering one—to me. Nor is it what you expected. To be brief, Lorna won't have me. Refused me—flat!"

Blank surprise portrayed itself upon the professor's face.

"The devil she did!"

"Confess now!" said Callandar, smiling. "You thought I was the one to blame? There was retributive justice in your eye, don't deny it!"

"But, I don't understand! I thought—I was sure—"

"I know. But she doesn't! Not in that way. As a sister—"

"That's enough! I—Accept my apology. I feel very sorry, Henry."

Again that look of embarrassment and guilt upon the doctor's face.

"No. Don't feel sorry! See here, let's be frank about the whole thing. It was a mistake, from the very beginning, a mistake. Miss Sinnet, Lorna, is a girl in a thousand. But—I did not care for her as a man should care for the woman he makes his wife. Nor did she care for me—wait, I'm not denying that there was a chance. We were very congenial. She might have cared if— if I had cared more greatly."

"Henry Callandar! Are you a cad?"

"No. Merely a man speaking the exact truth. I thought I might risk it, with you. Lorna Sinnet is not a woman to give her love and take a half-love in return. She was more clear-sighted than you or I. We should both have been very miserable."

Elliott Willits sighed. He was a very sensible man. He prided himself upon being devoid of sentiment, but even the most sensible of men, entirely devoid of sentiment, do not like to see their well laid plans go wrong.

"Well," he said, "I was mistaken. Let us say no more about it."

Callandar's eyes softened, melted into misty grey. He laid his arm affectionately over the other's thin shoulders. "Only this," he said. "That no man ever had a better friend! I know you, old Button-Moulder. I know your ambition to make of me a 'shining button on the vest of the world!' You thought that Lorna might help. But I failed you there. I'm sorry. That was really the bitterness of the whole thing—-to fail you!"

"You owe me nothing," gruffly.

"Only my life—my sanity."

"I shall doubt the latter if you stay here."

"No, you will see it triumphantly vindicated. I tell you I am better already. Look at my hand! Do you remember how it shook the last time I held it out for you. A few more months of this and it will be steady as a rock. Ah! it's good to be feeling fit again! And it isn't only a physical improvement." His smile faded and rising he began to pace the room. "I doubt if even you fully understand the mental depression that was dragging me down. No wonder Lorna would have none of me! Strange, that I cannot understand my own case as I understand the cases of others. Do what I would, I could not heal myself, the soul of the matter persistently escaped me. I was beginning to be as much the victim of an obsession as any of the poor creatures whom I tried to cure."

"You never told me of that."

"No, I was afraid to speak of it. It would have made it seem more real. But I can tell you now, if you are sure you will not be bored."

"I shall not be bored," said Willits quietly.

CHAPTER VII

"In order to make you understand, I'll have to go back," said the doctor musingly, "a long way back. Some of the story you already know, but now I want you to know it all. But first—when you found me in that hospital, a useless bit of human wreckage, and forced me back into life with your scorn of a coward and your cutting words, what did you think? What did I tell you? It is all hazy to me."

"You told me very little. It was plain enough. You had come a bad cropper. Some girl, I gathered. You had lost her, you blamed yourself. You talked a great deal of nonsense. I inferred—the usual thing!"

"You were mistaken. It was at once better and worse than that. But let's begin at the beginning. My father was a fairly wealthy man—but a dreamer. He made his money by a clever invention and lost it by an investment little short of idiotic. Like many unpractical men he had rather fancied himself as a man of business and the disillusion killed him. He—shot himself. My mother, my sister and myself were left, with nothing save a small sum in the bank and the deed of the modest house we lived in. Adela was twenty-one and I was nineteen. We sold the house, moved into rooms; Adela learned shorthand and went into an office. I wanted to do the same. But mother was adamant. I must finish my college course and take my degree; she and Adela could manage until I could make it up to them later. It was hard, but it seemed the only sensible thing to do—

"I faced the task of working my way through college with a thankful heart, for though I pretended that I did not care, it would have been a terrible thing to have given up my life's ambition. The thought of Adela trudging to the office hurt—it was the touch of the spur. I needn't tell you, you can guess how I worked! People were kind. One summer, old Doctor Inglis, whose amiable hobby it was to help young medical students, engaged me for the holidays as his chauffeur and general helper at a wage which would see me through my next term. It seemed an unusual piece of luck, for he lived only twenty miles from my mother's home and an electric tram connected the towns. One night I went with Adela to a Church Social—of all places—and that is where the story really begins, for it was at the Social that I met Molly Weston. It seemed the most casual of all accidents, for you can imagine that

I did not frequent churches in those days, and Molly, too, had come there by chance. She was dressed in pink, her cheeks were pink, she wore a pink rose in her hair. She was the prettiest little fairy that ever smiled and pouted her way into a boy's heart. Before I left her I was madly in love—a boy's first headlong passion. Adela was amazed, teased me in her elderly sister way but never for a moment took it seriously. Molly was a mere bird of passage, an American girl staying with friends for a brief time, therefore my infatuation was a humorous thing. But it was not so simple as that. Molly stayed on, Dr. Inglis was indulgent, we met continually. If her friends knew of it they did not care. It was just a flirtation of their pretty guest's. As a serious factor I was quite beneath the horizon, a young fellow working his way through college, and with, later on, a mother and sister to support.

"Molly understood the situation. At least she knew all the facts. I doubt if she ever understood them. She was one of those helpless, clinging girls who never seem to understand anything clearly. I remember well how I used to agonise in explanation, trying to make her see our difficulties and to face them with me. But when I had talked myself into helpless silence she would ruffle my hair and say, 'But you really do love me, don't you, Harry?' or 'I don't care what we have to do, so long as mother doesn't know.'

"I soon found out that her one strong emotion was fear of her mother. She was fond of her but she feared her as weak natures fear the strong, especially when bound to them by ties of blood. I was allowed to see her photograph—the picture of a grim hard face instinct with an almost terrible strength. No wonder my pretty Molly was her slave. One would have deemed it impossible that they were mother and daughter. Molly, it appears, was like her father, and he, poor man, had been long dead. Molly would do anything, promise anything, if only her mother might not know. She had not the faintest scruple in deceiving her, but this I laid, and still lay, to the strength of her love for me.

"She did love me. She must have loved me—else how could her timid nature have taken the risk it did?

"Summer fled by like a flash. Molly stayed with her friends as long as she could find an excuse and then went on for a brief week in Toronto. It was the week, of course, that I returned to college. We hoped that she could extend her stay, but her mother wrote 'Come home,' and there was no appeal from that. Then I did a desperate thing. Without Molly's knowledge I wrote to her mother telling her that I loved her daughter and begging, as a man begs for his life, to be allowed to ask her to wait for me. The letter was a lie in that it concealed the fact that my love was already confessed but I felt it necessary to shield Molly. I received no answer to the letter, but Molly received a telegram, 'Come home at once.'

"I can leave you to imagine the scene—my despair, Molly's tears! Never for an instant did she dream of disobeying and I—I felt that if she went I should lose her forever.

"Willits, there is something in me, devil or angel, which will not give up. Nothing has ever conquered it yet and Molly was like wax in my hands—so long as 'Mother' need not know. I do not attempt to excuse myself; what I did was dastardly, but it did not seem so then. The night before she left, she stole away from home. I had a license and we were married by a Methodist minister. He knew neither of us and probably forgot the whole incident immediately. It was a marriage only in name for we said good-bye at Molly's door. She left next morning. I never saw her again."

Into the silence which followed, the professor's words dropped dryly.

"What was your idea in forcing a meaningless marriage?"

"I loved her. I knew that it was the only way. Madly as I loved her, I knew that Molly was weak as water. I could not, would not, run the risk of letting her leave me without the legal tie. But I justified it to myself—I could have justified anything, I fear! I vowed a vow that she would be repaid for the waiting as never woman yet was paid. She wept on my shoulder and said, 'And you really do love me, Harry—and you'll swear mother need never know?'

"I swore it. There were to be no letters. Molly was too terrified to write and still more terrified of receiving a letter. She would live in constant dread, she said, if there were a possibility of such a thing. Weak in everything else she was adamant in this.

"I went back to work. I worked with the strength of ten. Health, comfort, pleasure, all were subordinated to the fever of work. I hoped that I might steal a glimpse of her sometimes. She promised to try to return to Toronto. But my letter must have alarmed the mother. I found out, indirectly, that shortly after her return, Mrs. Weston whisked her off to Europe. They were gone a year. When they returned I was in the far west with a government surveying party, earning something to help me with my last year's college expenses. When I was again in Toronto she had vanished. Gone, as I afterward learned, to stay with an aunt in California. Her mother, alive to danger, was not going to risk a meeting, and my vow to Molly left me helpless. But how I worked!

"That last year things began to come my way. Adela married a fine young fellow, wealthy and generous. My mother went to live with them in their western home, Calgary, where they still are. Then Thomas Callandar, my mother's brother, who had never bothered about any of us living, died, and left me a handsome property, adding, as you already know, the condition that I take the family name. You remember that my father's name, the name under which I married Molly, was Chedridge.

"Nothing now held me from Molly—in another month I would have my degree, and free and rich I could go to claim her. It seemed like a fairy tale! In my great happiness I broke my promise and wrote to her, to the California address, hoping to catch her there. In three weeks' time the letter came back from the dead letter office. I wrote again, this time to the Cleveland address, a short note only, telling her I was free at last. Then, next day, I followed the letter to Cleveland, wealth in one hand, the assurance of an honourable degree in the other.

"I had no trouble in finding the house. It was one of a row of houses, nondescript but comfortable, in a pleasant street. It seemed familiar—I had seen Molly's snapshots of it often. I cannot tell you what it felt like to be really there—to walk down the street, up the path, up the steps to the veranda. I was trembling as with ague, I was chalk-white I knew—was I not in another moment to see my wife!

"I could hear the electric bell tingle somewhere inside. Then an awful pause. What if they were not at home? What if they lived there no longer? I knew with a pang of fear that I could not bear another disappointment.

"There was a sound in the hall, the door knob moved—the door opened. I gasped in the greatness of my relief for the face in the opening was undoubtedly the face of Molly's mother. They were at home. They must have had my letter—they must be expecting me—

"Something in the woman's face daunted me. It was deathly and strained. Surely she did not intend to continue her opposition? Yet it confused me. I forgot all that I had intended to say, I stammered:

"'I am Henry Chedridge. I want to see Molly. I am rich, I have my degree—'

"'You cannot see her!' she said. Just that! The door began to close. But I had myself in hand now. I laid hold of the door and spoke in a different tone. The tone of a master.

"'This is foolish, Mrs. Weston. I thought you understood. I can and I will see your daughter. Molly is my wife!'

"She gave way at that. The door opened wide, showing a long empty hall. The woman stood aside, made no effort to stop me, but looking me in the eyes she said: 'You come too late. Your wife is not here. Molly is dead!'

"Then, in one second, it seemed that all the years of overwork, of mental strain and bodily deprivation rose up and took their due. I tried to speak, stuttered foolishly, and fell like dead over the door-sill of the house I was never to enter.

"You know the rest, for you saved me. When I struggled back to life, without the will to live, you shamed and stung me into effort. You brought the new master-influence into my life, taught me that the old ambition, the old work-ardour was not dead. Those months with you in Paris, in Germany, in London at the feet of great men saw a veritable new birth. I ceased to be Henry Chedridge, lover, and became Henry Callandar, scientist. All this I owe to you."

The other raised his hand.

"No, not that. Some impulse I may have given you, but you have made yourself what you are. But—you have not told me all yet?"

"No." Again the doctor began his uneasy pacing of the room. "The rest is harder to tell. It is not so clear. It has nothing to do with facts at all. It is just that when I first began to show signs of overwork this last time I became troubled with an idea, an obsession. It had no foundation. It persisted without reason. It was fast becoming unbearable!"

He paused in his restless pacing and Willits' keen eyes noticed the look of strain which had aroused his alarm some months ago. Nevertheless he asked in his most matter-of-fact tone, "And the idea was—?"

Callandar hesitated. "I can hardly speak of it yet in the past tense. The idea is—that Molly is not dead!"

"Good Heavens!" ejaculated the professor, startled out of his calm. "But have you any reason to doubt? To—to base—"

"None whatever. No enquiries which I have made cast doubt upon the mother's words. But on the other hand I have been unable to confirm them. I cannot find where my wife died—except that there is no record of her death in the Cleveland registries. She did not die in Cleveland."

"But you have told me that they were seldom at home. That the mother was a great traveller."

"Yes. The want of evidence in Cleveland proves nothing."

"Did you feel any doubt at first?"

"Absolutely none. The gloomy house, the empty hall, the white face and black dress of the woman in the door, the look of horror and anger in her eyes—yes, and a kind of grim triumph too—all served to drive the fatal message home. Dead!—There was death in the air of that house, death in the ghastly face—in the cruel, toneless words!—After my tedious recovery

I made an effort to see Mrs. Weston, although I had conceived a horror of the woman, but she was gone. The house had been sold. I tried to trace her without result. She seemed to have vanished off the face of the earth."

"And how long ago did the whole thing happen?"

"Twelve years. I was twenty-three when I went to claim my bride. I am thirty-five now."

"Dear me!" said the little man sincerely, "I have always thought you older than that! But twelve years is—twelve years! And you say this doubt is a very recent thing?"

"Yes. I have told you the thing is absurd. But I can't help it."

"Have you made any further enquiries?"

"Yes, uselessly. There is a rumour that Mrs. Weston, too, is dead. A lady who used to know them tells me that she is certain she heard of her death—in England, she thinks, but upon being questioned was quite at sea as to where or when or even as to the original source of her information. She remembers 'hearing it' and that's all. Then I sought for the aunts, the maiden ladies whom Molly visited in California. They too are gone, the older died during the time I lay ill in the hospital. The younger one was not quite bright, I believe, and was taken away to live with some relatives in the East. It was not Molly's mother who fetched her. It was a man, a very kind man whom the old lady, my informant, had never seen before. She said he had a queer name. She could not remember it, but thought he was a physician. I imagine that the kind friend was an asylum doctor."

"Very likely. And could your informant tell you nothing of the niece—if Molly had visited there?"

"She remembered her last visit very well but her memories were of no value. She was a sweet, pretty child, she said, and she often wondered how she came to have such a homely mother. She evidently disliked Mrs. Weston very much, and when I asked her if she had ever heard of Molly's death she said no, but that she was not a bit surprised as she had always predicted that the pretty, little, white thing would be worried into an early grave. I noticed the word 'white' and asked her about it, for the Molly I knew had a lovely colour. Her memory became confused when I pressed her, but she seemed quite sure that the girl who came that winter with her mother was a very pale girl—looked as if she might have come south for her health."

"All of which goes to prove—"

"Yes—I know. Poor Molly! Poor little girl! I believe in my heart that our mad marriage killed her. Without me constantly with her, the fear of her mother, perhaps the doubt of me, the burden of the whole disastrous secret was too much. And it was my fault, Willits—all my fault!" He turned to the window to hide his working face. "Do you wonder," he added softly, "that her poor little wraith comes back to trouble me?"

"Come, come, no need to be morbid! You made a mistake, but you have paid. As for the doubt which troubles you—it is but the figment of a tired brain. The mother could have had no possible reason for deceiving you. You were no longer an ineligible student—and the girl loved you. Besides, there was the legal tie. Would any woman condemn her daughter to a false position for life? And without reason? The idea is preposterous. Come now, admit it!"

"Oh, I admit it! My reasoning powers are still unimpaired. But reason has nothing to do with that kind of mental torture. It is my soul that has been sick; it is my soul that must be cured. And to come back to the very point from which we started, I believe I shall find that cure here—in Coombe."

"With Mrs. Sykes?" dryly.

"Certainly. Mrs. Sykes is part of the cure."

"And the other part?"

"Oh—just everything. I hardly know why I like the place. But I do. Why analyse? I can sleep here. I wake in the morning like a man with the right to live, and for the first time in a year, Willits, a long torturing year, I am beginning to feel free of that oppression, that haunting sense that somewhere Molly is alive, that she needs me and that I cannot get to her. I had begun to fear that it would drive me mad. But, here, it is going. Yesterday I was walking down a country road and suddenly I felt free— exquisitely, gloriously free—the past wiped out! That—that was why I almost feared to see you, Elliott, you bring the past so close."

The hands of the friends met in a firm handclasp.

"Have it your own way," said the professor, smiling his grim smile. "Consider me silenced."

The doctor's answer was cut off by the jingling entrance of Mrs. Sykes bearing before her a large tray upon which stood tall glasses, a beaded pitcher of ice cold lemonade and some cake with white frosting.

"Seeing as it's so hot," said she amiably, "I thought a cold drink might cool you off some. Especially as breakfast will be five minutes late owing to the chicken. I thought maybe as you had a friend, doctor, a chicken—"

"A chicken will be delicious," said the doctor, answering the question in her voice. "Mrs. Sykes, let me present Professor Willits; Willits, Mrs. Sykes! Let me take the tray."

Mrs. Sykes shook hands cordially. "Land sakes!" she said. "I thought you were a priest! Not that I really suspicioned that the doctor, good Presbyterian as he is, would know any such. But priests is terrible wily. They deceive the very elect—and it's best to be prepared. As it is, any friend of the doctor's is a friend of mine. You're kindly welcome, I'm sure."

"Thank you," said the professor limply.

The doctor handed them each a glass and raised his own.

"Let us drink," he said, "to Coombe. 'Coombe and the Soul cure!'"

"Amen!" said Willits.

"Land sakes!" said Mrs. Sykes. "I thought it was his spine!"

CHAPTER VIII

Zerubbabel Burk sat upon his stool of office in the doctor's consulting room, swinging his legs. Would-be discoverers of perpetual motion might have received many hints from Bubble, though he himself would have scorned to consider the swinging of legs as motion. He was under the delusion that he was sitting perfectly still. For the doctor was asleep.

Asleep, at four o'clock on a glorious summer day! No wonder his friend and partner wore a tragic face.

"Doesn't seem to care a hang if he never gets any patients!" mused Bubble, resentfully, stealing a half fond, half angry glance at the placid face of the sleeper. "Only two folks in all day and one a kid with a pin in its throat. And all he says is, 'Don't worry, son, we're getting on fine!' We'll go smash one of these days, that's what we'll do—just smash!"

"Tap-tap" sounded the blinds which were drawn over the western windows. A pleasant little breeze was trying to come in. "Buzz" sounded a fly on the wall. Bubble arose noisily and killed it with a resounding "thwack."

"Wake the doctor, would you?" he said. "Take that!"

But even the pistol-like report which accompanied the fly's demise failed to ruffle the sleeper. Bubble returned disconsolate to his stool.

"Smash," he repeated, "smash is the word. I see our finish."

The pronoun which Bubble used nowadays was always "we." He belonged to the doctor body and soul, but it was no servile giving. The doctor also belonged to him, and it was with this privilege of ownership that he now found fault with his idol. Had any one else objected to the doctor's afternoon rest he would have found reason and excuse enough; but in his own heart he was puzzled. Such indifference to the appearances, such wilful disregard of "business" could hardly, he thought, be real; yet, for an imitation, it was remarkably well done. Bubble admired even while he deprecated.

Why, he did not even go to church so that the minister might introduce him around as "Dr. Callandar, the new brother who has come amongst us."

Neither did he walk down Main Street, nor show himself in public places. When he went walking he went early in the morning and directed his steps toward the country. About all the usual means of harmless and necessary advertising he did not seem to know Beans! Bubble looked disconsolately out of the window. There was Ann, now, coming across the yard. School must be out, and still the doctor slept.

"Anybody in?" asked Ann in a stage whisper.

"Not just now. Been very busy though. Doctor's resting. Stop that noise."

"I'm not making any noise! He's part my doctor anyway. I'll make a noise if I like—"

"No you won't, miss!"

"But I don't *like*," added Ann with her impish smile. "If he's asleep what are you staying here for? Come on out."

Bubble regarded the tempter with scornful amazement.

"That's it!" he exclaimed, "jest like I always said, women haven't any sense of honour. What d'ye suppose I'm here for?"

"Not just to swing your legs," placidly. "He doesn't need you when he's asleep, does he? Come on and let's get some water-cress. He'd like some for his tea—dinner I mean. Say, Bubble, why does he call it dinner?"

"Because he comes from the city, Silly! They don't have any tea in the city. They have breakfast when they get up and lunch at noon and dinner about seven or eight or nine at night. Then if they get hungry before bed-time they have supper. The doctor says he never gets hungry after dinner so he don't have that."

Ann considered this a moment.

"They do so have tea!" she declared. "I heard Mrs. Andrew West telling about it. She said her sister in Toronto had a tea specially for her."

"Oh," with superb disdain, "that's just for women. If they can't wait for dinner they get bread and butter and tea in the afternoon. But they have to eat it walking around and they only get it when they go out to call."

Ann sighed. "I'd like to live in the city," she murmured. "Say, don't you feel as if you'd like a cookie right now?"

Bubble squirmed. But his Spartan fortitude held.

"In business hours? No, thank you. 'Tisn't professional. Look silly, wouldn't I, if one of our patients caught me eating?"

"How many to-day?"

"That'd be telling. 'Tisn't professional to tell. Doctor says if a man wants to succeed, he's got to be as dumb as a noyster in business!"

"Pshaw!" said Ann, "Aunty'll tell. She always counts. Then you don't want a cookie?"

"Well—later on—Cricky! here's some one coming! You scoot—pike it!"

"I won't!" Ann stood her ground, peering eagerly around the rose bush. "It's only Esther Coombe. She'll be coming to see Aunt—no—she's coming here! Hi, Bubble, wake him up—quick!"

"Hum, Hum!" said Bubble in a loud voice, rattling a chair. The sleeper made no movement.

Ann, brave through anxiety, flew across the room and shook him with all the strength of her small hands. The heavy lids lifted and still Ann shook.

"Is it an earthquake?" asked the victim politely.

"No—it's a patient! Oh, do get up. Oh, goodness gracious, look at your hair!"

The doctor passed his hand absently over a disordered head. "Yes," he said, "I have always thought that shaking is not good for hair. Dear me! I believe I have been asleep!"

Ann threw him a glance of mingled admiration and reproach and vanished through the parlour door just as the step of the patient sounded upon the stone steps.

"Why, Bubble Burk!" said a voice. "What are you doing here?"

At the sound of the voice, sleep fled from the doctor's eyes. He arose precipitately.

"I'm workin'," Bubble's voice was not as confident as usual. "This here is Dr. Callandar's office. Mrs. Sykes' visitors go round to the front door."

"Oh! But it's the doctor I wish to see. Is he in?"

Bubble was now plainly agitated.

"If you'll just wait a moment, I'll—I'll see."

Leaving Esther smiling upon the steps he disappeared into the shaded office and pulled up the blinds. The couch had been decorously straightened. The office was empty! Bubble gave a sigh of relief and his professional manner returned.

"He isn't just what you might call in," he explained affably to Esther. "But he'll be down directly. Walk in."

Esther walked in and took the seat which Bubble indicated.

"Somebody sick over at your house?" with ill-concealed hope.

Esther dimpled. "Not dangerously, thank you."

"Then it's just tickets for the choir concert. I might have known. But you're too late. Doctor's got half a dozen already. He—"

Further revelations were cut short by the entrance of the doctor himself. A doctor with sleep-cleared eyes, fresh collar, and newly brushed hair. A doctor who shook hands with his caller in a manner which even the professional Bubble felt to be irreproachable.

"Bubble, you may go."

With a grin of satisfied pride the junior partner departed, but once outside the gloomy expression returned.

"It's only choir-tickets!" he told Ann, who was waiting around the corner of the house. "Come on—let's go fishin'."

Inside the office Esther and the doctor looked at each other and smiled. He, because he felt like smiling; she, because she felt nervous. Yet it was not going to be as awkward as she had feared. With a decided sense of relief she realised that Dr. Callandar looked exactly like a doctor after all! Convention, even in clothes, has a calming effect. There was little of the weary tramp who had quenched his throat at the school pump in the well groomed and quietly capable looking doctor. With a notable decrease of tension Esther saw that the man before her was a stranger, a pleasant, professional stranger, with whom no embarrassment was possible.

As for him he realised nothing except that Coombe was really a delightful place. He felt glad that he had stayed.

"No one ill, I hope, Miss Coombe?" His tone, even, seemed to have lost the whimsical inflection of the tramp.

"No, Doctor. Not ill exactly. It is Aunt Amy. We cannot understand just what is the matter. You see, Aunty imagines things. She is not quite like other people. Perhaps," with a quick smile as she thought of Mrs. Sykes, "perhaps you may have heard of her—of her fantastic ideas? They are really quite harmless and apart from them she is the most sensible person I know. But lately, just the other day, something happened—"

He checked her with an almost imperceptible gesture. "Could you tell me about it from the beginning?"

Esther looked troubled. "I do not know much about the beginning. You see, Aunt Amy is my step-mother's aunt, and I have only known her since she came to live with us shortly after my father's second marriage. But I know that she has been subject to delusions since she was a young girl. She was to have been married and on the wedding day her lover became ill with scarlet fever, a most malignant type. She also sickened with it a little later; it killed him and left her mentally twisted—as she is now. Her health is good and the—strangeness—is not very noticeable. It has usually to do with unimportant things. She is really," with a little burst of enthusiasm, "a Perfect Dear!"

The doctor smiled. "And the new development?"

"It is not exactly new. She has always had one delusion more serious than the others. She believes that she has enemies somewhere who would do her harm if they got the chance. She is quite vague as to who or what they are. She refers to them as 'They.' Once, when she came to us first, she was frightened of poison and, although my father, who had great influence over her, seemed to cure her of any active fear, for years she has persisted in a curious habit of drinking her coffee without setting down the cup. The idea seemed to be that if she let it out of her hands 'They,' the mysterious persecutors, might avail themselves of the opportunity to drug it. Does it sound too fantastic?"

"No. It is not unusual—a fairly common delusion, in fact. There is a distinct type of brain trouble, one of whose symptoms is a conviction of persecution. The results are fantastic to a degree."

Well, the day before yesterday Aunt Amy was drinking her coffee as usual, when she heard Jane scream in the garden. She is very fond of Jane, and it startled her so that she jumped up at once, forgetting all about the coffee, and ran out to see what was the matter. Jane had cut her finger and the tiniest scratch upsets poor Auntie terribly. She is terrified of blood. When she came back she felt faint and at once picked up the cup and drank the remaining coffee. I hoped she had not noticed the slip but she must have done so, subconsciously, for when I was helping her with the dishes she turned suddenly white—ghastly. She had just remembered!

'They've got me at last, Esther!' she said with a kind of proud despair. 'I've been pretty smart, but not quite smart enough.'

I pretended not to understand and she explained quite seriously that while she had been absent in the garden 'They' had seen her half-filled cup and seized their opportunity. It was quite useless to point out that there was no one in the house but ourselves. She only said, 'Oh, "They" would not let me see them "They" are too smart for that.' Overwhelming smartness is one of the attributes of the mysterious 'They.'

"I hoped that the idea would wear away but it didn't; it strengthened. In vain I pointed out that she was perfectly well, with no symptom of poisoning. She merely answered that naturally 'They' would be too smart to use ordinary poisons with symptoms. 'I shall just grow weaker and weaker,' she said, 'and in a week or a month I shall die!' I tried to laugh but I was frightened. Mother advised taking no notice at all and I have tried not to, but I can't keep it up. She is certainly weaker and so strange and hopeless. I am terrified. Can mind really affect matter, Doctor Callandar?"

"No. As a scientific fact, it cannot. But it is true that certain states of mind and certain conditions of matter always correspond. Why this is so, no one knows, when we do know we shall hold the key to many mysteries. The understanding, even partial, of this correspondence will be a long step in a long new road. Meanwhile we speak loosely of mind influencing matter, ignoring the impossibility. And, however it happens, it is undoubtedly true that if we can, by mental suggestion, influence your Aunt's mind into a more healthy attitude the corresponding change will take place physically."

"But I have tried to reason with her."

"You can't reason with her. She is beyond mere reason. I might as well try to reason you out of your conviction that the sun is shining. A delusion like hers has all the stability of a perfectly sane belief."

"Then what can we do?"

"Since that delusion is a fact for her we must treat it as if it were a fact for us."

"You mean we must pretend to believe that the danger is real?"

"It is real. People have died before now of nothing save a fixed idea of death."

"Oh!"

"But don't worry. Aunt Amy is not going to die. When may I see her? If I come over in a half an hour will that be convenient?"

Esther rose with relief. How kind he had been! How completely he had understood! She had been right, perfectly right, in coming to him. In spite of Mrs. Coombe's ridicule, Aunt Amy's need had been no fancy. And there was another thing; he was coming to the house. Her mother would see him—and presto! her prejudice against doctors would vanish—he would cure the headaches, and everything would be happy again.

The doctor, watching keenly, thought that she must have been troubled greatly to show such evident relief.

"One thing more," he said. "Was there, do you know, any history of insanity in your aunt's family?"

The girl paled. The idea was a disturbing one.

"Why—no—I think not. I never heard. You see, she is not my Aunt, really, but my step-mother's aunt. There was a brother, I think, who died in—in an institution. He was not quite responsible, but in his case it was drink. That is different, isn't it? Does it make any difference?"

"No—only it may help me to understand the case. Good-afternoon."

He watched her go, through a peep-hole made by Bubble in the blind.

"Pretty, isn't she?" said a reflective voice below him.

The doctor started. But it was only Mrs. Sykes who had stepped around the house corner to pluck some flowers from the bed beneath the window. As he did not answer, the voice continued, "That boy Burk has gone fishing. I told you you'd regret putting that new suit on to him, brass buttons and all! Not that I want to say anything against the lad and his mother a widow, but when a person's dealing with a limb of mischief a person ought to know what to expect. Anybody sick over at Esther's house?"

The doctor, leaning against the door in deep reverie, did not seem to hear. Mrs. Sykes, after a suspicious glance, decided that perhaps he really had not heard, and proceeded.

"Not that I'm asking out of curiosity, Land sakes! But I've got some black currant jelly that sick folks fancy. I could spare a jar as well as not."

A pause.

The flower picker bunched her flowers into a tight round knot which she surveyed with pride. "That step-mother of Esther's now," she said. "I don't hold much with her. Flighty, I call her. Delicate, too, if looks don't lie. Men are queer. The only thing queerer is women. What d'ye suppose a sensible middle-aged man like Doctor Coombe ever saw in that pretty doll? And what did she see in him—old enough to be her father? A queer match, I call it. But they do say that her side of it is easy explained. Anyway it must have been a trying thing when the doctor's gold mine didn't—"

Mrs. Sykes' flow of words ceased abruptly, for rising from a last descent upon the rose bush she saw that her audience had vanished.

"Dear me! I hope he didn't think I was trying to be curious," said Mrs. Sykes.

CHAPTER IX

It required some persuasion to induce Aunt Amy to consent to see the doctor. Doctors, she had found (with the single exception of Dr. Coombe), were terribly unreasonable. They asked all kinds of questions, and never believed a word of the answers.

"And if I have a doctor," she declared tearfully, "I shall have to go to bed. And if I go to bed who will get supper? The sprigged tea-set—"

"But you won't need to go to bed, Auntie. You aren't ill, you know; just a little bit upset. If you feel like lying down why not use the sofa in my room? And even if you do not wish to see the doctor for yourself," Esther's tone was reproachful, "think what a good opportunity it is for us to get an opinion about mother. Don't you remember saying just the other day that you thought mother was foolish to be so nervous about doctors?"

"Yes, but she needn't stay in the room, need she, Esther? I don't want her in the room. She laughs. But I would like to lie on your sofa and if I must see him I had better wear my lavender cap."

"Yes, dear, and you will not mind mother staying—"

"But I do mind, Esther. And anyway she can't," triumphantly, "because she has gone out."

"Gone out? Mother? But she knew the doctor was coming and she promised—"

"Yes, I know. She said to tell you she had fully intended staying in until the doctor had been, but she had forgotten about the Ladies' Aid Meeting. She simply had to go to that. She said you could attend to the doctor quite as well as she could and that it was all nonsense anyway, because there was nothing whatever the matter with me." The faded eyes filled with tears again and Esther had much ado to prevent their imminent overflow.

She settled Aunt Amy upon the couch and adjusted the lavender cap without further betrayal of her own feelings, but in her heart she was both angry and hurt. Her mother had known of the doctor's intended visit and had distinctly promised to remain in to receive him. What would Dr. Callandar think? It was most humiliating.

The Ladies' Aid Meeting was plainly an excuse for a deliberate shirking of responsibility. Or, worse still, Mrs. Coombe, divining Esther's double motive, may have left the house purposely to escape seeing the doctor on her own account. Esther well knew the stubbornness of which she was capable upon this one question, and the cunningness of it was like her. She had made no objections; she had not troubled to refuse or to argue—she had simply gone out.

Well, it was something to feel that she, Esther, had done what she could. At any rate, there was no time to worry, for the doctor was already coming up the walk.

Esther hurried to the door. It relieved her to find that he seemed to expect her, and showed no offence on realising that the patient's nearest relative was not at home to receive him. Indeed, he seemed to think of no one save the patient herself. His manner, Esther thought, was perfect. Had she been a little older she might have suspected such perfection, deducing from it that Callandar, like herself, was subconsciously aware of an interest in the situation not altogether professional. But the girl made no deductions and certainly there was no trace of any embarrassment in the doctor's way with his patient. It took only a moment for Esther to decide that here, at least, she had done the right thing. She waited only long enough to see the frightened look in Aunt Amy's eyes replaced by one of timid confidence and then, murmuring an excuse, slipped away, leaving them together.

Callandar also waited while the startled eyes grew quiet and then lifted the fluttering hand into his own firm one.

"Creatures of habit, we doctors, aren't we?" he said, smiling. "Always taking people's temperatures."

Aunt Amy ventured upon a vague answering smile.

"I understand," continued the doctor, "that you have reason to fear that you have been poisoned?"

The hand began to flutter again, but quieted as the pleasant, confident voice went on:

"Your niece has told me something of the case but no details. Perhaps you can supply them for me. When exactly did it happen and what kind of poison was it?"

The fluttering hand became quite still and the eyes of Aunt Amy slowly filled with a great amazement. Here was an unbelievable thing—a doctor who did not argue or deny or playfully scold her for "fancies." A doctor who took her seriously and showed every intention of believing what she said. No one, save Dr. Coombe, had ever done that—

"It is always best in these cases to get the details from the patient herself," went on the doctor, encouragingly.

No, he was not laughing! Aunt Amy could detect nothing save the gravest of interest in his kindly eyes. An immense relief stole over her. A relief so great that Callandar, watching, felt his heart grow hot with pity.

"Oh, doctor!" she cried feebly, "I—" a rush of easy tears drowned the rest of the sentence.

Callandar let her cry. He knew the value of those tears. Presently when she grew more quiet he exchanged her soaking bit of cambric for his own more serviceable square. Aunt Amy dried her eyes on it and handed it back as simply as a child.

"Pray excuse me," she begged, "but—the relief! I might have died if you had not come." She went on brokenly. "You see," dropping her voice, "my relatives are *queer*. They have strange ideas. When I know things quite well they tell me I am mistaken. Mary, my niece, laughs. Even Esther, who tries to help me, thinks I do not know what I am talking about. They all argue in the most absurd manner. If I do not pretend always that I agree with them I have no peace. Sometimes when I tell some of the things I know, Esther looks frightened and says I am not to tell Jane. So I try to keep everything to myself. I don't want the children to be frightened. They are young and ought to be happy. I was happy when I was young—at least, I think it was I. Sometimes I'm not sure whether it wasn't some other girl—I get confused—"

"Don't worry about it," said the doctor calmly. "Or about Miss Esther either. I want to hear all about the poison."

Aunt Amy remembered her precarious condition with a start. Her eyes grew vague.

"I don't know how They put it in," she said. "I didn't see Them, you know. I left my cup of coffee standing while I went to find Jane. I heard her crying. She had cut her finger and when I had bound it up I felt faint, so I foolishly forgot and picked up the coffee and drank it. I wasn't quite myself or I should never have been so careless."

The doctor seemed to appreciate this point. "Did you taste anything in the coffee?" he asked.

"No. Of course They would be too clever for that!"

"And when did you begin to feel ill?"

"Just as soon as I remembered that I had forgotten to pour out a fresh cup." The naïveté of this statement was quite lost upon the eager speaker.

Esther, who had re-entered the room, opened her lips to improve this opportunity for argument but, meeting the doctor's eye, refrained. Callandar took no notice of the significant admission.

"Where do you feel the pain now?" he asked.

Aunt Amy appeared disturbed.

"Mostly in my head—I—I think." She moved restlessly.

Callandar appeared to consider this.

"But I suppose," he said thoughtfully, "that you really feel very little actual pain. None at all perhaps?"

Aunt Amy admitted that she could not locate any particular pain.

"Weakness is the predominating symptom," went on the doctor. "It is, in fact, a very simple case. All the more serious, of course, for being so simple, *if* we did not understand it. But now that we know exactly what is wrong we need have no fear."

Aunt Amy's vague eyes began to shine.

"Shall we get the better of them again?" she asked eagerly.

"We certainly shall," kindly. "Miss Esther, I am going to leave some medicine for your aunt; these little pink tablets. She must have one every two hours and two at bedtime. When she has taken them for two days I shall send something else. You will notice an improvement almost at once. Even in an hour or two, perhaps. By the end of the week all medicine may be discontinued."

He crushed a little pink tablet in a spoon, mixed it with water, and watched the old lady while she eagerly swallowed it.

"There!" he exclaimed. "That is the beginning! All we need now is a little rest and quiet. Nothing to excite the patient and a tablet regularly every two hours." He arose, affecting not to see Aunt Amy's grateful tears. "And of course," he added as if by an afterthought, "*They* won't know anything about this. They will think that, having taken the coffee, the result is certain. They will take for granted that They have finished you, in fact! So cheer up, it is worth a little illness to be rid of the fear of Them forever."

A lightning flash of hope lit up the worn face upon the pillow. "Oh, Doctor! Do you really think I am free?"

"Sure of it."

Aunt Amy sank back with a long sigh; her lined face grew suddenly peaceful. Esther, who had observed the little scene with wonder, said nothing, but taking the tablets, kissed her Aunt, and led the way out in silence.

"Well?"

As they stood together in the hall she could see the amused twinkle in the doctor's eye.

"I don't like it! You lied to her!"

"So I did," cheerfully.

"These tablets," holding up the glass vial, "what are they?"

"Tonic."

"And the medicine which you are going to send later?"

"More tonic."

"But she thinks—you gave her to understand that they are the antidote for the poison which you know does not exist."

"No. They are the antidote for a poison which does exist—medicine for a mind diseased."

"It's—it's like taking advantage of a child."

"So it is, exactly. I suppose you have never taken advantage of a child, for the child's good?"

"Certainly not."

"Never told one, gave one to understand, so to speak, that a kiss will cure a bumped head?"

"That's different!"

"Never told your school class during a thunderstorm that lightning never hurts good children?"

"That's very different."

"And yet all the time you know that lightning falls upon the just and unjust equally."

Esther was silent. The doctor laughed.

"I fear we are both sad story-tellers," he said gaily. "But in Aunt Amy's case the fibbing will all be charged to my account, you are merely the nurse. A nurse's duty is to obey orders and not frown (as you are doing now) upon the doctor. You will find that I shall effect a cure. Seriously, I do not believe that you have any idea of what that poor woman has been suffering. If the delusion of living in continual danger can be lifted in any way even for a time, it will make life over for her. You would not really allow a scruple to prevent some alleviation of your Aunt's condition, would you?"

The girl's downcast eyes flashed up to his, startlingly blue.

"No. I would not. I love her. I would tell all the fibs in the world to help her. But all the time I should have a queer idea that *I* was doing wrong. It would be common sense against instinct."

"Against prejudice," he corrected. "The prejudice which always insists that truth consists in a form of words."

They were now in the cool green light of the living room. Esther stood with her back to the table, leaning slightly backward, supporting herself by one hand. She looked tired. There were shadows under her eyes. The doctor felt an impulse of irritation against the absent mother who let the girl outwear her strength.

"My advice to you is not to worry," he said abruptly. "You are tired. More tired than a young girl of your age ought to be. You cannot teach those imps of Satan—I mean those charming children—all day and come back to home cares at night. Will it be possible for me to speak to Mrs. Coombe before I go?"

Watching her keenly he saw that now he had touched the real cause of the trouble.

"I am sorry," began Esther, but meeting his look, the prim words of conventional excuse halted. A little smile curled the end of her lips and she added, "Since she went out purposely to escape you, it is not likely."

"Your mother went out to escape me?" in surprise.

"In your capacity of doctor only. You see," with a certain childish naïveté, "she hasn't seen you yet. And mother dislikes doctors very much. Oh!" with a hot blush, "you will think we are a queer family, all of us!"

"It is not at all queer to dislike doctors," he answered her cheerfully. "I dislike them myself. At the very best they are necessary evils."

"Indeed no! And when one is ill it seems so foolish—"

"Is Mrs. Coombe ill?"

"I don't know. I think so. She has headaches. She is not at all like herself. I hoped so much that you would meet her this afternoon, and then she—she went out!"

"And this is really what is troubling you, and not Aunt Amy?"

"Yes. You see, Aunt Amy has been quite all right until the last two days. But mother—that has been troubling us a long time."

"How long?"

"Almost since father died—a year ago."

"But—don't you think that if Mrs. Coombe were really ill her prejudice would disappear? People do not suffer from choice, usually."

"No. That is just what puzzles me!" She did indeed look puzzled, very puzzled and very young.

"If I could help you in any way?" suggested Callandar. "You may be worrying quite needlessly."

"Do people ever consult you about their mothers behind their mother's back?"

"Often. Why not?"

"Only that it doesn't seem natural. Grown-up people—"

"Are often just as foolish as anybody else!"

"Besides, I doubt if I can make you understand." Now that the ice was broken Esther's voice was eager. "I know very little of the real trouble myself. It seems to be just a general state of health. But it varies so. Sometimes she seems quite well, bright, cheerful, ready for anything! Then again she is depressed, nervous, irritable. She has desperate headaches which come on at intervals. They are nervous headaches, she says, and are so bad that she shuts herself up in her room and will not let any of us in. She will not eat. I—I don't know very much about it, you see."

"You know a little more than that, I think, perhaps when you know me better?—It is, after all, a matter of trusting one's doctor."

"I do trust you. But feelings are so difficult to put into words. And the greatest dread I have about mother's illness is only a feeling, a feeling as if I knew, without quite knowing, that the trouble is deeper than appears. Jane feels it too, so it can't be all imagination. It is caused, I think, by a change in mother herself. She seems to be growing into another person—don't laugh!"

"I am not laughing. Please go on."

"Well, one thing more tangible is that the headaches, which seem to mark a kind of nervous crisis, are becoming more frequent. And the medicine—"

"But you told me that she took no medicine!"

"Did I? Then I am telling my story very badly. She has some medicine which she always takes. It is a prescription which my father gave her a few months before he died. She had a bad attack of some nervous trouble then which seems to have been the beginning of everything. But that time she recovered and it was not until after father's death that the headaches began again. Father's prescription must, long ago, have lost all effect, or why should the trouble get worse rather than better? But mother will not hear a word on the subject. She will take that medicine and nothing else."

"Do you know what the medicine is?"

"No. Father used to fill it for her himself. She says it is a very difficult prescription and she never has it filled in town, always in the city."

"But why? Taylor, here, is quite capable of filling any prescription. He is a most capable dispenser."

"Yes—I know. But mother will not believe it."

"And you say it does her no good whatever?"

"She thinks that it does. She has a wonderful belief in it. But she gets no better."

The doctor looked very thoughtful.

"She will not allow you to try any kind of compress for her head?"

"No. She locks her door. And I am sure she suffers, for sometimes when I have gone up hoping to help I have heard such strange sounds, as if she were delirious. It frightens me!"

"Does she talk of her illness?"

"Never, and she is furious if I do. She says she is quite well and indeed no one would think that anything serious was wrong unless they lived in the house. Any one outside would be sure that I am worrying needlessly. Am I, do you think?"

"I can't think until I know more. But from what you tell me, it looks as if this medicine she is taking might have something to do with it. If it does no good, it probably does harm. Perhaps it was never intended to be used as she is using it. Otherwise, as you say, the attacks would diminish. At the same time a blind faith in a certain medicine is not at all uncommon. One meets it constantly. Also the prejudice against consulting a physician. It is probable that Mrs. Coombe does not realise that she is steadily growing worse. Could you let me examine the medicine?"

Esther hesitated.

"It is kept locked up. But, I might manage it. If I asked her for it she would certainly refuse. I—I should hate to steal it," miserably.

"I see. Well, try asking first. It is just a question of how far one has the right to interfere with another's deliberately chosen course of action. The medicine is probably injurious, even dangerous. I should warn her, at least. If she will do nothing and you still feel responsible I should say that you have a moral right to have your own mind reassured upon the matter."

Esther smiled. "I believe I feel reassured already. Perhaps I have been foolishly apprehensive and it never occurred to me that the medicine might be at fault; at the worst I thought it might be useless, not harmful. If I could only manage to have you see it without *taking* it! There must be a way. I'll think of something and let you know."

"Do." The doctor picked up his hat for the second time. He was genuinely interested. He had not expected to find a problem of any complexity in sleepy Coombe. The cases of Aunt Amy and the peculiar Mrs. Coombe seemed to justify his staying on. It was pleasant also to help this charming young girl—although that, naturally, was a secondary consideration!

Esther ran upstairs with a lightened heart.

CHAPTER X

"I really could not help being late, Esther! I tried to hurry them but Mrs. Lewis was there. You know what *she* is!"

Mrs. Coombe sank gracefully into a veranda chair. Out of the corners of her eyes she cast a swift glance at the face of her step-daughter and, as the girl was not looking, permitted herself a tiny smile of malicious amusement. She was a small woman but one in whom smallness was charm and not defect. Once she had been exceedingly pretty; she was moderately pretty still. The narrow oval of her face remained unspoiled but the small features, once delicately clear, appeared in some strange way to be blurred and coarsened. The fine grained skin which should have been delicate and firm had coarsened also and upon close inspection showed multitudes of tiny lines. Her fluffy hair was very fair, ashy fair almost, and would have been startlingly lovely only that it, too, was spoiled by a dryness and lack of gloss which spoke of careless treatment or ill health, or both. Still, at a little distance, Mary Coombe appeared a young and attractive woman. The surprise came when one looked into her eyes. Her eyes did not fit the face at all; they were old eyes, tired yet restless, and clouded with a peculiar film which robbed them of all depth. Curiously disturbing eyes they were, like windows with the blinds down!

If her eyes were restless, her hands were restless too and she kept snapping the catch of her hand-bag with an irritating click as she spoke.

"I know I ought to have been here when the doctor called to see Amy," she went on, "but I could not get away. Mrs. Lewis talked and talked. That woman is worse than Tennyson's brook. She makes me want to scream! I wonder," musingly, "what would happen if I should jump up some day and scream and scream? I think I'll try it."

"Do!"

"What did Doctor Paragon-what's-his-name say about Amy?"

"He thinks we have been treating Aunt Amy wrongly. He thinks she should be humoured more. His name is Callandar."

"Callandar? What an odd name! It sounds half-familiar. I must have heard it somewhere. There is a Dr. Callandar in Montreal, isn't there? A specialist or something."

"I think this is the same man. But if it is he, doesn't want it known. He is here for his health, and he has never taken the trouble to correct the impression that he is a beginner working up a practice. I thought so myself at first."

"At first?"

"When I first saw him. I have met him several times."

Mrs. Coombe was evidently not sufficiently interested to pursue the subject. "Whoever he is," she said fretfully, "I hope he is not going to allow Amy to fancy herself an invalid."

"He is going to cure the fancy."

"Oh!" dubiously. "Well, I hope he does! I find I must run over to Detroit for a few days."

"What?"

"It would be provoking to have her ill while I'm away. No one else can manage Jane properly while you're at school. Where is Jane?"

"I don't know. You are not speaking seriously, are you?"

"I certainly am. At a pinch I suppose I could take Jane with me. She needs new clothes. But I'd rather not bother with her. Her measure will do quite as well. I wish you would call her. I've got some butterscotch somewhere. Here it is." The restless hands fumbled in the hand-bag. "No, it isn't here, how odd! I promised Jane—"

"Mother, when did you decide to go away?"

"Some time ago. It doesn't matter, does it? I had a letter from Jessica Bremner to-day. She asks me to come at once. It's in this bag somewhere. I declare I never can find anything! Anyway, she wants me to come."

"When did you get the letter?"

"On the noon mail, of course."

Esther turned away. She knew very well that there had been no letter from Detroit on the noon mail. But there seemed no use in saying so. These little "inaccuracies" were becoming common enough. At first Esther had exposed and laughed at them as merely humorous mistakes; but that attitude had long been replaced by a cold disgust which did not scruple to call things by their right names. She knew very well that Mary Coombe had developed the habit of lying.

"You see," went on the prevaricator cheerfully, "it would be necessary to run down to Toronto soon anyway. I haven't a rag fit to wear and neither has Jane. But Detroit is better. Things are much cheaper across the line. And easy as anything to smuggle. All you need to do is to wear them once and swear they're old."

"An oath is nothing? But where is the money coming from?"

Mrs. Coombe shrugged her shoulders. "One can't get along without clothes! And even if I could, there is another reason for the trip. My medicine is almost finished. I can't risk being without that."

It was the opportunity for which Esther had waited. She spoke eagerly.

"Why not try getting it filled here? I'm sure they are as careful as possible at Taylor's."

The hand-bag shut with a particularly emphatic click. Mrs. Coombe rose.

"We have discussed that before," she said coldly. "It is a very particular prescription and hard to fill. As it means so much to me in my wretched health to have it exactly right, I am surprised at you, Esther!"

Esther put the surprise aside.

"You could get it by mail, couldn't you?"

"I shall not try to get it by mail."

"But Taylor's are absolutely reliable. Why not give them a chance? If it is not satisfactory I shall never say another word. It seems so senseless going to Detroit for a few drugs which may be had around the corner. Perhaps it is not as difficult to fill as you think. Let me show the prescription to Dr. Callandar—" She stopped suddenly for Mrs. Coombe had grown white, a pasty white, and she broke in upon the girl's suggestion with a little inarticulate cry of rage, so uncalled for, so utterly unexpected, that Esther was frightened. For a moment the film seemed brushed from the hazel eyes—the blinds were raised and angry fear peeped out.

"You wouldn't dare!" The words were a mere breath. Then meeting the girl's look of blank amazement she caught herself from the brink of hysteria and added more calmly, "What an impossible suggestion! I need no second opinion upon the remedy which your father prescribed for me and I shall take none. As for the journey, I shall ask your advice when I wish it. At present I am capable of managing my own affairs. I shall come and go as I like."

The would-be firm voice wavered wrathed badly toward the end of this defiance, but the widely opened eyes were still shining and as she turned to enter the house, Esther caught a look in them, a gleam of something very like hate.

"So that is what comes of asking," said Esther sombrely.

She did not follow her step-mother into the house but remained for a while on the veranda, thinking. It was clearly useless to reopen the subject of the prescription. For some reason Mrs. Coombe regarded it as a fetish. She would not trust it to Taylor's. She would not allow a doctor to see it; there remained only the suggestion of Dr. Callandar that it be inspected without her consent. Esther knew where the prescription was kept, but—

Women are supposed, by men, to have a defective sense of loyalty and it is a belief fairly well established, also among men, that there is a fundamental difference in the attitude of the sexes to that high thing called honour. Esther was both loyal and honourable. To deceive her step-mother, however good the motive, could not but be horrible to her and just now, being angry with a very young and healthy anger, she was less willing than ever to lose her own self-respect in the service of Mary Coombe.

"I won't!" said Esther firmly, and went in to prepare Aunt Amy's supper.

"I don't feel like I ought to be eating upstairs this way," fussed the invalid as Esther came in with the tray. "I am so much better. That medicine the doctor gave me helped me right away. He must be a very smart man, Esther."

"It looks like it, Auntie."

"I don't doubt I'll be around to-morrow just like he said. So I don't want you staying home from school. That girl you get to take your place is kind of cross with the children, isn't she?"

"She is strict."

"Well, don't get her. I don't like to think about the children being scared out of their lives on my account. So I'll just get up as usual. I could get up now if necessary. And my mind feels better."

"Your *mind*?" Never before had Esther heard Aunt Amy refer to "her" mind as being in any way troublesome.

"Yes. I suppose you never knew, but sometimes I have felt a little worried about my mind."

"Whatever for?" The surprise which still lingered on the girl's voice was balm to Aunt Amy's soul. She laughed nervously.

"Of course it was foolish," she said, "but really there have been times when I have felt—felt, I can hardly express it, but as if there were a little something *wrong*, you know. Did you ever guess that I felt like that, Esther?"

"No, Auntie."

Aunt Amy shivered. For a moment her faded eyes grew large and dark. "I'm glad you did not guess it. It is a dreadful feeling, like night and thunder and no place to go. A black feeling! I used to be afraid I might get caught in the blackness and never find a way out and then—"

"And then what, dear?"

"Why, then—I'd be mad, Esther!"

"Oh, darling, how awful!" Esther's warm young arms clasped the trembling old creature close. "You must never, never be afraid again! Why didn't you tell me and let me help?"

"I couldn't. You would not have believed me. And it would have frightened you. And you might have told Mary. If Mary knew of it she would be certain to be frightened and if she was frightened she would send me away. Then the darkness would get me."

"It never shall, Auntie. No one shall ever send you away! And you won't be afraid any more, will you?"

"No, not if you don't keep telling me that things I know aren't true. I know they are true, you see, but when you say they aren't it makes my head go round."

"We'll be more careful, dear! And here is your medicine before you have your supper."

Aunt Amy turned cheerfully to the supper tray.

"Your mother need not be told about it," she observed. "She wouldn't understand. She was in a while ago to say she hoped I'd be better in the morning. She is going to the city. What she came for was to ask me to lend her my ruby ring. She never understands why I can't lend it to her. I told her she might have the string of pearls and the pearl brooch and the ring with the little diamonds and anything else except the ruby. You see, I might die before she got back, and I couldn't die without the ruby ring on my finger. I promised somebody—I can't remember whom—"

"I know, dear, don't try to remember."

"Mary says it is shameful waste to leave it lying shut up in the box in my drawer. But it has to lie there. If I took it out now it would stop shining immediately. And it must be all red and bright when I die, like a shining star in the dark. Then, afterwards, you can have it, Esther. You don't mind waiting, do you?"

"Gracious! I hope I'll be an old woman before then! So old that I shan't care for ruby rings at all."

Aunt Amy looked at the girl's pretty hand wistfully. "I'd like to give it to you right now, Esther. But you know how it is. I can't. If the red star did not shine I might lose my way. Some one told me—"

"I know, Auntie. I quite understand. And you have given me so many pretty things that I don't need the ruby."

"You may have anything else you want. But of course the ruby is the loveliest of all. If I could only remember who gave it to me—"

"Perhaps you always had it," suggested Esther, hastily, for she knew quite well the tragic history of the ruby.

"Perhaps. But I don't think so. I love it but I never dare to look at it. It makes the blackness come so near. Does it make you feel that way?"

"No—I don't know—large jewels often give people strange feelings they say."

"Do they?" hopefully. "Go and look at it now. Don't lift it out of the box. Just open the lid and look in. Perhaps you will feel something."

Esther went obediently to the drawer where the beautiful jewel had lain ever since Aunt Amy's arrival. As no one outside knew of its existence it was considered quite safe to keep it in the house. The box lay in a corner under a spotless pile of sweet smelling handkerchiefs. Esther snapped open the lid of the case and looked in. She looked close, closer still, bending over the open drawer—

"Do you feel anything, Esther?"

The girl's answer came, after a second's pause, in a strained voice. "The drawer is so dark, I can't tell!"

"Take it to the window," said Aunt Amy.

Esther lifted the case from the drawer and carried it into a better light. Her eyes were panic-stricken. For her indecision had been only a ruse to give herself time to think. She had known the moment she opened the case that the ruby was gone!

"It does make me feel queer," she said, closing the case. "I'll put it away."

"Is it a black feeling?" with interest.

"I think it is."

"Then you are kin to it," said Aunt Amy sagely. "Your mother never has any feeling about it at all. Except that she would like to wear it. She was looking at it when she was in. She was as cross as possible when I told her she could not take it with her."

Esther gathered up the tea things without a word. Her curved mouth was set in a hard red line. At the door she paused and turning back as if upon impulse, said: "If it makes you feel like that, I would advise you not to look at it, Auntie. It will be quite safe. I'll see to that. I'll appoint myself 'Guardian of the Ring.'"

CHAPTER XI

Esther carried the tea-tray into the kitchen and stood for a moment beside the open window letting the sweet air from the garden cool the colour in her cheeks. Through the doorway into the hall she could see into the living room where Jane sat at the table in a little yellow pool of lamplight, busy with her school home work. Farther back, near the dusk of one of the veranda windows, Mrs. Coombe reclined in an easy chair. Her eyes were closed; in the half light she looked very pretty, very fragile; her relaxed pose suggested helplessness. Unconsciously Esther's innate strength answered to the call; her hard gaze softened. To apply the terms liar and thief to that dainty figure in the chair seemed little short of brutality. Mary was weak, that was all—just weak!

At the sound of the girl's step in the doorway Mrs. Coombe opened her eyes. They were very filmy to-night, blank, contented. Her nervousness seemed to have left her. Perhaps she was half asleep, for she yawned, an open, ugly yawn, which she did not trouble to raise her hand to hide.

"I have decided to take Jane with me, Esther."

"I don't want to go," said Jane.

"Well, you are going—that's enough."

"If you have really decided to go," began Esther slowly, "I think you are wise to take Jane. We cannot tell yet just how Aunt Amy may be."

The child returned to her book with a discontented sigh. Esther came nearer and spoke in a lower tone. "But before you go," she said, "please don't forget to replace Aunt Amy's ring. If she were to find it gone it would be no joke but a serious shock, as I suppose you know."

Mrs. Coombe laughed. And Esther realised that a laugh was the last thing she had expected. For anger, evasion, denial, she had been prepared. Mary would probably storm and bluster in her ineffective way—and return the ring. Instead—

"How did you know I had it?" she asked good humouredly.

"I saw that it was gone."

"And the deduction was obvious? Well, this time you are right. I did take it. I expect I have a right to borrow my own Aunt's things if she is too mean to lend them. It's a shame of her to want to keep the only decent jewel we have shut up. Amy gets more selfish every day."

"But you will put it back before she misses it?"

Mrs. Coombe could see her step-daughter's face quite plainly and its expression made her wince, but she was reckless to-night. After all, why pretend? If Esther intended to eternally interfere with her affairs the sooner an open break came, the better.

"Perhaps, perhaps not. Certainly not until I return from my visit."

Esther fought down her rising dismay.

"Mother, don't you understand what you are doing? The ring is Aunt Amy's You have no right to take it!"

"I've a right if I choose to make one."

"If Auntie finds out it is not in its box, we cannot tell what the effect may be!"

"She needn't find out. What she doesn't know won't hurt her!"

"But—it is stealing!"

Mrs. Coombe laughed. "What a baby you are, Esther, for all your solemn eyes and grown-up airs. Stealing—the idea! Anyway you need not worry since you are not the thief." She yawned again, rose, and declared that she felt quite tired enough to go to bed.

When she had gone, Jane left her lessons and came to her sister's side.

"Esther, do I really have to go away with Mother?"

"It looks like it, Janie. But you'll like it. Mrs. Bremner has a little girl."

"I don't like little girls."

"Then you ought to! The change will probably do you good."

Jane looked dubious. "Things that I don't want never do me any good. Will you help me with my 'rithmetic?"

"I will when I come back."

"Where're you going?"

"Out. I'll not be long. Answer Aunt Amy's bell if it rings, like a dear child."

Esther's decision had been made, as many important decisions are, suddenly, and without conscious thought. All the puzzling over what was right and wrong seemed no longer necessary. Without knowing why, she knew that it had become imperative to get some good advice and get it at once. If she had been disturbed and uneasy before, she was frightened now. Something must be done, if not for Mary's sake at least for the sake of the honoured name she bore, and for Jane's sake!

"Mother doesn't seem to *know* when a thing is wrong any more!" was the burden of the girl's thought as she hurried upstairs.

She knew where the prescription was kept—in a little drawer of her father's old desk, a drawer supposed to be secret. To-morrow Mary would take it away with her. Esther opened the drawer without allowing herself a moment for thought or regret. The paper was there, folded, in its usual place.

With a sigh of relief she seized it, hurried to her own room for her hat and then out into the summer night. A brisk five minute walk brought her to Mrs. Sykes' gate, and there, for the first time, she hesitated.

"Evening, Esther!" called Mrs. Sykes cheerfully from the veranda. "Come right along in. Mrs. Coombe told Ann you might be over to borrow the telescope valise if she decided to take Jane. Rather sudden, her going away, isn't it? Hadn't heard a word about it until the Ladies' Aid—come up and sit on the veranda and I'll get it."

"I didn't come for the telescope," said Esther. "I came to see Dr. Callandar."

"Oh," with renewed interest. "Well, he's in. At least he's in unless he went out while I was upstairs putting Ann to bed. That's his consulting room where the light is. It's got a door of its own so folks won't be tramping up the hall—but of course you know. You were here this afternoon. Funny, Mrs. Coombe going away with your poor Auntie sick and all! I suppose it *is* your Auntie, since it can't be Jane or Mrs. Coombe?"

"Yes, it is Aunt Amy. She has not been very well."

"The heat, likely. Heat is hard on folks with weak heads. Not that your Auntie's head ever seems weaker than lots of other folks. Won't you come up and sit awhile?—Well, ring the bell."

Mrs. Sykes voice trailed off indistinctly as Esther rounded the veranda corner and stood by the rose bush before the doctor's door. She pushed the new electric bell timidly.

"You'll have to push harder than that!" called Mrs. Sykes. "It sticks some!"

But the door had opened at once, letting out a flood of yellow light.

"Miss Coombe—you?"

"It's Esther Coombe come about her Aunt Amy," called the voice from the veranda.

Hastily the doctor drew her in and closed the door with an emphatic bang. Then for the second time that day they looked into each other's eyes and laughed.

"Do you think my patients will stand that?" he asked her ruefully.

"Oh, we are used to Mrs. Sykes, we don't mind."

"That's good! Ah, I see you have the mysterious prescription. It wasn't so hard after all, was it? Probably your mother was quite as anxious as you."

"No, she refused to let me show it you. I took it. To-night was the only chance, for she is going away to-morrow and will take it with her."

"And how about your Presbyterian conscience?" Still with a twinkle.

"Silenced, for the present. But look at it quickly for the silence may not last. It seemed that I simply had to help mother, in spite of herself. And there was no other way. All the same I shall despise myself when I get time to think."

The doctor took the paper with a smile. "When that time comes I shall argue with you, though argument rarely affects feeling. To my mind you are doing an eminently sensible thing."

He opened the paper and peered at it under the lamp; looked quickly up at the girl's eager face and then from her to the paper again.

"What is it?" she asked anxiously.

"Why—I don't know. Where did you get this?"

"In the secret drawer of father's desk."

"Was the prescription always kept there?"

"Yes."

The doctor folded the paper again and handed it to her. "Does this look like the prescription?"

"Yes, of course. It is the prescription."

"I'm afraid not. Come and look."

Esther seized the paper eagerly and saw—a neatly written recipe for salad dressing!

Hot and cold with mortification, she stared at it blankly. "I have been nicely fooled," she said in a low voice.

"Am I permitted to smile, or would it hurt your feelings?"

"It is not at all funny! Of course the real prescription has been removed. She must have suspected. You see, I asked her to let me have it. Oh!" with sudden shame and anger. "She guessed that I might take it, don't you see?"

"I am afraid you are right. But now at least I should think that you have done your whole duty. It would look as if Mrs. Coombe was herself aware of the inadvisability of continuing this prescription. Why else should she be so careful to prevent you showing it to me? At the same time she is determined to go on using it. We cannot prevent her."

"Can we do nothing?"

"When I see her I shall be better able to judge."

"But she is going away."

"Then we must wait. If it is, as I suspect, a case of disordered nerves aggravated by improper treatment, the instinct is strongly for concealment. Do you find, for instance, that Mrs. Coombe is not as frank in other matters as she used to be?"

A shamed blush crimsoned the girl's cheek, but the doctor's tone was compelling and she answered in a low voice: "Yes, I think so."

"Don't look like that. It is only a symptom of something rotten in the nervous system."

"Isn't there such a thing as character?" bluntly.

"As distinct from the nervous system? Some say not. But we do not need to venture such a devastating belief to know, well, that a dyspeptic is usually disagreeable. In potential character he may be equal to the cheeriest man who ever ate a hearty dinner. Think of Carlyle."

"I don't like Carlyle."

"But don't you admire him?"

"No. Do you remember the story of the beggar who picked up his hat one day and instead of giving him sixpence, Carlyle said, 'Mon, ye may say ye hae picked up the hat of Thomas Carlyle.'"

The doctor laughed. "Oh he had a guid conceit o' himself—must you go?" For Esther had risen.

"Yes, thank you. Oh, please do not come with me. It is only a step. I'd much rather not. Mrs. Sykes would conclude that the whole family were in danger of immediate extinction."

She was so evidently perturbed that the doctor laid down his hat, but for the first time it occurred to him that Mrs. Sykes was not an unmixed blessing.

Esther was holding out her hand.

"Then you think we can safely leave it until mother returns?"

"I think we shall have to, and if things have been going on as long as you think, a week more or less will make no very material difference. In any case we cannot examine a lady by force or prevent her from getting a prescription until one knows it to be dangerous."

"No, of course not. Good-night, and—thank you, Doctor!"

"And I am not to be allowed to walk home with you?"

"Truly, I would rather not."

"Then good-night, and don't worry."

He watched her flit down the dusky path, heard the click of the gate latch, and turned back into the office to wonder why it seemed suddenly bare and empty!

CHAPTER XII

Mrs. Coombe had been in the city a week when one morning Ann, who was feeling lonely without Jane, sat swinging upon the five-barred gate and whistling intermittently for Bubble. She had become very tired of waiting. She knew that Bubble could hear. The five-barred gate was within easy hearing distance of the house, and both doors and windows of the office were open. Therefore it became each moment more evident that the whistles were being deliberately ignored.

"Horrid, nasty boy!" exclaimed Ann, climbing to a precarious seat on the highest of the five bars. "Well, if he waits until I come to get him, he'll—just wait!"

It was very hot on the gate. The vacant field on the other side, where the Widow Peel pastured her cow, was hot, too, but if one cut across the field and circled the back of the Widow Peel's cottage one substantially lessened the distance between oneself and the cool deliciousness of the river. The Widow Peel was near-sighted and hardly ever noticed one rushing over her beds of lettuce and carrots and onions, or if she did, she could not "fit a name to 'em."

Ann sighed and swung her brown legs. Should she or should she not go in search of Bubble? Going would mean a distasteful swallowing of proper pride; not going would mean—no Bubble. It would be a case of cutting off one's nose—Ann's small white teeth came together with a little click.

"I'll go. But I'll pay him out afterwards."

With this thoroughly feminine decision she tumbled off the gate, raced across the orchard and, having paused a moment to regain breath and poise, appeared casually at the office door. The office looked cool and empty; Bubble was not upon his official stool. Perhaps, after all, he had not heard the whistles! Perhaps—

"What d'ye want?" asked a gruff voice from behind the desk.

Ann jumped, and then tried to look as if she hadn't.

"I knew you were there!" she said. "But just you wait till the doctor catches you at it!" Mounting the step she frowned across at Bubble who, in the doctor's favourite attitude, was reclining in the doctor's chair. "I suppose you think you look like him, but you don't, nor act like him either. If he was sitting there and a lady came in, he'd be up too quick for anything. And if the lady was polite and stayed on the doorstep (just like I am) he would say, 'Pray come in, madam,' and then he'd set a chair and—"

"Oh, cut it out!" Bubble's dignity collapsed with his attitude. The tilted chair came down with a bang and its occupant settled himself more naturally upon a corner of the desk. "Don't bother me! I can't come out. Doctor's away. Some one's got to attend to business. See those medicines? Well, don't you go handling them! This here is for Lizzie Stephens (measles), and that there is for Mrs. Nixon (twins). If they got mixed I'd be responsible. Run away!"

"Where's the doctor?" asked Ann, ignoring.

"The doctor is out. You needn't wait. He won't be back all day."

"Where'd he go?"

"Little girls mustn't ask questions!"

Ann's small face wrinkled into an elfish grin. "I know where he's gone," she said slyly.

"Yes, you do!" This sarcastic comment was Bubble's most emphatic negative.

"Very well, then, I don't."

Not to be outdone, Ann volunteered no further information. She sat down on the step and waited.

Bubble busied himself with tying up the bottles. Presently he stepped out from behind the desk.

"Think you can mind the office while I run around with these medicines?" he asked sternly.

"Sure!" Ann's assent was placid.

"What'll you say if any one comes and asks for the doctor—or me?"

"You're out delivering medicines and the doctor's been called away very sudden."

"What'll you tell them if they ask you what he's been called away to?"

"Oh, I'll just say they needn't worry, 'tisn't anything catching."

Bubble allowed his face to relax. He even displayed a grudging admiration for this feminine diplomacy.

"And you wouldn't be telling lies, either," he remarked approvingly. "All the same," with a return to gloom, "we can't keep it a secret. Folks are bound to find out. You can bet your eyes on that!"

Ann nodded. "I expect most of them know by now. Any one that wanted to could see them. *He* didn't seem to care. They drove right down the main street and you could see the picnic basket sticking out at the side!"

"O cricky! Isn't that just like him? You'd think he wanted the whole town to know he'd gone off picnicking with a girl. But I'd have thought Esther Coombe would have better sense!"

"It wasn't Esther's fault. She couldn't act as if she was ashamed of him, could she? When a gentleman asks a lady to go out in his automobile she can't ask him to drive down the back streets."

"If he had only taken her at night!" groaned the harassed junior partner. "But no, he must take a whole day off and him with two patients on his hands. Look at me! Have I ever asked off to go on any picnics? Not on your tintype. Business is business. Doctors can't fool round like other folks."

Ann nodded agreement. Things were coming her way very nicely. She glanced at the wrathy Bubble out of the corners of her eyes. "I didn't think he'd be mean like that," she remarked craftily.

"Like what? He isn't mean!"

"To make you stay in all day."

"He didn't. Not him! He gave me fifty cents and told me to take a day off. 'Just run around with the medicine, Bubble,' says he, 'and then you can hike it. I have a feeling in my bones,' he says, 'that nobody's going to die to-day.'"

"Well, then —"

"A man has a sense of duty for all that."

"Well," rising with a dejected air, "if you're not coming, good-bye. It will be lovely paddling! Aunt's given me some lettuce sandwiches and two apple turnovers. One was for you, but I suppose I can eat them both. The sugar's leaked all round the edge—lovely!"

The stern disciple of business watched her tie on her sun-bonnet with mingled feelings. It began to look as if she was really going!

"Good-bye," said Ann.

Bubble's red face grew a shade redder.

"Just like a girl!" he said bitterly. "Because a man's got to deliver two medicine bottles, off she goes and won't wait for him. And the farthest I've got to go is over to Mrs. Nixon's. The whole thing won't take five minutes."

Sun-bonnets are splendid things for hiding the face! Had Bubble seen that slow smile of victory there is no telling what might have happened. But he did not see it. And Ann was too good a general to exult openly. Her answer was carefully careless. "I'll wait—if you'll hurry up!"

But the look which she threw after his hastily retreating figure was as old as Eve.

Meanwhile the doctor and Esther, who had been so criminally careless of professional appearances as to drive down Main Street with a picnic basket protruding, were enjoying themselves with an enjoyment peculiar to careless people. Esther had forgotten about the pile of uncorrected school exercises which were supposed to form her Saturday's work; the doctor had forgotten about the measles and the twins. Rain had fallen in the night and the dust was laid, the trees were intensely green.

Neither of them knew exactly how this pleasant thing had come about, although, as a matter of crude fact, Mrs. Sykes had played the part of the god from the machine. This energetic lady had made the doctor's professional career her peculiar care and it had occurred to her that, as a resident physician, he was disgracefully ignorant of the surrounding country. At the same moment she had remembered that to-morrow was Saturday, and that for trapesing the country and meandering around in outlandish places there was no one in town equal to Esther Coombe.

"But," objected the doctor, "I hardly know Miss Coombe well enough to ask a favour of her."

Mrs. Sykes opined that that didn't matter. "Land sakes," she declared, "it would be a nice state of affairs if one huming-being couldn't do a kindness to another without being acquainted a year or two." Besides, Esther, as the old doctor's daughter, might almost be said to have a duty toward the newcomer. Mrs. Sykes felt sure that Dr. Coombe would have insisted upon proper attentions being shown, since he was always "the politest man you ever saw, and terrible nice to strangers."

Mrs. Sykes also, with the assistance of Aunt Amy, had provided the large basket. They might not need it all, but then again they might. It was best to be prepared. And, anyway, no one should ever say that she, Mrs. Sykes, "skimped" her boarders' meals. As for the big shawl, once belonging to a venerated ancestress, it is always safe to take a big shawl on a country trip even in June heat with the thermometer going up.

The doctor agreed to everything, even the shawl. Whether one is taking a rest cure or not, it is distinctly pleasant to look forward to a day in the country with a lovely girl. Esther had taken his request quite simply. It seemed only natural to her that he should wish to explore, while the invitation to act as guide was frankly welcomed. Indeed her girlish gaiety in the prospect had shown very plainly that such holidays had been rare of late. School did not "keep" on Saturday, Jane was away, and Aunt Amy was so much better that she could leave her without misgiving. Bubble alone prophesied disaster, and at him they all laughed.

There is a little folder published by the Town Council which gives a very good idea of the country around Coombe. We might quote this, but it will be much better for you to go some time and see things for yourself. Dr. Callandar saw a great deal that day, but was never very clear afterwards in his descriptions. It was rocky in spots, he knew, and wild and sweet and piney. And there were little lakes. He remembered the lakes particularly because—well, because of what came later.

> They had their lunch on the shores of a jewel-like bay, sitting upon the shawl of Mrs. Sykes' grandmother. Esther had many memories of the place. She had often camped there with her father. But it had been wilder then. Once a bear had come right up to the door of her tent.

"By Jove!" said the doctor enviously, "what did you do?"

"I said 'shoo'!"

"And did he?"

"Yes, he did. He was a nice bear, very obedient. Some days later father and I saw Mrs. Bear trot across the clearing with two baby bears behind. They were moving. I think Mr. Bear was looking for a house when he called on me."

Altogether it was a magic day. There is an erroneous belief that magic has died out of the world. But in our hearts we all know better. Which of us has not lived through the magic hours of a magic day? Which of us does not know that land, unmapped, unnamed, a land whose sun is brighter, whose grass is greener, whose sky is bluer, and whose every road runs into a golden mist? Magic land it must be, for much seeking cannot find it. No one, not the wisest nor the best, may enter it at will; but for every one at some time the unseen gate swings open, birds sing, flowers bloom, the glory and the dream descend! Poor indeed, unutterably poor and cheated of his heritage is he who has not passed that way.

They were not in love, of course. They were too happy for that. Love is the greatest thing in the world, but it is seldom quite happy. Esther and the doctor were not lovers but lingered in that deliciously unconscious state of "going-to-be-in-love-presently" which is nothing less than heavenly. Therefore they ate their lunch with appetite and laughed about the story of the bear. Both were surprised when the doctor's watch told them it was time to think of home.

They came back very slowly along the shaded trail to where the car stood waiting in the brilliant light of the declining sun.

"Just a moment," said the doctor, and cranked vigorously. A confusion of odd noises ensued, from which, somehow, the right noise did not emerge.

"Just a moment," he repeated. "There appears to be something loose—or tight—or something. If you'll just sit out on the grass a moment, Miss Esther, I'll see what it is."

Esther descended. The grass was just as pleasant to sit upon as the car seat and she knew nothing whatever about the tricky ways of motors.

"Just a moment," said Callandar for the third time, and disappeared behind the bonnet. Fifteen minutes after, he reappeared with a very hot face decorated fantastically with black.

"She's sulking," he announced gloomily.

"Is she?" Esther's tone held nothing save placid amusement.

"Just a moment." The doctor banged down the bonnet and effaced himself once more. This time under the body of the car.

Motors are mysterious things. Why a well-treated, not to say pampered, car which some hours before had been left in perfect condition and excellent temper should abruptly turn stubborn and refuse to fulfil its chief end is a problem which we shall not attempt to solve. Every one who has ever owned a motor knows that these things be.

The doctor, a modest man, considered himself a fair mechanician. In expansive moments he, who made nothing of his undoubted excellence in his own profession, was wont to boast that you couldn't teach him much about motors! He had laughed to scorn the remark of his Scotch chauffeur that "they things need a deal o' humourin'!" Humour a thing of cogs and screws? Absurd! One must master a motor, not humour her.

Half an hour later he emerged from the car's eclipse and sank, a pitiable figure, upon the grass beside Esther.

"Won't it go?" asked Esther dreamily. It had been very pleasant sitting there watching the sun set.

The master of motors made a tragic gesture. "No," he said, "she won't."

"Shake her," said Esther.

Dr. Callandar pushed back his sweat-bedewed hair with fingers which left a fearsome streak above his left eyebrow. The girl laughed. But the doctor's decorated face was rueful.

"Do you know, Miss Esther, I'm afraid it isn't a bit funny." His tone, too, was sober; and Esther, suddenly more fully alive to the situation, noticed that the hands clasped recklessly about the knees of once spotless trousers were shaking, just a little. He must be awfully tired!

"That's because you can't see yourself. Give the motor a rest. There is plenty of time. Let's have tea here instead of on the way home. There is cold tea and chicken-loaf, bread and butter, and half a tart."

The doctor brightened. "You may have the half-tart," he concluded generously. "And in return you will forgive me my pessimism. I believe I am hungry and thirsty and—if I could only swear I should be all right presently."

Esther put her small fingers in her ears and directed an absorbed gaze toward the sunset.

Callandar laughed.

"All over!" he called. "Richard is himself again. And now we have got to be serious. Painful as it is, I admit defeat. I can't make that car budge an inch. It won't move. We can't push it. We have no other means of conveyance. Deduction—we must walk!"

"Yes, only like most deductions, it doesn't get us anywhere. We *can't* walk."

"Not to Coombe of course. Merely to the nearest farm house."

"There isn't any nearest farm house."

"Then to the nearest common or garden house."

"I thought we were going to be serious. Really, there is no house within reasonable walking distance. We are quite in the wilds here. Don't you remember the long stretches of waste land we came through? No one builds on useless ground. The nearest houses of any kind are over on the other side of the lake. The beach is good there and there are a few summer cottages and a boarding house. Farther in is the little railway station of Pine Lake—"

"Jove! That's what we want! Why did you try to frighten me? Once let us reach the station and our troubles are over. There is probably an evening train into Coombe."

"There is. But we shall never catch it. We are on the wrong side of the lake. We have no boat. There is a trail around but it is absolutely out of the question, too far and too rough, even if we knew it, which we do not. It would take a woodsman to follow it even in daylight."

"But—" The doctor hesitated. He was beginning to feel seriously disturbed. It seemed impossible that they could be as isolated as Esther seemed to think. Distance is a small thing to a powerful motor eating up space with an effortless appetite, which deceives novice and expert alike. It is only when one looks back that one counts the miles. He remembered vaguely that the nearest house was a long way back.

"I'll have another try," he answered soberly, "and in the meantime, think—think hard! There may be some place you have forgotten. If not, we are in rather a serious fix."

"There are no bears now," said Esther.

"There are gossips!" briefly.

The girl laughed. The thought of possible gossip seemed to disturb her not at all. "Oh, it will be all right as soon as we explain," confidently. "But Aunt Amy will be terrified. If we could only get word to Aunt Amy! I don't mind so much about Mrs. Sykes, for she is always prepared for everything. She will comfort herself with remembering how she said when she saw it was going to be a lovely day: 'It may be a fine enough morning, Esther, but I have a feeling that something will happen before night. I have put in an umbrella in case of rain and a pair of rubbers and a rug and you'd better take my smelling salts. I hope you won't have an accident, I'm sure, but it's best to be forewarned.'"

The doctor glanced up from his tinkering to join in her laugh. He felt ashamed of himself. The possibility of evil tongues making capital of their enforced position had certainly never entered into the thought of this smiling girl. Yet that such a possibility might exist in Coombe as well as in other places he did not doubt. And she was in his charge. The thought of her clear eyes looking upon the thing which she did not know enough to dread made him feel positively sick!

When he spoke to her again there was a subtle change in his manner. He had become at once her senior, the physician, and man of the world.

"Miss Esther," he said, leaving his futile tampering with the machine, "I can see no way out of this but one. I am a good walker and a fast one. I shall leave you here with the car and the rugs and a revolver (there is one in the tool box), and go back along the road. I shall walk until I come to somewhere and then get a carriage or wagon—also a chaperone—and come back for you. It is positively the only thing to do."

Esther's charming mouth drooped delicately at the corners. "Oh no! That's not at all a nice plan. I'm afraid to stay here. Not of bears, but of tramps—or—or something."

"Where there are no houses there will be no tramps."

"There may be. You never can tell about tramps. And I couldn't shoot a tramp. The very best I could do would be to shoot myself—"

"But—"

"And I might bungle even that!" pathetically.

"But, my dear girl—"

"And anyway, I've thought of another plan. There is a place on the lake, on this side. Not a house exactly, but a log cabin, where old Prue lives. Did you ever hear of old Prue? She is a man-hater and a recluse and lives all by herself in the bush. It is a dreadful place and she keeps a fierce dog! But perhaps she keeps a boat, too. She must keep a boat," cheerfully, "because she lives right by the water and I know she fishes. If she would only let us have the boat! But I warn you she may refuse. She is like the witch in 'Hansel and Gretel.' Do you remember—"

But at the first mention of the boat, the doctor had sprung to action and was now standing ready laden with the basket and the rug. With the air of a man who has never heard of "Hansel and Gretel" he slipped a most businesslike revolver into a pocket of his coat. "For the dog, if necessary," he said. "We must have that boat! Is it far?"

"Quite a walk. About two miles through the bush. But I know the way and the trail is fairly good, or should be. It branches off from the one we took this morning."

The sun was gone when they turned back into the woods but the wonderful after-light of the long Canadian sunset would be with them for a good time yet. There was no breeze to stir the trees, but the air had cooled. It was not unpleasantly hot, now, even in the thickest places. The doctor stepped out briskly.

"Listen!" Esther paused with uplifted finger. The trees were very still but in the undergrowth the life of the woods was beginning to stir. Startled squirrels raced up the fallen logs, glancing backward with curious but resentful eyes. Hidden skirmishings and rustlings were everywhere and something brown and furry darted across the path with a faint cry.

"Don't you feel as if you were in some fairy country?" asked the girl. "You can feel and hear them all about you though they keep well hidden. A million eager eyes are watching, Lilliputian armies lie in ambush beneath the leaves. How quiet they are now that we have stopped moving, but as soon as we go on the hurry and skurry will break out afresh! We are the invading army and the fairies fly to help the wood-folk protect their homes."

As they branched into the deeper path the light grew dimmer. Outside, it would still be clear golden twilight but here the grey had come. And now the trees grew closer together and a whispering began—a weird and wonderful sighing from the soul of the forest; the old, primeval cry to the night and to the stars.

It was almost dark when they reached the tiny clearing by the lake. Across the cleared space the water could be seen, faintly luminous, with the black square of the cabin outlined against it. There was no sign of life or light from the dark windows. A dog began to bark sharply.

"He is chained!" said Callandar. "We are fortunate."

"How can you tell?"

"A free dog never barks in that tone. I think he has been a bad dog to-day. Killing chickens, perhaps, or chasing cats. A man-hater, like your old witch, is certain to have cats! I wonder where she is? Does she count going to bed at sundown as one of her endearing peculiarities?"

"Quite the contrary, I imagine. Let's knock."

They raced up the path to the door like children and struck some lusty blows. No one answered. The door was locked and every window was blank.

"Knock again!"

They knocked again, banged in fact, and then rattled the windows.

"She could never sleep through all that racket!" said Callandar with conviction. "She must be out. Well, out or in, we've got to get that boat. Let's explore—this path ought to lead to the lake."

"Shall we steal it?" in a delighted whisper.

"We probably shall. You won't mind going to jail, I hope?"

"Not at all!" The doctor was walking so rapidly that Esther was a little out of breath. "Only, the oars—are certain—to be locked—in the house!" she warned jerkily.

"Then we shall serve sentence for house breaking also."

"Oh, gracious!" Esther stumbled over the root of a tree and nearly fell. But the doctor only walked the faster. They scrambled together down the steep path and over the stretch of rocky beach to where the tiny float lay a black oblong on the water. The boat house was beside it.

"Eureka!" cried the doctor, springing forward.

But the door of the boat house was open and the boat was gone.

CHAPTER XIII

It is a fact infinitely to be regretted, but the doctor swore!

"Well, did you *ever!*" exclaimed Esther. She was a little tired and more than a little excited, a condition which conduces to hysteria, and collapsing upon the end of the float she began to laugh.

"I wish," said the doctor judicially, "that I knew exactly what you find to laugh at."

"Oh, nothing! Your face—I think you looked so very murderous. And you did swear—didn't you?"

"Beg your pardon, I'm sure," stiffly.

For an instant they gazed resentfully at each other. The doctor was seriously worried. Esther felt extremely frivolous. But if he wanted to be stiff and horrid,—let him be stiff and horrid.

"I declare you act as if it were my fault the old boat is gone!" she remarked aggrievedly.

"Don't be silly!"

An uncomfortable silence followed. Esther began to realise how tired she was. Callandar stared out gloomily over the darkening lake.

"Anyway it's bad enough without your being cross," said Esther in a small voice.

"Cross—my dear child! Did I seem cross? What a brute you must think me. But to get you into this infernal tangle!—If this old woman is out in the boat she'll have to come back some time. She can't stay out on the lake all night."

Esther, who thought privately that this was exactly what the old woman might do, made no reply. She rather liked the tone of his apology and was feeling better.

"Then there is the dog. If she is anywhere near, she will be sure to hear the dog. From the noise he is making she will deduce burglars and return to protect her property. As a man-hater she will have no fear of a mere burglar. Luckily for us, that dog has a carrying voice!"

Scarcely had he spoken than the dog ceased to bark.

"Shall I go and throw sticks at it?" asked Esther helpfully.

"Hush! The dog must have heard something. Let's listen!"

In the silence they listened intently. Certainly there was something, a faint indeterminate sound, a sound not in the bush but in the lake, a sound of disturbed water.

"The dip of a paddle," whispered Callandar. "Some one is coming in a canoe. The dog heard it before we did—recognised it, too, probably. It must be the witch!"

The dipping sound came nearer and presently there slipped from the shadow of the trees a darker shadow, moving. A canoe with one paddle was coming toward them.

Esther with undignified haste scrambled up from the float, abandoning her position in the line of battle in favour of the doctor. The dog broke into a chorus of ear-splitting yelps of warning and welcome. The moving shadow loomed larger and a calm though harsh voice demanded, "Be quiet, General! Who is there?"

"We are!" answered Callandar, stepping as far from the tree shadow as possible. "Picnickers from Coombe, in an unfortunate predicament. Our motor has broken down, and we want the loan of a boat to get over to Pine Lake station."

As he spoke he was vividly conscious of Esther close behind. So near was she that he felt her warm breath on his neck. She was breathing quickly. Was the child really frightened? Instinctively he put out his hand, backward, and thrilled through every nerve when something cool and small and tremulous slipped into it.

The canoe shot up to the float.

"You can't get any boat here."

There was no surprise or resentment in the harsh level voice. Only determination, final and unshakable.

Esther felt the doctor's hand close around her own. Its clasp meant everything, reassurance, protection, strength. In the darkness she exulted and even ventured to frown belligerently in the direction of the disagreeable canoeist. They could see her plainly now. A tall woman in a man's coat with the sleeves rolled up displaying muscular arms. Her face, even in the half-light, looked harsh and gaunt. With a skill, which spoke of long practice, she sprang from the canoe, scarcely rocking it, and proceeded to tie the painter securely to a heavy ring in the float. Then she straightened herself and turned.

"I'll loose the dog!" she announced calmly.

Just that and no more! No arguments, no revilings, no display of any human quality. There was something uncanny in her ruthlessness.

"If you do, it will be bad for the dog," said Callandar coldly. "Who are you who threaten decent people?"

It was the tone of authority and for an instant she answered to it. Her harsh voice held a faint Scotch accent.

"There'll be no decent people here at this hour o' the nicht. Be off. You'll get no boat. Nor the hussy either. The dog's well used to guarding it."

"How dare you!" Esther was so angry at being called a hussy that she forgot how frightened she was and faced the woman boldly. But the old hard eyes stared straight into her young indignant ones and showed no softening. Next moment old Prue had pushed the girl aside and disappeared in the darkness of the wooded path.

"Quick!" The doctor's tone was crisp and steady. "The canoe is our chance. Jump in, while I hold it—in the bow, anywhere!"

"But the paddle! She has taken the paddle!" Even as she objected she obeyed. The frail craft rocked as she slid into it, careful only not to overbalance; next moment it rocked more dangerously and then settled evenly into the water under the doctor's added weight.

"Sit tight!" Carefully he leaned over her, steadying the canoe with one hand on the float. In the other she saw the glint of a knife, felt the confining rope sever, felt the strong push which separated them from the float and then, just as a great dog, fiercely silent now, bounded from the path above, a paddle rose and dipped and they shot out into the lake.

"If he follows and tries to overturn us I'll have to shoot him," said the doctor cheerfully. "But he won't. Hark to him!"

The long bay of the baffled dog rose to the stars.

"There was an extra paddle in the boat-house," he explained. "I took it out when we first came down—in case of accident. Old She-who-must-be-obeyed must have forgotten it. It is a spliced paddle but we shall manage excellently. Luckily I know how to use it. All I need now is direction. Lady, 'where lies the land to which this ship must go?'"

"'Far, far away is all the seamen know,'" capped Esther, laughing. "But if you will keep on around that next point and then straight across I think we ought to get there—Oh, look! there is the moon! We had forgotten about the moon!"

They had indeed forgotten the moon. And the moon had been part of their programme too. Both remembered at the same moment that, according to schedule, they were now supposed to be almost home, running down Coombe hill by moonlight.

"This is much nicer," said Esther, comfortably.

"But—" he did not finish his sentence. Why disturb her? Besides it certainly was much nicer! The forgotten moon bore them no malice. A soft radiance grew and spread around them, the whole sky and lake were faintly shining though the goddess herself had not yet topped the trees. The shadows were becoming blacker and more sharply defined. In front of them the point loomed, inky black. Like a bird of the night the little canoe shot towards it, skimmed its darkness and then slipped, effortless, into shining silver space. The smile of the moon! Pleasing old hypocrite! Always she smiles the same upon two in a canoe!

They were paddling toward her so that her light fell full on the doctor's face—a clean cut, virile face, manly, stern, yet with a whimsical sweetness hidden somewhere.

"How handsome he is!" thought Esther, exactly as the moon intended.

"Strong, too," her thought added as the light picked out his well-set shoulders and the sweep of the arm which sped the paddle so lightly yet so strongly up and down. Clear, yet soft, the moon showed no touch of grey in the hair (although the grey was there) nor did she point out the markings which were the legacy of strenuous years. Seen so, he appeared no older than she who watched shyly from girlish eyes.

With a little shiver of utmost content Esther settled herself against the thwart of the canoe.

Manlike he did not know the meaning of that shiver.

"Fool that I am!" he exclaimed. "You are cold, and behold we have left behind the shawl of Mrs. Sykes' grandmother!"

"Indeed we have not! The dog would have torn it to bits. I assure you the shawl of the venerated ancestress was in the canoe before I was."

"Then wrap yourself up. It is wonderful how cool the nights are."

Esther was not cold. But it is sometimes pleasant to be commanded. This is what enables man to persist in a certain pleasing delusion regarding woman's natural attitude. When she occasionally pleases herself by a simulation of subjection he immediately thrills with pride, crying, "Aha! I have her mastered!" Of course he finds out his mistake later.

It pleased Esther, though not cold, to wrap herself in the shawl and it pleased Callandar to see her do it. I assure you it left the whole question of the subjection of women quite untouched.

The moon knew all about it but, feminine herself, she favoured the deception. Around the girl's dark head she drew a circle of light. The branching tendrils of her hair, all alive and fanlike now in the coolness of the night, made a nimbus of black and silver from which her shadowed face shone like a faint pure pearl. As he seemed younger, so did she seem older; under the moon she was no longer a child, but a woman with mysterious eyes.

An impulse came to him—the rare impulse of confidence! Suddenly it seemed that what he had mistaken for self-sufficiency had been in reality loneliness. He had learned to live to himself not because he was of himself sufficient but because no one else, save the Button Moulder, had ever come within speaking distance. Lorna Sinnet, for all his admiration of her, had established no claim upon his confidence, yet now, with this young girl, whom he had known but a few weeks, a new need developed—a need to talk of himself! A primitive need indeed, but, like all primitive needs, compelling.

We need not follow the history. Perhaps, reported, it would not seem very lucid. There were blanks, unsaid things, twists of phrase, eloquent nothings which, wonderfully understandable in themselves, do not report well. Somehow he must have made it plain, for Esther understood it and understood him, too, in a way which we, who have never sailed with him under the moon, cannot hope to do. Faults of expression are no hindrance to this kind of understanding. He did not talk well, was clumsy, not at all eloquent, but magically she reconstructed the hopes and dreams of his ambitious youth. From a few bald phrases she fashioned the thunderbolt which shattered them, saw him stunned, then alive again, struggling. With every ready imagination she leaped full upon the fires of an ambition which accepted no check but fed upon difficulty and overleapt obstacles. Between stories of his early college life, her sympathy sensed the deadly strain which his narrative missed and, long before he mentioned it, her foresight had descried the coming of hard won success.

But the really vital thing, the core of the short history, she followed slowly word by word, anxiously. It told of wonders which she did not know—love, passion, despair! Now indeed he seemed to be speaking in a strange language—yet not strange entirely. She hid each broken phrase in her heart, knowing them rare, and wondering at the treasure entrusted to her. Some of her girlhood she left behind her as she listened. Something new, yet surely old, stirred faintly. What was this love he spoke of? The breath of bygone passion brushed across her untouched soul and left it trembling!

Into the long silence which followed the story her voice drifted like a sigh.

"If she could only have lived until you came!"

It was of the girl wife she thought. Her heart was full of an aching pity for that other girl whom life had cheated of her sweetest gift. More than the man who had lived out a bitter expiation, did she pity her who had missed the fight, slipped out of the struggle. Death seemed to Esther such a terrible thing. The new life stirring in her shuddered at the thought of mortality. That breath of the divine which we name Love began already to proclaim itself immortal.

Yet Molly, that other girl, had loved — and died.

The doctor, too, was lost in self communings. Already, with the words not cold upon his lips, he was surprised that he had told the story. How could he? Why had he? That pitiful little story of Molly which had been too sacred for the touch of a word. Above all, why had the telling been a relief? It was a relief, he knew that. Somewhere, in the silver waters of Pine Lake he had buried a burden. He felt lighter, younger. Had his very love for Molly become a load whose proper name was remorse? Had his heart harboured regret and fear under the name of sorrow? Or had he never loved at all, never really sorrowed? Had the thing he called love been but a boy's hot passion caught in the grip of a man's awakening will, a mistake made irrevocable by a stubbornness of purpose which could not face defeat? Whatever it had been, it had come to be a burden. And the burden had lightened — it pressed no longer. In a word, he was free! He was his own man again, unafraid, able to look into his heart, to open all the windows — no dark corners, no haunting ghosts! He could enter now without the dread of echoing footsteps or wistful, half-heard whisperings. The shade of pretty, childish Molly would vex no more.

The relief of it — the pain of it! It was like a new birth.

Meanwhile the strong, sure strokes were bringing them swiftly nearer the opposite shore where yellow dots of light proclaimed the position of the summer cottages. One dot, larger, detached itself from the others and indicated the flare on the end of the landing float. Outlines began to be darkly discernible, the moon's silver mirror was shivered by lances of gold. Very soon their journey would be ended.

The paddle dipped more slowly. Esther sighed, and sat up straighter. Considering all the trouble they had taken, neither of them seemed overjoyed to be so near the desired haven.

"We are nearly there," said Callandar obviously.

Esther looked backward over their shining wake. Something precious seemed to be slipping away on those fairy ripples. Yet all she could find to say was—

"We have come very fast. You must be tired."

Strange little commonplaces, how they take their due of all the wonderful hours of life! Esther wriggled out of the shawl, smoothed her hair, arranged her ruffled collar. Callandar shipped his paddle and resumed his coat.

"Where to, now?" he asked practically.

"There is only one landing, we shall be right on it in a moment. Then— there are several of the cottagers whom I know. But I think Mrs. Burton will be the best. She has often asked me to visit her and is such a dear that the present unexpected arrival will not make me less welcome."

"That's good! As for me, I'll make for the station and send the telegrams. They won't be seriously anxious yet, do you think? Then—there is a train I think you said?"

"You have missed that. But there is a very early morning train, a milk train—O gracious!" Esther broke off with a start of genuine consternation. "To-morrow is Sunday!"

"Naturally!" in surprise.

"How horribly unfortunate! The milk train doesn't run on Sunday!"

"Does the milk object to Sunday travelling?"

"Don't joke!" forlornly. "It's dreadful that it should be Sunday. People will talk!"

"Oh, will they?" The doctor was immensely surprised. "Why?"

"Because it's Sunday."

"What has Sunday got to do with it? They can't talk. Here you are safe and sound with your friend Mrs. Burton by 9 o'clock, an intensely respectable hour even in Coombe. What can they say?"

"But it's Sunday! You will return home, by rail, on Sunday. Every one will know. Your breaking of the Sabbath will be put down to careless pleasuring. It will hurt your practice terribly!"

Callandar laughed heartily. But before he could reply the quick bursting out of a blaze upon the shore startled them both. "What is it?" he asked apprehensively.

"Only a bonfire! Some one is giving a bonfire party. It is quite the fashionable thing. There will be songs and speeches with lemonade and cake. Oh, hurry! We shall be in time for the programme."

The mysterious woman, born of the moon, was gone. In her place was a rumple-haired, bright-eyed child. Callandar took up the paddle with a whimsical smile.

"Sit still or you'll overturn the canoe!" he said warningly. And across the narrowing stretch of water floated the opening sentiments of the patriotic cottagers.

"O Cana_dah_, our heritage, our love—"

CHAPTER XIV

Henry Callandar, resting neck-deep in the cool green swimming pool, tossed the wet hair out of his eyes and whistled ingratiatingly to a watching robin. A delightful sense of guilt enveloped him, for it was Sunday morning and, since his experience at Pine Lake a week ago, he had learned a little of what Sunday means in Coombe. Esther had been quite right in fearing that his return by train upon that sacred day might deal a severe blow to his prestige—at least until Mrs. Sykes had had time to explain to every one how unavoidable it had been—and he knew that if he were to be caught in his present delightful occupation his Presbyterian reputation might be considered lost forever.

The robin twittered at him prettily but refused to be beguiled. Sunday bathing was not among its weaknesses. Presently it flew away.

"Gone to tell the minister, I'll be bound!" murmured Callandar. "'Twill be a scandal in the kirk. I'll lose all my five patients. Horrid little bird!"

Smiling, he drew himself from the embrace of the faintly shining water and retiring to the willow screen began to dress with that virtuous leisureliness which characterises those who rise before their fellows. He had the world to himself; a world of cool, sweet scents, pure light and Sabbath quiet—that wonderful quiet which seems a living thing with a personality of its own, so different is it from the ordinary quiet of work-a-day mornings.

The primrose sky gave promise of a beautiful day. The blue grey vault overhead was already filling with shimmering golden light, the drooping willows and the dew-wet grass were stirring in the breeze of dawn, the voice of the water sang in the stillness.

Callandar slipped his blue tie snugly under the collar of his white flannel shirt and sighed with the ecstasy of health renewed. A half-forgotten couplet hummed through his brain.

"Sweet day, so cool, so calm, so bright!
The bridal of the earth and sky—"

"And it's a hymn, too, or I'm a Dutchman," he declared, much edified. "That proves that swimming on Sunday is quite compatible with proper orthodoxy of mind. Shouldn't wonder if the Johnnie who wrote that wrote it on Sunday morning after a dip. I'll tell Mrs. Sykes he did anyway—where in thunder did I put my boots?"

The missing articles had apparently fulfilled the purpose of their being by walking away, or else the robin had collected them as evidence! Callandar chuckled at a whimsical vision of them in a church court, damningly marked "Exhibit 1." But as he searched for them the utter peace of the morning fled and suddenly he became conscious that he and the willows no longer divided the world between them. Some one was near. He felt eyes watching. The curious half-lost instinct which warns man of the approach of his kind, told him that he was no longer alone. The doctor fixed a stern eye on the screening willows.

"Zerubbabel!" he commanded, "come out of there at once, sir!"

A stirring in the bushes was the only answer.

The doctor glanced at his bootless feet.

"Bubble," more mildly, "if you want a swim—"

"It isn't Bubble," said a meek voice, "it's me. Are you dressed enough for me to come out?" Without waiting for an answer the elfish face of Ann appeared through the willow tangle. "If you're looking for your boots," she remarked kindly, "they're hanging on that limb behind you."

But boots no longer absorbed the doctor.

"Come out of those willows, both of you!"

"There's only me," still meekly. "And I didn't come to swim. I came for you. Honour bright! The Button Man's here."

"What?"

"Yes, he is. He came in a big grey car and was sitting on the doorstep when Aunt got up. He told her not to disturb you, but of course Aunt thought that you ought to know at once and when she found that you were gone"—a poignant pause!

"Yes, when she found me gone—"

"When she found you gone," slowly, "she said you must have been called up in the night to a patient!"

"Did she really?" The doctor's laugh rang out.

"And I hope the Lord will forgive her for such a nawful lie!" finished Ann piously.

"He will, Ann, He will! You can depend on that. He has a proper respect for loyalty between friends. Did I understand you to say that you had seen my boots? Oh, yes, thanks! Now I wonder what can have brought our Button Man back so soon? He didn't by any chance say, I suppose?"

"Him?" with scorn. "Not much fear! I'll do up your boots if you like."

"Thanks, no. That would be using unseemly haste. Button-men who go visiting on Sunday must learn to wait. Don't you want to have a splash, Ann? I'll walk on slowly, you can easily catch me up!"

The child looked enviously at the now sparkling water, but shook her head.

"I'd love to. But I dasn't. Aunt always knows when I've been in. Even if I go and muddy myself afterwards, she knows. She says a little bird tells her."

"A robin, I'll bet. I know that bird! Sanctimonious thing! He was watching me this morning and went off as fast as he knew how, to spread the news. Ann, you have lived in this remarkable town all your life. Can you tell me just why it is wicked to go swimming on Sunday?"

Ann looked blank. "No. But it is. You're likely to get drowned any minute! Not but what I'd risk it if it wasn't for Aunt. I'm far more scared of Aunt than I am of God," she added reflectively.

"Why, Ann! What do you mean?"

"Well, you never can tell about God, but Aunt's a dead sure thing! If she says you'll get a smack for going in the river you'll get it—but God only drowns a few here and there, for examples like."

"Look here!" Callandar paused in his stride and fixed her dark eyes by the sudden seriousness in his own. "You've got the thing all wrong. God doesn't drown people for swimming on Sunday. He isn't that sort at all. He—He—" the unaccustomed teacher of youth faltered hopelessly in his effort to instruct the budding mind, but Ann's eyes were questioning and at their bidding the essential truth of his own childhood came back to him. "God is Love," he declared firmly. "Great Scott! a person would think that we lived in the Dark Ages! Don't you let 'em frighten you, Ann. What are you allowed to do on Sunday anyway?"

"Church," succinctly. "And Sunday-school and church and the 'Pilgrim's Progress.'"

"Well, that's something. Jolly good book, the 'Pilgrim's Progress'!"

"Yes," dubiously. "If it didn't use such a nawful lot of big words. And if he'd only get on a little faster. He was terrible slow."

"So he was. Well, let us be merry while we can. I'll race you to the orchard gate."

At the gate they paused to regain their lost breath and sense of decorum for, across the orchard, the veranda could be plainly seen with the trim figure of Professor Willits in close proximity to the taller and gaunter outline of Mrs. Sykes. With one of her shy quick gestures, the child slipped her fingers from the doctor's hold and sped away through the trees. Her friendship with Callandar was the most wonderful thing that had ever happened to Ann, but she was not of the kind which parades intimacy.

"Patient dead?" asked Willits dryly after they had shaken hands.

"Patient?" Then, catching sight of the flaming red in the cheeks of his landlady, "Dead? Certainly not. Even my patients know better than to die on a morning like this. But whatever possessed you to disturb a righteous household? Mrs. Sykes, he doesn't deserve breakfast, but I do. When do you think—"

"In just about five minutes, Doctor. Soon's I get the coffee boiling and the cream skimmed. I didn't know," with an anxiously reproving glance, "but what you might want to get washed up after you got in."

"I—no, I think I'm quite clean enough, Mrs. Sykes. But it was very thoughtful of you to wait—"

"Aunt, the coffee's boiling over!" The warning was distinctly audible and, with a gesture of one who abandons an untenable position, Mrs. Sykes retreated upon the kitchen.

The visitor watched her flight with mild amaze.

"I suppose I should seem curious if I were to ask why the excellent Mrs. Sykes imperils her immortal soul in your behalf? But why in the name of common sense is the peril necessary? It isn't a crime, is it, for a medical man to get up early and go for a swim?"

"You forget what day it is," said Callandar solemnly. "Or rather, you never knew. I myself was not properly acquainted with Sunday until I came to this place. Your presence here is in itself a scandal. People do not visit upon the Seventh day in Coombe."

"No? You should have informed me of the town's eccentricities. As it is, if my presence imperils your social standing you can seclude me until the next train."

"Better than that," cheerfully, "I can take you to church."

The alarmed look upon the professor's face was so enticing that Callandar continued with glee:

"Why not? I have always thought your objection to church-going a blot upon an otherwise estimable character. Hitherto I have been too busy to attend to it, but now—"

"Quit chaffing, Harry! I came up because I had to see you. You pay no attention to my letters. I never dreamed that you would stay a month in this backwater. What is wrong? What is the matter with you?"

"Look at me—and ask those questions again."

The keen eyes of the Button-Moulder looked deep into the doctor's steady ones. There was a slight pause. Then—

"Yes, I see what you mean. I saw it as you came across the orchard." The sharp voice softened. "My anxiety for your health could hardly survive the way in which you leaped that fence! But all this makes it only the more mysterious. Have you found the fountain of youth or—or what?"

Callandar threw an affectionate arm over the other man's shoulders.

"I *am* young, amn't I! Trouble is, I didn't know it." He ruffled his hair at the side so that the grey showed plainly. "Terrible thing when one loses the realisation of youth! But I've had my lesson. I'll never be old again, never!"

In spite of himself the professor's straight mouth curved a little. A spark of pride glowed in his cool eyes as he bent them upon the smiling face of his friend. Yet his tone was mocking as he said, "Then it is the fountain of youth? One is never too old to find that chimera."

"It's not something that I've found, old cynic. It's something that I've lost. Look at me hard! Don't you notice something missing? Did you ever read the 'Pilgrim's Progress'?"

"The Pilgrim's—"

"Breakfast is ready!" called Ann, teetering on her toes in the doorway.

"The Pil—"

"And   Aunt—says—will—you—please—come—at—once—so's—the coff—ee—won't—be—cold!" chanted Ann.

"Yes, Ann. We're coming."

"But I want to know—"

"Old man, I'll tell you after breakfast. I want you to see me eat. I wish to demonstrate that there is no deception. A miracle has really happened. No one could observe me breakfasting and doubt it!"

When they were seated he looked guilelessly into the still disapproving face of Mrs. Sykes. "Perhaps you are wondering, as I did, what has brought Professor Willits back to Coombe," he said, "but time and space mean little to professors, and the fact is that Willits has long wished to hear a sermon by the Reverend Mr. Macnair. He is coming with me this morning. Perhaps you hadn't better mention it, though. It might disturb Mr. Macnair to know that so eminent a critic was listening to him."

The eminent critic frowned grimly and took a fourth cream biscuit without noticing it.

"Not a mite!" declared Mrs. Sykes. "The man ain't born that can fluster Mr. Macnair. Nor yet the woman, unless it's Esther Coombe—Land sakes, Doctor! I forgot to tell you how that cup tips! Ann, get a clean table napkin. I hope your nice white pants ain't ruined, Doctor? I really ought to put that cup away but it's a good cup if it's held steady and I hate to waste good things. Last time it tipped was when the Ladies' Aid met here. Mrs. Coombe had it and the whole cup spilled right over her dress. I was that mortified! But she didn't seem to care. I can't imagine what's the matter with that woman. She's getting dreadful careless about her clothes. Next time I met her she wore that same dress, splash an' all! 'Tisn't as if she hadn't plenty of new things,—more than they can afford, if what folks say is true. You haven't met Mrs. Coombe yet, have you, Doctor?"

"She is away from home."

"Well, when you do meet her you'll see what I mean, or like as not you won't, being a man. Men never seem to see anything wrong with Mary Coombe. But Esther must feel dreadful mortified sometimes when her Ma forgets to get hooked up behind. Esther's as neat as a pin. Always was. Why, even when she got home last week after that awful time you and she had up at Pine Lake, and her having to stay overnight without so much as a clean collar, she walked in here as fresh as a daisy—won't you let me give you some more coffee, Professor?"

"Thank you, yes. You were saying—"

"Willits, do you think so much coffee is good for you?"

"Land sakes, Doctor, my coffee won't hurt him! It never seems to trouble you any. As I was saying, one would almost have thought that what with picnicking in the bush all day and trapesing around in a canoe half the night and having to stay where she wasn't expected and wouldn't like to ask the loan of the flat-irons—"

"Please, Mrs. Sykes, don't let Ann eat another biscuit. I don't want her to be ill just when I want a day off to take Willits to church. Willits, as your medical adviser, I forbid more coffee. He will really injure himself, Mrs. Sykes, if I do not take him away. He isn't used to breakfasts like this and his constitution won't stand it."

Mrs. Sykes beamed graciously under this delicate compliment and confiscated Ann's latest biscuit with a ruthless hand. "If you gentlemen would like to sit in the parlour—" she offered graciously. But Callandar with equal graciousness declined. The office would do quite well enough. Willits might want to smoke. "And as it-seems that my watch has stopped," he added, "perhaps you would be so kind as to tell us when it is time to change for church."

The professor settled himself primly upon the hardest chair which the office contained and refused a cigar.

"You seem to have acquired a reprehensible habit of fooling, Henry," he said. "Your language also is strange. When, for instance, you say 'change for church,' to what sort of transformation do you refer?"

Callandar chuckled.

"Only to your clothes, old chap. Don't worry. You wouldn't expect me to go to church in flannels?"

"I should not expect you to go to church at all."

"Well, the fact is, old man, you are painfully ignorant. I do go to church, and the proper church costume for a professional man is a frock coat and silk hat. But as you are a traveller, and as you are not exactly a professional man, I shall not lose caste by taking you as you are."

The imperturbable Willits waived the point. "I understood you to say, also, that your watch had stopped. Was that a joke?"

"No such luck!" The doctor took out his watch and shook it. "Mainspring gone, I'm afraid!"

"A month ago," said the professor, "if your watch had stopped you would have had a fit."

"Really! Was I ever such an ass? Well, I'm not the slave of my watch any longer. Time goes softly in Coombe. Aren't you glad I'm not taking a fit?"

"I am glad. But I want to understand."

"Then let's return to the 'Pilgrim's Progress.' Ann and I were talking about it this morning. Do you remember the man with the pack on his back and how when he reached a certain spot the pack, seemingly without effort of his own, fell off and was seen no more?"

Willits reflected. The doctor was thoroughly in earnest now. "I seem to recollect the incident to which you refer," he said after a pause. "If I remember rightly it is an allegory and is used in a definitely religious sense. The man with the pack meets a certain spiritual crisis. Do I understand that you—er—that you have experienced conversion? I am not guilty of speaking lightly of so important a matter, but I hardly know how to frame my question."

The doctor tilted back his chair and looked dreamily out of the window. "I did not mean you to take my illustration literally. My religious beliefs are very much the same as they have always been. To a materialist like you they seem, I know, absurdly orthodox; to a church member in good standing they might seem fatally lax; but such as they are I have not changed them. Still, I was, as you know, a man with a burden. You may call the burden consequence or what you will, the name doesn't matter. The weight of that youthful, selfish, unpardonable act which bound a young girl to me without giving her the protection which that bond demanded, was always upon me, crushing out the joy of life. The news of her death made no difference, except to render me hopeless of ever making up to her for the wrong I had done. Her death did not set me free, it bound me closer.

"I seemed like one caught in the tow of some swift tide, always fighting to get back, yet eternally being drawn away. The tide still flows out, for the tide of human life is the only tide which never returns, but I have ceased to struggle. I no longer look back. It is not that God has forgiven me (I have never been able to think of God as otherwise than forgiving), it is that I have forgiven myself."

CHAPTER XV

"It amounts to this, then," said Willits presently. "You are cured. The balance is swinging true again. It has taken a long time, but the cure is all the more complete for that. Now, when are you coming back to us?"

Callandar did not answer.

"You are needed. Not a day passes that your absence is not felt. You used to have a strong sense of responsibility toward your work. What has become of it?"

"I have it still. I am not slighting my work by taking time to build myself into better shape for it."

"But you will simply stagnate here!" querulously. "You are becoming slack already. You let your watch run down."

The doctor laughed.

"If many of my patients could do the same without worry they would not need a doctor. Half of the nervous trouble of the age can be ultimately traced to watches which won't run down. Leisure—unhurried leisure—that is what we want. We've got to have it!"

"Piffle! I shall hear you talk about inviting your soul next."

"Well, if I do he is in better shape to accept the invitation than he used to be."

The professor's gesture was sufficiently expressive.

"Very well. I give up. Remember, I advise against it. I think you are making a mistake!—I'll have that cigar now. I suppose one is allowed to smoke in the garden?"

"Yes, do, that's a good fellow! I must run up and make myself presentable. I suppose you haven't seen Lorna lately?"

"I have seen her very lately. She asked to be remembered."

"Oh, you old prevaricator! Lorna never asked to be remembered in her life. What she really said was, 'If you see Harry give him my love!'"

"If she did, you don't deserve it! Oh, boy," with sudden earnestness, "why will you make a fool of yourself? She's a woman in a thousand. Others see it if you don't. Since you've been away, MacGregor is paying her marked attention."

"Good old Gregor!" The doctor's exclamation was one of pure pleasure. "And yet you say my absence isn't doing any good? Go along with you! Take your cigar and wait for me underneath the Bough. I'll not be long."

He was long, however. The professor's cigar and his cogitations came to an end together without the promised reappearance. Even when he returned to the office it was empty except for Ann, who in the stiffest of starched muslin and whitest of stockings was spread out carefully upon the widest chair. Her black hair was parted as if by a razor blade and plastered tightly in slablike masses while the tension of the braids was such that they stuck out on either side of the small head like decorated sign posts. Weariness, disgust and defiance were painted visibly upon the elfish face.

"This is the best chair!" said Ann politely, "but if you'll excuse me I shan't get up. Every time I sit down it makes a crease in a fresh place. By the time church is over I look like I was crumpled all over. It's the starch!" she added in sullen explanation.

Willits, who liked children but did not understand them, essayed a mild joke.

"Did you put some starch in your hair too?"

Ann flushed scarlet with anger and mortification and made no answer.

"It looked much nicer at breakfast," blundered on the professor genially. "If I were you I should unstarch it—" he paused abashed by the glare in Ann's black eyes and turned helplessly to Callandar, who had just come in, resplendent in faultless church attire.

"Don't listen to him, Ann!" said the doctor. "Button moulders are so ignorant. They know absolutely nothing about hair or the necessity for special tidiness on Sundays. All the same, I'm afraid we shall have a headache if we don't let a reef out somewhere. Sit still a moment, Ann. I was always intended for a barber."

To the fresh astonishment of Willits his friend's skilful hands busied themselves with the tightly drawn hair which, only too eager for freedom, soon fell into some of its usual curves. With a quick, shy gesture the child drew the adored hand to her lips and kissed it. Callandar turned a deep red. The professor chuckled, and Ann, furious at betraying herself before him, fled precipitately, the crackling starch of her stiff skirts rattling as she ran.

For a moment Willits enjoyed his friend's embarrassment and then, as the probable meaning of the frock coat began to dawn upon him, his expression changed to one of apprehension.

"You weren't in earnest about that church nonsense, were you?"

"Certainly. If you need a clean collar take one of mine, and hurry up. The first bell has stopped ringing."

"But I'm not going!"

"Not if I ask you nicely?"

"But why? What are you going for?"

"Come and see."

The shrewd eyes of the professor grew coldly thoughtful.

"That is exactly what I shall do," he decided.

From the home of Mrs. Sykes upon Duke Street to the First Presbyterian Church upon Oliver's Hill is a brisk walk of fifteen minutes. As Coombe lies in a valley, Oliver's Hill is not a hill, really, but a gentle eminence. It is a charming, tree-lined street bordered by the homes and gardens of the well-to-do. It is, in fact, *the* street of Coombe, and to live upon Oliver's Hill is a social passport seldom mentioned but never ignored.

As if social prominence were not enough, it had another claim upon the affections and memories of many, for up this hill every Sunday in a long and goodly stream poured the first Presbyterians who were not only the elect but also the elite of Coombe. To see Knox Church "come out" was one of the sights of the town and, decorously hidden behind a muslin curtain, a stranger might feast his eyes upon greatness unrebuked. It was said at one time that every silk hat in Coombe attended Knox Church, but this was vainglory, for it was afterwards proved that several repaired to St. Michael's and at least one to the Baptist tabernacle. With this explanation you will at once understand why the sidewalk was a few feet broader upon the church side of Oliver's Hill, and if this circumstance savours to you of ecclesiastical privilege we can only conclude that you are not Presbyterian, and request you not to be so narrow-minded.

As the doctor and his half-reluctant friend turned at the foot of the hill they were immediately absorbed by the stream pressing upwards, for the last bell had already begun to ring.

"We're all right," whispered Callandar encouragingly. "It rings for five minutes."

The professor opened his lips to say something, but shut them with a snap. There was probably method in the doctor's madness but it was method which would never be disclosed through much questioning. With an expression of intense solemnity he fixed his eyes, gimlet-like, upon the middle button of the Sunday blouse of the lady in front of him and followed up the hill. To the absurdly low-toned remarks of his companion he vouchsafed no reply whatever.

They entered the church to the subdued rustle of Sunday silks and the whisper of Sunday voices. At the door some one shook hands with Callandar and remarked in a ghostly whisper that it was a fine day. A grave young man, in black, led them to a pew half way down the aisle. Most of the pews were already full, the latest comers showing slight signs of hurry; and as they seated themselves the bell stopped and the organ began.

There was a moment's expectant interval and then two doors, one at either side of the pulpit, opened simultaneously and the minister entered from one side, the choir from the other. Before the minister walked a very solemn man with abnormally long upper lip. This was Elder John MacTavish, a man of large substance, of great piety and poor digestion. It was upon this latter account that the doctor always observed him with peculiar interest, for had not Mrs. Sykes declared that if he should only be called in once to prescribe for John MacTavish's stomach his future in Coombe was secure?

"Doctor Parker is doing him just no good at all," she reported. "So keep an eye on him. If he looks especially dour it's a good sign."

"Would you say that he looks especially 'dour'?"
whispered Callandar to Willits.

"I should. Why?"

"Oh, nothing—only it's a good sign! Hush!"

When the minister has entered the pulpit at Knox Church there is a moment during which you may bow your head, or, if you consider this popish, you may cover your face with your gloved hand. It is a moment of severe quiet. One does not dare even to cough. Hence the doctor's warning "hush!"

But this morning the quiet was rudely broken. Somewhere, just outside the open windows, sounded a laugh; a young, clear, unrestrained laugh, then the call of a sharp whistle, and next moment, through the doors not yet closed, hurtled something yellow and long-legged! With a joyous bark it rushed along the nearest aisle, across the front of the pulpit, down the other aisle and out at the door again.

The congregation was amazed and grieved. Its serenity was shaken, even the minister seemed disturbed. Some younger members of the choir giggled. It was most unseemly.

"Naughty dog!" said the voice outside the window. "Go home! Don't dare to lick my hand!"

One of the choir members grew red in the face and choked. It was outrageous! And then, as if nothing at all had happened, the girl who had been the cause of the whole unfortunate incident entered and walked down the aisle. She appeared to be quite undisturbed; was, in fact, smiling. Every eye in the church followed her as, a little out of breath, a little flushed, with dark hair slightly disarranged as if from an exciting chase, she took her seat, unconscious, or careless, of them all. The minister, who had paused with almost reproachful obviousness, gave out the opening psalm and the congregation freed itself from embarrassment with an accustomed flutter of hymn-books.

Going to church was somewhat interesting after all, thought Professor Willits. Then, in common with the rest of the congregation, he detached his eyes from the girl's exquisite profile and focused them upon the minister.

Friends of the Rev. Angus Macnair asserted that he was a man in a thousand. For that matter he was a man in any number of thousands; for his was a personality, true to type, yet not likely to be duplicated. Born of a Highland Scotch father and a Lowland Scotch mother, he developed almost exclusively in his father's vein. Loyal in the extreme, narrow to fanaticism, passionate, emotional, yet trained to the cold control of a red Indian, he was a man of power, at once the victim and the triumph of his creed.

Early in life he had come under a conviction of sin, had received assurance of forgiveness and of election and, before he had left the Public School, his Call had come. From that time forward he had burnt with a fierce fire of godliness which, together with a natural incapacity for seeing two sides to anything, had carried him safely through the manifold temptations to unbelief and heresy which beset a modern college education. Many wondered that a man so gifted should remain in Coombe, but the explanation is simple. He suited Coombe; the larger churches of the larger cities he did not suit. Lax opinions, heretical doctrines, outlooks appallingly wide were creeping in everywhere. It is safe to say that in most of the churches of his own faith he would have seemed bravely but hopelessly behind the times. But in Coombe he had found his place. Coombe was conservative. Coombe Presbyterians were still content to do without frills in the matter of doctrine. Coombe could still listen to hell fire and, if not unduly disturbed, did not at least smile behind its hand.

Something of all this the Button-Moulder, student of men, felt as he watched the sombre yet glowing face of the preacher.

The sermon that morning was one of a series dealing with the Commandments and the text was, "Thou shalt not bear false witness against thy neighbour." The speaker had the scholar's power of concentration, the orator's power of delivery. He was both poignant and personal. He seemed to do everything save mention names. Some sinners in that congregation, thought Willits, had undoubtedly been bearing false witness, and were now listening to a few plain words! Cautiously he glanced around, almost expecting to see the tale of guilt and sorrow legibly imprinted upon some culprit's face. But no one seemed at all disturbed, save one old lady who glared back at him an unmistakable "Thou art the man!" The congregation sat, serenely, soberly attentive, testifying their entire agreement with the speaker by an occasional sigh or nod. The more fiery the preacher's denunciations, the more complacent his hearers. In astonishment Willits realised that, if appearances go for anything, no one in Knox Presbyterian Church had ever borne false witness against anybody!

The collecting of the offering was somewhat of an anti-climax, as was also the anthem by the choir, the latter consisting of a complicated arrangement of the question, "If a man die shall he live again?" reiterated singly by all parts in succession, by duets and quartets and finally by the whole choir, without so much as a shadow of an answer appearing anywhere.

Willits gave a long sigh as they stepped into the summer day again. It had not been uninteresting, but he was quite ready for lunch. The doctor, on the contrary, seemed unaccountably to linger. He even paused to talk to a fat lady in mauve velvet who had mauve cheeks to match.

"So glad to see you in church, Doctor! Young men, you know, are inclined to be young men! And these nice days—very tempting, I'm sure! Is your friend a stranger?"

Callandar gravely introduced Willits, who became immediately convinced that this mauve lady was the most unpleasant person he had ever seen and doubtless the very person to whom the minister had spoken in his sermon.

Why had Callandar let him in for this? Why was he waiting around for anyway? There he was, shaking hands with some one else—this time it was the girl who had laughed.

"May I present my friend, Professor Willits, Miss Coombe?"

The girl extended a graceful hand and for an instant the professor was permitted a look into eyes which caused him to set his firm lips somewhat grimly.

"And I know, Willits, you will be delighted to meet our pastor, Mr. Macnair."

A spark began to glow in the professor's eye, but Callandar's face was guileless. The minister shook hands with professional heartiness, but his gaze, Willits thought, was wandering. He began to feel interested.

"Very fine day," he remarked imperturbably.

"Lovely, lovely," agreed the minister, still heartily. The mauve lady was waiting for the pastoral handshake, but he did not notice her. He was watching the dark girl talking to Callandar.

"What is so rare as a day in June?" said Willits, with deliberate malice.

"Ah, yes, very much so. Delighted to have met you. You will excuse me, I'm sure. Annabel," with an impatient glance toward a stout, awkward woman in the background, "if you are not quite ready I think Miss Coombe and I will walk on." He moved toward the dark girl as he spoke and Willits followed.

"Then I'll have to come some other day to get the roses," they heard Callandar say. "But remember I haven't a single flower in the office. So it will have to be soon."

"At any time," answered the girl, flushing slightly.

"No flowers?" repeated the minister, a little fussily, "dear me, I will speak to my sister. Annabel will be delighted to send you any quantity, Doctor. You must really drop in to see our garden, some day. Sunday, of course, is a busy day with me. Come, Miss Esther. Good morning, Doctor. Good morning, Professor. Glad to see you at our services any time—"

Bowing courteously, the minister moved away, followed perforce by Miss Coombe. (An invitation to lunch at the manse is an honour not to be trifled with.) Perforce also the doctor stood aside and Willits caught the look, half shy, half merry, which the girl threw him from the depths of her remarkable eyes. It was really quite interesting, and rather funny. Not often had he seen fair ladies carried off from under the nose of Henry Callandar. Transferring his glance quickly to the face of his friend, he hoped to surprise a look of chagrin upon his abashed countenance, but the countenance was not abashed, and the look which he did surprise there startled him considerably. Henry Callandar, of all men, to be looking after any girl with a look like that!

Well, he had been invited to come and see. And he had seen.

CHAPTER XVI

As Esther walked away, demurely acquiescent, by the side of the Rev. Mr. Macnair she was conscious of a conflict of emotions. The sight of the doctor's disappointed face as he stood hat in hand, awoke regret and perhaps a trifle of girlish gratification. She had been sorry herself to miss that half hour among the roses but she was still too young and too happy to know how few are such hours, how irrevocable such losses. Also, it had seemed good to her maidenly pride that Dr. Callandar should know—well, that he should see—just exactly what he should know and see she did not formulate. But underneath her temporary disappointment she felt as light and glad as a bird in springtime.

The minister was speaking, but he had been speaking for several moments before Esther's delighted flutter would permit of her listening to him. When at last her thoughts came back she noticed, with a happy-guilty start, that his tone was one of dignified reproof.

"Naturally we all understand," he was saying, "at least I hope we all understand, that you are not primarily to blame. At the worst one can only impute carelessness—"

"Oh, but it wasn't carelessness! You don't know Buster. He's the *cleverest* dog! He hid. I had no idea that he was with me until he bounded past me at the church door. And though I whistled and tried to grab him he was in before I knew it. I'll make him sit up meekly and beg your pardon."

A flush of what in a layman might have been anger crimsoned the minister's cheek.

"You are well aware," stiffly, "that I am not referring to the incident of the dog."

"To what then? I am sorry I wasn't listening but you seemed to be scolding and I couldn't think of anything else." Even the abstruse Mr. Macnair saw that her surprise was genuine. His tone grew gentler.

"You are very young, Miss Esther. But since I must speak more plainly, I was referring to that mad escapade of a week ago. Don't misunderstand me, the blame undoubtedly rests upon the man who was thoughtless enough, selfish enough, to put you in such a position."

"Whatever do you mean?" Esther was torn between anger and a desire to laugh. But seeing the earnestness in his face, anger predominated. "Can you possibly be referring to the breakdown of Dr. Callandar's motor?" she asked coldly.

"I refer to the whole unfortunate adventure. If your step-mother had been at home I feel sure it would not have happened. She would never have permitted the excursion to take place."

The girl's dark brows drew together in their own peculiar manner.

"Let us be honest," she suggested. "You know quite well that my step-mother would not have bothered about it in the least."

"I feel it my duty," went on the minister, "to tell you that there were some peculiar features in connection with the disablement of the motor. I understand from the mechanician who accompanied Dr. Callandar to the spot for the recovery of the machine that there was really very little the matter. A short ten minutes completed the necessary repairs."

"Ten minutes? Oh, how silly he must have felt—the doctor I mean. After all the hours he spent and the things he said." She laughed with reminiscent amusement. "He threw the monkey wrench at it, too. And he thought he knew so much about motors!"

Her companion observed her with sombre eyes. Was it possible that she had actually missed the point of his remark?

"Can you understand," he said slowly, "how a man used to driving a motor car can have been entirely baffled by so slight an accident? To me it seems—odd!"

"So Dr. Callandar thought, only he expressed it more forcibly."

"And you?"

"Well, I suppose I was heartless. But it was the funniest thing I ever saw!" Esther's laughter bubbled again.

They were now at the manse gate. He saw that he must hasten.

"My dear Miss Esther, let us be serious. I do not like to disturb your mind but I have a duty in this matter. Has it never occurred to you that this so-called accident may not have been so—so—er—entirely—er—irremediable, so to speak, as it was made to appear?"

"Do you mean that he did it on purpose?" The tone was one of blank amazement. Esther's hand was upon the gate but forgot to press the latch. She was a quick brained girl and the insinuation in the minister's words had been patent. Yet that he should be capable of such an idea seemed incredible! Had he been looking at her he would have seen the clear red surge over her face from neck to brow and then recede, but not before it had lighted a danger spark in her eyes.

"You did mean that!" She went on before he could answer. The scorn in her voice stung. But the Reverend Angus was not a coward.

"That was my meaning. You are a young and inexperienced girl. You go upon an excursion with a man whom none of us know. An accident, a very peculiar accident, happens. You are led to believe that the damage is serious, but later, when the matter is investigated, it is found to have been trifling. What is the natural inference? What have you to say?"

"It has been said before," calmly.

"Well—"

"Thou shalt not bear false witness against thy neighbor."

They faced each other, the man and the girl. And the man's eyes fell.

"God forbid that I should do so," he murmured.

Esther's face softened. Her anger was not proof against humility.

"If you are really disturbed about it," she said slowly, "I can reassure you. You say that you do not know Dr. Callandar. But I do know him. The whole situation rests upon that. He is a man incapable of the caddish villainy you impute. Why he could not repair the car, I cannot say. I think," with a smile, "that he does not know quite as much about cars as he thinks he does. But he did his best, I know that! When we found his efforts useless we took the only course possible and made at once for the canoe. We had to steal it, you remember, but the doctor showed no faltering in that. He was also prepared to shoot the dog. And you have my word for it that he made no attempt to swamp the canoe or to otherwise complicate matters. I arrived at Mrs. Burton's by ten minutes past nine. She was delighted to see me. Dr. Callandar walked over to the station and sent telegrams to Aunt Amy and Mrs. Sykes. He returned to Coombe upon the morning train. I remained with Mrs. Burton and came back in time for school on the milk train Monday morning. That is the whole story of the adventure and, to be frank, I enjoyed it immensely."

The minister shook his head, but he could say no more. His attitude had not changed, yet he felt a sense of shame before the straightforward honesty of Esther's outlook. She had no sense of the evil of the world. That very fact seemed to make the world less evil.

"When will Mrs. Coombe be back?" he asked abruptly.

Immediately the girl's frank look clouded. "I do not know," she said. "She hardly ever tells me when she is returning. She may be at home any day now. You know how impulsively she acts."

"Yes—just so." The minister's manner was absent. "The fact is I wish very much to speak with your mother regarding a certain matter. Not the matter we have been discussing, we will say no more of that, but a matter of great importance to—er—to me. The importance is such indeed that I doubt if I am justified in delaying longer if you have no idea of when I may expect to see her."

Had Esther been noticing she must have remarked the unusual agitation of his manner, but Esther was not noticing.

"Is it anything you could discuss with me?" she asked innocently. "Mother cares less and less for business. Unless it is something quite private she will probably turn it over to me in any case."

"But this is not—er—a matter of business. Not exactly. Not a business matter at all, in fact. It is a matter which—"

"Oh, there you are!" Miss Annabel's voice was breathless but gratified and free from the faintest suspicion of having arrived, as usual, at exactly the wrong moment. "Are you showing Esther the new rose, Angus? Such a disappointment, Esther, my dear! I had quite made up my mind that it was to be red. It came out pink, and such a beautifully strong plant—such a waste! I simply can't make myself care for pink roses. They are so common. Was I very long? You must both be starved. I know I am. Won't you come upstairs, Esther, and put off your hat?"

Esther intimated that she would. Just now, she had no desire for the further company of Mr. Macnair. She was conscious even of a faint stirring of dislike. Therefore the eagerness with which she followed Miss Annabel filled that good lady with hospitable reproach.

"I didn't intend to be so long," she apologised, "but you know what choir-leaders are? And Angus won't speak to him. I can't make Angus out lately. Tell me," abruptly, as they stood in the cool front room with its closed green shutters, "did *you* notice anything peculiar about Angus?"

"No," in surprise, "is he peculiar?"

"Quite. He's getting fussy. He never used to be fussy. The trouble was to induce him to be fussy enough. Except over church matters. But this morning he was just like an ordinary man. About his collar" (Miss Annabel had a fascinating habit of disjointing her sentences anywhere) "nothing suited him. And you know, Esther, what care I always take with his collars.

He said they were too shiny. Of course they're shiny. Why not? He said he noticed that men weren't wearing shine on their collars now. Fancy that!"

"Not really?" Esther's fresh laugh rang out.

"Well, words to that effect. He asked me if I wanted to make him a laughing stock before the congregation. Did you ever? And he *banged the door!*"

"Does he not bang doors usually?"

"Never. And he banged it hard. It shook the house."

"But people have to bang doors, hard, sometimes, even ministers. I wouldn't worry if I were you. It probably did him the world of good. As for the collars—he may have been noticing Dr. Callandar's. Mrs. Sykes says the doctor sends all his laundry to the city."

"You don't say? And is it different from ours?"

"I—yes, I think it does look different."

"How did you happen to notice it? Oh, Esther, you aren't really carrying on with that strange young man, are you?"

The girl's cheek flamed. The question, she knew, was void of offence. "Carrying on" meant nothing, but the homely phrase seemed suddenly very displeasing—horribly vulgar! Her very ears burned. What if, some time, he should hear a like phrase used to describe their wonderful friendship? The thought was acute discomfort. Oh, how mean and small and misunderstanding people were!

She took off her hat and smoothed her hair without answering. But Miss Annabel was so used to having her anxious queries unanswered that she did not notice the lack.

"I know you haven't, of course," she went on. "But Coombe is such a place for gossip. Ever since you and he had that smash-up with the automobile, people have kind of got it into their heads that you're keeping company. But I said to Mrs. Miller, 'I know Esther Coombe better than you do and it isn't at all likely that a girl who can pick and choose will go off with a stranger—even if he is a doctor. And,' I said, 'how do we know he is a doctor anyway?' Goodness knows he came into the place like a tramp. You've heard, haven't you, Esther, how he came into the Imperial with nothing but a knapsack and riding in Mournful Mark's democrat?"

This time she did pause for an answer and Esther said "Yes," shortly.

"Then that settles it. I knew you had some sense. Just like I said to Mrs. Miller. Next time I see her I'll tell her what you say. 'Tisn't as if we knew anything about the man. No wonder you feel vexed about it."

"I hope you will not mention the subject at all."

"Of course not. Except to tell them how silly they are. You're sure you didn't notice anything queer about Angus when you were walking home from church?"

"Nothing at all." Yet, as she said it, it occurred to her that she had noticed something unusual in the minister's manner—an agitation, a lack of poise! "Perhaps he is disturbed about church matters," she suggested, thinking of the interrupted conversation about the important matter which was not business. "Why don't you ask him?"

Miss Annabel shook her head. "Oh, I never ask him anything! But," cheerfully, "I almost always manage to find out. I'm rather good at finding out things. But this isn't a church matter. I know all the symptoms of that. This is different. It's—it's more human!"

"Liver?" suggested Esther.

"No. I know the symptoms of liver too, Esther! What if it should be *Love!*"

The idea was so daring that Miss Macnair justly spoke it in italics. But the attitude of her listener was disappointing. Esther looked as if it might be quite a natural thing for the minister of Knox Church to fall in love.

"Love!" she said the word caressingly. "Perhaps it is. They say love is a disturbing thing. But—does it usually make a man bang doors?"

"It often turns a sensible man into a fool." Miss Annabel's tone held bitterness. "But what I can't discover is this! If Angus is in love, whom is he in love with?" The question was delivered with such force that Esther jumped.

"I'm sure I don't know!"

"Nor do I. And that is what I must find out. I have my suspicions. My dear, don't let me startle you, but have you ever thought that it might possibly be—your mother?"

"Gracious! So it might! I never thought of it."

"I have not been blind," went on Miss Annabel complacently. "I have noticed how often he calls at the Elms and how long he stays. Also how very considerate he is of Mrs. Coombe, how patient with Jane, how indulgent with you—"

"Indulgent with me!" indignantly. "Why should he be 'indulgent' with me?"

"Why, indeed," asked Miss Macnair pointedly, "unless on account of your mother?"

Esther subdued a desire to laugh. Many little things, half-observed, seemed to fit in with Miss Annabel's theory. Yet, somehow, instinct told her that the theory was wrong.

"I don't believe it," she declared finally. "At first I thought it possible but now I seem to know that we're on the wrong track. Mr. Macnair is not in love with mother, and as for mother—Oh, the thing is absurd! Aren't you awfully hungry, Miss Annabel?"

CHAPTER XVII

It was a curious luncheon party. The host was abstracted, nervous, far from being his usual bland self. The guest was subdued, silent, uneasy for no reason at all. The hostess, usually an ever-springing well of comment and question, had decided upon quiet dignity as the most fitting expression of sensibilities ignored by the banging of doors.

> "I think, Angus," she ventured once, "that you ought to remonstrate with Mr. McCandless in regard to 'If a man die.' An Easter Anthem is an Easter Anthem, but after five renderings it is hardly fair to expect the congregation to behave as if they had never heard it before."

"Quite so," said the minister absently.

"Then may I tell him myself that it is your special request—"

"Certainly not. I wish you would not interfere, Annabel. The choir does very well. I think I have told you before that your continual desire for something novel in music has not my sympathy. I am not sure that I approve of this growing craze for anthems. They seem to me, sometimes, wholly unconnected with worship. We do not ask for new hymns every Sunday, nor do we ever become weary of the psalms. Indeed, familiarity seems often the measure of our affection."

"Net with anthems," firmly. "Anthems are different. Aren't anthems different, Esther?"

"I have known familiarity to breed something besides affection in the case of anthems," agreed Esther.

In the ordinary course of things this remark would have aroused her host into delivering a neat and timely discourse upon the proper relation of music to the service of the Protestant Church and the tendency of the present age to unduly exalt the former at the expense of the latter. But to-day he merely upset the salt and looked things at the innocent salt-cellar which his conscience, or his cloth, did not allow him to utter.

Miss Annabel raised her eyebrows at Esther in a significant way, telegraphing, "What did I tell you?" And Esther signaled back, "You were right. He is certainly not himself."

Several other topics were introduced with no better result and every one felt relieved when lunch was over.

"I think," said the Reverend Angus, as they arose, "that it is probably pleasanter in the garden."

Esther glanced at Miss Annabel. She wanted very much to go home. Yet in Coombe it was distinctly bad mannered to leave hurriedly, after a meal. She thought of pleading a headache, but the excuse seemed too transparent and she could think of nothing better. Miss Annabel was unresponsive. Her host was already moving toward the door. Now he held it open for her. There was nothing to do but go. If she were clever she could keep the conversation in Miss Annabel's hands.

But Miss Annabel's brother had other ideas. "I think," he suggested with the soft authority which in that house was law, "that as you are taking Mrs. Miller's class, Annabel, it might be well for you to look over the Sabbath School lesson. Our guest will excuse you, I know."

"Why, I've hardly seen her at all, Angus."

"There will be time later. I am sure Miss Esther understands."

Esther understood very well and her heart sank. She was probably in for another scolding. However, as politeness required, she murmured that on no account would she wish to interfere with the proper religious instruction of Mrs. Miller's class. Miss Annabel looked rebellious, but as usual found discretion the better part and contented herself with another facial telegram to Esther: "Find out what is the matter with him." And Esther smiled and nodded: "I'll try."

"Perhaps you would like to see the rose bush to which my sister referred," began the minister nervously as they stepped out upon the lawn. "It is a very fine rose, but pink, I regret to say, pink. It is unfortunate that Annabel should dislike pink so much. I think myself that a pink rose is very pretty. Something a little different from the red and white varieties."

Esther murmured, "Naturally," and opened her strange eyes widely so that he could see the mischief which was like a blue flash in the depths of them. He coloured faintly.

"I fear I am talking nonsense! The fact is that I am thinking of something else. Something so important that it occupies my mind completely. That is why, Esther, I wished to speak with you alone."

The girl was thoroughly interested now. She was flattered also. Miss Annabel had been right. Something was troubling the minister. And she,

Esther, was to be his confidant. To her untroubled, girlish conceit (girls are very wise!) it seemed natural enough. She had no doubt of her ability to help him. Therefore her face and her answering "Yes?" were warmly encouraging.

It is a general belief that a woman always knows, instinctively, when a man is going to propose to her. She cannot be taken unawares; her flutter, her surprise, her hesitancy are assumed as being artistically suitable, but her unpreparedness is never bona fide. If this be the true psychology of the matter then Esther's case was the exception which proves the rule. No warning came to her, no intuition. She was still looking at the minister with that warm expression of impersonal interest, when, without further preliminaries, he began his halting avowal of love.

Had the poor pink rose-bush suddenly flamed into crimson she could scarcely have been more surprised. She caught her breath with the shock of it! But shocks are quickly over. One adjusts one's self with incredible swiftness. A moment—and it seemed to Esther that she ought to have been expecting this. That she ought to have known it all along. Thousands of trifles mocked at her for her blindness, thousands of unheeded voices shrieked the truth into her opened ears. She felt miserably guilty. Not yet had she arrived at the stage when she could justify her blindness and deafness to herself. Later, she would understand how custom, the life-long habit of regarding the minister as a man apart, had helped to dull her perception. Later, common sense would prove her innocent of any wilful blunder. But just now, in her first bewilderment, it seemed that nothing could ever excuse that lack of understanding which had made this declaration possible!

"I love you, Esther! I have loved you for two years." (It was like the Reverend Angus to refer to the exact period.) "You must have seen it. This can be no surprise to you. You may blame me in your heart for not speaking sooner. But you were young. There seemed time enough. Then, lately, when I saw that you were no longer a child, I decided to speak as soon as your mother should have returned. But to-day I felt that I could not wait longer. I must know at once—now! I must hear you say that you love me. That you will be my wife. You will—Esther?"

His impassioned tones lingered on the name with ecstasy.

The startled girl forced herself to look at him, a look swift as a swallow's dart, but in it she saw everything—the light on his face—the love in his eyes! And something else she saw, something of which she did not know the name but from which, not loving him, she shrank with an instinctive shiver of revolt. He seemed a different man. The minister, the teacher, was gone, and in his place stood the lover, the claimer. Yes—that was it. He claimed her, his glance, his voice—somewhere in the girl's heart a red spark of anger began to glow.

She tried to speak, but he silenced her by a gesture. "No, do not answer yet. Although you must have known what I have felt for you, you are startled by my suddenness, I can see that. I have told you that it was not my intention to speak so soon. Circumstances have hurried me. I felt that I must have this settled. That—that episode of last week alone would have determined me. Things like that must not recur. I must have the right to advise, to—to protect you. You are so young. You do not know the world, its wickedness, its incredible vileness." His face was white with intense inward passion. "With me you will be safe. My God! to think of you at the mercy of that man—of any man! It stirs a madness of hate in me. Hate is a sin, I know, but God will understand—it is born of love, of my love for you."

Again the girl tried to force some words from her trembling lips. And again he stopped her.

"Do not speak yet. I apologise for my violence. Forgive it. We need not refer to this aspect of the matter again. Let us dwell only upon the sweeter idea of our love—for you do love me? You will love me—Esther?"

But the time for speech had gone. To her own intense surprise and to the minister's consternation, Esther burst into tears.

She was frightened, angry, stung with pity and a kind of horror. She felt herself honoured and insulted at the same time; and with this strange medley of emotions was a consciousness of youth and inexperience very different from the calm, untried confidence of a few minutes before.

"Forgive me, forgive me!" pleaded the conscience stricken suitor. "I have been too sudden! I should have prepared you. I should have allowed you to see more plainly." With a lover's first, fond air of possession he attempted to take her hand.

"Don't!" The word was sharp as a pistol shot. Esther's tears were suddenly stayed. Furtively she slipped the hand he had touched behind her. With the other she felt for her handkerchief and frankly wiped her eyes.

"You startled me," she explained presently. "And I am so sorry, so very sorry! I never dreamed that you thought of me at all—in that way, any more than I have thought of you. You honour me very much. But it is impossible. Quite, quite impossible."

"You mean my position here, as minister? Believe me, I have thought of all that. There may be difficulties but we will conquer them together. Nothing is impossible if you love me, dear."

"Oh!" She turned wide blue eyes upon him. "That is just it. I do not love you."

The blow fell swift, unerring, dealt by the mercilessly honest hand of youth. Esther's eyes were quite dry now. Her nervousness was passing. Regret and pity were merged in one overpowering, instinctive desire: the desire to show him beyond all manner of doubt that she repudiated that possessive touch upon her hand. "I could not ever possibly marry you," she said, as calmly as if she had been accustomed to dismissing suitors all her life.

They were still standing by the rose-bush whose desperate fate it was to produce pink roses. With incredulous dismay, the minister saw her turn from him and take a step toward the house.

She had refused him! She was leaving him! At any moment Annabel might finish her Sunday School lesson and come out upon the lawn—all his self-possession vanished like a puff of smoke.

"Esther!" he cried, "Esther! wait. Give me a moment."

She paused, but did not turn.

"I think there is nothing more to say—I am very sorry."

Sorry! She was sorry. This young girl upon whom he had set his desire, of whom he had felt so sure, to whom his love should have come as a crown, was sorry. King Cophetua, flouted by the beggar maid, could not have been more astonished, more deeply humiliated!

But the greater wound was not to his pride. At any cost to his dignity and self-respect he could not let her go like this. His ministerial manner fell away, his readiness deserted him. In a moment he became all lover, pleading, entreating, with the one great abandon of his life, with the stammering eloquence of unspeakable desire!

Slowly the girl turned to him. He saw her pure profile, then the full charm of her changing face. The blue eyes, widely open, were darker, lovelier than ever—Surely there was softening in their depths....

"Es—ther, Es—ther!" Miss Annabel's voice broke upon the tense moment with cheerful insistence, and Miss Annabel herself appeared at the turn of the walk, waving a slip of paper. She saw them at once.

"You're wanted at home, Esther. Your mother's come back. To-day! Think of that! On the noon train. In face of the whole town. And all she said when Elder MacTavish met her coming up from the station was that she had forgotten it was Sunday. Fancy!"

CHAPTER XVIII

Perhaps never, in all her life of inopportune arrivals, had Miss Annabel been so truly welcome—or so bitterly resented! Esther turned to her with a heart-sob of relief, the minister walked away without a word.

"Dear me! What's the matter?" said the good lady. "You seem all excited. Perhaps I shouldn't have shouted out the news so abruptly. But it never occurred to me that you might be startled. 'Tisn't as if your mother had been away a year. Jane's waiting for you down by the gate. Such a peculiar child! Nothing I could say will induce her to come in. Don't you find Jane is a peculiar child, Esther?"

"Only a little shy," said Esther, quickening her steps.

"Shy! Mercy, I shouldn't call her shy. That child has the self-possession of a Chinee! I hope you won't mind me saying it, but a little shyness is exactly what Jane needs."

Esther, whose shaken nerves threatened hysterical laughter, made no reply to this, but hurried toward the small figure by the garden gate.

"Oh, Jane!" she called, somewhat shakily.

At her voice, the Shy One stopped kicking holes in the turf with the toes of her new boots and executing a bearlike rush, threw herself into her sister's arms.

"I'm home, Esther! So's mother! And she says I don't have to go to Sunday School. That's why I didn't want to come in. Let's hurry before the minister comes."

"Listen to that!" said Miss Annabel in indignation. "Any one would think my brother was an ogre. Angus! Why, he's gone! I thought he was following us."

"I think Mr. Macnair went into the house."

"Did he? What did I tell you? Perhaps my news surprised him as well as you. I thought he looked as pale as a plate. What do you think?"

"I think it is none of our business."

Miss Annabel gave her a shrewd look. "Perhaps not your business. You don't have to live with him. But I do. Well, good-bye, my dear. Tell your mother," significantly, "that I'll be over to see her soon."

Both girls were relieved that the minister did not leave his study to say good-bye. They breathed more freely and their steps slackened as soon as the corner which hid the manse had been safely passed.

"I've got new boots," began Jane. "See them? And Fred's new dog has got puppies! He calls her Pickles. She got the puppies this morning. Oh! they're darlings! But Fred is horrid. He says he is going to give me one for my own, to make up for Timothy. Just as if anything ever could! I never knew any one so heartless as Fred—except Job."

"Job who?" It was a relief to Esther to let the childish chatter run on.

"Why, *Job*. Job was just like Fred. When all his wives died and his little children and his cows, he felt bad, but when God gave him more wives and more children and lots of cows he was pleased as Punch. I always thought that so strange of God," in a reflective tone, "but I expect he knew what kind of man Job was and that he didn't have any real feelings. Do you think I ought to take the puppy, Esther? I shouldn't like to be like Job."

"I think there is no danger, dear. But how is mother? Better?"

"Was she sick?" in surprise.

"Her headaches, you know."

"Oh, yes. I don't know whether they are better or not," carelessly. "I didn't see much of mother while we were away. I played all day with Mrs. Bremner's little girl. Except when we went shopping. I think she must be better, for she did such lots of shopping."

Esther smiled. "Not very much, I think, Janie. Shopping takes money."

"But she did! I have lots and lots of new clothes. Only," discontentedly, "most of them don't fit. Mother could never be bothered trying them on. She's got some lovely things, too. Dresses and hats and piles of new shoes and heaps of silk stockings—"

"Jane, why do you say 'lots' and 'piles' and 'heaps' when you know you are exaggerating?"

But there was a note of anxiety in the reproof nevertheless.

"I'm not exaggerating, Esther! She did. Even Miss Bremner asked her what she was going to do with them all."

The elder girl's fingers tightened upon the small hand she held. Her red lips set themselves in a firm line. In face of a danger which she could see and measure Esther had courage enough. And she had faced this particular danger before.

"Mother will tell me all about it, no doubt," she said calmly. "Did she get me something pretty, too?"

"Yes. It's a surprise."

"And when she got all the pretty things I suppose she told the clerks to charge them?"

"Oh, no. She paid for them out of her purse."

Esther was conscious of a swift reaction. The things were paid for. Of course Jane had exaggerated. Children have no sense of value. Some dainty things, Mrs. Coombe was sure to buy; but, as Esther well knew, her slender stock of money would hardly have run to "piles" and "heaps." And of course she had been unjust in fearing that Mary had gone into debt. They had one experience of that kind, an experience which had ended in a solemn promise that it would never happen again. Mary understood the position as well as she did.

As the girl's thought trailed naturally into the problem paths of every day, her weeks of freedom, her new interests, the strange experience in the manse garden seemed already remote. With the little frown of accustomed perplexity slipping in between her straight, black brows, her deeper agitation quieted. The unusual has no antidote so effective as the commonplace.

They found Mrs. Coombe waiting for them on the veranda. Lying back in the shade, in her white dress she looked very much at her ease. Yet a quick observer might have noticed a certain anxiety in the glance she tried to render merely welcoming. She was thinner than she had been; tired lines dragged at the corners of the pouting mouth and dark circles showed plainly through their dusting of pearl powder. Changes which creep in unnoticed when one sees a person every day are startlingly apparent when absence has forced a clearer focus. Esther had known that her step-mother had changed, was changing, but as she bent over her now, the extent of the change shocked her. With a tightening at her heart she wondered what her father would say if he could see the difference wrought by one short year. Pearl powder, lavishly used, is not becoming, especially when it sifts into multitudes of fine lines; nor can powder or anything else brighten a dull, yellowing skin which in health would still be delicately clear and firm.

But the dulled eyes and the faded face were only the symptoms of the real change in Mary Coombe. The thing itself lay deeper. Striving to express a subtlety which would not lend itself to words, Esther had more than once told herself that her mother was "not the same woman." Yet it was only to-day, as she stooped to kiss her, that the startling, literal truth of the phrase struck home. The outside changes were nothing—it was the woman herself who had changed.

"Well, Esther!" The sweet high voice with its impatient note was the same as ever. "Here we are home again. Fancy me forgetting it was Sunday! Wasn't it funny? We met old MacTavish coming up from the station (not a single cab down to meet the train, of course!) and he looked so shocked. Really, this place grows more insufferable every day. It seems to agree with you, though, you're looking awfully well. Amy looks well, too. The new doctor must be something of a wonder."

"He is considered very clever. Aunt Amy is certainly better. Now that you are home you must let him see what he can do for you."

Mrs. Coombe's pouting lips lengthened into a hard line.

"I won't see a doctor. And that's flat."

"Are you feeling better, then?"

As was always the case, her mother's perversity dissipated Esther's sympathy and left her tone cold. It was all the colder probably because just at that moment she had noticed that the simple white frock Mrs. Coombe was wearing was not simple at all. The delicate embroidery on it was all hand work. And French embroidery is no inexpensive trifle. It was probably a new "best" gown; but if so, why had it been worn on the train, why was it soiled in places and carelessly put on? The skirt was not even, the collar, having lost a support, sagged at one side and just below the girdle belt there was a small, jagged rent. Esther noticed these details with vexation and discomfort, for it was part of the change in Mary Coombe that from being one of the most carefully gowned women in town she had become one of the most slovenly. All her natty, pretty, American "style" which the plainer Canadians had sometimes envied was gone. But this—this was worse than usual! The girl's quick eyes travelled downward, noting the increased signs of deterioration with something like distress.

"Why, mother," she exclaimed involuntarily, "there is a hole in your stocking!"

"Is there?" Mary Coombe thrust out a small and elegant foot clad in thinnest silk and shod with pretty slippers not very clean and turning over at the heel.

"Dear me!" she said. "So there is. I need new slippers too. I quite forgot to get any."

"Oh, mother!" Jane's cry was instant. "You got heaps. Tan ones and brown ones and white ones and black ones with silver buckles—"

"Jane!" interrupted Esther, laughing. "Give your imagination a rest."

"But you did, didn't you, mother?"

"Did I? Why, yes—I did buy a few shoes. I had forgotten. The Customs man didn't find them either. Run and fetch me a clean white pair, Jane, and bring down the surprise we got for Esther—see how disapproving she looks. I declare, Esther, it would be just like you to make things disagreeable the moment I get home. I didn't charge a cent, if that's what you're afraid of."

"I knew you wouldn't do that," gravely. "And of course I'm glad you got the things. But I can't see how you managed."

"Oh, sales," vaguely. "Things are so cheap in Detroit and Jessica Bremner is a born shopper. She gets wonderful bargains. Anyway, I got them, and I'm not a cent in debt."

"What's debt?" asked Jane.

"Buying what you can't pay for, Janie."

"Oh, mother paid for everything. I saw her. It's Mrs. Bremner that's in debt, isn't she, mother?"

"Don't be silly, Jane, of course not. Jessica is far better off than we are."

"But she only gave you half the money for the ring. I heard her say—"

"Jane, get those slippers at once."

"I'm going. But Mrs. Bremner said—"

Mrs. Coombe's hand came down with stinging force upon the child's ear.

"Will you obey me—or will you not?"

Jane retired wailing and her mother sank back into her veranda chair, red spots burning through the powder on her cheeks.

Esther sat very still for a moment, and then, without looking at the other, she asked in a low voice:

"What did she mean?"

"How should I know?" fretfully.

"What ring did Mrs. Bremner give you money for? Did—you have to sell one of your rings?"

"Yes, I did."

"Which one?"

"Oh, don't bother me, Esther."

"But I want to know which one."

"It was the big red one!" called Jane from the hallway, where she had waited, safely out of reach.

Mary Coombe sprang up, fury blazing in her eyes, but Jane had fled, and Esther, cool and capable, was blocking the doorway.

"Sit down, mother. I've got to know about this. What ring does she mean?"

For an instant the older woman hesitated, then with a little shrug she turned back to the chair. The fury had died away as quickly as it had arisen.

"I knew you would be disagreeable," she said. "And you were bound to hear about the ring some time. Jane is the most ungrateful child, and a little tell-tale; the makings of a regular little cat! I'm sure I spent her full share on her, and I've brought you something nice, too. Not that I expect to be thanked for it. Of course I had to have some money. I hadn't a rag to wear, not a rag. And I got everything ready made. It's cheaper. Anyway, I can't stand dressmakers any more. They paw one so. I can't bear to be touched, my wretched nerves! And I remembered the fuss you made about the bills last time. You know you did make a fuss, Esther, as if all your dear father left belonged to you and not to me—"

"But what did you *do*?"

"I'm telling you, amn't I? I sold the ring, of course."

"Which ring?"

"The ruby ring. It's the only one that is worth anything!"

"You sold Aunt Amy's ring?"

"If you wish to put it that way, yes. I consider it is as much my ring as hers. She is my aunt and it is understood that all her things will come to me. She has lived here ever since I was married and I think it's a funny thing if she can't help me out occasionally. I simply had to have money and the ruby was the only thing worth selling. Good Heavens! Don't look so crazy. One would think I had stolen it!"

"You have."

Again Mrs. Coombe arose; this time without flurry. The little excitement had done her good. The dull eyes were actually sparkling, the sallow cheeks were flushed. She looked just as she used to look in one of her little rages before the great change came.

"That's enough, Esther. I'll take no more from you. I did what seemed to me right. If Amy were in her right mind I should not have had to take the ring, she would have offered it. Under the circumstances I did the only sensible thing. Amy will never discover the loss. I am getting a very good price for it from Jessica Bremner. It is a valuable jewel. She snatched at the chance of getting it."

Behind its whiteness Esther's face seemed to glow with pale flame. "Is it possible that you have forgotten the history of that ring?" she asked. "That it was poor Auntie's engagement ring and that, although she can't remember anything about it, she knows it means something more than life to her. And that she always says that she cannot die without the ruby on her finger?"

Mrs. Coombe looked uncomfortable, but kept her poise.

"It's all rubbish. She'll forget all about it. Dying people don't think of ruby rings. And anyway, she will probably outlive all of us. If not—we can easily divert her attention."

The girl looked at her step-mother in horror, half believing that this must be some cruel joke. The callousness of the words seemed unbelievable. But the reality of them could no longer be doubted and the pale glow died out of her face, leaving it white and hard.

"I do not understand you," she said slowly. "Somehow you do not seem quite—human. But be sure of this, Aunt Amy shall have back her lover's ring. Jane says it has not all been paid for. How much did you receive?"

"I shall not tell you. And I warn you, Esther, not to waste your money. If you buy it back, I shall sell it again."

They were standing now facing each other. Esther took a step forward and looked down steadily into her step-mother's face. Her own curious eyes were wide open, they looked like blue stars, bright, cold and powerful as flame.

"No! You shall not."

For a space Mary Coombe met that sword-like look, then her weaker will gave way. Her eyes shifted and fell. Her hands began to pluck nervously at the embroidery of her dress. She laughed, a little, affected laugh with no mirth in it, turned and entered the house.

CHAPTER XIX

We have stated elsewhere that Coombe was conservative, but by this we do not mean to imply that it was benighted. Far from it! True, it talked a great deal before it ventured upon anything strange or new, referred constantly to the tax rate and ran no risks, but at the time of which we write it had decided to take a plebescite upon the matter of Local Option and, a little later, the council wished to go so far as to present Andrew MacCandless, who had served them five times as mayor, with an address and a purse of fifty dollars.

The Presbyterian church, too, although still clinging to solid doctrine, was far removed from the tuning-fork stage. Through throes of terrible convulsion it had come to possess an organ, a paid soloist, and a Ladies' Aid, that insidious first thing in women's clubs.

The first meeting of the Knox Church Ladies' Aid, after the return of Mrs. Coombe and Jane, was held for the purpose of putting together a quilt, not the old-fashioned kind, of course, but something quite new—an autograph quilt, very chaste.

It was a large meeting and, providentially, Mrs. Coombe was late. I say providentially because, had she been early, it is difficult to imagine how her fellow members would have eased their minds of the load of comment justified by her indiscreet home-coming, and several other things equally painful but interesting. The Ladies' Aid had its printed constitution but it also had its unwritten laws and one of these laws was that strictest courtesy must always be observed. No member, whatever her failings, was ever discussed in meeting—when she was present.

"What I cannot excuse," said Mrs. Bartley Simson, "is the tone of levity in which she answered Mr. MacTavish when he met her on the way from the station. It is possible that she had some good reason for coming on that particular train. I am not one of those who hold that nothing can ever justify Sunday travel. Exceptional cases must be allowed for. But the frivolity of her excuse nothing can justify."

"Besides," said Miss Atkins, the secretary, "it was a—it sounded like—what I mean to say is that she could not possibly, *no one* could possibly, have forgotten what day of the week it was."

A subdued chorus of "Certainly not" and "Absurd" showed the trend of public opinion upon this point.

"I once forgot that Wednesday was Thursday," said the youngest Miss Sinclair, who always stood for peace at any price.

"Don't be silly, Jessie!" The elder Miss Sinclair, who believed in war with honour, jogged her sister's elbow none too gently. "That's a different thing altogether. For my own part," raising her voice, "I think that as a society we cannot be too careful how we minimise the fact itself. To us, as a society, it is the fact itself that matters, and not what Mrs. Coombe said about it. That, to a certain extent, may be her own affair. But I hold, and I say it without fear of successful contradiction, that no member of a community can disregard the Sabbath in a public way without affecting the community at large. That is why I feel justified in criticising Mrs. Coombe's behaviour. And I hope," here she raised a piercing eye and let it range triumphantly over the circle, "I sincerely hope that the minister has been told of this occurrence!"

The meeting rustled with approbation. This, it felt, was something like a proper spirit. There was no compromise here. A thrill of conscious virtue, raised to the _n_th power, shot through the circle.

"You think that Mr. Macnair ought to take cognizance of it officially?" asked Miss Atkins. (Being the secretary she used many beautiful words.)

"I do."

"But he and Mrs. Coombe are such friends!" objected the younger Miss Sinclair, who was a kindly creature.

An electric silence fell upon the quilters. Every one looked toward the president.

"I cannot allow such insinuations to be made at this meeting," said the President firmly.

"But—but I did not insinuate anything!" stammered poor Miss Jessie who, severely jogged by her sister and transfixed by the President's eye, had turned the colour of the crimson square before her.

"We all know," went on the President more mildly, "that Mr. Macnair calls fairly often at the Elms. We may even have heard rumours to the effect that he intends—I hardly know how to phrase it, but as our minister is unmarried and Mrs. Coombe is a widow you will understand what I mean. But, ladies, I may state on no less an authority than Miss Annabel that Mr. Macnair has no such intentions. There is absolutely nothing in it. His calls no doubt may be accounted for by the presence of—er—affliction in the house."

"Do you mean Aunt Amy?" A younger woman with a clever and rather pretty face looked up. "Why, can't you see that there is a much simpler explanation than that?"

It was certainly unfortunate that Mrs. Coombe should have chosen this moment to arrive. But the Ladies' Aid were used to interrupted statements. It was felt to be very convenient that one of the windows looked out directly upon the steps so that the meeting was never quite taken by surprise. A sudden pause there might be, but late arrivals had learned to expect that. It was the penalty for being late.

"Dear Mrs. Coombe, so glad you have come!" said the hostess pleasantly. "No, you are not very late. We are only just beginning."

Every one nodded and smiled. Chairs were moved and sewing shifted to provide space for the newcomer. A few left their work in order to shake hands and there was a general readjustment of everything, including topics of conversation. In the space of a few seconds it was noticed that Mrs. Coombe wore a new hat, a new gown, new slippers and silk stockings and that in spite of all these advantages they had never seen her look worse.

"Dear Mrs. Coombe, I think your belt-pin has become—allow me!" Miss Milligan, dressmaker in private life, with a discreet swiftness, twitched the blouse and skirt into place and deftly fastened it. At the same time she closed a gap in the fastening of the blouse itself.

Mary Coombe laughed. "Dear me! Am I undone? I must have forgotten to ask Amy to fix me. These blouses that fasten in the back are such a nuisance!"

The President smiled politely, but with evident effort. Mrs. Coombe was a prominent member. Still, on principle, she, a president, could not be expected to approve of people who forgot to have themselves done up. Supposing the minister had been present!

"What are we doing this afternoon?" asked the unconscious delinquent languidly. "Autograph quilts? I've got a lot of blocks for you—friends of mine in the city." She began to fumble in the pretty workbag she carried. "Gracious, I was sure I had them with me! Isn't that odd? I can't find them."

"Let me look," suggested Miss Jessie Sinclair kindly.

But the other snatched back the open bag with a gesture which was almost rude.

"Oh, no—they are not there! I can't imagine what I have done with them." She looked up in a bewildered way. Indeed the perturbation was so out of proportion to the size of the calamity that the ladies questioned each other with their eyes.

The President tapped with her thimble upon the quilting frame and every one became very busy. "I hope," she said, taking the conversation into her own hands for safe keeping, "that you found all well upon your return, Mrs. Coombe? I hardly ever seem to see Esther now. Did you know that we have been talking of changing our meeting to Saturday afternoon so that Esther and some more of our younger folk may join us? We thought that it would be so nice for them—and for us too," she finished graciously.

Mrs. Coombe looked surprised. "I can hardly see Esther at a Ladies' Aid Meeting," she said. "Did she tell you she would come?"

"No. We have not yet told any one of the proposed change. But we all felt—"

"We all felt," interrupted Miss Sinclair, who was fairly sniffing the air with the spirit of glorious war, "that the less time our young girls have to go off philandering with young fools whom no one knows anything about, the better it will be for everybody concerned!"

Mary looked up with an air of pleased surprise.

"Has Esther been philandering?" she asked eagerly.

The President frowned. This was hardly according to Hoyle.

"I really think," began Miss Jessie Sinclair indignantly, "that Esther ought to be allowed to tell her mother—"

"Gracious! Esther never tells me anything. And I'm dying to know. Who is the 'young fool'?—do tell me, somebody."

Strangely enough, now that the way was open, no one seemed to have anything to say.

"You've simply got to tell me now," urged Mary delightedly. "Unless it's only a silly bit of gossip."

This fillip had the desired effect. Everybody began to talk at once and in five minutes Esther's step-mother knew all about the new doctor and the broken motor. When they paused for breath, she laughed softly.

"It's the most amusing thing I've heard in ages. Fancy—Esther! Oh, it's delicious." She looked around the circle of surprised and disappointed faces and laughed again. "Oh, don't pretend! You know very well that you're not a bit shocked, really. And surely you don't think that I ought to scold Esther? Why," with a little flare of her old-time loyalty, "Esther is worth a dozen ordinary girls. I'd trust Esther with Apollo on a desert island. But I'll admit I'm rather anxious to see the young man. He must be rather nice if Esther agreed to show him around. As for the accident," she shrugged her shoulders, "I know enough about motors to know that that might happen any time."

"You are right, of course," the President's tone was more cordial. "And anyway we have no right to discuss Esther's affairs. The reference to it grew out of the proposed change of meeting. And the change of meeting was thought of chiefly because when Mr. Macnair heard about the escapade he seemed much worried. Naturally, as he says, he carries all his young people on his heart, and Dr. Callandar being such a newcomer—"

"Oh, yes, naturally." Mary Coombe's little gurgle of amusement had a note of cruelty in it, for she alone of all these women had guessed why the Rev. Angus Macnair should have taken Esther's escapade so much to heart. She knew, too, that the minister had no chance, but the idea of a rival was novel—and entertaining. Could Esther really have taken a fancy to this young doctor? Mary knew the Coombe gossips too well to take their chatter seriously, but there might be something in it. At any rate, there was enough to use as a conversational weapon against Esther. She was becoming a little nervous of Esther lately. The girl was positively growing up. Somehow, almost overnight it seemed, a new strength had come to her, a strength which her step-mother's weakness felt and resented. But now with this nice little story in reserve, things might be more even. Mary's eyes sparkled as she thought of some of the smart things she could say the next time Esther began to make a fuss about—about the matter of the ruby ring, for instance. Esther had been most disagreeable about that. Just as if any one could have foreseen that Amy would miss it so soon, or indeed at all, since it had been her fancy to keep it shut up in a stupid box.

As a matter of fact, the affair of the ring had assumed the proportions of a small catastrophe. Aunt Amy had been feeling so much better that it had occurred to her to see if the ring were feeling better too. Only one peep she would take, hopeful that at last its strange enchantment might be past. If she could look into its depths without the blackness coming close she would know, with utter certainty, that Dr. Callandar's cleverness had circumvented the power of her old enemies. "They" would trouble her no more.

But when, flushed with hope, she looked—the ring was gone!

Esther, reading in the sitting room, was startled beyond words by the scream which rang through the house. She seemed to know at once what had happened and her gaze flew to her step-mother, laden with bitter reproach, before she sped up the stairs to Aunt Amy's room. The door was open and the tragedy was plain to see. Aunt Amy stood by the bureau with the empty box in her hand and on her face an expression so dreadful, so hopeless that, with a sob, the girl tried to crush it out against her breast.

"What is it, dear? Don't look like that."

"The ring, Esther! 'They' have taken the ring!"

For an instant the girl hesitated, but common justice demanded that the sordid truth be told.

"No, dear. The ring is safe. It was taken from the box, but in quite an ordinary, simple way. Don't tremble so! It is not lost. It is just as if I had gone to the box and borrowed it—"

As she faltered, the poor woman raised her head in an agony of hope. "Have you got it, Esther? Oh, Esther, give it to me! I love you, Esther! You shall have it when I am dead. But I can't die without it. I promised somebody—I—I can't remember. Oh, Esther, don't keep it away from me—give it to me now!"

Bitter, angry tears filled the girl's eyes as she took the pleading, fluttering hands in hers.

"Don't, dear! Listen. It is quite safe. But I haven't got it. I promise you solemnly I will get it back. You'll believe me, won't you? You know I would not deceive you. And you won't be frightened? No one had anything to do with taking it but ourselves. I am going to tell you just how it happened—"

"Don't bother. I'll tell her myself."

In the doorway stood Mrs. Coombe, her eyes venomous with the anger of tortured nerves. Her high voice trembled on the verge of hysteria, yet she tried to speak with her usual mocking lightness.

"There is no need to make a mystery of the thing, I'm sure. I took the ring because I was hard up—needed money at once. You understand what that means, I suppose, Amy? You never wore the ring, nor would you allow me to wear it. It was simply wasted lying in that silly box. My own jewelry is of much less value. Besides, I use it. One would have thought that you would be glad to assist in some way with the—er—household expenses. In any case, no such fuss is necessary, and I should advise you," her voice grew suddenly cold and menacing, "not to scream like that again. A few more such shrieks and—people will begin to wonder." Without so much as a glance at Esther she passed on to her own room.

"Don't mind her!" The indignant girl tried to draw the trembling woman close. But Aunt Amy cowered away. Five minutes had undone the work of weeks. All the doctor's carefully laid foundations were crumbling. Esther, wrung with pity and remorse, stroked the grey hair in silence. She expected an outbreak of childish tears, but it did not come. Rather, the shivering grew less and presently Aunt Amy raised her head.

"It was she—Mary—who took it?" she asked in a whisper.

"Yes. But remember I have promised to get it back."

Aunt Amy looked at her blankly. She did not seem to hear.

"I never guessed it was Mary. Never! But now I know. I'll never be fooled again."

"Know what?" asked Esther uneasily. There was a look in Aunt Amy's eyes which she disliked, a sly, cool look—more nearly mad than any look she had ever surprised there. "Tell me what it is that you know," she repeated coaxingly.

But Aunt Amy would not tell. It was just as well, she thought, that Esther should not know that at last, after many years, she had found out the agent employed by "they" for her undoing. Ah, if she had only found out sooner. The ruby ring might still be shining in its box. But of course "they" knew that she would never suspect Mary, her own niece. They were so clever! But now she could be as clever as they—oh, very, very clever!

"What did she mean about my screaming?" she asked, looking at Esther cunningly.

"Nothing, nothing at all! Don't think of it."

"But she did. I know what she meant. She meant that if I get—troublesome—she will shut me up!"

"Nonsense!" declared Esther, thrilled to the heart with pity. "You must never think such a thought, dear. You shall never live anywhere but here with us. Why, you are our good angel, Auntie. We could never get on without you—you know that."

Aunt Amy nodded, stroking the girl's soft hand with her work-worn one. "You are good and kind, Esther. I know you will take care of me, if you can. And I'm not afraid just now. It will be all right if I am clever. I must not be troublesome. If I am, she will put me away with the mad people. The people that make faces and scream. I never scream. Until to-day I haven't screamed for a long time. And I'll be more careful. Oh, I can be very careful, now that I know!"

Again the strange mad look. It flitted across her lifted eyes like a dark shadow behind a window shade. And again Esther tried gently to question her, but Aunt Amy was "clever." She didn't intend that Esther should find out.

The girl left her at last feeling both troubled and sad, but Mary Coombe laughed at her fears. She was in one of her most difficult moods.

"It was all a tempest in a tea cup, as usual," she declared pettishly. "I do wish, Esther, that you would not be so disagreeable. She will have forgotten all about the ring by to-morrow. All she needs is a little plain speaking, and firmness."

"Firmness! Cruelty, you mean. You terrified her."

"Well, it had a good effect. She quieted down at once."

"She is too quiet. It's that which troubles me. Surely you can see the damage that has been done? All her new cheerfulness is gone. She is back to where she was before the doctor helped her."

"I never believed that any real improvement was possible. Insane people never recover."

"She is not insane! How can you say so? But how shall we explain the change in her to Dr. Callandar? We can't tell him that—that you—"

"Oh, don't mind me!" flippantly.

"Anyway, the ring will soon be back, thank heaven! I have written to Mrs. Bremner."

"You wrote to Jessica?"

"Certainly. I told you I should. It was the only thing to do."

Mary Coombe's rage flickered and sank before the quiet force in the girl's face and voice. With all the will in the world she was too weak to oppose this new strength in Esther. And before her mortified pride could frame a retort, the girl had left the room.

It was of this quiet exit of Esther's that Mary was thinking as she sewed on the autograph quilt. Better than anything else it typified the change in the girl. It meant decision, and decision meant action. Mary shrugged her shoulders and frowned over the quilt. Yes, undoubtedly, Esther was getting troublesome. It might be well if she were married.

CHAPTER XX

Meanwhile, unconscious of her step-mother's troubled musings, Esther was loitering delightfully on her way from school. Aunt Amy, who never looked at a clock, but who always knew the time by what Jane called "magic," was beginning to wonder what had kept her. Strain her eyes as she would, there was no glint of a blue dress upon the long straight road, and Dr. Callandar, who in passing had stopped by the gate, declared that he had noticed a similar absence of that delectable colour between the cross roads and the school house.

"I thought that I might meet her," he confessed ingenuously, "but when she was not in sight, I concluded that I was too late. Some of those angel children have probably had to be kept in. Could you make use of me instead? I run errands very nicely."

"Oh, it isn't an errand." Aunt Amy smiled, for she liked Dr. Callandar and was always as simple as a child with him. His easy, courteous manner, which was the same to her as to every one else, helped her to be at once more like other people and more like herself. "It's a letter. I wanted Esther to read it to me. Of course I can read myself," as she saw his look of surprise, "but sometimes I do not read exactly what is written. My imagination bothers me. Do you ever have any trouble with your imagination, Doctor?"

"I have known it to play me tricks."

"But you can read a letter just as it's written, can't you?"

"Yes. I can do that."

"Then your imagination cannot be as large as mine. Mine is very large. It interferes with everything, even letters. When I read a letter myself I sometimes read things which aren't there. At least," with a faint show of doubt, "people say they aren't there."

"In other words," said Callandar, "you read between the lines."

Aunt Amy's plain face brightened. It was so seldom that any one understood.

"Yes, that's it! You won't laugh at me when I tell you that everything, letters, handkerchiefs, dresses and everything belonging to people have a feeling in them—something that tells secrets? I can't quite explain."

"I have heard very sensitive people express some such idea. It sounds very fascinating. I should like very much to hear about it."

"Would you? You are sure you won't think me queer? My niece, Mary Coombe, does not like me to tell people about it. She has no imagination herself, none at all. She says it is all nonsense. But I think," shrewdly, "that she would like to know some of the things that I know. Won't you come in, Doctor? Come in and sit under the tree where it is cooler."

The doctor's hesitation was but momentary. He was keenly interested. And at the back of his mind was the thought that Esther must certainly be along presently. Fate had not favoured him of late. He had not seen her for five days. It is foolish to leave meetings to fate anyway. Then, if another reason were needed it was probable that if he stayed he would meet Esther's mother. He was beginning to feel quite curious about Mrs. Coombe.

"Thanks. I think I will come in. All the trees in Coombe are cool, but your elm is the coolest of them all. Let me arrange this cushion for you. Is that right?"

He settled Aunt Amy comfortably upon the least sloping portion of the old circular bench and, not wishing to trust it with his own weight, sat down upon the grass at her feet.

"Now," he said cheerfully, "let us have a regular psychic research meeting. Tell me all about it."

"What's that?" suspiciously.

"Psychic research? Oh, just finding out all about the queer things that happen to people."

"Do queer things happen to other people besides me?"

"Why, of course! Queer things happen to everybody."

Aunt Amy seemed glad to know this.

"They never talk about them," she said wistfully. "But, then, neither do I. Except to you. What was it you wanted me to tell you?"

"Tell me what you mean when you say that you read in a letter what is not written there. You see I haven't much imagination myself and I don't understand it."

"Neither do I," naively. "But it seems to be like this—take this letter, for instance, when I found it in—well, it doesn't matter where I found it—but as soon as I picked it up, I knew that it was a love letter. I felt it. It is an old letter, I think. And some one has been angry with it. See, it is all crumpled. But it is a real love letter. All the love is there yet. When I took it in my hands it all came out to me, sweet and strong. Like—like the scent of something keen, fragrant, on a swift wind. I can't explain it!"

"You explain it very beautifully," gravely. "I can quite understand that love might be like that."

"Can you?" with a pleased smile. "And can you understand how I feel it? I can feel things in people, too. Love and hate and envy and all kinds of things. I never say so. I used to, but people did not like it. They always looked queer, or got angry. They seemed to think I had no right to see inside of them. So I soon pretended not to see anything. But a letter doesn't mind. This one," swinging the crumpled paper swiftly close to his face, "is glad I found it. Can't you feel it yourself?"

Callandar shook his head. "I am far too dull and commonplace for that!" He smiled. "But I have no doubt it is all there, just as you say. Why not? Our knowledge of such things is in its infancy."

Aunt Amy stroked the paper with gentle fingers. "Yes, yes, it is all there," she murmured. "But I may have read it wrongly for all that. The written words I mean. I can't help reading what I feel. Once I felt a letter that was full of hate, dreadful! And I read quite shocking things in it. But when Esther read it, it was just a polite note, beginning 'Dear' and ending 'Your affectionate friend.'"

"It might have been very hateful for all that."

"But no one knew it. That is why I am so anxious always to know if I read things right. Will you read this letter to me?"

"With pleasure—if I may."

"Oh, it doesn't belong to any one. It isn't Esther's because it's too old and it begins 'Dearest wife' and it isn't Mary's because it isn't Doctor Coombe's writing; so you see I thought it might not hurt anybody if I pretended it was mine."

"No," gently, "I do not see why it would."

"I never had a love letter of my own. Or if I did I cannot find it. The only thing I ever had with love in it was the ruby ring, and that—"

She checked herself suddenly; her small face freezing into such a mask of tragedy that Callandar was alarmed. But to his quick "What is it?" she returned no answer and the expression passed as quickly as it had come.

When he held out his hand for the letter, she seemed to have forgotten it. Her gaze had again grown restless and vague. It would do no good to question further, the rare hour of confession was past.

"You both look very comfortable, I'm sure!" It was Esther's laughing voice. She had come so quietly that neither of them had heard her. Aunt Amy's vagueness vanished in a pleased smile and Callandar, as he sprang to open the gate, forgot all about the unread letter and everything else, save that she had come.

Why was it, he wondered, that he could never recall her, save in dulled tints. Lovely as she had lingered in his memory, her living beauty was so much lovelier. There, in the shade of the elm, her blue dress flecked with gold, the warm pallor of heat upon her face, her hair lying close and heavy, a little pulse beating where the low collar softly disclosed the slim roundness of her white throat, she was not only beautiful, she was Beauty. She was not only Beauty, she was Herself, the one woman in the world! He acknowledged it now, with all humility.

The girl greeted him quietly. She did not, as was her custom, look up at him with that sweet widening of the eyes which he had learned to hunger for. The truth was that she, too, was moving slowly toward her awakening. The days in which they had not met had been full of thoughts of him. Dreams had come to her, vague, delicious bits of fancy which had whispered in her ear and passed, leaving a new softness in her eyes, a new flush upon her cheek. There was about her a dewy freshness which seemed to brighten up the world. Vaguely her girl friends wondered what had "come over" Esther Coombe, and at home Aunt Amy's pathetic eyes followed her, dim with a half-memory of long past joy. But it was Mrs. Sykes' Ann who best expressed the change in her beauty when, one day, she said to Bubble: "Esther Coombe looks like she was all lighted up inside and when she walks you'd think the wind was blowing her."

So it happened that while yesterday she might still have smiled into the doctor's eyes as she greeted him, to-day she shook hands without looking at his face at all.

Callandar found himself remarking that it was a fine day. Esther said that it was beautiful—but dusty. A little rain would do good. She fanned herself with her broad hat, and stopped fanning to examine closely a tiny stain on the hem of her frock.

"Dear me," she said, "I'm afraid it's axle grease! Mournful Mark gave me a lift this morning."

"Oh, I hope not!" anxiously from Aunt Amy, and referring, presumably, to the grease.

The doctor looked at the little stray curl on the nape of the graceful neck and wished—all the foolish things that lovers have wished since the world began. But he had a great longing to see her eyes. If he were to say sharply, "Look at me!" would she look up? Absurd idea! And anyway he couldn't say it, or anything else, for the first time in his life Henry Callandar was tongue-tied.

Did she, too, feel strange? Was that why she kept her eyes so persistently lowered? No, it could hardly be that. She laughed and talked quite naturally—seemed entire mistress of herself.

"I know I am late, Auntie. It's Friday, you know, and I walked slowly. I forgot that I had promised to help Jane wash the new pup. But there is time yet. Supposing we have tea, English fashion, out here. I'll tell mother—"

"She is at the Ladies Aid, Esther."

"Oh, yes. I forgot. Well, then you must entertain Dr. Callandar while I see about tea."

"No tea for me, thanks," said the doctor hastily. He didn't know why he said it except that he wanted to say something, something which might make her look at him.

But she did not look. His refusal lost him a cup of tea and gained him nothing whatever.

"No tea?" Her tone was mildly wondering, but she was looking at Aunt Amy while she spoke. "I'm sorry you are in a hurry. Bubble said you were busy."

"Not busy exactly. But it's office hours, you know. My partner grows quite waxy if I'm late, and I'm late now."

"Another day, then?" Esther's tone was charmingly gracious, but she seemed to be addressing the gate post, as far as he could judge from the direction of her gaze.

Callandar picked up his hat, gloomily. There was nothing to do now but take his leave. And if he had had any sense he might have been going to stay for tea. Office hours be hanged!

"Thank you, another day I shall be delighted." He took the hand she offered and bowed over it. Delightful custom this of shaking hands! Esther's hand was cool as a wind-blown leaf. Would she actually say good-bye without looking at him? He held the hand firmly but she did not seem to be conscious that he held it. She was smiling at some children who were going by on the sidewalk.

"Good-bye," said Callandar in a subdued voice.

"Good-bye," said Esther sweetly.

He dropped her hand, they bowed formally, and the foolish, poignant little tragedy of parting was over. Not once had they looked into each other's eyes.

When he had gone Esther sank down upon the elm tree seat.

"Oh, Auntie!" she said with a little sob in her voice. "I want—some tea!"

Aunt Amy glanced irresolutely from the open letter in her hand to the girl's face, and decided to postpone the matter of the letter. "I'll get it, Esther. You sit here and rest."

When she returned the girl seemed herself again. She took the tea-tray and kissed the bearer with a fervour born of remorse. "I am a Pig," she declared, "and you are a darling! Never mind, we'll even up some day."

"When you have had your tea, Esther, I've got a letter I want you to read."

"A letter? Who from? I mean, from whom? Gracious! I'll have to be more careful of the King's English, now that I'm a school teacher."

"I don't know. It is signed just 'H' and it's written to 'Dearest wife.' You don't know who that could be, do you?"

"Mother, perhaps?"

"No. It's not in your father's writing and his name did not begin with 'H.'"

"Where did you find it, dear?"

"Up in an old trunk of your grandma's—I mean of Mary's mother's. One of the trunks that were sent here after she died. Mary asked me to put moth balls in it. This letter was all crushed up in a corner. I took it out to smooth it, because I knew it was a love letter. You don't think any one would mind?"

"N—o." Esther, who knew Aunt Amy's feeling about love letters, could not find it in her heart to disagree. "I think we may fairly call it treasure-trove. It's only a note anyway." Her eyes ran swiftly over the two short paragraphs upon the open sheet.

"Dearest wife:—

"At last I can call you 'wife' without fear. Our waiting is over. Brave girl! If it has been as long to you as to me, you have been brave indeed. But it is our day now. Even your mother cannot object any longer. I am coming for you to-morrow. Only one more day!

"Dear, I think that in my wild impatience I did you wrong. But love does not blame love. No wife shall ever be so loved as you. May God forget me if I forget what you have done for me...."

"What a strange letter!" Esther looked up wonderingly.

"Is that all, Esther?" Aunt Amy's face was vaguely disappointed. "The one I read was much longer than that."

"That is all that is written here, Auntie. But it is a beautiful letter. They had been separated, you see, and she had been brave and waited. One can imagine—"

The click of the garden gate interrupted her.

"Here's your mother," said Aunt Amy, in a flurried tone. "Don't let her—"

"Is that the mail, Esther?" Mrs. Coombe's high voice held a fretful intonation. Aunt Amy seized the letter and hid it in her dress. "She shan't see it," she whispered childishly.

"Is that the mail?" repeated Mrs. Coombe, coming up the walk.

"No, there is no mail," said Esther, "No one has been to the post office. Perhaps Jane had better run down now."

"But you had a letter," suspiciously. "I'm sure I saw it. Where is it?"

"Don't be absurd, mother. I have no letter. Nor would I think it necessary to show it to you if I had. I am not a child."

"You are a child. And let me tell you, a clandestine correspondence is something which I shall not tolerate. Let me see the letter."

Esther was feeling too happy to be cross. Besides it was rather funny to be accused of clandestine correspondence.

"I think I'll go and help Jane with the pup," she said cheerfully. "Too bad you didn't come in sooner, mother. Dr. Callandar was here."

"Then you do refuse to show me the letter?"

"If I had one I should certainly refuse to show it. Why do you let yourself get so excited, mother? You never used to act like this. It must be nerves. Every one notices how changed you are." She paused, arrested by the frightened look which replaced the futile anger on her step-mother's face.

"I'm not different. Who says I am different? It is you who are trying to make a fuss. I'm sure I do not care about your letter. Why should I? Your father always seemed to think you needed no advice from any one. Only don't imagine that I am blind. I *saw* you with a letter."

Having triumphantly secured the last word, she turned to busy herself with the tea-tray, and Esther, knowing the uselessness of argument, went on toward the house. Aunt Amy attempted to follow but was stopped by Mary.

"Amy, what did that doctor want here?"

"He came to see me."

Mary laughed. "Likely!" she said. "This tea is quite cold. Was it he who left the letter for Esther?"

"Esther didn't have a letter. I had one."

Again the incredulous laugh, and the dull red mounted into Aunt Amy's faded cheeks. She clutched the treasured letter tightly under her dress. This mocking woman should never see it! But as she turned again to leave her, another consideration appealed to her unstable mind. Mary suspected Esther—and nothing would annoy her more than to find herself mistaken. On impulse Aunt Amy flung the letter upon the tea-tray.

"There it is. Read it, if you like. It has nothing to do with Esther. Or any one else. I found it in one of your mother's old trunks."

Left alone, Mary Coombe drank her tea, which after all was not very cold. She was not really interested in the letter, now that she had got it. Had not a vagrant breeze tossed it, obtrusively, upon her lap, she would probably not have looked at it.

Listlessly she picked it up, opened it, glanced at the firm, clear writing....

A sharp, tingling shock ran through her. It was as if some one had knocked, loudly, at dead of night at a closed door! That writing—how absurdly fanciful she was getting!

"Dearest wife," she read, "at last I can call you 'wife' without fear"—the vagrant breeze, which had tossed the letter into her lap, tossed it off again. Her glance followed it, fascinated!

Of course she had dreamed the writing? She had been terribly troubled by dreams of late. But what had Amy said about finding the paper in her mother's trunk? The whole thing was a fantastic nightmare. She had but to lean forward, pick up the letter, read it properly and laugh at her foolishness.

But it was a long time before she found the strength to pick it up. When she did, she read it quietly to the end with its scrawled "H." Then she read it over again, word by word. Her expression was one of terror and amaze.

When she had finished she looked up, over the pleasant garden, with blank eyes. Her face was ashen.

"He came," she said aloud. "He came! But—*what did she tell him when he came?*"

The garden had no answer to the question. Somewhere could be heard a girl's laugh and the sharp bark of a protesting puppy. Mary Coombe drew her hand across her eyes as if to clear them of film and, trying to rise, slipped down beside the elm-tree seat, a soft blot of whiteness on the green.

They found her there when they had finished washing the puppy, but though she came quickly to herself under their eager ministrations, she would not tell them what had caused her sudden illness. To all their questionings she answered pettishly, "Nothing! Nothing but the heat."

CHAPTER XXI

When a man of thirty-five has at last shaken himself free from the burden of an unhappy love affair, he is not particularly disposed to welcome an emotional reawakening. He knows the pains and penalties too well; the fire of Spring, he has learned, can burn as well as brighten. Callandar thought that he had done with love, and a growing suspicion that love had not done with him brought little less than panic. Upon the occasion of Willits' second visit he had begun to realise his danger and the professor never guessed how nearly he had persuaded him to leave Coombe. Some deep instinct was urging flight, but the impulse had come just a little bit too late. He could not go, because he wanted so very much to stay.

After Willits' departure he had deliberately tested himself. For five days he did not try to see Esther and upon the sixth he realised finally that seeing Esther was the only thing that mattered. Then had come the short interview under the elm tree—an interview which had shown him a new Esther, demure, adorable, with eyes which refused to look at him. He had come away from that meeting with a new pulse beating in his heart.

To doubt was no longer possible. He loved her.

But she? Lovers are proverbially modest, but their modesty is fear disguised. They hope so much that they fear to hope at all; it seemed impossible to Callandar that Esther should not love him and yet it seemed impossible that she should. Only one thing emerged clearly from the chaos—the immediate necessity of finding out.

"Why don't you ask her?" demanded Common Sense in that wearily patient way with which Common Sense meets the vagaries of lovers.

"But it is so soon," objected Caution, while Fear, aroused, whispered, "Be careful. Give her time." Even Mrs. Grundy made herself heard with her usual references to what people, represented by Mrs. Sykes, might say, adding scornfully, "Why, you haven't met the girl's mother yet. Don't make a fool of yourself, please."

But over all these voices rose another voice, insistent, demanding to be satisfied. It might be premature, it might be all that was rash and foolish but he simply had to find out at once whether or not Esther Coombe loved him.

His final decision came one morning when driving slowly home from an all night fight with death. He was tired but exultant, because he had won the fight, and life, which slips so easily away, seemed doubly precious. After all, he was no longer a boy. If life still held something beautiful for him, why should he wait? He had waited so many years already.

Guiding the car with one hand, he slipped the other into his pocket and opening a small locket which he found there, gazed long and earnestly at the picture it contained. The face it showed him was a young face, fair, rounded, childish. Dear Molly! his thought of her was infinitely tender. He loved her all the more for the knowledge that he had not loved her enough. Well, he could never atone now. She was gone—slipped away, he thought, with but little more knowledge of living than the tiny baby he had just helped to bring into the world. Brushing away the mist which for a moment blurred his sight, Callandar kissed the picture gently and shut the case.

The dawn was golden now. The motor began to gather speed. An early farmer getting into market with a load of hay, drew amiably to one side to let it pass. From a, wayside house came the cheerful noise of opening shutters; a milk cart rattled out of a nearby gate; the motor sped still faster— the new day was fairly begun.

Early as it was, Mrs. Sykes was busy washing the veranda. This was a ritual, rigorously observed twice every day; in the morning with a pail and broom, in the evening with the hose. Par be it from us to malign the excellent Mrs. Sykes or to suggest that her opportune presence on the front steps was due to anything save the virtue of cleanliness. Mrs. Sykes, as she often said, couldn't abide curiosity. Still, it would be very interesting to know whether Amelia Hill's latest was a boy or a girl. Mrs. Hill had already been blessed with nine olive branches, all girls, and had confided to Mrs. Sykes that if the tenth presented no variation, she didn't know what on earth Hill would do—he having acted so kind of wild-like last time. Mrs. Sykes, unable to resist the trend of her nature, had advised that no variation could be looked for. "It may be," she had said, "but after a run of nine, it isn't to be expected. There's no denying that girls run in some families. I know jest how you feel, Mrs. Hill, and, if I could, I'd encourage you, for I'm a great believer in speaking the truth in kindness. But it's best to be prepared, and a girl it will be, you may be sure."

"You are up early, Mrs. Sykes," said the doctor cheerfully. "Wait till I take the car around and I'll finish up those steps for you."

"Land no! I won't let you, Doctor. You're clean tired out. I've got a cup of hot coffee waiting. I don't suppose, with Amelia laid aside, any of them Hills would think to give you so much as a bite. All girls too."

"Not all girls now, Mrs. Sykes," said the doctor cheerfully. "A son and heir arrived this morning. Fine little fellow. They appear to be delighted."

The discomfited prophet leaned against the door-post for support.

"A boy? It can't be a boy! It doesn't stand to reason!"

"It never does, Mrs. Sykes."

"And I was so sure 'twould be another girl!" There was an infinitesimal pause during which Mrs. Sykes' whole outlook readjusted itself, and then with a heavy sigh she continued, "Poor Amelia Hill! She'll certainly have her troubles now. I shouldn't wonder a mite if it didn't live. Miracles like that seldom do. And if it does, it will be spoiled to death. No boy can come along after nine sisters and not be made a sissy of. Far better if it had been a girl in the first place. And yet I suppose Amelia's just as chirpy as possible? She never was one to look ahead to see what's coming."

"Lucky for her!" murmured Callandar, as he picked his way over the shining wetness of the veranda. "And now, Mrs. Sykes, I want you to do me a favour. Don't go predicting to my patient that her boy baby will die, or if he doesn't it would be better for him if he did. A woman who has mothered nine children is entitled to a little peace of mind with the tenth. Don't you think so?"

"Land sakes, yes. If you put it that way. But the shock will be all the worse when it comes. Still, if you want the poor thing left in a fool's paradise I don't object. Perhaps it would be a good thing to have the three littlest Hills over here to spend a week with Ann. I can stand them if you can."

"Good idea!" Callandar smiled at her, but attempted no thanks. He had learned early that she was as shy about doing a kindness as a child who hides its face, while offering you half of its lolly-pop. "I'll fetch them. But some one will have to pick them out. Likely as not I'd bring the middle three instead."

"They are dreadful similar," assented Mrs. Sykes, pouring coffee. "I don't know but what it was them Hill children that made me a suffragette!"

"What?"

Mrs. Sykes did not notice the unflattering (or flattering) surprise in the doctor's voice.

"Yes. I think it was the Hill children as much as anything. There they are, nine of them, like as peas in a pod, and all healthy. I shouldn't wonder if the whole nine grows up—and what then? Amelia Hill just can't hope to marry nine of them. Three out of the bunch would be about her limit. And what are the others going to get? I say, give them the vote. Land sakes! Why not? I ain't one to refuse to others what I don't want myself."

CHAPTER XXII

Tired though he must have been, the doctor had never felt less like sleep. There was a fever in his blood which the cool quietness of the spare room could not soothe. The lavendered freshness of the bed invited in vain. Crossing to the western window, he threw up the blind and looked out to where, peeping out between roofs and trees, the gable window of the Elms glittered in the early sun. The morning breeze blew softly on his face, sweet with the scent of flowering pinks and mignonette. In the orchard all the birds were up and singing. Every blade of grass was gemmed with dew, sparkling through the yellow glory of dawn like diamonds through a primrose veil. But Callandar, usually so alive to every manifestation of beauty, saw nothing save the distant glitter of the gable window. The morning, in which he could hardly hope to see Esther, stretched before him intolerably long.

Upon impulse he drew his desk to the window and, sitting down, began to write:

"Dear Old Button-Moulder—

"Behold the faulty button about to be recast! This is to be a big day. I am writing you now because if she refuses me, I shan't be able to tell you of it, and if she accepts me I shan't have time. I fancy you know who she is, old man. I saw enlightenment grow in your eyes that day after church. I hardly knew it myself, then, but now I am sure. Do you remember that house we looked at one day? I have forgotten even the street, but we can find it again. It had a long sloping lawn, you remember, and stone steps and a beautiful panelled hall running straight through to a walled garden which might well have fallen there by some Arabian Nights enchantment. That is the house I mean to have for Esther. I can see her there quite plainly, in her blue dress, filling the rose bowl which stands upon the round table in a dusky corner of the hall. Over her shoulder, through the open door, glows the riotous colour of the garden. Her pure profile gleams like mother-o'-pearl against the dark panelling—say, Willits, just go and look up that house, will you? I am going to ask her to marry me. And I never knew before what a coward I am. Was there ever a chap named Callandar who quoted uppish remarks about being Captain of his Soul? If so, let me apologise for him. I think the chap who wrote those verses could never have been in love—or perhaps he wrote them after she said 'yes.' I'll telegraph the news. Don't expect me to write. And don't dare to come down to see me. H.C.

"P.S.—I came upon a good thing the other day. It is by Galsworthy, the chap who writes English problem novels:

"'If on a spring night I went by
And God were standing there,
What is the prayer that I would cry
To Him? This is the prayer:
O Lord of courage grave,
  O Master of this night of spring,
Make firm in me a heart too brave
  To ask Thee anything!'"

"Rather fine, don't you think? Or is it just a madness of pride? On second thought, I don't believe that I have arrived at the stage when I can do without God. H."

He folded the letter, stamped and addressed it and placed it upon the table in the hall where Ann would find and post it. Then, lighting a cigar, he sat down beside the open window and began to wonder how the momentous meeting with Esther could be best arranged. Perhaps if he walked out to the schoolhouse and waited until lunch time? No, it was Saturday morning and there was no school. The obvious thing was to call at the house, but this, the doctor felt, was sure to be unsatisfactory. Not only was there Jane to think of and Aunt Amy—but there was also the as-yet-unknown Mrs. Coombe. The visit would almost certainly end in a formal call upon the family. He might perhaps send Bubble over with an invitation to go fishing. No, that was too risky. Esther might refuse to go fishing and that would be a bad omen.

In a sudden spasm of nervousness Callandar threw the half-burned cigar out of the window and, following it with his eyes, was not sorry to be distracted by the sight of Ann in her night-dress, crying under the pear tree. Ann crying was an unusual sight, but Ann in a night-dress was almost unbelievable. The doctor knew at once that something serious must have happened and went down to see.

The child looked up at his approach, all the natural impishness of her small face drowned in sorrow. In her open hand she held the body of a tiny bird, all that was left of a fledgling which had tried its wings too soon.

"It toppled off and died," said Ann. "All its brothers and sisters flewed away."

"Heartless things!" said Callandar, and then seeing that comfort was imperative he sat down beside the mourner and tried to do the proper thing. He explained to her that the dead bird was only one of a nest-full and that the dew was wet and that she was getting green stains on her nightie. He reminded her that birds' lives, for all their seeming brightness, are full of danger and trouble. Perhaps the baby bird was just as well out of it. At least it would never know the lack of a worm in season, nor the bitterness of early snow. This particular style of comfort he had found very effective in cases other than baby birds, but it didn't work with Ann.

"I don't care," she sobbed, "it might have lived anyway. It never had a chance to live."

Living, just living, was with Ann clearly the great thing to be desired.

Callandar stopped comforting and took the child on his knee.

"I believe you've got the right idea, little Ann," he said. "It isn't so much the sorrow that counts or the joy either, but just the living through it. We're bound to get somewhere if we keep on. Don't cry any more and we'll bury the little bird all done up in nice white fluffy cotton. As Mrs. Burns says when any one dies: 'It's such a comfort to have 'em put away proper.' And then after a while you and Bubble might go fishing."

"I can't." Ann showed signs of returning tears. "If Aunt lets me go anywhere, I promised to go and help Esther Coombe pick daisies to fix the church for to-morrow."

Here was chance being kind indeed! But the doctor dissembled his exultation.

"Hum! too bad. Where did Miss Esther tell you to go?" he asked guilelessly.

"To the meadow over against the school."

"What time?"

"Half past two."

"Well, cheer up, I'll tell you what—I'll go and help Miss Esther pick the daisies. I can pick quite as fast as you. And I'll speak to Aunt Sykes and make it right with her. So if you run now and get dressed you and Bubble may go just as soon as you've had breakfast. And stay all day. Be sure you stay all day, mind."

A good sound hug was the natural answer to this and when the conspirators met at breakfast everything had been satisfactorily arranged. Ann had her holiday and the doctor's way lay clear before him. For all his apparent ignorance Callandar knew that daisy field quite as well as Ann. It was wild and lonely, yet full of cosy nooks and hollows. Mild-eyed cows sometimes pastured there. It was a perfect paradise for meadow-larks. Could any man ask better than to meet the girl he loved in a field like that?

"You're not eating a mite, Doctor."

With a start, Callandar helped himself to marmalade.

So much for the morning of the eventful day. We have given it in detail because it was so commonplace, so empty of any incident which might have foreshadowed the happenings of the afternoon. Callandar was restless, but any man is restless under such circumstances. He found the morning long, but that was natural. Long afterwards he thought of its slow moving hours, lost in wonder that he should have caught no glimpse, heard no whisper, while all the time, through the beauty of the scented, summer day, the footsteps of inescapable fate drew so swiftly near. Fortunate indeed for us that the fragile house we dwell in is provided with no windows on the future side, and that the veil of the next moment is as impenetrable as the veil of years.

What are they, anyway, these curious combinations of unforeseen incidents which under the name of "coincidence" startle us out of our dull acceptance of things? Can it be that, after all, space and circumstance are but pieces in a puzzle to which the key is lost, so that, playing blindly, we are startled by the *click* which announces the falling of some corner of the puzzle into place? Or is it merely that we are all more closely linked than we know, and is "coincidence" but the flashing of one of numberless invisible links into the light of common day? Some day we shall know all about it; in the meantime a little wonder will do us good.

It was, of course, coincidence that this afternoon Mary Coombe should offer to gather the marguerites for Esther and that, the Saturday help having failed to materialise, Esther was glad of the offer which left her free to help Aunt Amy in the kitchen. It was also coincidence that Mary should choose to wear her one blue dress and her shady hat which looked a little like Esther's. But, given these coincidences, it is easy to understand why the doctor, passing slowly by the field of marguerites, felt his heart bound at the supposed sight of Esther among the flowers.

Now that the moment had really come, his restlessness fell from him. He felt cool, confident, happy! The world, the beautiful world, was gay in gold and green. Over the rise, half hidden by its gentle undulation, he caught the glint of a blue gown—

Running his car under the shade of some nearby trees, the doctor leapt the pasture fence in one fine bound. The blue figure among the daisies was stooping, her face hidden by a shady hat. No one else was in sight—just he and she in all the lovely, sunny, breeze-swept earth! He came towards her softly; called her name, but so low that she did not hear. Then a meadow-lark, disturbed, flew up with his piercing "sweet!" the stooping figure turned and he saw, in the clear sunlight, the face under the shady hat—

Had something in his brain snapped? Or was he living through a nightmare from which he would awake presently? The world, the daisy field, the figure in blue, himself, all seemed but baseless fabrics of some fantastic vision!

For, by a strange enchantment, the face which should have been Esther's face was the face of Molly Weston, his lost wife!

It could not be! But it was.

Incredible the swiftness with which nature rights herself after a stunning shock. Only for a moment was Callandar left in his paradise of uncertainty. The next moment, he knew that he beheld no vision, knew it and accepted it as certainly and completely as if all his life had been but a preparation for the revelation.

"You!" he said. It was only a whisper but it seemed to fill the universe. "You—Molly!"

At the name, the hazel eyes which had met his so blankly sprang suddenly alive—recognition, knowledge, fear, entreaty, flashed across them in one moment's breathless space—then they grew blank again and Mary Coombe fell senseless beside her sheaf of daisies.

CHAPTER XXIII

Bending over the form of his lost wife, Henry Callandar forgot Esther. His mind, careful of its sanity, removed her instantly from the possibility of thought. She was gone—whisked away by some swift genie and, with her, vanished the world of blue and gold inhabited by lovers.

There remained only that white, faded face among the daisies. With careful hands he removed the crushed hat and loosened the collar at the neck. It was Molly. Not a doubt of that. Not Molly as he remembered her but Molly from whom the years had taken more than their toll, giving but little in return. He could not think beyond this fact, as yet. And he felt nothing, nothing at all. Both heart and mind lay mercifully numb under the anaesthetic of the shock.

Deftly he did the few things necessary to restore the swooning woman, noting with a doctor's eye the first faint flush of pink under the dead white nails, then the flutter of breath through the parted lips and the slow unclosing of the hazel eyes which, at sight of him, sprang widely, vividly into life.

"Harry!" The name was the merest whisper and held a quiver of fear. He remembered, stolidly, that just so had she whispered it upon the evening of their hurried marriage.

"Yes, Molly. It is all right. Don't be frightened!"—Just so had he soothed her.

She closed her eyes a moment while strength came back and then, raising herself, slipped out of his arms with a little breathless movement of avoidance. She seemed indeed to cower away and the fear in her eyes hurt him with a physical pang. Instinctively he put out his hand to reassure her, repeating his entreaty that she should not be frightened.

"But I am frightened!" Her voice was hoarse. "You terrified me! You had no right to come like that. You should have let me know—sent word—or—or something."

"Sent word?" He repeated the words, in a dazed way. "How could I? How could I know?"

"How could you come if you didn't know?" Already the miracle of readjustment which in women is so marvellously quick, had given back to Mary Coombe something of her natural manner. Besides, she had always known that some day he might find her—if he cared to look.

"Why should you come at all?" she flashed, raising defiant eyes. "The time to come was long ago."

"I did come." Callandar spoke slowly. "I came—" he paused, for how could he tell her that his coming had been to a house of death.

The bald answer, the strangeness of his gaze stirred her fear again. For a moment they stared at each other, each busy with the shifting puzzle. Then her quicker intuition abandoned the mystery of the present meeting to straighten out the past.

"Then you followed the letter?"

"Yes, I followed the letter."

"And you saw her—my mother?"

"Yes, I saw your mother."

Impulsively he moved toward her but she shrank back, plainly terrified.

"Don't! I didn't know. I swear I did not know. I never saw the letter— until last night. And I don't understand. What—what did my mother tell you when you came?"

"There was only one thing which would have kept me from you, Molly."

"Only one thing? What?" she almost whispered.

"She told me you were dead."

The flash of understanding on her face showed that she, at least, had shifted part of the puzzle into place.

"I see now," she said slowly, "I have wondered ever since I saw the letter. But I did not think she would go that far. Yet it was the simplest way. There was no date on the letter—but I guessed that it must have come too late."

"Too late?"

"Yes, or she would never have dared. Besides she might not have wanted to. She didn't know. I never had the courage to tell her. But if the letter had come in time—"

She faltered, growing confused under his intense gaze.

"In time for what?" he prompted patiently.

She brushed the question aside.

"Did you believe her when she said that?"

"Yes. Why should I have doubted? It seemed to be the end. I fainted on the doorstep. A long illness followed, when it was at its worst a friend came—helped me to pull out. When I was well again, I searched for your mother, employed detectives, but we never found her. Neither did we find anything upon which to hang a doubt of what she had told me."

"No. She was very clever."

"But *why*? For God's sake, why? Why should she lie to me? I had never harmed her. We were married. I could give you a home. She knew it. I told her. Why should she do this senseless, horrible thing?"

She looked at him with wide eyes and stammered,

"Don't—don't you know?"

A sense of some hitherto undreamed horror came to him with that stammering whisper. The spur of it brought some of his firmness back.

"I do not know. There must have been a reason. You must tell me."

He forced her, through sheer will, to lift her eyes to his. They were startled and sullen. With a start he saw, what he had missed before, that this woman, his wife, was a stranger. But he had himself well in hand now and his gaze did not falter. There was no escaping its demands. Her answer came in a little burst of defiance.

"Yes, there was a reason. You may as well know it. Your letter and your coming were both too late. I was married."

The doctor was not quick enough for this—

"Yes, of course you were, but—"

"Oh, not to you! Can't you understand? I was married to another man.... You need not look like that! What did you expect? I warned you. I knew I could never defy mother. I told you so. But you said it wouldn't be long—that she need never know. And I waited and waited. I could have married more than once but I wouldn't. I faced mother and said I wouldn't. But every time it was harder. I couldn't keep it up. And you didn't come. Then when he came and we thought he was so rich she made me marry him. She *made* me. I thought you were never coming back anyway. I wrote you once telling you to come. You didn't answer."

She paused breathless but he could find nothing to say. It seemed a small thing that the letter must have missed him somewhere, his whole mind was absorbed in trying to comprehend one stupendous fact. The puzzle had shifted into place indeed.

"I thought you didn't care any more," her words raced as if eager to be done, "and mother gave me no peace. You will never understand how terrified I was of mother. And he seemed so kind and was going to be rich. He owned part of a gold mine—mother was sure it would mean millions. But it didn't. Mother was fooled there!" with a gleam of malice. "The mine turned out to be worthless—after we were married."

Callandar drew a sharp breath and shook himself as if to throw off the horror of some enthralling nightmare.

"You married him—this man—knowing that you were a wife already?"

"A fine sort of wife!" He quivered at the coarseness of meaning in her tone. "We were never really married."

"What do you mean?"

"I mean that it was all a farce. What's a ceremony? For all I knew it wasn't even legal. When you did not answer my letter I thought that was what your silence meant. I asked a girl to ask her father who was a lawyer if a marriage was legal when the girl was under age and the parents didn't know about it. He said sometimes it wasn't."

Callandar groaned. "And you married again—on that?"

"Yes. I had to, anyway. I couldn't hold out against mother. I daren't tell her. She left us after the wedding, when the mine failed, and went back to Cleveland. It was there she must have got your letter, and the note I found last night. And when you came, she told you I was dead—to save the scandal. She was always different after that, though I never guessed why. It was a lie, you see, and mother was terrified of telling lies. It was the only thing she was afraid of. She believed that liars go to hell."

The tone in which she spoke of the probable torment of her mother was quite without feeling. Callandar listened in fascinated wonder. Was this Molly?—Pretty, kind-hearted Molly?

"I cannot understand," he said in a stifled voice. "It is all too horrible! This man you married—"

"He is dead. He died a year ago. I thought at first that you must have found out and that was why you came. I should have died of fright if you had come while he was alive. He would never have understood—never! He didn't like mother but he wasn't afraid of her. And I think that at last he suspected that she had made me marry him for his money. But he was always good. At first I was afraid all the time—oh, it was dreadful! I think

I have always been afraid—all my life—" Without warning she threw her hands out wildly and broke into choking sobs, crying with the abandon of a frightened child. Yet no one could have mistaken the impulse of her grief. It was for herself she wept.

Was it possible that she was a child still? A child in spite of her woman's knowledge, and the dulled lustre of her hair? Callandar remembered grimly that Molly's views of right and wrong had always been peculiarly simple. She had never wished to do wrong, but when she had done it, it had never seemed so very wrong to her. Her greatest dread had always been the dread of other people's censure.

"Don't cry," he said gently.

She must have felt the change in his voice, for although her sobs redoubled she did not again shrink from the hand he laid upon her hair. It was all over. She had told him the truth. Surely he must see that he was the one to blame, not she.

After a while she dried her eyes and looked up at him timidly but with restored confidence.

"People need never know now!" she said more calmly.

"People? Do people matter?"

She picked a daisy and began nervously to strip it of its petals—a pang of agony caught at the man's heart. So, only that morning, had he imagined himself consulting the daisy oracle. "She loves me, she loves me not." Absolutely he put the memory from him. Molly was speaking.

"People do matter. They make things so unpleasant. Not that I care as much about them as I used to; but still, one has to be careful. People are so prying, always wanting to know things," she glanced around nervously, "but let's not talk about them. I don't understand things yet. How did you find me, if you thought I was—dead?"

"Accident, if there be such a thing. I was driving down the road. I am living in the town near here—in Coombe!"

"But you can't! I live in Coombe. It is my home. There isn't a Chedridge in the place."

"My name is not Chedridge now. I took my uncle's name when I inherited his money. I am called Henry Callandar."

"Callandar!" Her voice rose shrilly on the word. "And you are living in Coombe? Why you are—you must be— Esther's Dr. Callandar!"

The man went deathly white, yet his enormous self-control, the fruit of years, held him steady.

Mary Coombe began to laugh weakly. "Why, of course, that explains it all, don't you see? Haven't you placed me yet? Esther is my step-daughter. The man I married was Doctor Coombe."

"Good God!" The exclamation was revelation enough had Mary Coombe heard it. But she did not hear it; this new aspect of the situation had seemed to her so farcical that her laughter threatened to become hysterical. "Oh, it's so funny!" she gasped.

It was certainly funny—such a good joke! The Doctor thought he might as well laugh too. But at the sound of his laughter, hers abruptly ceased.

"Don't do that!"

He tried to control himself. It was hard. He wanted to shriek with laughter. Esther's step-mother, the mysterious Mrs. Coombe, was Molly— his wife! Some mocking demon shouted into his ears the words he had intended to say to her when he came to tell her that he and Esther loved each other. He thought of his own high mood of the morning, of the tender regret which he had laid away with the dead of the dead past. It seemed as if all the world were rocking with diabolic laughter—Fate plans such amusing things!

He caught himself up—madness lay that way.

"Please don't laugh!" said Mrs. Coombe a trifle fretfully. "At least not so loudly. You startle me. My nerves are so wretched. And anyway it's more serious than you seem to think. We shall have to discuss ways of managing so that people will not know. Your being already acquainted with Esther will help. It will make your coming to the house quite natural. But it will be better to admit that we knew each other years ago, were boy and girl friends or something like that. Your change of name and my marriage will explain perfectly why we did not know each other until we met. Nobody will go behind that. They will think it quite romantic. The only one we need be afraid of is Esther. She is so quick to notice—"

She did not know about Esther then? She had never guessed that the girl was more to him than a mere acquaintance. Thank God for that! And thank God, above all, that the worst had not happened—Esther herself did not know, would never know now—

"I believe it can come quite naturally after all," Mary went on more cheerfully. "No one will wonder at anything if we say we are old friends. And we can be specially careful with Esther. I wouldn't have her know for anything. She is like her father. She would never understand. She doesn't know what it is to be afraid, as I was afraid of my mother. Do you think it is wicked that sometimes I'm glad she is dead, mother, I mean?"

He answered with an effort. "You used to be fond of your mother, Molly."

"Oh, don't call me Molly. Call me Mary. It will sound much better. No one has ever heard me called Molly here. If Esther heard it she would wonder at once. You will be careful, won't you?"

"Yes. I shall be careful." He had not heard what she said, save that she had mentioned Esther's name. Rather he was thinking with a gratitude which shook his very soul that fate had at least spared the innocent. Esther was safe. She did not love him. He felt sure of that now. Strange irony, that his deepest thankfulness should be that Esther did not love him.

A small hand fell like a feather upon his arm.

"Harry!"

"Yes, Molly!"

He looked down into her quivering face and saw in it, dimly, the face of the girl in his locket, not a mere outward semblance this time but the soul of Molly Weston, reaching out to him across the years. Her light touch on his arm was the very shackle of fate. Her glance claimed him. Nothing that she had done could modify that claim—the terrible claim of weakness upon the strength which has misled it.

Vaguely he felt that this was the test, the ultimate test. If he failed now he was lost indeed. Something within him reached out blindly for the strength he had dreamed was his, found it, clutched it desperately—knew that it held firm.

He took the slight figure in his arms, felt that it still trembled and said the most comforting thing he could think of. "Don't worry, Molly. No one will ever know."

CHAPTER XXIV

Ester was sitting upon the back porch, hulling strawberries and watching with absent amusement the tireless efforts of Jane to induce a very fat and entirely brainless pup to shake hands. It had been a busy day, for owing to the absence of the free and independent "Saturday Help" Esther had insisted upon helping Aunt Amy in the kitchen. Now the Saturday pies and cakes were accomplished and only the strawberries lay between Esther and freedom.

She had intended, a little later, to walk out along the river road in search of marguerites, but when Mary, more than usually restless after her fainting spell of yesterday, had offered to go instead, she had not demurred. It would be quite as pleasant to take a book and sit out under the big elm. Esther was at that stage when everything seems to be for the best in this "best of all possible worlds." She was living through those suspended moments when life stands tiptoe, breathless with expectancy, yet calm with an assurance of joy to come.

With the knowledge that Henry Callandar was not quite as other men, had come an intense, delicious shyness; the aloofness of the maiden who feels love near yet cannot, through her very nature, take one step to meet it.

There was no hurry. She was surrounded with a roseate haze, lapped in deep content; for, while the doctor had learned nothing from their last meeting under the elm, Esther had learned everything. She had not seemed to look at him as they parted, yet she had known, oh, she had known very well, how he had looked at her! All she wanted, now, was to be alone with that look; to hold it there in her memory, not to analyse or question, but to glance at it shyly now and again, feeding with quick glimpses the new strange joy at the heart.

"D'ye think He ever forgets to put brains into dogs?" asked Jane suddenly. "Oh, you silly thing, don't roll over like that! Stop wriggling and give me your paw!"

"He, who?" vaguely.

Jane made a disgusted gesture. "You're not listening, Esther! You know there is only one Person who puts brains into dogs!"

"But Pickles is such a puppy, Jane. Give him time."

"It's not age," gloomily. "It's stupidness. All puppies are stupid, but Pickles is the most abnormously stupid puppy I ever saw."

Esther laughed. "Where did you get the word, ducky?"

"From the doctor. It was something he said about Aunt Amy. Say, Esther, isn't he going to take you driving any more? I saw him going past this very afternoon. He turned down towards the river road. There was lots of room. Next time he takes you, may Pickles and me go too?"

"Pickles and I, Jane."

"Well, may we?"

"I don't know. Perhaps. When did the doctor go past?"

"Nearly two hours ago. I wonder if there's some one kick down there? Bubble says they're getting a tremenjous practice. I don't like Bubble any more. He thinks he's smart. I don't like Ann, either. I shan't ask her to my birthday party."

"I thought you loved Ann."

"Well, I don't. She thinks she's smart!"

"Ann, too? Smartness must be epidemic."

"It's all on account of the doctor," gloomily. "They can't get over having him boarding at their place. I told Ann that my own father was a doctor, but she said dead ones didn't count. Then I told her that my mother didn't have to keep boarders anyway."

"That was a naughty, snobbish thing to say. I'm ashamed of you!"

"What's 'snobbish'?"

"What you said was snobbish. Think it over and find out."

Jane was silent, apparently thinking it over. The fat pup, tired with unwonted mental exertions, curled up and went to sleep. Esther returned to her dreams. Then, into the warm hush of the late afternoon came the quick panting of a motor car.

"There he is!" cried Jane excitedly. "Let's both run down to the gate to see him."

"Jane!" Esther's cheeks were the colour of her ripest berry. "Jane, come here! I forbid you—Jane!"

"He's stopping anyway. He'll be coming in. You had better take off that apron.—Oh, look! Some one's with him. Why," with some disappointment, "it's mother! He is letting her out. I don't believe he is coming in at all—let go! Esther, you pig, let me go!"

She wriggled out of her sister's firm hold but not before the motor had started again; when she reached the gate it was out of sight.

Mrs. Coombe surveyed her daughter coldly. "You are a very ill-mannered child," she said, and putting her aside walked slowly up the path and around the house to where Esther sat on the back porch.

"Where are the daisies?" asked Esther, looking up from her berries.

"The daisies?" vaguely. "Good gracious! I forgot all about the daisies."

"Didn't you get any?"

"Heaps, but the fact is I didn't bring them home. I felt so tired. I don't know how I should have managed to get home myself if Dr. Callandar hadn't picked me up."

"Dr. Callandar?" Esther's voice was mildly questioning.

"Yes, why not?"

"I thought you had not met him."

"Neither I had—at least I hadn't met him for a good many years." Mary gave a little excited laugh. "But that's the funny part of it—he is an old friend."

Esther looked up with her characteristic widening of the eyes. The news was genuinely surprising. And how agitated her mother seemed!

"It is really quite a remarkable coincidence," went on Mary nervously. "I was so surprised, startled indeed. Although it's pleasant, of course, to meet an old schoolmate."

"You and Doctor Callandar schoolmates?" The eyes were very wide now.

Mary grew more and more confused.

"Yes—that is, not exactly. I mean his name wasn't Callandar then. His name was Chedridge. Did you never hear me speak of Harry Chedridge?"

"Never."

"Well, you never listen to half I say. And how was I to know that Doctor Callandar was the Harry Chedridge I used to know? He took the name of Callandar from an uncle—or something. Anyway it isn't his own."

Esther hulled a particularly fine berry and carefully putting the hull in the pan, threw the berry away.

"Curiouser and curiouser!" she said, quoting the immortal Alice. "Did you recognise him at once?"

If it be possible for a lady of this enlightened age to simper, Mrs. Coombe simpered. "He recognised me at once!" with faint emphasis on the pronouns.

The girl choked down a rising inclination to laugh.

"Why shouldn't he? I suppose you haven't changed very much."

"Hardly at all, he says; at least he says he would have known me anywhere. But it's quite a long time, you know, terribly long. I was a young girl then. Naturally, he was much older."

"I should have thought so. That's why it seems queer—your having been schoolmates."

Mrs. Coombe looked cross. "I did not mean schoolmates in that sense."

"Oh, merely in a Pickwickian sense!" Esther's laugh bubbled out.

Mary arose. She was afraid to risk more at present, until she had been to her room and—rested awhile. "You are rude, as usual," she said with dignity. "When I said that Dr. Callandar and I were schoolmates I meant simply that we were old friends, that we knew each other when we were both younger. I do not see anything at all humorous in the statement."

"No, of course not!" with quick compunction. "It's quite lovely. Just like a book. Why didn't he come in?"

The question was so cleverly casual that no one could have guessed the girl's consuming interest in the answer. But its cleverness had overshot the mark, for so colourless was the tone in which it was asked that Mary did not notice it at all. Instead she retreated steadily along her own line.

"I hope I always treat your friends with proper courtesy, Esther. And I shall expect you to do the same with mine. Dr. Callandar is a very old friend indeed. Should he call to-night I wish you to receive him as such."

"I'll try," said the girl demurely.

The way of escape was now open, but Mrs. Coombe hesitated. She seemed to have something else to say. Something which did not come easily. "It's horrid living in a town like Coombe," she burst out. "People always want to know everything. We met the elder Miss Sinclair on the river road—you know what that means! If people ask you any question—or anything—you had better tell them at once that Dr. Callandar is not a stranger."

"I should not dream of suppressing the fact."

"You see," again that odd hesitation, "he may call—rather often. And—people talk so easily."

Despite her care, Esther's sensitive face flamed in answer to the quickened beat of her heart. What an odd thing for her mother to say! What did she mean? Was it possible that he had already told her—asked her? Or had she merely guessed? There was a moment's pause, and then, "Let them talk!" said the girl softly. "It can't make any difference, to them, how often Dr. Callandar calls."

Mrs. Coombe looked doubtful, hesitated once more, but finally turned away without speaking. As she went, she cast a careless glance at Aunt Amy, who stood just within the kitchen doorway, a curiously watchful look in her usually expressionless eyes.

"Berries all ready, Auntie," said Esther cheerfully. "What's the matter with me as a Saturday Help?"

But Aunt Amy did not smile as she usually did.

"She's gone to get dressed," she said abruptly, indicating with a backward gesture Mrs. Coombe's retiring figure.

"Well?"

"For him. She's gone to get dressed for him."

Esther was puzzled. "Why shouldn't she? Oh, I forget you didn't know! It's quite a romance. Mother used to know Dr. Callandar when she was a girl. 'We twa hae rin aboot the braes,' you know. Only it seems so funny. Fancy, Dr. Callandar and mother! But we shan't have to worry any more about her health. She can't possibly avoid him now."

Aunt Amy was not listening. The curiously watchful look was still in her eyes and suddenly, apropos of nothing, she began to wring her hands in the strange, dumb way which always preceded one of her characteristic mental agonies,—agonies which, far beyond her understanding as they were, never failed to awake profound compassion in Esther.

"What is it, dear?" she asked gently. "Are you not so well?"

"Don't you ever feel things, Esther? Don't you ever sense things— coming?"

"No, dear. And neither do you, when you are well. You are tired." She placed her hands firmly upon the locked hands of Aunt Amy and with tender force attempted to separate them. But Jane, who had been a silent but interested spectator, spoke eagerly.

"Don't, Esther! Do let her tell us what is coming. You know she always tells right when she wrings her hands. Go on, Auntie—"

"Jane, be quiet! I'll tell you why afterwards. Auntie dear, sit down."

'Aunt Amy's hands relaxed and the strange look faded. "It's nothing," she said. "It's gone! I must be more careful. Do not mention it to your mother, children. She might think me queer again, and I am not at all queer any more. You have noticed that I'm not, haven't you, Esther? I'll do anything you say, my dear."

"Then lie out in the hammock while I get supper. The berries are all ready. Then we'll all get dressed. Jane may wear one of her new frocks and you shall wear your grey voile. It will be quite a party."

"Will there be ice cream? Because if there isn't I don't want to get dressed," sighed Jane. "My new things don't fit. They look like bags."

"It will soon be holidays and then I'll fix them for you."

Jane laid a childish cheek to her sister's hand.

"Nice Esther," she cooed. "I'm sorry I called you a pig." Then, in a change of tone as they left Aunt Amy resting in the hammock, "Esther, why is Auntie so afraid of mother lately? She says such queer things I don't know what she means."

"Neither do I, dear. But I think it is just a passing fancy. She was very much hurt about the ring being sold. When she gets it back she will forget about it."

"She looks at mother as if she hates her."

"Oh, no!" in a startled tone. "How can you say such a thing, Jane?"

"But she does. I've seen her. I don't blame her. I think it was horrid—"

"That's enough. You know nothing about it. Little girls who do not understand have no right to criticise."

"Fred says it was the most underhan—"

"Jane, one word more and you shall have no berries to-night. Duck, don't you realise that you are speaking in a very unkind way of your own mother."

The child's eyes filled with ready tears, but her little mouth was stubborn. "Auntie's more my mother, Esther, and so are you. And it was mean to take the ring and I don't care whether I have any berries or not."

Supper was a very quiet meal that night. Mrs. Coombe, interrupted in the process of dressing, came down in an old kimono, but ate almost nothing, Jane was sullen, Aunt Amy silent and Esther happily oblivious to everything save her own happy thoughts.

As soon as she could, she slipped away to her own room, and, choosing everything with care, began to dress herself as a maiden dresses for the eye of her lover. She was to be all in white, her dainty dress, her petticoats, stockings and shoes. White made her look younger than ever, absurdly young. He had never seen her all in white and she knew quite well how soft it made the shadows of her hair, how startlingly blue her eyes, how warm and living the ivory of her lovely neck.

"Oh, I am glad I am pretty!" she whispered to her mirror. "Glad, glad!" Then with a laugh at her own childishness she "touched wood" to propitiate the jealous fates and ran down stairs to hide herself in the duskiest corner of the veranda.

It was delightful there. The cooling air was sweet with the mingled perfumes of the garden border below, an early star had fallen, sparkling, upon the blue-grey train of departing day, a whispering breeze crept, soft-footed, through the shrubbery. Esther lay back in the long chair and closed her eyes. For thirty perfect moments she waited until the click of the garden gate announced his coming. Then she sprang up, smiling, blushing,— peering through the screen of vines—

A man was coming up the path. At first sight he seemed a stranger, some one who walked heavily, slowly—the doctor's step was quick and springing. Yet it was he! She drew back, shyly, yet looked again. Some one, in a pretty green silk gown, had slipped out from under the big elm and was meeting him with outstretched hands.

"Mother," thought Esther, "how strange!"

They had paused and were talking together. Mary's high, sweet laugh floated over the flowers, then her voice, a mere murmur. His voice, lower still. Then silence. They had turned back, together, down the lilac walk.

Esther sat down again. She felt numb. She closed her eyes as she had done before. But all the dreams, all the happy thoughts were gone. She opened them abruptly to find Aunt Amy staring down upon her, dumbly, wringing her hands. In the warm summer air the girl shivered.

"What is it?" she asked a little sharply. But Aunt Amy seemed neither to see nor hear her. She flitted by like some wandering grey moth into the dim garden, still wringing her hands.

Esther sat up. "How utterly absurd," she said aloud. Indeed she felt heartily ashamed of herself. To behave like a foolish child, to startle Aunt

Amy into a fit and all because her mother and Dr. Callandar had gone for a stroll down the lilac walk—the most natural thing in the world. They would return presently. She had only to wait. But the waiting was not quite the same. Those golden moments already sparkled in the past. Nothing could ever be quite the same as if he had come straight up the path to where she waited for him in the dusk.

In the living-room, Jane who had small patience with twilight, had lighted the lamp. Its shaded beams fell in golden bars across the veranda floor. The sky was full of stars, now, but the voice of the breeze was growing shrill, as if whistling up the rain.

They were coming back along the side of the house. Esther rose quickly and slipped into the safety of the commonplace with Jane and the lighted lamp. Mrs. Coombe entered first, there was an instant to observe and wonder at her. She seemed a different woman, young, pretty, sparkling; even her hair seemed brighter. Behind her came Callandar and when Esther saw his face her heart seemed to stop. It was the face, almost, of a man of middle age, a firm, quiet face with cold eyes.

"Esther!" Mrs. Coombe's voice held incipient reproof.

The girl came forward and offered her hand. The doctor, this new doctor, took it, let it drop and said, "Good evening, Miss Esther," then turned to Jane with a politely worded message from Ann and Bubble.

"You can tell them I won't go," said Jane crossly. "They think they are smart. Just because—"

Esther slipped quietly from the room. In the hall outside she paused, breathless. She felt as if she had run a long way. Shame enveloped her, a shame whose cause she could not put into words. She only knew that she had, in the few seconds of that cold greeting, been profoundly humiliated. She quivered with the sting of unwarranted expectancy. But if this had been all, it would have been well. There was something else, some deeper pain surging through the smart of wounded pride, something which led her with blind steps into a dark corner of the stairs where she sat very quiet and still.

Through the open front door, she could see the bars of lamplight on the deserted veranda, and hear from the open windows of the living-room a hum of conversation in which Jane seemed to be taking a leading part. Then came the tinkle of the old piano and Mary's voice, singing, or attempting to sing, for it was soon apparent that her voice sagged pitifully on the high notes.

Presently Jane came out, banging the door. Jane's manners, Esther thought, were really very bad. She had probably banged the door because she had been sent to bed and she had probably been sent to bed because she had been saucy. Esther wondered what particular form her sauciness had taken, but when Jane called softly, "Esther!" she did not answer. She did not want to put Jane to bed to-night. The child flashed past her up the stairs and soon could be heard from an upstair window calling imperatively for Aunt Amy. But Aunt Amy, flitting through the dim garden wringing her hands, did not hear. Jane, much injured, went to bed by herself that night.

In the lamp-lit room there was no more music. The murmur of voices grew less distinct. There were intervals of silence. (Only very old friends can support a silence gracefully—but of course these two were very old friends.) Esther wondered, idly, how it would be best to explain her absence to her mother. Toothache, perhaps? Not that the excuse mattered. Mary never listened to excuses. She would be cross and fretful anyway and complain that Esther never treated her friends with proper courtesy. The best thing she could do would be to go to bed. But she made no movement to go; the moments ticked by on the hall clock unnoticed.

After a time, which might have been long or short, there was a stir in the room and her mother's voice called "Esther! Esther!"

The girl stood up, smoothed her white dress, slipped out on to the veranda and into the garden. From there she answered the call. "Yes, Mother?"

"Where are you? You sound as if you had been asleep. Doctor Callandar is going."

Esther came lightly up the steps.

"So soon?"

"It is early," agreed Mrs. Coombe playfully, "but I can't keep him."

Esther, herself in shadow, could see the doctor's face as he stood quietly beside his hostess. It was full of an endless weariness. Her pride melted. Impulsively she put out a warm hand—

"Good night, Miss Esther. How very sweet your garden is at night. But it feels as if our fine weather were over. The wind begins to blow like rain."

Esther's hand dropped to her side. Perhaps he had not seen it in the dusk.

CHAPTER XXV

We all know that strange remoteness into which one wakes from out deep sleep. Though the eye be open, the Ego is not there to use it. For an immeasurable second, the awakener knows not who he is, nor why, nor where. Only there is, faintly perceptible, a reminiscent consciousness whether of joy or sorrow, a certain flavour of the soul, sweet or bitter, into which the Ego, slipping back, announces, "I am happy" or "I am miserable."

Esther had not hoped to sleep that night but she did sleep and heavily. When she awoke it was to blankness, a cold throbbing blankness of undefined ill being. Then her Ego, with a sigh, came back from far places; the busy brain shot into focus; all the memories, fears, humiliation of the night before stood forth clear and poignant. She buried her face in the pillow.

Yet, after the first rush of consciousness, there came a difference. There always is a difference between night and day thoughts. Fresh from its wonder-journey, the soul is braver in the morning, the brain is calmer, the spirit more hopeful. After a half-hour's self-examination with her face in the pillow Esther began to wonder if she had not been foolishly apprehensive and whether it were not possible that half her fears were bogies. The weight began to lighten, she breathed more freely. Looking over the rim of the sheltering pillow the morning seemed no longer hateful.

Foremost of all comforting thoughts was the conviction that instinct must still be trusted against evidence. Through all her speculations as to the unexplained happenings of the previous day, she found that instinct held firmly to its former belief regarding the doctor's feelings toward herself. There are some things which one knows absolutely and Esther knew that Henry Callandar had looked upon her as a man looks upon the woman he loves. He had loved her that night when they paddled through the moonlight; he had loved her when he watched for her coming along the road, but most of all he had loved her when, under the eye of Aunt Amy, they had said good-bye at the garden gate. This much was sure, else all her instincts were foresworn.

After this came chaos. She could not in any way read the riddle of his manner of last night. Had the sudden resumption of his old friendship with her mother absorbed his mind to the exclusion of everything else?

Impossible, if he loved her. Had purely physical weariness or mental worry blotted her out completely for the time being? Impossible, if he loved her. Then what had happened?

Doubtless it would all be simple enough when she understood. She sighed and raised her head from the pillow. At any rate it was morning. The day must be faced and lived through. Any one of its hours might bring happiness again.

The rainstorm which had swept up during the night had passed, leaving the morning clean. She needed no recollection to tell her that it was Sunday. The Sabbath hush was on everything; no milkman's cans jingled down the street; no playing children called or shouted; there was a bell ringing somewhere for early service. Esther sighed again. She was sorry it was Sunday. Work-a-day times are easiest.

A rich odour of coffee, insinuating itself through the half open door, testified mutely to the fact that Aunt Amy was getting breakfast. It was later than usual. After breakfast it would be time to dress for church. Every one in Coombe dressed for church. It was a sacred rite. One and all, they had clothes which were strictly Sabbatarian, known indeed by the name of Sunday Best.

Esther's Sunday best was a blue, voile, a lovely blue, the colour of her eyes when in soft shadow. It was made with a long straight skirt slightly high at the waist, round neck and elbow sleeves and with it went soft, wrinkly gloves and a wide hat trimmed with cornflowers. She knew that she looked well in it—and the doctor would be in church.

On this thought which flew into her mind like a swift swallow through an open window, her lethargy fled and in its place came nervous haste; a feverish impatience which brought her with a bound out of bed, flushed and eager. Philosophy is all very well but it never yet stilled the heart-beat of the young.

Aunt Amy looked up in mild surprise as she hurried into the kitchen in time to butter toast and poach the eggs.

"Why, Esther!" she said in her bewildered way. "I thought—I didn't think that you would get up this morning."

"Why? I am perfectly well, Auntie. Where is mother?"

"Oh, she's up! Picking flowers."

Esther looked slightly surprised. It was not Mrs. Coombe's habit to rise early or to pick flowers, but before she had time to comment, Mary herself entered the kitchen with an armful of roses.

"Hurry with your breakfast, Jane," she said, "I want you to take these over to the doctor's office. I wonder you have not sent some to the poor man before this, Esther. Mrs. Sykes' roses never amount to anything. Shall I pour the coffee? I suppose you felt that you did not know him well enough. But flowers sent in a neighbourly way would have been quite all right. If you weren't always so stiff, people would like you better. I felt quite ashamed of your behaviour last night. Of course it wasn't necessary for you to stay in the room *all* the evening, but it was simply rude to run away as you did. You needn't make Jane an excuse. Jane could put herself to bed, for once."

"I did—" began Jane, but catching sight of her sister's face, went no further. And Mrs. Coombe, who was always talkative when airing a grievance, paid no attention.

"If you are feeling huffy about the motor breaking down, you'll just have to get over it," she went on. "It couldn't possibly have been Dr. Callandar's fault anyway."

"I am quite sure that it wasn't."

"Then don't sulk. He is rather fine looking, don't you think? Though as a boy he was almost ugly. It doesn't seem to matter in men—ugliness, I mean. And of course in those days he could not afford to dress; dress makes such a difference. I shouldn't be a bit surprised if his clothes are English made. That baggy look that isn't really baggy, you know. When I knew him his people were quite poor. Only a mother and sister. The father shot himself. People said suicide ran in that family. But Harry—Henry said that if it did, it was going to stop running. He said such odd things. I was staying with friends when I met him, at a church social. One meets all kinds at an affair like that. My friends didn't ask him to the party they gave for me. For although they were a very good family, the Chedridges, Henry was almost a hired man at that time, working for old Dr. Inglis, to put himself through college. His mother and sister never went out."

"Were they both invalids?"

"Don't be clever, Esther! I mean socially, of course. Jane, run up to my dresser and look in the second drawer on the right hand side and bring down my small photo case. I think I have a photo somewhere, not a very good one, but enough to show how homely he was.... Amy, aren't you going to eat any breakfast this morning?"

Aunt Amy, who had been following her niece's unusual flow of talk with fascinated attention, returned with a start to her untasted egg. Esther tried to eat some toast and choked. In spite of all her resolutions she felt coldly and bitterly angry. That her mother should dare to gossip about him like that! That she should call him "ugly," that she should speak with that air of almost insolent proprietorship of those wonderful early years long, long before she, Esther, had come into his life at all, it was unendurable!

Do not smile, sophisticated young person. When you are in love you will know, only too well, this jealousy of youless years; this tenderness for photos and trifling remembrances of the youth of the one you love. You will envy his very mother, who, presumably, knew him fairly well in the nursery, and that first dreadful picture of him in plaid dress and plastered hair will seem a sacred relic.

In the meantime you may take my word for it, and try to understand how Esther felt as she bent, perforce, over the photo of a dark-browed lad whose very expression was in itself a valid protest against photography.

"Ugly, wasn't he?" asked Mrs. Coombe.

"Very," said Esther.

"Perfectly fierce," said Jane, peering over her shoulder. "Really fierce, I mean, not slang. He looks as if he would love to bite somebody."

"The photographer, probably."

Esther shrugged her shoulders and laid the photo carelessly upon the table. So careless was she, in fact, that a sharp "Look out!" from Jane did not prevent a sudden jerk of her elbow upsetting her steaming cup of coffee right over the pictured face.

With an angry exclamation, Mary sprang forward to rescue her property but Esther had already picked it up and was endeavouring to repair the damage with her table napkin.

"Oh, do take care!" said Mary irritably. "Don't rub so *hard*—you'll rub all the film off—there! What did I tell you?"

"Dear me! who would ever have dreamed it would rub off that easily?" Esther surveyed the crumpled bits of photo with convincing dismay.

"Any one, with sense. It's ruined—how utterly stupid of you, Esther." Mary's voice quivered with anger. "You provoking thing! I believe you did it on purpose."

The cold stare from the girl's eyes stopped her, but she added fretfully, "You are always doing things to annoy me. I can't think why, I'm sure."

"She was trying to dry it," declared Jane, belligerently. "She didn't mean to hurt the old photo. Did you, darling?"

"I can hardly see what my motive could have been," said Esther politely, rising from the table. She had deliberately tried to destroy the photograph and was exultantly glad that she had succeeded, yet, so quickly does the actress instinct develop under the spur of necessity, that her face and manner showed only amused tolerance of such a foolish suspicion.

Later, the culprit smiled understandingly at her image in the mirror as she dressed for church. "I did not know I could be so catty," she told her reflection, "but I don't care. She hadn't any right to have that darling picture. Ugly, indeed!" The blue eyes snapped and then became reflective. "Only she didn't think it ugly any more than I did. It was just talk. She was certainly furious when the film rubbed off. I wonder—" She fastened the last dark tress of hair, still wondering.

All the way to church she wondered, walking demurely with Jane up Oliver's Hill, while Mary, nervously gay, fluttered on a step or two ahead. Jane found her unresponsive that morning. The acquaintances they passed found her distant. They wondered if Esther Coombe were becoming "stuck up" since she had a school of her own? For although, as Miss Agnes Smith said, it is not quite the thing to do more than nod and smile on the way to church, one doesn't need to pass one's friends looking like an absent-minded funeral.

Poor Esther! She saw nobody because she looked for only one.

"Oh, Esther, Mrs. Sykes has a new bonnet. There she is, Esther, look!"

"Very pretty," murmured Esther absently.

Jane dropped her hand. "You're blind as well as deaf, Esther. It's perfectly, dreadfully awful, and you know it!"

Thus abjured, Esther managed to look at Mrs. Sykes' bonnet. And, having looked, she laughed. Mrs. Sykes had certainly surpassed herself in bonnets. And poor Ann, her skirts were stiffer, her pig-tails tighter and her small face more mutinous than ever. The doctor was not of the party. Esther had known that, long before Jane had noticed the bonnet.

Still, there was nothing in that. He did not always walk with Ann to church. He might not come up Oliver's Hill at all. He might come from the opposite direction. He might be in church already. Esther's step quickened. But she had no excuse for hurry. Unless one sang in the choir or were threatened with lateness it was not etiquette to push ahead of any one on Oliver's Hill. Decently and in order was the motto, so Esther was sharply reminded when she had almost trodden on the unhastening heels of Mrs. Elder MacTavish.

Mrs. MacTavish turned in surprise but, seeing Esther, relaxed into the usual Sunday smile and bow.

"Good morning, Esther. Good morning, Mrs. Coombe. Good morning, Jane. What perfect weather we are having. You are all well, I hope?"

"Very well, thank you."

"And dear Miss Amy?"

"Very well indeed."

"So sad that she never cares to come to church. But of course one understands. And it must be a satisfaction to you all that she keeps so well. I said to Mr. MacTavish only last night that I felt sure Dr. Callandar was not being called in professionally. That is the worst of being a doctor. One can hardly attend to one's social duties without arousing fear for the health of one's friends. Not that Dr. Callandar is overly sociable, usually."

The last word, delivered as if by an afterthought, said everything which she wished it to say. Esther's lips shut tightly. Mary Coombe flushed. But she was quick to seize the opening nevertheless.

"Such an odd thing, dear Mrs. MacTavish! Dr. Callandar turns out to be quite an old friend of—of my family. We knew each other as boy and girl. In his college days, you know."

"How very pleasant. But I always understood your family lived in Cleveland. Did Dr. Callandar take his degree in the States?"

"Oh, no, of course not, but I was visiting in Canada when we knew each other. Mutual friends and—and all that, you know."

"Very romantic," said Mrs. MacTavish. Her tone was pleasantly cordial, yet there was a something, a tinge—her quick glance took in Mrs. Coombe's pretty dress and flowered hat, and the beginning of a smile moved her thin lips. She said nothing. But then she did not need to say anything. Mind reading is common with women.

Mrs. Coombe was furious. Esther laughed suddenly, a bubbling, girlish laugh, and then pretended that she had laughed because Jane had stubbed her toe. Jane looked hurt, Mrs. Coombe suspicious and Mrs. MacTavish amused. So in anything but a properly Sabbatical frame of mind the little party arrived at the church door.

Who does not know, if only in memory, that exquisite thrill of fear and expectation with which Esther entered the place which might contain the man she loved? Another moment, a breath, and she might see him!... And who has not known that stab of pain, that awful darkness of the spirit, which came upon her as, instantly, she knew that he was not there?

He was not in the church. Mental telepathy is recognised as well by its absence as by its presence. Esther knew that the church was empty of her lover and that it would remain empty. He was not coming to church to-day. Fortunate indeed that Mrs. MacTavish was not looking, for the girl's lip quivered, an unnatural darkness deepened the blue of her eyes. Then, smiling, she followed her mother up the aisle. Girls are wonderfully brave and if language is given us to conceal our thoughts smiles are very convenient also.

Mary Coombe settled herself with a flutter and a rustle, and then, behind the decorous shield of a hymn book, she whispered,

"Did you see Dr. Callandar as we came in?"

"No."

"Look and see if he is here."

The girl glanced perfunctorily around.

"No," she said.

Mrs. Coombe frowned. She was patiently annoyed and Esther felt cold anger stir again. What difference could the doctor's absence possibly make to Mary Coombe?

The singing of the psalm and the reading were long drawn out wearinesses. Esther had not come to church to worship that morning. We do not comment upon her attitude. We merely state it. To-day, church, the service and all that it stood for had been absolutely outside of her emotions. Yet with the prayer came the thought of God and with the thought a thrill of angry fear—a fear which was an inevitable after effect of her very orthodox training. God, she felt dimly, did not like people to be very happy. He was a jealous God. He was probably angry now because she had come to church thinking more of Dr. Callandar than of Him. "Thou shalt have no other Gods before me!" Awful, mystical words! Did they mean that one couldn't have any human god at all? Not even a near, kind protecting god—like the doctor? It frightened her.

She found herself explaining to God that her lover was not really a rival. That although she loved him so terribly it was in quite a different way and would never interfere with her religious duties. Then, feeling the futility of this, she pretended carelessness, trying to deceive God into the belief that she didn't think so very much of the doctor anyway.

This was in the prayer, while she sat with her eyes decorously shaded by her hand. Above her in the pulpit, the minister in an ecstasy of petition set forth the needs of the church, the state and the individual. Esther did not hear a word until a sudden dropping of his voice forced a certain phrase upon her attention. He was praying, with an especial poignancy for "that blessing which maketh rich and addeth no sorrow."

Was there such a blessing? A blessing which would make rich and add no sorrow? No wonder the minister prayed for it. To Esther, whose mind was saturated with the idea of God as the author of chastenings, the possibility came with a shock of joy. She, too, began to pray, and she prayed for one thing only, over and over—the blessing that maketh rich and addeth no sorrow. There was no need, she felt, to specify further. God was sure to guess what blessing she meant.

A subdued rustle, a swaying as of barley in a gentle breeze and the prayer was over. Esther removed her hand from her eyes and looked up at the minister. For a tiny second his glance met hers. A thrill shot through her, a thrill of dismay. With all the force of a new idea, it came to her that she and he were in the same parlous case. He loved her, as she loved—somebody else.

And that meant that he must suffer, suffer as she had suffered last night. Last week when he had told her of his love she had been surprised, sorry and a little angry. But last week he had spoken of unknown things. Love and suffering had been words to her then, now they were realities.

Then, for she was learning quickly now, came another flash of enlightenment. They had been praying for the same thing. He, too, had prayed for the blessing which maketh rich—and he had meant *her*. She knew it. He had been asking God to give her to him. Horrible!

Common sense shrank back before the invading flood of fear. What if God had listened? What if He had answered? Ministers, she knew, have great influence with God. What if He had said, "Yes"? What if all the trouble of last night, the blankness of to-day, were part of the answer?

"Never! Never!" she said. She almost said it aloud, so real had her fear been. Her eyes, fixed upon the minister's face, were terrified, but her soul was strong. Fearful of blasphemy, yet brave, she faced the bogie of a God her thought had evoked, saying, "I make my own choice. Take my lover from me if you will—I shall never give myself to another."

All this was very wrong, shocking even, especially in church. But it really happened and is apt to happen any Sunday in any church so long as human love rebels at the idea of a Divine love less tender than itself.

Gradually the panic fear died down. Esther's sane and well-balanced nature began to assert itself. Some voice, small but insistent, began to say, "God is not like that," and she listened and was comforted. She had not yet come to the love which casts out fear, but she was done with the fear which casts out love.

So that when on the church steps in the sunshine she felt Angus Macnair's hand tremble in hers, she was able to meet his eyes, straightly, understandingly, but unafraid.

CHAPTER XXVI

The manner in which Dr. Callandar spent that tragic Sunday is not clearly on record. We have watched Esther so closely that he has been permitted to escape our observation, and it would be manifestly unfair to expect any coherent account of the day from him. He knows that he went for a walk, early, and that he walked all day. He remembers once resting by the willow-fringed pool which had seen his introduction into Coombe, but he could not stay there. Between him and that hot June day lay the wreck of a world. Once he stumbled upon the Pine Lake road and followed it a little way. But here, too, memory came too close and drove him aside into the fields. There he tried to face his future fairly, under the calm sky. But it was hard work. With such a riot of feeling, it was difficult to think. His mind continually fell away into the contemplation of his own misery. It was a bad day, a day which left an ineffaceable mark.

With night came the first sign of peace, or rather of capitulation. He fought no more because he realised that there was nothing for which to fight. There had never been, from the very first moment, a possibility of escape, the smallest ray of hope. Fate had met him squarely and the issue had never been in doubt.

It was a "wonderful clear night of stars" when, having circled the town in his aimless wandering, he found himself opposite the schoolhouse gate and calm enough to allow his thoughts to dwell definitely upon Esther. She, at least, was safe, and the knowledge brought pure thankfulness. Not for anything in the world would he have had her entangled in this tragic coil. Leaning over the gate he saw the school steps, faintly white in the starlight. It needed small effort of imagination to see her there as he had seen her that first day—a happy girl, looking at him with the long, straight glance of unawakened youth. A great wave of protecting love went out to meet that vision. Self was lost in its immensity. As he had found her, so, please God, she was still and so he would leave her.

Then, somewhere in the back of his brain, a question sprang to vivid life. Was she the same? He knew that all day he had been fighting back that question. Last night something had frightened him—something glimpsed for a moment in Esther's face when she had come in from the garden to say good-night. Fancy, perhaps, or a trick of the lamplight. She could not really have changed. He would not allow himself even to dream that she had changed.

By this time she would know about himself and Mary—know all that any one was to know. He had insisted upon that. Mary had promised to tell her to-day that they were to be married soon. Next time he saw her she would look upon him with different eyes; eyes which would see not her sometime friend and companion but her step-mother's future husband. He must steel himself for this. Probably she would laugh a little. He hoped she would laugh. Last night she had looked so—she had not looked like laughter. If she should laugh it would answer the last doubt in his heart. He would know that she was free.

Presently he felt himself to be unbearably weary. Physical needs, ignored all day, began to clamour. He must get home at once. No *outré* proceedings must raise the easy breath of gossip. He must not flinch, he dared not run away, all must be done decently and in order. Let him only keep his head now—the bravest man need not look too far into the morrow.

It must be late, he knew. The road into Coombe was deserted. All the buggies of the country folk returning from evening service had passed long ago and even the happy young couples indulging in a Sunday night "after church" flirtation had decorously sought their homes. He looked at his watch by the clear starlight. It was later even than he had thought. No need to avoid passing the Elms, now; they would all be asleep—he might perhaps be able to sleep himself if he knew that no light burned in Esther's window.

There was no light in the house anywhere. It stood black in the shadow of its trees. The doctor found himself walking softly. His steps grew slower, paused. Irresistibly the "spirit in his feet" drew him to the closed gate from where he could see the black oblong of her window.

"She is asleep," he thought. "Of course she is asleep. Thank God!"

Then, on the instant of dropping his eyes from the window, he saw her. She was standing quite near, in the shadow of the elm.

"Esther!" The one word leaped from his lips like a cry.

"Yes, it is I," she said.

She offered no word of explanation nor did any need of one occur to him. Moving from the shadow into the soft starlight she came toward him like the spirit of the night. But when she paused, so close that only the gate divided them, he saw that her eyes were wide and dark with trouble.

"I am so glad you came. I wanted to see you. I—I could not sleep." She spoke with the direct simplicity of a child, yet nothing could have shown more plainly that she was a child no longer. All her pretty girlish hesitation, all her happy shyness had passed away on the breath of the great awakening. It was a woman who stood there, pale, remote, with a woman's question in her eyes.

The keen shock of the change in her filled Callandar with rebellious joy; it would be pain presently, but, just for the moment, love exulted shamelessly, claiming her own. He tried to answer her but no words came.

"You look very tired." She seemed not to notice his silence. "I must not keep you. But there is a question I want to ask. Mother told me to-night that you and she are to be married. Is it true?"

How incredible she was, he thought. How perfect in her direct and simple dignity. Yet there had crept into her tone a wistfulness which broke his heart.

"Yes. It is true." He could do no less than meet her on her own high ground.

"She said," the girl's sweet, remote voice went on, "that you had loved each other all your lives. Is that true, too?"

He had hoped that he might be spared the bitterness of this, but since only one answer was possible, "It is true," he said hoarsely, "it is true that we loved each other—long ago."

"Long ago—and now?" He was to be spared nothing, it seemed. Her wide eyes searched his face. Lest she should read it too plainly, he bowed his head.

Then suddenly, even as she drew back from him, hurt to the heart, some trick of moonlight on his half-hidden face, linked to swift memory, showed her another moonlight night, a canoe, a story told—and in a flash the miracle had happened. Intuition had leaped the gulf of his enforced silence—Esther knew.

A great wonder grew in her eyes, an immense relief.

"Why," she spoke whisperingly, "I see, I know! She, my mother, is the girl you told me of. The girl you married—"

She did not need the confirmation of his miserable eyes. It was all quite plain. With a little broken sigh of understanding, she leaned her head against the gate post and, all child again, began to cry softly behind the shelter of her hands.

"Esther!"

He could say nothing, do nothing. He dared not even touch the dark, bent head. But we may well pity him as he watched her.

The girl's sobbing wore itself out and presently she lifted tear-drenched eyes, like the blue of the sky after rain. Her tragic, unnatural composure had all been wept away.

"I understand—now," she faltered. "Before, I didn't. I thought dreadful things. I thought that I—that you—oh, I couldn't bear the things I thought! But it's better now. You did love me—didn't you?"

"Before God—yes!"

She went on dreamily. "It would have been too terrible if you hadn't—if you had just pretended—had been amusing yourself—been false and base. But I felt all along that you were never that. I knew there must be some explanation and it didn't seem wrong to ask. Instead of pretending that I didn't know all the things you had not time to say. Forgive me for ever doubting that you were brave and good."

"Spare me—"

She was not yet old enough to understand the tragic appeal. For she leaned nearer, laying her soft hand over his clenched ones.

"It is all so very, very sad," she said with quaint simplicity which was part of her, "but not so bad—oh, not nearly so bad as if you had been pretending—or I mistaken. Think!—How terrible to give one's love unworthily or unasked!"

"But you do not love me," he burst out, "you cannot! You must not!"

Never had he seen her eyes so sweet, so dark.

"I do love you. And I honour you above all men."

Before he could prevent her, she had stooped—her lips brushed his hand.

"Oh, my Dear!"—He had reached the limit of his strength—instant flight alone remained if he would keep the precious flower of her trust. And she, too, was trembling. But in the soft starlight they looked into each other's eyes, and what they saw there helped. Their hands clasped, but in that moment of parting neither thought of self, so both were strong.

CHAPTER XXVII

Mrs. Sykes thought much about her boarder in those days and, for a wonder, said very little. Gossip as she was, she could, in the service of one she liked, be both wise and reticent. Perhaps she knew that oracles are valued partly for their silences. At any rate her prestige suffered nothing, for the less she said, the more certain Coombe became that she could, if she would, say a great deal. Of course her pretence of seeing nothing unusual in the doctor's engagement was simply absurd. Coombe felt sure that like the pig-baby in "Alice," she only did it "to annoy because she knows it teases."

One by one the most expert gossips of the town charged down upon the doctor's landlady and one by one they returned defeated.

"True about the doctor and Mary Coombe? Why, yes of course it's true. Land sakes, it's no secret." Mrs. Sykes would look at her visitor in innocent astonishment. "Queer? No. I don't see anything queer about it. Mary Coombe's a nice looking woman, if she is sloppy, and I guess she ain't any older than the doctor, if it comes to that. No, the doctor doesn't say much about it. He ain't a talking man. Sudden? Oh, I don't know. 'Tisn't as if they'd met like strangers. As you say, they *might* have kept company before. But I never heard of it. I always forget, Mrs. MacTavish, if you take sugar? One spoon or two? As you say, old friends sometimes take up with old friends. But sometimes they don't. My Aunt Susan found her second in a man who used to weed their garden. But it's not safe to judge by that. Ann, hand Mrs. MacTavish this cup, and go tell Bubble Burk that if he doesn't stop aggravating that dog, it'll bite him some day, and nobody sorry."

In this manner did Mrs. Sykes hold the fort. Not from her would Coombe hear of those "blue things of the soul" which her quick eye divined behind the quiet front of her favourite. But with the doctor himself she had no reserves, it being one of her many maxims that "what you up and say to a person's face doesn't hurt them any." The doctor was made well aware that her unvarnished opinion of his prospective marriage was at his disposal at any time.

"I'm not one as gives advice that ain't asked," declared Mrs. Sykes with sincere self-deception. "But what sensible folks see in Mary Coombe I can't imagine. I may be biased, not having ever liked her from the very first, but being always willing to give her a chance—which I may say she never took. There's a verse in the Bible she reminds me of, 'Unstable as water'—Ann, what tribe was it that the Lord addressed them words to?"

"I don't know, Aunt."

"There, you see! She doesn't know! That's what happens along of all these Sunday Schools. In my day I'd be spanked and sent to bed if I didn't know every last thing about the tribes."

"Ann and I will go and look it up," said the doctor hastily, hoping to escape; "it will be good discipline for both of us."

"Land sakes! I'm not blaming you, Doctor. Naturally you haven't got your mind on texts, and I don't blame you about the other thing either. Men are awful easy taken in. My Aunt Susan used to say that the cleverer a man was the more he didn't understand a woman. Dr. Coombe was what you'd call clever, too, but it didn't help him any. Mind you, I'm not criticising, far from it, but I suppose a person may wonder what a man's eyes are for, without offence. No one knows better than you, Doctor, that I'm not an interfering woman and I'd never dream of saying a word against Mary Coombe to the face of her intended husband, but if I did say anything it would have to be the truth and the truth is that a more thorough-paced bit of uselessness I never saw."

"Mrs. Sykes," the doctor's voice was dangerously quiet, "am I to understand that you are tired of your boarder?"

Mrs. Sykes jumped.

"Land, Doctor, don't get ruffled! I'm real sorry if I've hurt your feelings. I didn't mean to say a word when I set out. My tongue just runs away. And naturally you have to stand up for Mrs. Coombe. I see that. That'll be the last you'll hear from me and 'tisn't as if I'd ever turn around and say 'I told you so' afterwards."

This was *amende honorable* and the doctor received it as such; but when he had gone into his office leaving his breakfast almost untouched, Mrs. Sykes shook her head gloomily.

"You needn't tell me!" she murmured, oblivious of the fact that no one was telling her anything. "You needn't tell me!" Then, with rare self-reproach, "Perhaps I hadn't ought to have said so much, but such blindness is enough to provoke a saint. If he'd any eyes—couldn't he see Esther?" Mrs. Sykes sighed as she emptied the doctor's untasted cup.

More frankly disconsolate, though not so outspoken, were Ann and Bubble. Not only did they dislike the bride elect but they objected to marriage in general. "A honeymoon will put the kibosh on this here practice, sure," moaned Bubble.

"Look at me. I'm not thinking of getting married, am I? No, and I'm never going to get married either."

"I am," said Ann, "and I'm going to have ten sons and the first one is going to be called 'Henry' after the doctor."

"Huh!" said Bubble, "bet you it isn't. Bet you go and call it after its father. They all do."

"No chance! Bet you I won't. I wouldn't call it 'Zerubbabel' for anything."

For an instant they glared at each other, and then as the awful implication dawned upon Bubble his round face grew crimson and his voice thrilled with just resentment.

"Well, if you think you're going to marry me, Miss Ann, you're jolly well mistaken."

"Will if I like," said Ann, retiring into her sun-bonnet.

Upon the whole, however, their affection for the doctor kept them friendly. Both children felt that something was wrong somewhere. Their idol was not happy. Bubble whispered to Ann of long hours when the doctor sat in his office with an open book before him, a book the pages of which were never turned. Ann told of weary walks when she trotted along by his side, wholly forgotten. Only between themselves did they ever speak of the change in him, and Henry Callandar was well repaid for the careless kindness of his brighter hours by a faithful guardianship, a quick-eyed consideration and a stout line of defence which protected his privacy and ignored his moods without his ever being aware of such a service.

Esther he seldom saw. She was remarkably clever, he thought, with a tinge of bitterness, in arranging duties and pleasures which would take her out of his way. It was better so, of course. It was the worst of injustice to feel hurt with her for doing what of all things he would have had her do. But one doesn't reason about these things, one feels.

Sometimes he wondered if that midnight interview with her at the gate had ever really taken place—or had it been midsummer madness, too sweet to exist even in memory? Certainly, in the Esther he saw now there was nothing of the Esther of the stars. She wore her mask well. School had closed for the holidays and the summer gaieties of Coombe were in full swing. Esther boated, picnicked, played croquet and tennis. If there was any change in her at all it showed only in a kind of feverish gaiety which seemed to wear her strength. She was certainly thinner. Callandar ventured to suggest to Mary that she was looking far from well. But Mary laughed at the idea. She was very much annoyed with Esther. The girl appeared to care nothing at all for the great event, refused to discuss it, declined absolutely to put herself out in the slightest for the entertainment of her mother's prospective husband, seemed to avoid him in fact. Moreover, she openly expressed her intention of leaving home immediately after the wedding. Mrs. Coombe was afraid people would talk.

Of them all, Aunt Amy was the only one who understood. How her poor, unsound brain arrived at the knowledge we cannot say. Perhaps Esther was more careless in her presence, dropping her mask almost as if alone, or perhaps Aunt Amy's strange psychic insight took no note of masks, or perhaps—account for it as you will, Aunt Amy knew! Esther and Dr. Callandar loved each other, and Mary stood between. This latter fact was not at all surprising to Aunt Amy. Was it not the special delight of the mysterious "They" to bring misery to all Aunt Amy loved, and was not Mary their accredited agent? The affair of the ruby ring had proved her that, though no one else must guess it. What would come of it all, Aunt Amy could not tell. Wring her hands as she might she could not see into the future. Often she would mutter a little as she went about her work, or stand still staring, straining into the dark. No one noted any difference in her save Jane, for Jane was as yet happily free to observe. The others, caught up in the whirl of their own destinies, saw nothing save the problems in their own anxious hearts.

"Esther," said Jane one evening, "Aunt Amy is odder and odder and you don't seem to care a bit."

Esther, who was preparing to go to a garden party, turned back, a little startled.

"What do you mean, Jane?"

"I don't know. Can't you see that she isn't happy?"

"But she is better. She never complains. She almost never fancies things now."

"She goes into corners and stares—and she wrings her hands."

"But she always did that, duck."

Jane was not equal to a more lucid explanation.

"It's not the same," she insisted. "I know it isn't. Esther, when you go away, will you take Aunt Amy and me?"

"How could I, dear? Your home is here. And you like Dr. Callandar, don't you?"

"I used to. But he never plays with the pup any more. He's different. And you're different and mother's different. I don't want to live with mother. That was a fib I told you the other day about the cut on my head. I didn't fall and hurt it. It was mother She threw her clothes brush at me."

"Jane!" There was pure horror in her sister's voice.

"Yes, she did. I went into her room when she was taking some medicine in a glass and I asked her what it was. Honest, Esther, that is all I did. And she screamed at me—and threw the brush."

Esther came back into the room and sat down.

"When was this?" in businesslike tones.

Jane considered. "It was that day she wasn't down stairs at all, and sent word to Dr. Callandar not to come—three days ago I think."

"Yes, I remember. O Janie dear, it looks as if things were going to be bad again! It must have been one of her very bad headaches. She was probably in great pain. Of course she did not mean to throw the brush Are you sure it was medicine she was taking?"

"It was something in a glass," vaguely, "she was mixing it—look out, Esther! You are spoiling your new gloves."

The girl threw the crumpled gloves aside and drawing the child to her knee kissed her gently.

"It seems to me," she said slowly, "that big sister has been losing her eyes lately. She must find them again; it isn't going to help to be a selfish pig."

"Help what, Esther?"

Esther's only answer was another kiss, but when she had hurried out of the room, Jane found something round and wet upon her hand.

CHAPTER XXVIII

Jane was still looking at the wet place on her hand when the doctor entered.

"Esther's been crying," she told him. In her voice was the awe which children feel at the phenomenon of tears in grown-ups.

Callandar felt his heart contract—Esther crying! But he could not question the child.

"I don't know why," went on Jane obligingly. "Esther's so strange lately. Every one is strange. You are strange too. Am I strange?"

"A little," said Callandar gravely.

"Perhaps it's catching? Do you want mother? She is upstairs and her door is locked. Perhaps she'll be down in a little while. She said Esther was to stay in and entertain you, but Esther wouldn't. She has gone to a garden party. I'll entertain you if you like."

"That will be very nice."

"Shall I play for you on the piano?"

"Thanks. And you won't mind if I sit in the corner here and close my eyes, until your mother comes?"

"No. You may go quite to sleep if you wish. I'm not sensitive about my playing. Bubble says you are nearly always tired now. He says you have such a 'normous practice that you hardly ever get a wink of sleep. That's what makes you look so kind of hollow-eyed, Bubble says."

"So Bubble has been diagnosing my case, has he?"

"Oh, he doesn't talk about professional cases usually. He said that about you because Mrs. Atkins said that being engaged didn't seem to agree with you. She said she was just as glad you didn't take a fancy to her Gracie if prospective matteromony made you look like the dead march in Saul."

"Observing woman!"

"What," resumed Jane, "is a dead march in Saul?"

"It is a musical composition."

Jane considered this and then dismissed it with a shrug. "It sounded as if it was something horrid. Mrs. Atkins thinks she's smart. Anyway, I didn't tell mother."

"Well, suppose you run now and tell her that I am here."

"Can't. The door is locked."

"Then let us have some of the music you promised. I'll sit here and wait."

Strange to say, Jane's music was not unsoothing. She had a smooth, light touch and the little airs she played tinkled sweetly enough from the old piano. The weary, nerve-wrung man was more than half asleep when she grew tired of playing and slipped off to bed without disturbing him. The moments ticked themselves away on the big hall clock. Mrs. Coombe did not come, nor did the doctor waken.

> He was aroused an hour later by a voice upon the
> veranda. It was Esther's voice and in response to it he
> heard a deeper murmur, a man's voice without doubt.
> There was a moment or two of low-toned talk, then
> "Good-night," and the girl came in alone.

She did not see him as she came slowly across to the table. He thought she looked grave and sad, older too—but, so dear! With a weary gesture she began to pull off her long gloves.

"Who was it with you, Esther?" He tried hard to make the inquiry, so devouringly eager, sound carelessly casual.

She looked up with a start.

"Oh—I didn't see you, Doctor! Mr. Macnair was with me. Did you wish to see him?" She could play at the game of carelessness better than he. "Where is mother?" she added quickly.

"In her room, I think. Esther, are you going to marry Macnair?"

The girl slipped off her second glove, blew gently into its fingers, smoothed them and laid it with nice care upon the table beside its fellow.

"I do not know."

He realised with a shock that he had expected an indignant denial.

"You do not love him!"

"No. Not now. He knows that. And I do not expect ever to love him. But perhaps, after a long while, if I could make him happy—it is so terrible not to be happy," she finished pathetically.

Callandar could have groaned aloud; the danger was so clear. And how could he, of all men, warn her. Yet he must try. He came quickly across to where she stood and compelled her gaze to his.

"Do not make that mistake, Esther! It is fatal. Try to believe that in spite of—of everything, I am speaking disinterestedly. You are young and the young hate suffering. You would marry him, out of pity. But I tell you that no man's happiness comes to him that way. You will have sacrificed yourself to no purpose. The risk is too awful. Wait. Time is kind. You will know it, some day. But even though you do not believe it now—wait. Wait forever, rather than marry a man to whom you cannot give your heart."

"That is your advice?" She spoke heavily. "You would like some day to see me marry a man I could—love?"

"Yes, a thousand times yes!"

"I shall think over what you say." She was still gravely controlled but it was a control which would not last much longer. She glanced around the empty room with a quick caught breath. "Why are you left all alone?"

"Is a keeper necessary?" Then, ashamed of his irritation and willing to end a scene which threatened to make things harder for both of them, he added in his ordinary tone, "I really do not know who is responsible for such unparalleled neglect. Jane played me to sleep, I fancy. She said her mother was upstairs but would be down presently. It must be late. I had better go."

"Wait a moment, I will see if there is any message from mother."

As she left the room her light scarf slipped from her shoulders and fell softly across his arm. Callandar crushed it passionately to his lips and then, folding it carefully, laid it beside the gloves upon the table. Even the scarf was not for him. Aunt Amy, passing through the hall on her way upstairs, saw the dumb caress and shivered anew at the mysterious power of "They" which could tear such a man as Callandar from the woman he loved.

Esther was gone only a moment and when she returned she brought with her a change of atmosphere. Something had banished every trace of self-consciousness from her manner. She looked anxious but it was an anxiety with which no embarrassment mingled.

"Doctor," she said at once, "mother seems to be ill. The door is locked and she did not answer my knocking. Yet she is not asleep. I could hear her talking. I think you ought to come up."

An indescribable look flitted across the doctor's face. He looked at the girl a moment in measuring silence and then pointed to a chair.

"Sit down," he said briefly, "I thought that this would come. I have been afraid of it for some time. Is it possible that you have no suspicion at all in regard to these peculiar—illnesses—of your mother's?"

The startled wonder in her eyes was answer enough even without the quick, "What do you mean?"

Callandar's face grew gravely compassionate. "I think you ought to know," he said. "I have put off saying anything because I was not absolutely sure myself. And I have never had quite the right opportunity of finding out. But I have had fears for some time now that your mother is in the habit of taking some drug which—well, which is certainly not good for her. Do not look so frightened. It may not be serious. Do you remember when you first consulted me about your mother and how we both agreed that the medicine she was taking for her nervous attacks might be harmful? I was suspicious then, but there was little to go on, only her fear of any one seeing the prescription, and a few general symptoms which might be due to various causes. Since then I—I have noticed things which have made me anxious. I think for her own sake as well as yours and mine, the sooner the truth is known the better. Are you sure the door is locked?"

"Yes," the girl's voice was tense, "but the window is open. It opens on the top of the veranda. You could enter there."

"If that is the only way, I must take it. I thought, I hoped that if things were as I feared she would tell me herself, but she never has. It is useless, now, to hope for her confidence. The instinct is so strongly for concealment. We must help her in spite of herself."

"Hurry then! I shall wait here. You will call me if necessary?"

She did not ask him exactly what it was that he feared nor did he tell her, but for the first time in many weeks they were able to look at each other as comrades look. The eruption of the old trouble into the new obscured the latter so that, for the time at least, the sick woman behind the locked door held first place in both their thoughts.

It seemed to Esther that she waited a long time before the summons came. Then she heard him call, "Esther!" It was a doctor's call, cool, passionless, commanding. She flew up the stairs, closing Jane's door as she hurried by. The door to her mother's room was open. It was brightly lighted. The shade of the lamp had been removed and its garish yellow fell full upon the bed and the strange figure which lay there.

Mary Coombe had apparently thrown herself down fully dressed—but in what a costume! Surely no nightmare held anything more bizarre. Esther had no time to notice details but she remembered afterwards how the feet were clothed in different coloured stockings and that while one displayed a gaily buckled slipper, the other was carefully laced into a tan walking boot. Just now she could see nothing but the face, for the greatest shock was there. It did not look like Mary's face at all—it was strange, old, yellow and repulsive. Her unbrushed, lustreless hair hung about it in a dull mat, one of her hands was clutched in it—the hand was dirty.

A terrible thought struck every vestige of colour from Esther's cheek. Her terrified gaze swept over the disordered room, up to the face of the man who stood there so silently, then down again to the inert woman upon the bed. Once, not long ago, she had seen a drunken man asleep upon the roadside grass—like this.

"Is it—is it drink?" The words were a whisper of horror.

The doctor shook his head.

"I wish it were. I wish it were only that. Have you never heard of the drug habit—morphia, opium? That is what we have to fight—and it is what I feared."

"Oh!" It was a breath of relief. To Esther, who knew nothing of drugs, or drug habits, the truth seemed less awful than the thing she had imagined.

"Is—is it serious?" she asked timidly.

The doctor smiled grimly. "You will see. No need to frighten you now. But it will be a fight from this on." He threw a light coverlet over the helpless figure and replacing the shade on the lamp, turned down the flaring wick. "I will tell you what I can, but at present it is very little. Probably this began long ago, before your father's death. In the first place there may have been a prescription—I think you said she had had an illness in which she suffered greatly. The drug, opium in some form probably, may have been given to reduce the pain—and continued after need for it was gone without knowledge of its dangerous qualities. Nervous people form the habit very quickly. Then—I am only guessing—as the amount contained in the original prescription ceased to produce the desired effect, she may have found out what drug it was that her appetite craved. If she saw the danger then, it was already too late. She could not give up voluntarily and was compelled to go on, shutting her eyes to the inevitable consequences, if indeed she ever clearly knew them."

"But now that you know? It ought not to be hard to help her now that you know. There are other drugs—"

"Yes. There is a frying-pan and a fire. In fact I fear that she has already tried that expedient herself. Some of the symptoms point to cocaine. No, our best hope is in the decreasing dose with proper auxiliary treatment. I cannot tell yet how serious the case may be. At any rate there must be an end of the mystery. Every one in the house must know, even Jane; for in this fight ignorance means danger. But," he hesitated and his face grew dark, "you cannot realise what this is going to mean. It is my burden, not yours. At least I have the right to save you that. We must have a nurse—"

A little eager cry burst from her. "Oh, no! Not that! You wouldn't do that. You can't mean not to let me help."

"You do not know—"

"I do not care what it means. But if you won't let me help, if you shut me out—" Her voice quivered dangerously, but with a spark of her old fire she recovered herself. "You cannot," she added more firmly, "because it is my burden as well as yours. Whatever she is to you, she was my father's wife and I am responsible to him. Unless extra help is really needed, no nurse shall take my place."

"Very well," quietly. "Call Aunt Amy, then, and search the room. She will sleep for a long time yet. When she wakes there must be no more of the drug within her reach. I must find out the amount to which she has been accustomed and arrange a decreasing dose. But if you are to be a nurse, you know, you must expect a bad time. It will not be easy."

Esther's reply was to call Aunt Amy and while the doctor explained to the bewildered old lady the danger in which her niece stood and the absolute importance of keeping all "medicine" away from her, Esther quietly and swiftly searched the room. Boxes and drawers she unlocked and opened, the dresser, the writing-table, the bureau, the long unused sewing basket, all were examined without success. But in the locked box which contained her father's portrait, she made another discovery which woke a little throb of angry pity in her heart. There, still wrapped in its carelessly torn off postal wrappings, lay the box containing the ruby ring which Jessica Bremner had returned. Mary must have got it from the post herself and had immediately hidden it, careless of the fact that all Esther's careful savings had been necessary to make the return possible. Without comment she slipped the ring into the bosom of her dress.

"Have you found anything?"

"Nothing yet."

Aunt Amy took a fascinated step nearer the figure on the bed. If Callandar could have intercepted the look she cast upon it he might have been warned of the subtle change which had taken place in her of late, but the doctor had turned to help Esther. Aunt Amy could gaze undisturbed.

"She looks like Richard," said Aunt Amy suddenly. "Do you remember Richard?" She brushed her hand over her eyes in a painful effort of memory. "He was a bad man, a very bad man."

"She means her brother Richard," explained Esther. "He has been dead for ages. I believe he was not a family ornament."

"Just like Richard," murmured Aunt Amy again with a quickly checked chuckle. "But you ought to be glad of that. You won't have to marry her now. You can marry Esther."

If a shell had burst in the quiet room, it could scarcely have caused more consternation. The doctor's stern face quivered, Esther's searching hand dropped paralysed. Here was a danger indeed! Was their secret really so patent? Or had it been but a vagrant guess of a clouded mind?

Callandar recovered himself first. Without glancing at the girl he walked quietly over to the bed and placing his hand upon Aunt Amy's shoulder compelled wavering eyes to his.

"Aunt Amy, you must never say that again." He spoke with the crisp incisiveness of a master, but for once his subject did not immediately respond. With a sulky look she tried to wrench herself free.

"Why?" she questioned. But Callandar knew his business too well to argue. "You must never say it again," he repeated. "You—must—never—say—it—again!"

The poor, weak lips began to quiver. Her own boldness had frightened her quite as much as his vehemence. Her eyes fluttered and fell.

"Very well, Doctor," she answered meekly.

They searched now in silence and presently Esther emerged from the closet with a pair of dainty slippers in her hand.

"I think I have found something," she said. "There are three pairs of party slippers and the toes of them are all stuffed with these." She handed the doctor a package of innocent looking tablets done up in purplish blue paper.

Callandar glanced at them, shook them out and counted their number.

"You are sure you have them all?"

"I can find no trace of more."

"Then I think we have a strong fight coming—but a good hope, too."

CHAPTER XXIX

Miss A. Milligan stood before the door of her select dressmaking parlours, meditatively picking her teeth with a needle. We hasten to observe that her teeth were quite clean and that this was merely a harmless habit denoting intense mental concentration. Miss Milligan was tall and full of figure with an elegant waist and a bust so like a pin-cushion that it fulfilled the duties of that article admirably. Her small bright eyes set in a wide expanse of face suggested nothing so much as currants in an underdone bun, and just now, as she watched the graceful figure of Mrs. Coombe, bride to be, disappear around the corner, they gave the impression of having been poked too far in while the bun was soft.

The door of Miss Milligan's select parlours did not open upon the main street, it being far from her desire to attract promiscuous trade. The parlours, indeed, were situated upon one of the "nicest" streets in Coombe and occupied a corner lot, so that a splendid view down two of the most genteel residential streets was obtainable from their windows. The only sign of business anywhere was a board of chaste design over the doorway, bearing the simple legend, "A. MILLIGAN." Even the word "Dressmaker" was considered superfluous. Also there was one window, near the door, which from time to time displayed wonderfully coloured plates of terribly twisting and elegantly elongated females purporting to be the very latest from Paris (*France*).

Mrs. Coombe was getting some "things" made at Miss Milligan's. It had been rumoured at first that she had contemplated running down to Toronto and Detroit, buying most of her trousseau there, but for some unexplained reason the plan had been given up. Doctor Callandar, it appeared, believed in patronising local tradesmen and had been sufficiently ungallant to veto the Detroit visit altogether. Everybody wondered why Mary Coombe stood it. Surely it was bad enough when a man sets up to be a domestic tyrant after marriage. They were surprised at Dr. Callandar—they hadn't thought it of him.

"It is women like Mary Coombe who submit tamely to such indignities," declared the eldest Miss Sinclair, "who have held back the emancipation of women from the beginning of time."

"She looks so poorly, too," agreed Miss Jessie. "I am sure she needs a change. I should think that Esther would insist upon it."

But Esther appeared in all things to back up Dr. Callandar. People admitted that they were disappointed in Esther and only hoped that the day would never come when she would be sorry. For if all the world loves a lover, all the world is indulgent to a prospective bride and any one could see that this particular bride was being denied her proper privileges. Any one would think she was a child and not to be trusted alone. Esther went with her everywhere, simply everywhere. Of course it was sweet of Esther to be so attentive, but people didn't wonder that her mother didn't like it.

Such were the current comments of the town, sent out somewhat in the nature of feelers, for behind them all, Coombe, having a very sensitive nose for gossip, was uneasily aware that their cleverest investigators were not yet in possession of the root of the matter. Every one seemed to know everything, and yet—no wonder that Miss Milligan picked her teeth in agonies of mental tumult at finding herself sole possessor of a satisfactory explanation which she was bound in honour not to disclose.

Mrs. Coombe had just been in. She had been having a "first fitting" and in the privacy of the fitting room she had been perfectly frank with Miss Milligan. She had told Miss Milligan "things." She had told her things which would move a heart of stone, regardless of the fact that Miss Milligan's heart was made of the softest of soft materials and beat warmly under her spiky pin cushion. The fact that her eyes were hard and black had nothing to do with it; mistakes in eyes occur constantly in the best regulated families. At this very moment when her eyes were more like currants than ever she was making up her mind that, come what might, doctors or no doctors, she was not going to see a fellow creature put upon.

For, you see, Mrs. Coombe, poor little thing, had confided in Miss Milligan. She had told her all about it, and like most mysteries, it had turned out to be very simple. It seemed that Dr. Callandar, such a perfectly charming man in most respects, had a most absurd prejudice against patent medicines. This prejudice, common to the medical profession on account of patents interfering with profits, was, in Dr. Callandar's case, almost an obsession. Miss Milligan, being a sensible person, knew very well that there are patents *and* patents. Some of them are frauds, of course, but there are others which are better than any prescription that any doctor ever wrote. Miss Milligan did not speak from hearsay, she had had an extensive experience the results of which lent themselves to conversational effort. Therefore it is easy to see how she understood and sympathised at once when Mrs. Coombe told her of a remedy which she had found to be quite excellent but which the doctor absolutely forbade her to use.

"Not that he means to be inconsiderate, dear Miss Milligan, only he is so very sure of his own point of view. Doctors have to be firm of course. But you can see it is rather hard on me. The trouble is that I cannot obtain the remedy I need in Coombe. It is a remedy very little known and useful only in obscure nerve troubles. I have been in the habit of getting it from a certain firm in Detroit, not a very well-known firm, and now, of course, that is impossible—without upsetting the doctor, which I hesitate to do."

Miss Milligan was of the opinion that a little upsetting was just what the doctor required.

"No—o." The visitor shook her head. She could not bring her mind to it. She would prefer to suffer herself. But did not Miss Milligan think that, in face of such an unreasonable and violent prejudice, a little innocent strategy might be justified?

Miss Milligan thought so, very emphatically.

Mrs. Coombe sighed. "I do so want to look well for the wedding, you know. And really, nothing seems to help me like my own particular medicine. It is hard, very hard, to be without it."

Miss Milligan did not doubt it. It seemed, to her, a perfect shame. But had Mrs. Coombe ever tried "Peebles' Perfect Pick-me-ups" for the nerves? They were certainly very excellent.

Yes. Mrs. Coombe had heard of them and no doubt they were very good for some people. But constitutions differ so. On the whole she felt sure that even "Peebles' Perfect Pick-me-ups" would not suit her nearly as well as her own particular remedy.

It was at this point that Miss Milligan stopped fitting and began to pick her teeth, a sign, as we have before stated, of great mental activity. If nothing would suit Mrs. Coombe but this one medicine and if the medicine could be obtained in Detroit and if Mrs. Coombe had the correct address—why not write for it? It was a brilliant idea, but Mrs. Coombe shook her head.

She had the address, naturally, and she had also thought of writing, but it would be of no use. Esther and the doctor actually watched her mail.

"Incredible!"

"Oh, not in any offensive way. They did not mean to be tyrannous. They were quite convinced that patent medicines were very injurious. But women suffering from nerves (like yourself, dear Miss Milligan) know that relief is often found in the least likely places and from remedies not mentioned in the Materia Medica."

Miss Milligan knew that very well. And people are so hard to convince. When Mrs. Barker, over the hill, had first recommended that new blood-purifier to Miss Milligan, Miss Milligan had laughed. But after taking only six bottles she had thanked Mrs. Barker with tears in her eyes. "And I must say," added she in a burst of virtuous indignation, "that if I were going to Detroit to-morrow I would bring you back all the patent medicine you wanted, Mrs. Coombe, and be very glad to do it."

This was most satisfactory save for one small fact, namely that Miss Milligan was not going to Detroit to-morrow. Mrs. Coombe thanked her very much and raised her arm (which shook sadly) while Miss Milligan pinned in the underarm seam.

"Even as it is," went on Miss Milligan, "I don't see why—a little higher please, and turn a trifle to the light, thank you!—I don't see why it can't be done. Nobody inspects my mail, thank heaven! and one address is as good to a druggist as another."

What a bright idea! Strange that it had never occurred to Mrs. Coombe to arrange things so easily. It was very, very clever and kind of Miss Milligan to think of it. But—people might talk! Think how upset the doctor would be if their innocent little plot were spoken of abroad. People are so unkind, quite horrid in fact. And as Esther and the doctor were doing it all for her good they would naturally hate to have their actions misunderstood. Of course, Mrs. Coombe knew that Miss Milligan herself would never mention it to a soul. She felt quite sure of that, still—as it did not appear how the little plot could be spread abroad under those circumstances unless the lay-figure in the corner should become communicative, Mrs. Coombe's sentence remained plaintively unfinished. Miss Milligan, in spite of its being so very unnecessary, found herself promising solemnly never to mention it.

As the whole thing was entirely unpremeditated it seemed like a special piece of good luck that Mrs. Coombe should have at that moment in her pocket a note to the druggists (who were not called druggists, exactly) and that all she needed to do was to add Miss Milligan's address, and hand to that lady sufficient money to secure a postal note as an enclosure. She did this very quickly and the whole little affair was satisfactorily disposed of when Esther was seen coming hurriedly down the street.

"I thought," said Esther, who entered a little out of breath and with a worried pucker between her eyes, "I thought that I would just run in and see how the linings look."

"You can never tell anything from linings," said Miss Milligan in an injured tone. "Gracious! I don't suppose any one would ever want a dress if they went by the way the linings look. I always advise my customers never to look in the glass until I get to the material, what with seams on the wrong side and all!"

"There is really nothing at all to see as yet," assented Mrs. Coombe crossly.

Esther seated herself by the open window.

"Very well," she said quietly. "I won't look. I'll just wait."

Mrs. Coombe shrugged her shoulders and displaced a pin or two. There was an injured look upon her face and Miss Milligan, replacing the pins, wondered how it is that nice girls like Esther Coombe never see when they're not wanted.

The fitting went quickly forward. Mrs. Coombe seemed to have lost all her genial expansiveness. Miss Milligan's pins had overflowed from her pin-cushion into her mouth and Esther, who appeared tired, gazed steadily out of the window. Only the humming of the machines in the adjoining workroom and the subdued talk and laughter of Miss Milligan's young ladies saved the silence from becoming oppressive. Occasionally, when her supply of pins became exhausted, Miss Milligan would contribute a cooing murmur to the effect that it did "set beautiful across the shoulders" or that "the long line over the hip was quite elegant."

Without doubt the atmosphere had changed with the coming of Esther. Mrs. Coombe became each moment more fidgety, she became, in fact, jerky! Her hands twitched, her head twitched, she could not stand still and suddenly she twitched herself out of Miss Milligan's hands altogether and flinging herself into a chair declared that she couldn't stand any more fitting that day. Even Miss Milligan's black currant eyes could see that her nerves were terribly wrong—she looked ghastly, poor thing! And all on account of a silly prejudice regarding patent medicines.

Esther, who exhibited no surprise at her mother's sudden collapse, helped Miss Milligan to unpin the linings.

"My mother has been a little longer than usual without her tonic," she calmly explained. "The other fittings can wait," and quickly, yet without flurry, she found Mary's hat, bag, gloves and parasol and picked up her handkerchief which she had flung upon the floor.

Mrs. Coombe accepted these services without thanks, indulging indeed in a little spiteful laugh which Miss Milligan obligingly attributed to her poor nerves. Things had come to a pretty pass indeed, thought the sympathetic dressmaker, when a grown woman is obliged to have her medicine chosen for her like a baby.

As she stood in the doorway watching the two ladies out of sight, a just indignation grew within the breast so strongly fortified outside, so vulnerable within; and without even waiting to call her giggling young ladies to order, she pinned on her hat and departed to send Mrs. Coombe's postal note to the Detroit druggist, who, oddly enough, was not a druggist at all.

CHAPTER XXX

Esther and her step-mother set out upon their homeward walk in silence. The older woman's face was drawn and bitter, Esther's thoughtful and sad. Though there seemed no reason for haste, Mrs. Coombe's steps grew constantly quicker until she was hurrying breathlessly.

More than once the girl glanced at her anxiously as if about to speak, yet hesitating. Then when the walk threatened to become a run she laid a detaining hand upon her arm.

"If you walk so very rapidly, mother, people will notice." It was the only argument which never failed of effect. Mrs. Coombe's steps slackened.

"Besides," went on Esther eagerly, "every moment is a gain. Ten minutes more will make this the longest interval yet. Don't you think you could try...."

"No!"

The word was only a gasp and the face Mary turned for a moment on the girl was livid. The eyes shone with hate. "You—you beast!" she muttered chokingly.

Esther turned a shade paler, but otherwise gave no sign that she had heard. "Mother, just try, you are doing so well, so splendidly. The doctor says ..."

"Be quiet—be quiet! I hate him. I won't try. I won't be tortured—oh, why can't you all leave me alone!" She began to sob and moan under her breath, careless even of a possible passerby. Fortunately there was no one, and they were already within sight of home. Esther, very white, supported the shaking woman with her arm and they hurried on together. At the door she would still have accompanied her but Mary flung herself angrily from her hold and ran up the stairs with sudden feverish strength. Esther turned into the living room and dropped into the nearest chair.

She was still sitting there without having removed either hat or gloves when, a little later, Callandar entered.

"Well, nurse," with a faint smile, "how are things to-day?" His quick eye had noticed in a moment the girl's closed eyes and listless attitude, but nothing in his tone betrayed it.

"Very well, I think, until a little while ago. We were late in getting home from the dressmaker's—"

"I see. You look rather done up. The fact is you are overdoing things. Rather foolish, don't you think?"

"No," stubbornly. "I am all right."

"You are exhausted and there is no need. Things are going well. The dose is steadily diminishing, more quickly than she suspects. It looks as if we might begin to breathe again. It is a great gain to feel reasonably sure that she has no more of the stuff hidden anywhere. If she had, she would have used it during that last crisis."

The girl in the chair winced. She hated even to think of the night to which his words referred. "Yes," she said, "but—but there won't be any more times like that, will there?"

"Yes," grimly. "We are not through yet. But every crisis will be a little easier—if things go as they are going."

Esther sighed. "It is very terrible, isn't it?" she said. "And really it doesn't seem fair, for it wasn't her fault; in the beginning she didn't know. And she does suffer so."

"We must not think of it in that way. It helps more to think of the suffering she is escaping. What she is going through now is saving her, body and soul. It is taking her out of torment and leading her back to life, and sanity. You don't know, but I do, and any struggle, any suffering is mild compared to the horrors before her if she kept on. She was taking some cocaine too. The word means nothing to you, but to a physician it spells hell. So you see—it gives one strength."

Esther sat up and straightened her collar. "I'm ashamed of myself," she said. "No wonder you want another nurse. But I won't resign yet. And I wanted to ask you—do you think it is necessary now to be with her whenever she goes out? She hates it so. I think she is getting to hate me, too. Where could she possibly get the stuff? None of our local stores would sell it without a prescription."

"I know. But in a case like this you can never be sure of anything. No, we must not relax in the slightest. Even as it is, I am continually afraid." He began to pace the room restlessly. "There may be a weak spot somewhere, some loop-hole we have forgotten. I think the druggists are safe and the mail is watched. That last supply, you are sure it was all destroyed?"

"Yes, I burned it. At least I gave it to Aunt Amy to burn. I couldn't leave mother."

"Well, let us call Aunt Amy, and make sure. I believe I am foolishly nervous, but—" without finishing his sentence the doctor walked to the door and waited there until Aunt Amy answered his call.

"Auntie," said Esther, "you remember the little package I gave you that night when mother was so ill? It was done up in purplish blue paper."

"Yes, Esther."

"Do you remember what you did with it, dear?"

Aunt Amy looked frightened.

"I—I don't know. I've a very good memory, Esther. But somehow I'm not quite sure."

"You will remember presently," said Callandar kindly. "We want to be quite sure that it was destroyed. You know, I explained to you, that Mary must take no more of that medicine. It is very dangerous...."

"What does it do?" unexpectedly.

"It is a kind of poison. It makes people very ill, so ill that in time they die."

"Mary likes it. She says it makes her nerves better and puts her to sleep."

"When did she say that?"

"When she asked me if I had any."

The doctor and the girl exchanged a quick look.

"And you gave her some?"

"Oh, no, I couldn't. I had burned it in the stove—I remember now."

They both drew a breath of intense relief. But when she had left them, Callandar looked very sober. "There, you see," he said, "was a possibility we had overlooked."

> "Yes, and it would have been my fault. I should have made sure long ago. It is hard to get out of the habit of taking things for granted."

"Yet it is the one thing we must never do. In this we must trust no one, and nothing. Then we shall win. If there is no relapse now, the worst, the slowest part, is over. Soon you will be free, dear girl—and God bless you forever for what you have been to her and to me."

She answered him only with a wistful smile and when he had gone, she sighed. She would be free soon, he said. Strange that he could not see that it was her freedom that she dreaded. Hard as it had been, hard as it was, there was a still harder time coming—the time when she would be free—free, to leave forever the man she loved.

The present with its load of duty and anxiety, the constant strain of watching, its bearing of poor Mary's thousand ingratitudes seemed dear and desirable when she thought of the black gulf of separation at the end of the tortuous way. But of course he could not guess. How could he? Men are so different from women.

She knew, though, that she was coming to the end of her strength. Not even the doctor guessed how great the strain of those past weeks had been.

When Mary had awakened to find that her secret was discovered she had been like a mad thing. There had been rage, tears, protestations, hysterical denials—finally confession and anguished promises. That she had never realised the reality of her danger, nor the extent of her servitude was plain. It seemed easy enough to promise. Esther and the doctor were making a terrible fuss about nothing, as usual. She grew sulky under Callandar's warnings and her fury knew no bounds when she found that certain of her hidden stores had been confiscated. She demanded that the supply be left in her hands; was not her promise enough?

But all this was before she knew what denial meant, before she realised that the way back along the path she had trodden so easily was thick-set with suffering; that every backward inch must be fought for with agony and tears. Then she had broken down altogether, had raved and pleaded. The very knowledge of the depth to which she had fallen, threatened to send her deeper still. Callandar soon realised that if she were to be saved it must be in spite of herself. There were but two points of strength in her weak nature; one the newly awakened, yet capricious passion for himself, and the other that ruling terror of her life, which of all her inherent safeguards was the last to give way under the assaults of the drug, namely, "What will people say?" but neither of these, nor both of them together, could stand for a moment before the terrible appetite when once its craving was denied.

Twice she failed her helpers just when they were beginning to hope. In her first search Esther had not exhausted the hiding places of the poison and, to retain the temptation by her, Mary had lied and lied again. Twice when the crises of her desire had come upon her she had given way, helplessly, completely; and twice they had begun all over again. The third time she had not been able to procure the drug, had been compelled to fight through on the decreasing dose which the doctor had allowed.

No wonder Esther shuddered when she thought of that night! Yet at the time she had stood beside the moaning woman, white and firm, when even Callandar had staggered for a moment from the room.

Next morning they had taken heart of hope again. Undoubtedly Mary had exhausted the supply, and the possibility of its being replenished seemed remote. It was only a matter of time now; of care, of unremitting, yet gentle vigilance and Mary would be cured. The bride could go to her husband, clean and in her right mind. And Esther would be free.

Strangely enough, it was Mary herself who objected to a hastening of their remarriage. Perhaps in spite of her inevitable deterioration there was that in her still which forbade her going to him as she was. Perhaps it was only another and more obscure effect of the drug; some downward instinct which made her dread the putting of herself within the circle of her husband's strength. She would fight her fight outside. Why? Was it because she would conquer of herself, or because she did not really wish to conquer at all?

To Esther, Mary's refusal came as a reprieve. But to Callandar it was but a lengthening out of torture. Man's love must always, in its essence, be different from woman's; though many women seem incapable of recognising this fact. To Esther, now that she had put aside her first half-understood glimpse of passion, it was sweet to be near him, to hear his voice, to touch his hand and, above all, to spend her strength in his service. But to him the strain was almost intolerable. The sight of her, the touch of her, the whole soul-shattering nearness of her beauty meant constant conflict; all the fiercer since it must be unsuspected.

Willits, the only man who had been told the truth, watched the fight with admiration, sharply touched with anxiety. Expert in the moulding of buttons, he knew very well that Callandar was drawing rather recklessly upon his newly acquired strength. If the tension did not slacken soon there might be another physical breakdown, and then—Willits shrugged his shoulders. It would be entirely too bad if this very fine button were to be spoiled after all. His heart was sore for his friend.

"You see," Callandar had written in one of his rare letters, "it was a right instinct which warned me that no man escapes the consequences of his own acts. There did come a short, golden time when I put the voice of instinct behind me and dared to think that I, at least, had shaken myself free. Closing the door of yesterday, I boldly knocked open the door of to-morrow—and lo, to-morrow and yesterday were one!

"I know, now, that even had poor Mary been dead, as I believed, the payment would have been exacted in some other way. When my brain is clear enough to think, I have flashes of thankfulness that payment is permitted to take the form of expiation. I can save Mary, and I will. In some strange and rather dreadful way her need is my salvation.

"I have said nothing of Esther. How can I? The other day I heard Miss Sinclair say that Esther Coombe was losing all her good looks. 'Thin as a rail, and peeked as a pin' were the words she used. To me she has never been so lovely. She is thinner; there are hollows in her cheeks; her lips are no longer a thread of scarlet. The transparent lids of her deep, wonderful eyes droop often and her hair seems to have lost its life and hangs soft and very close to her face. I love her. I love her as a man loves a woman, as a knight loves his lady, as a Catholic loves the Madonna! This terrible strain must soon be over for her. I am doing all in my power to hurry on the marriage. She is young. She is bound to forget. When she leaves here she goes out of my life—and may God speed her!

"She is to go to Toronto. Lorna Sinnet has good friends there and they will take her into their circle. She will begin to taste a fuller life, and as her interests expand the old wound will heal. She will find happiness yet. When Mary recovers, she and I will return to Montreal. I am quite fit now. I feel that I can never work hard enough. Mary will like the excitement of city life, and I rely upon you and Lorna to make our coming as easy as possible. How is Lorna? A talk with her will be a tonic.

"Does not all this sound admirably lucid and sensible? I want you to see that I am not losing my hold—that I have finally faced down the problem of the future. And there is one thing that has come to me out of all this, a wonderful thing; I have forgotten Fear. It seems to me that all my life I have lived in fear. Now I am not afraid...."

It was when Bubble was entering the post office for the purpose of posting this letter that he met Miss Milligan, coming out. Miss Milligan was evidently in a hurry, so great a hurry that she had not time to question Bubble upon affairs in general as was her usual custom. Instead she asked him to do something for her. It was a trifling service, only to deliver to Mrs. Coombe a small postal packet which she held in her hand.

"It will only take you a few moments, Zerubbabel," she said. "I was going to deliver it myself but Mrs. Stanton wants a fitting right away. I ought not to have come down to the post at all. But I promised Mrs. Coombe— does Dr. Callandar permit you to run messages in your spare time?"

"Sure," declared the youth, "only I don't get much spare time. The doctor's terrible busy. Since we got the phone in, it's ringing all the time! But I guess I can slip over to Mrs. Coombe's or if I see Jane I can give the parcel to her."

"No!" Miss Milligan seemed struck with a sudden hesitancy. "You must not give it to Jane, you must give it to Mrs. Coombe. Dear me, I believe I had better take it myself."

Without listening to the boy's polite protests she hurried off again. Bubble gazed after her with relieved astonishment.

"Guess it must be something for the wedding," declared he, sapiently.

CHAPTER XXXI

The next day was the day of the Presbyterian Sunday school picnic. It was bound to be beautiful weather, because it always was. The Presbyterians seemed to have an understanding with Providence to that effect. But Jane, who must have been born a sceptic, was up very early just to see that there was no mistake.

There was a hint, just a hint, of autumn in the air. On the window-sill lay a golden leaf. It was the forerunner. The garden lay quiet, brooding; the rising sun shone softly through a yellow haze.

Jane shivered deliciously in her thin night gown. It was going to be a perfectly glorious, scrumptious day. She leaned farther out to make sure that the leaves of the small silver maple beneath her window were not turned wrong side up—a sure sign of rain. And as she looked, she noticed a curious thing—the side door was open.

Somebody else must be up. If it were Esther, Jane decided that she would call "Boo" very loudly and surprise her; but it was her mother and not Esther who came out of the open door. Jane drew back, watching through the curtains. She thought her mother looked very pretty in her dressing gown with her hair down and her bare feet thrust into pink satin mules. It was a pity, Jane thought, that she wasn't as nice as she looked. And how curiously she was acting. She was actually climbing up the little ladder which led to the bird house by the side of the lawn. Jane knew there was nothing at all in the bird house, for she herself had placed the ladder there the day before. Whatever was she doing? Jane giggled, for one of Mary's slippers had fallen off leaving her foot bare. But she didn't seem to care. She was putting her hand far into the bird house. Jane watched the hand carefully to see what it might bring out. But it came out empty. Mary hurriedly climbed down the ladder, picked up her slipper, glanced quickly around the empty garden and ran back into the house closing the door without a sound.

Jane was puzzled. What had her mother hoped to find in the bird house? She crept back into bed, wondering, and just as she was slipping off to sleep, the solution came. "She was hiding something," thought Jane, sleepily, "and when I get up I'll find out what it is."

Little things are the levers which move the big things of life. Had it been any other day save the day of the picnic, Jane would certainly have found out what Mary hid in the bird house and many things might have been different. But there was so much to do that morning and Ann and Bubble came over before Jane finished breakfast so that in the delightful hurry of getting ready and packing baskets, she forgot all about it.

There was a disappointment, too, at the last moment, for just when they were all ready and the doctor had come with the motor, Mrs. Coombe decided that she really did not feel equal to going and that meant that Esther had to stay behind. Jane showed signs of tears. Ann and Bubble protested volubly. Even the doctor did his best to change Mary's decision.

"You really ought to come, Mary," he said, "the drive alone will do you good, and if you get tired of it, I can bring you home early." He looked at her rather anxiously as he spoke but she did not seem ill. She looked better than usual for her eyes were brighter and her face was faintly flushed.

"No, I won't come to-day. I'm tired. There is not the slightest need for Esther to stay. I am going to stay in my room with a good book."

"Oh, Esther, do come! Oh, Esther, you promised!" Thus Ann and Bubble, while Jane pulled at her frock.

Mary looked on with a slightly acid smile. The doctor drew her aside.

"Won't you come?" he asked patiently. "You see how disappointed the children are."

"Yes, about Esther. And Esther does not need to stay. It's absurd. Are you never going to trust me?"

"You know it isn't you that we distrust. It is something stronger than you, or any of us. Mary, be patient, just a little longer. You want to be free, don't you?"

She hid the glitter in her eyes, against his coat. "Yes, of course. Only don't ask me to go to-day. It excites me. I want to be quiet."

"Very well, and you promise—"

"Yes, I'll promise anything. And if Esther stays I'll be decent to her. Though why you bother about her so much, I don't see. She is nothing to you."

"She is very much to you," sternly.

"Yes—a spy! Oh, well, don't let's quarrel. Be sure to be back early for the supper party to-night. Mr. Macnair and Annabel are invited. You can bring them with you in the motor. It is just as well Esther isn't going. There'll be lots of little things to attend to."

"That's settled then." Knowing that further persuasion was useless, he kissed her and turned to quiet the eager children.

Almost she held her breath as she watched him go. Her small hands twisted, a pulse beat visibly in her temple, her lips worked, she shook from head to foot. Nevertheless she stood there, controlling herself, until the motor horn had honked its farewell to a chorus of children's laughter. Then, as one released from some desperate strain, she turned and fled to her room....

"Mother!" Esther came in slowly, unpinning her hat. There was no answer to her call. But she had not expected any. In her sulky moods Mrs. Coombe often went for days without speaking to her step-daughter. When the girl saw that she had gone to her room she was rather relieved than otherwise; it meant at least a peaceful afternoon. Mary, in her room, was considered safe and all that Esther need do was to be ready in order to accompany her if she decided to go out.

She was not disappointed at missing the picnic. It was getting rather hard to be gay. And it would be nice to have everything ready when the party returned.

It was a quietly beautiful afternoon and as the girl went about her simple tasks she was not unhappy. Already she was learning the great lesson which many more fortunate lovers miss, that the rarest fragrance of love lies in its bestowal. That is why love is of all things most securely ours.

Once she called up to the blowing curtains of Mrs. Coombe's window.

"Mother, won't you come and help me with the flowers?" But no hand pushed the curtain aside, nor did she receive any answer. Perhaps Mary was really asleep. In that case she was sure to be amiable at supper time.

Everything was daintily ready and Esther had had time to slip on her prettiest frock when the "honk" of the returning motor brought a faint colour into her pale cheeks.

"Dear me, you've got quite a colour, Esther," said Miss Annabel Macnair in a slightly injured voice. She had come intending to tell Esther how badly she was looking and to recommend a tonic.

"I don't see why you didn't come to the picnic."

"Oh, Esther," Jane's plain little face was radiant, "you missed it! It was the nicest picnic yet. I won one race and Bubble won another, and Ann won't speak to either of us. She says she hates her aunt because she'd have won a race too if she hadn't had so much starch in her petticoats. But Mrs. Sykes says she wouldn't be a mite surprised if Ann has a bad heart—not a wicked heart, just a bad one, the kind that makes you drop down dead. Some of Ann's folks died of bad hearts, Mrs. Sykes says. But the doctor says it's all nonsense. He agreed with Ann that it wasn't anything but petticoats— Oh, say! how pretty the table looks. Did mother say you could use the best china?"

"Seeing that it's Esther's china on her own mother's side, I guess she can use it if she likes," said Aunt Amy, mildly belligerent. "I thought you might want to set the table before we got home, Esther, and I was so afraid you might forget and use the sprigged tea set. But the doctor said you'd be sure not to."

"That's one of her queer notions, I suppose?" said Miss Annabel in a stage whisper plainly heard by every one. "How odd! Can you come upstairs with me, Esther? I want to speak to you most particularly and I haven't seen you for ages.

"Not that I haven't tried," she continued in her jerky way as they went up the stairs together; "but you seem to be always with your mother. Going to lose her soon. Natural enough. I said to Mrs. Miller, 'There's real devotion.' Possible to overdo it though. Marriage is terribly trying. For relatives. But long engagements are worse. How was it you didn't get to the picnic?"

Esther murmured that she hadn't quite felt like going to the picnic.

"Well, you didn't miss much. Even Angus wasn't as cheerful as usual. Inclined to be moody. And that brings me to what I wanted to tell you. Remember that last time you had lunch with us?"

"Yes."

"Remember me saying that I never ask questions, but that I always find out? Well—I have."

"Have what?" asked Esther, who had not been following.

"Found out. Found out what is the matter with my brother. Exactly what I thought. He is the victim of an unhappy attachment. Unreciprocated!"

"But—"

"You remember you laughed at me, Esther. Suggested liver. And when I mentioned your mother you almost convinced me that I was wrong. Although I am never wrong. It *is* your mother, Esther. My poor brother, brokenhearted, quite—utterly!"

This was so amazing that Esther waited for more.

"I suppose he felt certain of her until Dr. Callandar stepped in. Could hardly believe it. When I told him of your mother's reputed engagement he was not in the least disturbed. Said 'Pshaw!' Couldn't imagine such a possibility. I said, 'I assure you it is the truth, Angus,' and he merely remarked, 'Well, what if it is?' in a most matter of fact way. Quite calm!"

"And you think—"

"My dear, I am sure. All put on. To deceive me. Although I never am deceived. So I waited. And then one night last week I happened to get home from a business session of the Ladies' Aid, early. I went in quietly. Angus was in his study, without a light, but the door was a little bit open, and I could hear his voice quite plainly. He was praying—"

"Oh, please—"

"My dear, I couldn't help hearing. I didn't listen. I was rooted to the spot. Positively! He—"

"You must not tell me, Miss Annabel, I won't listen."

"Very well, my dear. Perhaps you are right. Couldn't tell you his very words anyway. I cannot remember them. He was very eloquent, terribly worked up! And he was praying for Her. That's what he called your mother, just Her. It sounded almost—almost popish, you know! Then suddenly he stopped as if something had cut him off—sharp. There was a silence. So long I began to be frightened and then he cried out loud, 'Not for me! Not for me!' It was dreadful! But it proves my point, I think. Why, my dear, whatever is the matter?"

Esther, leaning against the window frame, was sobbing weakly.

"Dear me! I had no idea you would feel it so badly. Take a sip of water— do!"

Esther struggled to regain her self-control.

"It seems so—sad," she faltered.

"Yes, of course. It is sad. And I have great sympathy with my poor brother," went on Miss Annabel pinning down her hair net. "But do you know, I sometimes think," she hesitated and a slow blush arose in her middle-aged cheek, "I sometimes think that people in love aren't to be pitied after all. Though it is hardly a thought to express to a young girl like you.

"You know," she went on awkwardly as Esther still made no remark, "they feel a great deal, of course, but it must be so very *interesting*. A little cold cream for my nose, Esther. If I leave it until I get home I shall certainly peel."

Esther provided the cream and a powder puff. She felt sick at heart. Her calmer world of the afternoon burst like a bubble leaving only a tear behind. The vision of Angus Macnair in the dark study reaching out frantic hands for the thing he knew could never be his, seemed a last touch of unendurable irony. Surely some one, somewhere, must be moved to dreadful mirth at these blunders of the fates. From the echo of such laughter commonplace was the only refuge. Esther bathed her eyes and called to Jane to let her mother know that supper was ready.

The sounds of the child's cheerful tattoos upon Mrs. Coombe's door accompanied them down the stairs, but when they had waited a few minutes, Jane came quietly into the room alone.

"Mother doesn't answer me, Esther."

Miss Annabel looked surprised, then curious. Esther felt her face flame. It was really too bad of Mary to make things so much harder than she need. Her refusal to answer could only mean that she had determined to be thoroughly disagreeable; and with company in the house. But her annoyance was abruptly checked by the effect of the news upon the doctor. It was not annoyance she read in his eyes. It was dismay. With a murmured sentence, which may or may not have been excuse, he turned from the room.

"I am so sorry," explained Esther smoothly. "Mother is not at all well, one of her old headaches. The doctor has gone up to see if he can be of any use."

Miss Annabel shook her head gloomily. "Mark my words," she said, "your mother ought to take those headaches of hers more seriously. A headache seems a little thing, but I know of a case—"

With Esther's sympathetic encouragement the good lady launched upon a recital of melancholy happenings more or less connected with headaches which occupied her attention very pleasantly and prevented any one else from saying anything until the return of the awaited guest. He came in looking as usual and bearing an apology from the hostess for her sudden indisposition. "Nothing at all serious," he added lightly. "It is possible that she may join us later." But it was noticeable that as he spoke he did not look at Esther nor could her anxious glance read the impassive sternness of his face.

It was not a successful meal. In spite of the pretty table, the dainty food, the well kept up fire of conversation, the beautiful evening out of doors, the softly shaded light inside, from first to last the supper was a nightmare. Of what avail the careful pretence that nothing was wrong? A very miasma of dread enveloped that table, a thing so palpable that Miss Annabel found herself starting at a sound, the minister's ready tongue faltered on a favourite phrase, Esther's clear voice grew blurred, Aunt Amy wrung her hands, Jane's eyes were wide with unchildlike care. Only Callandar seemed undisturbed, courteous, interested.

It was a relief to them all when after an uncomfortable half-hour with coffee on the veranda the minister suddenly remembered a forgotten committee meeting and hurried Miss Annabel away with half her parting words unspoken. The doctor, still courteous and interested, walked down with them to the gate. He would wait, he said, a little longer to see how Mrs. Coombe found herself. Esther carried off a subdued and silent Jane to bed.

"Esther," whispered Jane as her sister bent to kiss her, "why do lovely, lovely days always end so badly?"

"They don't, Janie."

The child sighed. "Mine do. I never had a perfect day in all my life."

"You will have. Every one has perfect days—sometime."

"Have you, Esther?"

"Yes, dear."

Jane looked up sleepily. "Perhaps mine will come to-morrow!"

Esther went slowly down stairs and out into the garden. Callandar was coming up the path from the gate. He walked slowly. When they met, he no longer avoided her glance.

"Well?" She had no need to ask. Yet she did ask, falteringly.

"We have failed," he said briefly.

The quiet hopelessness of his voice left no room for argument. Esther opened her lips to protest, but found nothing to say.

"She has outwitted us," he went on. "How? who can say? They have the cunning of the devil! There is only one thing to do now. Only one way—"

"You mean?—"

"The wedding must take place at once. I suppose the farce is really necessary. But there must be no more delay. Only the unsparing use of a husband's authority can save her now. I shall take her away. I must be with her day and night. In France there is a place I know, beautiful, isolated. I shall take her there. If all else fails there is the treatment of hypnotic suggestion. But—I shall not fail, I dare not!"

Blindly she put out her hand—he clasped it gently—yet not as if he knew whose hand it was. Then, laying it aside, he passed by, and, leaving her sobbing in the dusk, went on into the house and up the stairs to the closed room.

CHAPTER XXXII

It became quickly known in Coombe that, owing to Mrs. Coombe's delicate health, the wedding would take place much sooner than had been expected. A sea voyage, it was conceded, was the necessary thing and as Dr. Callandar would not allow his fiancée to go away alone it seemed only fair that he should make haste to go with her. Comment on all these points was much more restrained than usual because, just at this time, Coombe withstood the shock of finding out that Dr. Callandar was no less than Dr. Henry Chedridge Callandar of Montreal. No, not his brother, nor his cousin, but the man himself!

Of course Coombe had suspected this all along. Never for a moment had it been really deceived. Over and over again it had said: "My dear, that young man is not a mere local practitioner, mark my words!" From the first, Coombe had observed the marks of true distinction in him. He was so odd! He seemed to care nothing at all for appearances, and, as everybody knows, this comfortable attitude of mind is the privilege of the famous few. Besides, there was the matter of the marriage. Coombe had been right in thinking that Mary Coombe had not gone into the matter blindfold. She had known very well upon which side her bread was buttered, and as to her giving way to his whims in the absurd way she did—that, too, was understandable under the circumstances.

What puzzled Coombe, now, was how she had managed it. She was not pretty, at least not very pretty. She was not young, at least only comparatively young. And goodness knows, she was not clever! Hardly a mother in Coombe but had at least one daughter prettier, younger and cleverer; a daughter, in fact, who could give Mary Coombe aces and kings and still win out. Why had the doctor not been attached to one of these? It was incomprehensible. Even if, through a misplaced devotion to his profession, he had determined to marry into a doctor's family—there was Esther! Esther Coombe was a fine girl and quite nice looking before she had begun to "go off." Even as it was she had more to recommend her than her step-mother. There seemed to be a general impression that all men are fools.

"If they would only let some woman with sense choose their wives for them," declared the eldest Miss Sinclair in a burst of confidence, "they might get along fairly well. But if ever a man gets married to the right woman, it happens by accident."

Nevertheless, at a special meeting of the Ladies' Aid, called for the purpose, it was decided to give the bride a present. They had not intended to do it for fear of establishing a precedent. But when it came out who Dr. Callandar was, it hardly seemed right to let one of their best known members go from them to a more exalted sphere in a city (which many of them might, from time to time, feel inclined to visit) without showing her by some small token how very highly she was held in their regard. Every one could see the sense of this and the vote was unanimous. In regard to the nature of the gift there was more diversity of opinion, but it was finally decided that, as the value of this kind of thing lies not in the gift but in the spirit of the giving, a brown jar with the word "Biscuits" in silver lettering would do very well. Carving knives were thought of but as Mrs. Atkins very fitly said, "Everybody is sure to give carving knives"—a phenomenon which all the ladies accepted as a commonplace.

Of the prospective bride herself, Coombe saw little. She remained very much at home. She had lost much of her spasmodic energy, was inclined to be moody and even rude. Her state of health accounted naturally for this and also for the arrival of a new inmate at the Elms, a cool and capable looking person who was discovered, after much amazed enquiry, to be a trained nurse. Not a hospital nurse exactly but a kind of special nurse whose duties included massage, and the giving of certain baths and things which the doctor thought strengthening. Her name was Miss Philps. Coombe never got behind that. No one could ever boast that she knew more of Miss Philps than her name. She was, and remains to this day, a mystery.

There are people like that, although this was Coombe's first experience of one. Miss Philps was not a recluse. Everywhere Mrs. Coombe went, Miss Philps went too. Even Esther was not more assiduous in her attentions. She was not a silent person either, far from it. She bubbled over with precise and cheerful comment, she appeared to talk even more than was absolutely necessary and it was only upon her departure that her entertainers noticed that she had said nothing at all. A very baffling person to deal with. Coombe could not manage to "take to" her at all and great sympathy was felt for Mrs. Coombe when she was reported to have said to Miss Milligan that going out with Miss Philps felt exactly like a jail delivery—whatever that might be!

But if Miss Philps was not appreciated at large it was different in her own immediate circle. She had not been at the Elms a day before Esther recognised the doctor's wisdom in getting her. She was discreet, capable, kindly. The burden upon the girl's shoulders grew momentarily lighter. Miss Philps, with her matter of fact cheeriness, her strength and her experience, was exactly what that house of overstrained nerves needed.

"Dear me," she said, "you're all as fidgety as corn in a popper. And no need for it. I've nursed dozens worse than your mother, Miss Esther, and had them right as a trivet before I got through. As long as we can keep her hands off the stuff—and that's what I'm here for. So don't worry!"

Esther drew a deep breath. It was certainly good to feel the strain lifting, to have time for dreams again. The time was so pitifully short now. Two more weeks and she would leave Coombe behind her. The old life would be definitely over and done with. Looking back, she could see that it had been a happy life, and the future looked so dark. In youth, all life's happenings seem so terribly final. Every parting feels like a parting forever. Esther felt quite sure that she would never return to Coombe.

In the week before the wedding, freed from her continual attendance upon her mother, she unobtrusively paid farewell to all her old haunts and favourite places. It was a sweet sadness. She did not taste the sweet, but it was there. As one grows older, one does not linger over sad moments. It is because the sweet has vanished, only the bitter remains. But in untried youth sadness has a touch of beauty, a glamour of romance which shrouds its deepest pain. It is as if something within us, infinitely wise, were smiling, knowing well that for the young there is always to-morrow.

The maple by the schoolhouse turned early that year. When Esther, in her pilgrimage, came to say good-bye it welcomed her with all the glory of autumn. Against its greener brothers it stood out, naming, defiant. Beside it, the red pump seemed no longer red. Red and yellow, its falling leaves tossed themselves into the girl's lap as she sat upon the porch steps. It is almost certain that, as Esther gathered them, she compared her sad heart to a leaf which had fluttered from the tree of happy life. There seemed no outlook for her. She could not see through winter into spring.

The school children with their new teacher (whom Esther could not help but feel was sadly incompetent) had all gone home and it was very quiet on the porch steps. She closed her eyes and dreamed and clearly through her dream she heard, as she had heard that first morning in early summer, a determinedly cheerful, yet husky, voice singing. Some one was coming down the hill.

"From Wimbleton to Wombleton is fifteen miles;
From Wombleton to Wimbleton is fifteen miles;
From Wimbleton to Wombleton, from Wombleton to

Wimbleton,
    From Wimbleton to Wombleton,—"

The song trailed off into silence as it had done before. The girl's closed eyes smarted with tears—"Oh, it is a very long way!" she murmured, and burying her face in fallen leaves she felt that at last she knew the meaning of despair.

But though his voice had echoed through Esther's dream, Callandar was not on the long hill nor anywhere near it. Unlike Esther, he paid no farewells during these last days. He avoided the hill particularly and drove past the schoolhouse seldom and always at top speed. If the sight of the turning maples moved him at all it was not because he compared his lost happiness to a fallen leaf. Callandar was long past such gentle sadnesses as these. Every day he filled as full of work as possible. He walked far and hard in hope of tiring himself into dreamless sleep at night. And every day his face grew older, greyer, more sternly set.

At the very last, and as if inspired by some special imp of the perverse, Mary declared that she must have a church wedding. Opposition was useless. With all the distorted force of her drug-ridden brain, she desired this one thing. She wept, she coaxed, she raved. Every woman, she stormed, had a right to a proper wedding. She had always been cheated, she had been a pawn shoved about at the bidding of others, her own wishes never consulted. Was there any reason, any reason at all, why she should not be properly married in the church?

He ventured quietly to remind her that there were peculiar circumstances in the case. But she burst out at that. He was ashamed of her. Ashamed of his own wife. If there were peculiar circumstances whose fault were they? Not hers, surely? Would she be where she was now if he had not neglected her all those years? Anyway, peculiar circumstances or not, she would be married decently or she would not be married at all.

With set lips, the doctor gave in. Opposition maddened her, and, after all, one farce more or less could not matter much.

"Very well," he said, "make your own arrangements."

Immediately, Mary became amiable. She was quite polite to Miss Philps, almost pleasant to Esther. Into the preparations for the wedding she entered with some of her old spasmodic energy. The occasion, she determined, should be a talked of one in Coombe. She made plans, a fresh one every day, and talked of them continually.

Only—there was one plan of which she did not speak. There was one unsaid thing which matured quietly, covered by the noise of much talking.

Yet this plan more than any other would have to do with the success of her last appearance in Coombe. It would be foolish indeed, she decided, to let any promise, however well-meant, stand in the way of this success. She could not, and would not, face a crowded church feeling as she felt now. That was absurd! She would need some little stimulant to help her carry it off. A very slightly increased dose would do it. Only sufficient to banish that horrible craving, to give her a long, satisfying sleep and then just a touch more, very little, to brace her in the morning. Enough to send warm tingling thrills of well being through her tired body, to brighten her eyes, to clear her brain and steady her shaking nerves—to make her young again, young and a bride.

Only this once! Never again.

Of what use to continue the sophistries which justified her treachery to herself! Perhaps of the three it was she who suffered most during that last week. She lived in an agony of anticipation, a hell of desire for which a sane pen has no description. Yet no one must suspect that she anticipated or desired anything—not the cool-eyed Miss Philps, not Esther, not the doctor, not even Jane. The mask must not slip for one single moment. So far, they suspected nothing; but they were always on their guard, always. A careless look, an unconsidered movement might betray her, and then—! She raved in her room sometimes when she thought of a possible balking of her purpose.

She was very clever. She still had self-control when it was necessary to have it in the furtherance of the one devouring passion. Only when she was quite alone did she ever give way. The doctor thought her wonderfully docile and took heart of hope. A month or two alone with her in Prance and all would be well. In the meantime, patience! Naturally she was full of childish whims. He smiled at her indulgently when she asked him to request Miss Philps to stay outside of the fitting room at Miss Milligan's. "For you know," she said, "it is bad luck, very bad luck, for any person to see one, in one's wedding gown before the proper time. And anyway," the grey eyes filled with easy tears, "I'm sure it isn't good for me never to be trusted, not even with silly Miss Milligan."

The plea seemed genuine. It was like Mary to be concerned about the wedding-dress superstition. And what possible danger could there be? Miss Milligan in all probability had never heard the fatal names of opium and cocaine save as unpleasant things associated with Chinese and tooth-drawing. It was absurd to imagine Mary coming to harm there.

From this you will see that, upon the occasion of the last discovery, Mary had lied desperately and well. The "cache" in the bird-house had been found, but Miss Milligan's name had never been connected in the most remote way with that relapse. Mary had sworn that the new supply had not been new at all but had formed part of an old cache which she had hidden, in a place which even she had forgotten, all quite accidentally. And although many supplementary enquiries were made, the real truth had remained undiscovered.

So in the simplest way in the world, Mary secured several uninterrupted "fittings" with Miss Milligan while the excellent Miss Philps sat without and waited.

"This is positively the last time I shall have to trouble you, dear Miss Milligan," said her customer sweetly. "Of course, as soon as we are married, I am going to tell Dr. Callandar all about it and when he sees how very much better my medicine has made me, he will be quite ready to withdraw his objections. In the meantime I am sure you feel, as I do, that our little ruse has been quite justifiable!"

Miss Milligan did. She felt quite proud of her part in it. It is something to help a fellow woman and still more to get the better of a fellow man. Especially such a celebrated man as Dr. Callandar! She would order the fresh supply at once, that very afternoon, by the first mail. And as soon as the packet came she would see that Mrs. Coombe had it in person. "There is certain to be a few last touches necessary to the dress after it has been sent home," she remarked with a smile of truly Machiavellian subtlety.

"Yes!" said Mary. "That night—after the dress comes home!" She spoke sharply, unnaturally. Her face turned a dull, pasty white. She shook so that Miss Milligan was thoroughly frightened. But presently she controlled herself and forced a pathetic smile.

"You see, dear Miss Milligan, how much I need it."

"Indeed a blind bat could see that!" said the dressmaker pityingly. "Shall I call the nurse?"

But Mrs. Coombe would not hear of Miss Milligan calling the nurse!

CHAPTER XXXIII

It is the onlooker who sees most of the game and Aunt Amy was an ideal onlooker. Always self-effacing and silent, she was now more silent and self-effacing still. Consequently the principal actors tended to forget their parts when in her presence. No one explained anything to Aunt Amy but no one concealed anything from her. She simply "didn't matter." So far as the playing out of the little drama was concerned, Aunt Amy was supposed to be safely off the stage. She looked and listened, had her strange flashes of psychic insight and came to her own conclusions about it all, quite undisturbed by facts as they appeared to others. Her conclusions were very simple. Esther loved the doctor. The doctor loved Esther. That, in spite of this, Callandar was deliberately planning to marry Mary she considered a purely arbitrary matter arranged by those mysteriously malignant powers known as "They." Callandar, himself, had clearly no choice, Esther was helpless, and Mary triumphed easily and inevitably because Mary was one of "Them" herself. Aunt Amy had become firmly convinced of this latter fact. Everything went to prove it—the theft of the ring, the threat to shut her (Amy) up, the easy triumph over Esther, and a thousand and one trifles all "confirmation strong as proofs of holy writ." Of course it would be impossible to make this clear to Esther or the doctor. Amy realised that and did not try. But in her own mind she thought of it continually. And her little pile of proof mounted higher day by day.

Esther, absorbed in the care of her step-mother, was not even aware that Aunt Amy noticed her growing listlessness, her heavy eyes, her fits of brooding. She did not know that a silent foot paused before her closed door, listening. All she knew was that it was relief unspeakable to be with Aunt Amy, to let drop the mask of cheerful energy without fear of questioning or of wonder. Aunt Amy didn't matter.

Mary, too, felt that it was needless to hoodwink Amy. No need to pretend with her. She might show herself as irritable, as conscienceless, as nerve-racked and disagreeable as she chose without fear of displaying "symptoms." Aunt Amy was not looking for symptoms, indeed Mary thought she grew more stupid daily. After her marriage something would really have to be done about Amy. She hoped the doctor wouldn't be silly about it.

Even Dr. Callandar was not careful to hide his burden from those faded eyes. He was more self-conscious even with Ann or Bubble than he was with her. What matter if she did see his mouth harden or his eyes burn?— Poor Aunt Amy, such things could have no meaning for her. She was a soul apart.

A soul apart indeed, how far apart none of them quite realised; yet near enough to love—and hate. As the days went by and Esther drooped like a graceful plant athirst for water there grew in Aunt Amy's twisted brain a slow corroding anger. The timid, bitter anger of a weak nature which is often more deadly than the lordly passion of the strong.

If she could only do something. If she could only outwit "Them"! She would do anything at all, if she could only find the thing to do. It was terrible to be so helpless. It was maddening to have to be so careful. Yet careful she must be, she never forgot that. Often as she went about the house or stood in the sunny kitchen rolling out her flaky pie-crust, she pondered over ways and means. But none seemed suitable. Some of her plans were fantastic to a degree, but she always had sense enough to reject them in the end. In her planning she was conscious of no sense of right or wrong but only of suitability. There could be no question of right or wrong in dealing with "Them." They were outside the pale. No. What she wanted was something simple and effective. A little poison, now—in a pie? But Amy knew nothing of poison, nor how to obtain any, nor how to use it effectively in a pie when once obtained. She might consult the doctor perhaps? But something warned Aunt Amy that the doctor would not take kindly to the idea of a little poison in a pie. So this beautiful scheme had to be given up. She sighed.

"What a big sigh, Auntie!" Esther, who was sitting at the table peeling apples, looked up questioningly. "A penny for your thoughts."

A look of cunning came over Aunt Amy's face. And instead of speaking her real thoughts she said, "I was thinking of weddings, Esther."

"But why the sigh?"

"I don't like weddings. Once there was a young girl going to be married. She was very happy. She was so happy that she was afraid to look at her own face in the glass. And it was eleven o'clock on Tuesday. I mean she was waiting for eleven o'clock on Tuesday. She was to be married then. But just one minute before the time, something happened—the clock stopped, I think. Anyway eleven o'clock on Tuesday never came. So she could not get married. And she grew old and her flowers fell to pieces. It was very sad."

"Poor Auntie!"

Aunt Amy moved uneasily. "Do you know who the girl was, Esther?"

"Don't you know, Auntie?"

"No, that is, I am never sure. Sometimes I think I used to know her. But she's gone. I never see her now. I'd like to find her if I could."

"You will find her some day, Auntie. Try not to fret about it."

It was seldom indeed that Aunt Amy spoke even thus vaguely of that other self of hers which she had lost in the tragedy of her youth. Esther's heart was full of pity as she listened. What was her own trouble compared to this? She at least would have her memories.

"There is just one chance," went on Aunt Amy, now gently excited. She had never spoken of this chance before but she felt that Esther might like to hear of it. "Just one chance! You see, the world being round—the world is round, isn't it, Esther?"

"Yes."

"Well, the world being round there is a chance that, if she waits long enough, eleven o'clock on Tuesday may come around again. Then if she is ready and if she has the ring he gave her, the red ring, and if they are both very quick they may be married after all."

"Oh, Aunt Amy, *dear*! That is why you love the ruby ring?"

But the old lady's memory was clouding again. She looked bewildered and would say no more. Esther kissed her with new tenderness. "I am so glad you have it safely back," she whispered. "You need never be afraid of losing it again."

Aunt Amy found it hard to make the pies that morning. She was enveloped in a deep sadness, a sadness which in some misunderstood way seemed inseparable from the idea of that lost friend of hers, the girl-bride whose marriage hour had never struck. It seemed to Aunt Amy that the girl had been waiting a very long time and was tired. Even if the world were round, it was a very big world and eleven o'clock on Tuesday took a wearisome time to travel around it. She could not understand why she should feel so terribly sorry for the waiting girl, but she did. A hot tear fell into the pie-crust. That would never do! The pie-maker furtively dried her eyes and came back to the consideration of more immediate problems.

It may seem strange that no one noticed the morbid state of Aunt Amy at this time. But it would have been more strange if any one had noticed it. Of outward signs there were practically none. Even the silent hand-wringing had ceased. She ceased to rebuke Jane for stepping upon the third stair; she ceased to talk of the peculiarities inherent in sprigged china. She was more and more careful not to mention "Them," and, as always, her housekeeping was a wonder and a delight.

She even offered to make Mary's wedding-cake. An offer which Mary received graciously. No one could make fruit cake like Aunt Amy and if it proved too big for the house oven the baker could bake it in his. Jane was delighted. She told Bubble that it was to be a "hugeous" cake, the like of which was never seen in Coombe and she defied Ann to produce any relative or ancestor whatever whose wedding-cake had even faintly approached such dimensions. Ann retorted that big wedding-cakes were vulgar and that her Aunt Sykes did not think it proper for a widow woman to have a wedding-cake at all.

The making of the cake was a great mental help to Aunt Amy. It seemed to ease her mind and aid her to think clearly. She thought of many things as she prepared the materials, made most clever plans. That all the plans had to do with the preventing of the marriage and the final circumventing of "Them" goes without saying. There was one especially good plan which came to her while she stoned the raisins. Still another, while the currants were being looked over, and a third, more brilliant than either, while she chopped the candied peel. The trouble was that when she came to mix all her ingredients into the batter, her plans began to mix up too, until all was hopeless confusion. It was most disheartening! And the wedding, now, only a few days off. She wanted to go away into a corner and wring her hands, but if she did, some one might notice—and then "They" would have the chance they were looking for. Aunt Amy was too clever for that!

CHAPTER XXXIV

The day before the wedding, the wedding dress came home. No one had seen it. Mary's superstition in regard to this point was indulgently smiled at by everybody.

"But hadn't I better see it on you just once," suggested Esther. "Some trifle may have been forgotten and a missing hook and eye might spoil the effect of the whole thing."

"Oh, I have thought of that. Miss Milligan is going to run in after supper to see that everything is right. Then if anything is needed she can attend to it at once. Of course, it doesn't matter about Miss Milligan seeing it—for bad luck I mean."

"How about me?" asked Callandar, smiling.

"You!" with a playful shriek, "you would be worse than anybody. You would hoodoo it entirely!"

"How about little girls?" asked Jane coaxingly.

Mary turned suddenly peevish. "Don't bother me, Jane. I shall not let any one see it and that's enough." But their combined suggestions had disturbed her, and it was only upon their serious assurance that of course her wishes would be respected that her amiability returned.

Yet it was apparent that she felt rather worried about the dress herself for she had worked herself into a small fever of nervous anxiety before the promised appearance of Miss Milligan for the last fitting. When at last that lady arrived, a trifle late, and very much out of breath, Mary would hardly let her say good evening to the others, before hurrying her upstairs.

"And I think," said she hesitatingly, "that I shan't come down again to-night. I am tired. If the doctor calls in, tell him that I am trying to get a good rest for to-morrow. Good night, Miss Philps. Good night, Esther!"

To the girl's astonishment she kissed her. A light, hot kiss which fell on her cheek like a fleck of glowing ash. Yet it was a real kiss and may have meant that the giver was not ungrateful. Jane, too, had a good night kiss that night; but Aunt Amy had already gone upstairs.

"Well?" They were safely in the upstairs room now and the door was closed.

"I've got it. It came on the afternoon mail. I went down to the post office specially. I knew you kind of counted on it for to-morrow."

With the glee of a child playing conspirator Miss Milligan dived into the recesses of the reticule she carried. "Here it is. No, that's peppermints. But it's here somewhere—"

"Oh, hurry!" Mary almost snatched the packet from the friendly hand. At sight of it she turned deathly white and began to shake as she had shaken that day in the fitting-room. But this time she recovered quickly, almost before Miss Milligan had noticed it.

"Thank you so much," she said. With the last effort of her self-control she forced herself to place the packet upon the dresser. She wanted to snatch at it to tear it open, to scream with the relief of the tablets in her hand, but she did none of these things. Instead she thanked Miss Milligan again and proceeded to talk of other things, anything that would do to fill up the short time necessary to conceal the real purpose of the visit so that Esther and Miss Philps would not suspect—never for a moment suspect!

"Do you think we really need try on the dress?" asked the conscientious Miss Milligan.

Mrs. Coombe thought not. It was quite all right, she felt sure of that. And really she was a little tired. It had been a trying day. She moistened her lips and tried to smile, keeping her eyes well away from the tempting heaven in the little pasteboard box. Would the woman never go!

Fortunately Miss Milligan was a lady who prided herself upon her good sense and also upon her proper pride. She always knew, she declared, when she was not wanted, and, strange as it may seem, it began to dawn upon her that this was one of those rare occasions. Mrs. Coombe was very pleasant, of course, but Miss Milligan missed something, a certain cordiality which might have tempted her to prolong her stay. She was not offended, for if she considered that her self-denying journeys to the post office were meeting with less than their just deserts, she was not a woman to insist upon gratitude where gratitude was not freely given. She stayed therefore no longer than the fiction of dress-fitting required and then with a somewhat strained "good night" passed down the stairs and out of the house.

Mary waited, rigid as a statue, until she heard the front gate close, then, the last defence down, she sprang to the dressing table—tearing off the paper from the package as a puppy dog might tear the covering from a bone. A glass of water stood ready. Her shaking hands reached for it, counted the number of tablets and slipped them in. Then, with a long breath of relief, the tension relaxed. She raised her eyes, triumphing eyes, to the mirror and saw—Aunt Amy watching her from the doorway.

She had forgotten to lock the door!

But it was only Aunt Amy.

Fear and relief came in almost the same breath. She steadied herself against the dresser.

"Shut the door!"

Aunt Amy obeyed. But she shut herself inside the door. "What do you want?" Mary never wasted words on Amy—"Ah!"

With a motion so swift that it seemed like a conjuror's miracle, Aunt Amy had slipped from her stand by the door, snatched up the open box, and was back again before the choking cry on the other's lips had formed itself.

"Esther says you musn't take these," said Aunt Amy in her colourless voice.

For a second Mary hesitated. If she made the murderous spring which every baffled nerve in her tortured body urged her to make, Amy would scream. A scream would mean, Miss Philps—Esther—the doctor: agony and defeat. With a mighty effort she held herself. She tried to speak quietly.

"Don't be a fool, Amy. This is some medicine the doctor gave me himself. Hand it to me at once."

Aunt Amy smiled. It was a sly little smile. It made Mary want to rave, for it said more plainly than words that Aunt Amy knew. Swiftly she changed her tactics. Her face softened, became gentle, entreating—

"Amy—dear. I am only going to use a little. If you love me, give me the box."

Useless! Aunt Amy still smiled. She put the box behind her. With her other hand she felt for the door knob.

"Amy, give it to me! What have I ever done to you?"

"You stole my ring." In exactly the same tone she might have said, "You are a murderess."

The ring! Mary had forgotten the ring. Wait, perhaps it was not hopeless even yet. Amy placed an absurd value on that ring—and she, Mary, had the gem in her possession. She did not know that Esther had found and restored it. To her it was still in the box at the bottom of her drawer. A dazzling plan flashed through her excited brain. She would bribe Amy with the ring. The thought nerved her.

"Do you really want your ring back?" she asked sweetly.

Aunt Amy paused with her hands on the door knob.

"I have it back."

"Oh, no. You haven't. It is in a box in my drawer."

"It is not. Esther gave it to me!" But there was a spark of fear in Amy's eyes. Contradiction so easily confused her. *Had* Esther given her the ring? She felt oddly uncertain.

Mary laughed, and the laugh increased Aunt Amy's confusion. After all it was quite possible that Mary had taken the ring again. It had been locked away and hidden, but locks and hiding-places were never an obstacle to "Them."

"I've got it safe enough!" taunted Mary, tormentingly.

The spark of fear flamed. Amy took a swift step forward. "Give it to me!"

"Give me the box—and I will."

Aunt Amy had ceased to care about the box. Almost she placed it in the outstretched hand, then, with quick cunning, caught it back.

"The ring first."

Mary shrugged her shoulders. She felt cool enough now. It was going to be easy. She turned to the bureau and began to pull things out of the drawer, scattering them anywhere. She could not remember exactly where she had put the ring. As she searched, she talked.

"There is nothing to be tragic about," she said. "I intended to give you your ring anyway—some day. And the medicine is nothing that will hurt. It is only something to make me sleep so that I shan't look a sight to-morrow. I am taking only a little. No one will know. I shall not even oversleep. But if Esther or any of them knew, they would make a fuss. You must promise not to tell them—before I give you the ring. Just tell Esther that I do not want to be disturbed early. I'll wake myself, in plenty of time for the wedding."

"In plenty of time for the wedding!" For a moment Amy wondered what it was about the phrase which sounded familiar? Then she seemed to see, as in a dream, the vision of a young girl all in white, with flowers in her hands, sitting alone in a room waiting, watching a clock—a clock which never quite came round to the hour of eleven on Tuesday. Time has a great deal to do with weddings, evidently. People who wish to be married must be ready at the fateful moment, otherwise they have to wait—forever, perhaps. "Plenty of time"—suddenly a flash of direct inspiration seemed to coordinate her scattered faculties. She saw clearly a plan, a beautiful, simple plan to prevent the marriage. What if Mary should *not* wake in plenty of time for the wedding? What if the hour, the wedding hour, should not find her ready? The thing was so simple! If one tablet would make Mary sleep, two would make her sleep longer. For the moment she forgot even the ruby ring in her childish pleasure at such a clever idea. Her worn face was lit by a satisfied smile as she swiftly, quietly dropped more tablets from the box into the glass—one—two—she was not quite sure how many!

"Here is the ring," said Mary turning at last from the disturbed drawer with a cardboard box in her hand. It was the box from which Esther had taken the ring long before, but Mary was in too great a hurry to open it. She did not doubt that it contained the ring. For once in her life Mary thought she was playing fair.

They completed the exchange in silence, Mary wondering a little at the pleasant change which she saw in Amy's face. But she was too hurried to enquire into the cause of it. She hardly waited to hear her promise not to tell Esther but fairly pushed her from the room. Then, secure behind her locked door, she wiped the perspiration from her forehead and sank exhausted into the nearest chair.

When her strength came back her first care was to hide the remaining tablets in a safe place in her travelling bag, she never intended to use them again, never! But it would do no harm to feel that she could trust herself to leave them alone, as of course she could. Then she loosened her hair, not pausing to brush it, and, slipping off her dress, wrapped herself in a certain flowered dressing gown. Not one of the dainty new ones, but a gown whose lace was yellowed and torn, a gown which felt like an old friend but which, after to-night, she would wear no more—

Listen! Was that some one at the door?

Only Miss Philps calling good-night. Mary answered "Good-night" in a sleepy voice, and the step passed on. It left her shaking like a leaf in the wind. What else indeed was she? A fluttering, fading leaf shaken in the teeth of a wind of dread and mad desire.

All was quiet now. She would be disturbed no more that night. Her shaking hands rattled the spoon which stirred the mixture in the glass. The familiar motion quieted her. Here, right in her hands, was peace, rest, a swift and magical release from the torment of appetite denied. To-morrow—but why think of to-morrow? She might be stronger then. Everything might be easier. All she really needed was a long night's sleep.

She turned out the light and throwing up the blind stood for a moment looking out into the soft moonlight. The moon was clear. It would be a beautiful day for the wedding! Smiling, she picked up the glass and with a whispered, "Here's to the bride!" raised it to her eager lips and drank.

Silence settled down upon the Elms. There was a harvest moon that night, a glorious rounded moon more golden than silver. The garden slumbered, wrapped in mellow light, even the shadows gleamed faintly luminous. The breeze, roaming at will, shook drowsy perfume from the lingering flowers, but for all it aped the summer it was unmistakably an autumn breeze, melancholy, earth-scented. It stirred the curtains at Mary's window; rustled through the great bowlful of crimson leaves upon Esther's writing table and softly stirred the dark hair of the girl as she sat with her face hidden in her curved arms. For a very long time she sat there while the moon looked in and looked away again and who can tell what her thoughts were, or if she thought at all.

By and by she rose and went to the window, looking out to where a month ago she had stood by the garden gate under the stars. It was drenched with moonlight now and the shadow under the elm tree was dark.

What was that? A darker shadow in the shadow? Esther's hand caught at the curtain, her heart gave a great leap and then grew still. She knew who stood there. This was the good-bye he could not speak. Tears fell unheeded down the girl's pale cheeks. If during those last days she had had any doubt of the love which loyalty to Mary had helped him hide so well, they were all swept away now. A warm spot grew and glowed in her heart and a line from that old immortal love lyric which she had learned in her school days came back vivid with eternal truth.

> "I had not loved thee, dear, so much
> Loved I not honour more."

CHAPTER XXXV

It was a perfect day for the wedding. Autumn at her brightest and gayest before her new bright robes began to brown. Soft air, mellow sun, cool-lipped breeze, horizon veiled in tinted mist—a gem of a day, the jewel of a season.

"Them as has, gets," murmured Mrs. Sykes, gloomily, as she tied on her Sunday bonnet. She rather resented the kindness of nature upon this present occasion. A nice rain would have suited her mood better.

Nevertheless, much as her mind misgave her in regard to the wedding, she was early on her way to the Elms to see if she could help.

"They're sure to be flustrated," she told herself. "Aunt Amy's just as likely as not to lose what little bit of head she has and hired help are broken reeds. Esther will have the brunt of it. She'll be glad enough to see me, I'll be bound."

Do not imagine that Mrs. Sykes was curious. Curiosity was a failing which she systematically repudiated. But she was a very helpful person and it was wonderful how many opportunities of helpfulness she found upon solemn or joyous occasions. If, while helping, her ears were open, and her eyes shrewd, can she be blamed for that? There may be people with ears who hear not but they do not live in Coombe. The only difficulty is to manage to be, like Mr. Micawber, on the spot.

Mrs. Sykes was early, but not too early. When she slipped in at the side door there was already a stir of unusual movement in the house but the final flutter was still measurably distant. Jane dashed past with crimped hair and white ribbons flying. Miss Philps, very stately in a new gown, was arranging flowers in geometrical patterns. Dr. Callandar, self-possessed as ever, talked upon the veranda with Professor Willits who had arrived the night before. Aunt Amy was busy in the kitchen. Esther, flushed and excited, with eyes that flashed blue fire, seemed everywhere at once.

"Oh, Mrs. Sykes," she exclaimed, "how nice of you to come! Won't you please get Jane and tie her up—her ribbons, I mean? It is almost time to dress."

"Would you like me to assist?" asked Miss Philps, looking up from a geometrical pattern.

"Oh, thanks, Miss Philps. There are some hooks I cannot manage. But mother will probably need a lot of help. I thought you were with her now."

"No. She has not yet sent for me." Miss Philps drew out her watch and consulted it. "Dear me!" with slight surprise, "it is much later than I thought. Perhaps I had better go up."

Esther looked worried. "I believe you had—if she hurries at the last she will be terribly excited. Aunt Amy told me she wished particularly not to be disturbed this morning, but surely she has forgotten how late it is getting."

"I'll go up," said Miss Philps. "It's time for her tonic anyway, and we must persuade her to eat something. When you are ready for me to hook your dress, call. I can easily manage you both."

This is all that Mrs. Sykes heard, for just then Jane flew by again like a returning comet and had to be captured and properly tied up. Mrs. Sykes, as she admitted herself, was no hand at fancy fixings but she was painstaking and conscientious and the bow-tying absorbed all her energies. She was getting on very well and had almost succeeded in adjusting the last bow when a cry from the room above startled her into the tying of a double knot.

"What was that?"

It was not a loud cry—but there was something in it which brought Mrs. Sykes' heart leaping into her throat, which sent Esther reeling against the stair baluster, which brought the doctor, white-faced from the veranda—it was the kind of cry which carries in its note the psychic essence of terror and disaster.

Mrs. Sykes for all her iron nerve felt suddenly faint. Jane began to cry. The doctor and Esther had raced up the stairs. But there was no repetition of the cry. Instead there was silence. Then a murmur of voices and sounds of ordered activity overhead.

Clearly something had happened. But what? Mrs. Sykes wanted very much to go and see. But the glimpse she had caught of Callandar's eyes as he sprang to the stair, the look of white horror in Esther's face as she followed him, and above all, that strange terrifying Something in the cry she had heard seemed to discourage enquiry. The good lady turned her attention to the comforting of Jane. After all, if she waited long enough she could hardly help hearing all about it. At first hand, too.

It seemed a long time that she waited. Miss Philps came up and down the stairs several times but she did not appear to see Mrs. Sykes. Jane stopped crying and wandered out into the garden. Still Mrs. Sykes waited and presently Aunt Amy came in, looking quite excited and asked eagerly what time it was. Mrs. Sykes told her, adding with asperity that these were fine goings-on, and that they'd all be late for the wedding if they didn't hurry up.

"Yes, I think they will. I'm almost sure they will," said Aunt Amy, and she laughed as a child laughs when it is greatly pleased.

"Dear me, she is much madder than I thought," murmured Mrs. Sykes. "Whatever is the matter? What are they doing?" she asked in a louder tone.

Aunt Amy raised a finger, "Hush! she's asleep. Let us tidy up the room. I don't think she is going to wake up for a long time yet. And then she'll have to wait till the world goes round again."

"Well of all the—" began Mrs. Sykes, but she was interrupted by the entrance of Professor Willits. With the virtuous air of one who strictly minds her own business she began to tie her bonnet strings.

"Don't go, Mrs. Sykes," said the professor gravely. "I think—I'm afraid you may be needed."

"I hope nothing serious has happened?" faltered Mrs. Sykes, now thoroughly disturbed, but he did not seem to hear her. He was listening intently to the sounds overhead. They were very slight sounds now and presently they ceased altogether. Willits looked more anxious. Then, in the midst of a new, heavier silence, Dr. Callandar himself came down the stairs.

At first sight he appeared almost as usual. He did not notice Mrs. Sykes but went straight across the room to Willits.

"Nothing—any use—" he began haltingly. Then suddenly the words ceased to come. His lips moved but there was no sound. With an expression of intense surprise he lifted his hand to his head, and swayed awkwardly into the nearest chair.

"Land sakes, look out! he's going to fall," cried Mrs. Sykes in terror.

"Breakdown," said the professor briefly. "I expected something of the kind. Help me to get him to the car."

"Oh, Land, Land," moaned; Mrs. Sykes, "whatever"—but realising that the time for questioning was not yet, she did what she was told without more words.

"Better send for Dr. Parker," said Willits crisply to Miss Philps who had come in quietly. "Better tell the minister, too. Keep the little girl down stairs. I'll be back as soon as I can. Mrs. Sykes, I shall want you to come with me."

"Oh, Land—" but she got no further, the car was off like the wind.

Later when the doctor had been put to bed like a child and telegrams dispatched which would bring a specialist and a nurse on the afternoon train, the good lady drew a long breath and decided that she couldn't "last out" a moment longer.

Drawing Willits from the room her questions burst forth in their unstemmed torrent.

The tall man listened at first in bewilderment. Then, as the true inwardness of the case dawned on him, a look which was almost admiration came over his angular countenance.

"Why, Mrs. Sykes," he said, "is it possible that you do not know? I would have told you before but I took your knowledge for granted. The poor lady whom my friend was to marry was found dead in her bed. She died during the night. An overdose of sleeping powder."

CHAPTER XXXVI

Autumn that year was short and golden. Winter came early. In November it stormed, thawed, stormed again and began to freeze in earnest. The frost bit deeply but one night when its grip was sure, the temperature rose a little and snow began to fall. For days and nights it snowed, softly, steadily, without wind, and then the clouds parted and the sun shone out—a far off sun in a sky as blue as summer and cold as polar seas. The air tingled and snapped with frost. In the azure cup of the sunlit sky it sparkled like golden wine, and, like wine, it thrilled and strengthened. People stamped their feet and beat their hands to keep warm but smiled the while and murmured: "Glorious!"

So much for the weather—since it was the weather which became the main factor in helping Coombe forget the tragedy at the Elms. Wonder is no nine-day affair in Coombe. One sensation is carefully conserved until the next one comes along, but in this case the early winter with its complete change of interests, its sleighing, skating and snow-shoeing, its reawakening of business and social bustle proved a distraction almost as effective as battle, murder or sudden death. The talk died down, the interest slackened, and the principal actors were once more permitted to become normal persons living in a normal world.

For a time it had seemed that this desired condition would never be obtained. Coombe had felt the breath of a mystery. It was supposed to know everything and suspected that it knew nothing—a state of things aggravating to any well regulated community.

There had been an inquest, of course, and at the inquest the whole sad affair was supposed to have been made plain. It was simplicity itself. Simplicity, in fact, was its most annoying characteristic. Mrs. Coombe, it appeared, had been for a long time somewhat of a sufferer from an obscure trouble, referred to generally as "nerves." For the relief of this trouble, one of whose symptoms was insomnia, she had, from time to time, had recourse to narcotics which, as everyone knows, are dangerous, if not, as many thought, positively immoral. Undoubtedly the poor lady had died from an overdose. It was easy, the coroner said, for a sympathetic mind to reconstruct the details of the terrible occurrence. It was the night before the wedding and the deceased had retired early. Miss Milligan, who had run in for a last look at the wedding gown, and who had been the very last person to see and speak with her, deposed that she had appeared more than ordinarily tired and seemed anxious to be alone. Asked if she detected any other signs of disordered nerves the witness had said, no. The deceased had not appeared worried about anything? No. The wedding gown had been quite satisfactory? Quite.

No more questions were asked and Miss Milligan had not thought it necessary to go into the matter of the getting of the nerve tonic. The dead woman's harmless little deception was safe in her hands. It hadn't anything to do with the case anyway. Although in her own heart Miss Milligan blamed Dr. Callandar severely for not allowing the poor woman to use her tonic constantly. Had he done so the final tragedy might never have happened. Needless to say this good lady never knew what she had done. The fact that Mary Coombe had been a drug victim under treatment did not come out at the inquest. The coroner knew, but he was a sensible man and a very kind one. It hardly needed the logical arguments of Miss Philps or the heart-broken entreaties of Esther to convince him that knowledge of this fact was not for the general public. The only legally necessary information was the cause of death and that was simple enough. Easily understood, too, for given a tendency to sleeplessness and the excitement incident to a wedding, what more natural than that the excited bride should have sought relief in her customary sleeping draught.

The mistake, the taking of a lethal dose, was, as all such mistakes are, inexplicable. Did her hand shake? Had she miscounted the number of tablets? Had she, in her nervous state, deliberately risked a larger dose whose danger she did not realise? These questions would never be answered. She had been alone in her room, nor was there a thread of evidence upon which to hang a theory. Esther, the nurse, Jane, Dr. Callandar (poor man!) had noticed nothing out of the ordinary when they had parted from her that last time. Aunt Amy's evidence was not taken. No one thought to question her and she volunteered no information. Of all the household at the Elms she was least disturbed by the tragedy, but, naturally, one does not expect the mentally weak to realise sorrow like ordinary people. This exemption was, as many did not fail to remark, one of their compensations. So in this, as in other things, Aunt Amy did not matter. She went her quiet way undisturbed, the one contented and peaceful person in that house of shock and horror.

Why, then, since all was so plain, did Coombe scent a mystery? It would be hard to say. Perhaps the curious behaviour of Dr. Callandar was partly responsible. When the news of his sudden breakdown became known the first natural comment was, "So, you see, he did love her after all." But, upon longer consideration this did not seem to meet the case. A man may be genuinely in love with a woman and yet not be stricken, as had the doctor, by her sudden death. Dimly, Coombe felt that there must be a cause behind the cause. Miss Sinclair, the eldest, even went so far as to quote Shakespeare to the effect that "men have died and the worms have eaten them, but not for love." True, the doctor was not dead but his illness was proving a very long and stubborn one. In its early stages he had been taken away to Toronto for special treatment and had been quite unable to see any one, even the minister, before he left. Mrs. Sykes alone, with the exception of the trained nurses, had laid eyes on him since his sudden collapse on the day of the wedding. And Mrs. Sykes, miraculously, had nothing to say.

It was rumoured, however, that his brain was affected, that he was paralysed, that he was deaf and blind, that he was dying of slow decline. Somehow the town felt that Mary Coombe, living or dead, did not loom large enough as a cause of such disintegration.

Esther's actions, too, were part of the puzzle. It had been confidently supposed that she would go away at once for a rest and change. Every one knew that the Hollises had offered to take her with them on a long trip to the Pacific Coast. But Esther had declined to go. She declined to go anywhere. Worn out as she was with strain and grief, she persisted in disregarding the advice of everybody. ("So headstrong in a young girl! But Doctor Coombe, her father, was always like that.") Apparently she intended to go on exactly as if nothing had happened and to all arguments said nothing save, "I think it will be best," or, "I am not fit for strange scenes just now," or something equally futile. Coombe was quite annoyed with Esther—so stubborn!

Only to Miss Annabel did the girl attempt to justify her attitude when that kind soul had exhausted persuasion and was inclined to feel both worried and hurt.

"Don't you see," she explained haltingly, "I can't go away. I don't want to. I can't make the effort. Here every one understands and will make allowances. I want to be quiet, to rest, to think. I want to get back to where I was before—if I can."

"Before what, my dear?"

"Before—everything! I can't explain. But I know it is the only way I shall ever be content. I want to take my school again and to go on working and looking after Jane and Aunt Amy. Although," with a little smile, "it is really Auntie who looks after Jane and me. Won't you help me, dear Miss Annabel? I am quite sure that this is the only thing to do."

"You are a strange girl, Esther. One would think you would be crazy to get away. Look at Angus! He's going. He has suddenly found out that a trip to the Holy Land is necessary if one is to speak intelligently upon many portions of the Bible. Absurd! But I never let him dream that I know that isn't his reason. And I hope you won't. It is all over now and the sooner he forgets the better. But I think even you are convinced, now, that I was right about—you know to what I refer!"

Esther murmured something indistinguishable and Miss Annabel departed much pleased with her own perspicacity. And she did help. She let it be known at the Ladies' Aid that she quite understood Esther and approved of her. After all, it was senseless to run away from trouble since trouble can run so much faster. And it was natural and right of Esther to feel that nowhere could she find so much sympathy and consideration as in her own town. Travelling was fatiguing anyway.

As for the school, that was easily arranged. A little discreet wire pulling and Esther was once more established as school mistress of District Number Fifteen. People shook their heads, but by the time of the first snowstorm they had ceased to prophesy nervous prostration, and by the time sleighing was fairly established they were ready to admit that the girl had acted sensibly after all.

No one guessed that there was another reason for Esther's refusal to go away. It was a simple reason and had to do with the fact that in Coombe the mails were sure and regular. Travellers miss letters and strange addresses are uncertain at best, but in Coombe there was small chance of any untoward accident befalling a certain weekly letter in the handwriting of Professor Willits. Esther lived upon these letters. Brief and dry though they were, they formed the motive power of her life and indeed it was from one of them that she had received the impetus which roused her from her first trance of grief and horror.

"My dear young lady (Willits had written).

"I believe that there are times when the truth is a good thing. It might be tactful to pretend that I do not know the real reason of Calendar's collapse but it would also be foolish. I think he is going to pull through. Now the question is—how about you? Are you going to be able to do your part?

"Let me be more explicit. It may be a long time before our friend is thoroughly re-established in health but it is quite probable that he will be well enough, and determined enough, to face some of his problems in the spring. He will turn to you. Are you going to be able to help him? When he comes to you will he find a silly, nervous girl, all horrors and regrets and useless might-have-beens or will he find you strong and sane, healthily poised, ready to face the future and let the dead past go? For the past is dead—believe me!

"You have seemed to me to be an excellently normal young person, but no doubt the shock and trouble of late events have done much to disturb your normality. Can you get it back? On the answer to that, depends Callandar's future. I shall keep you informed, weekly, of his progress."

Esther had thought deeply over this letter. Its brief, stern truth was exactly the tonic she needed. Like a strong hand it reached down into her direful pit of morbid musings, and, clinging to it, she struggled back into the sunlight. Above all and in spite of everything, she must not fail the man she loved!

At first she had to fight with terrors. She feared she knew not what. The vision of Mary upon the bed, still and ghastly in the golden light of morning, came back to shake her heart. The memory of Callandar's face, of the frantic struggle to drag the dead woman back to life, made many a night hideous. The endless questioning, Could it have been prevented? Could I have done more? tortured her, but by and by, as she faced them bravely, these terrors lost their baleful power. Her youth and common-sense triumphed.

The school helped. One cannot continue very morbid with a roomful of happy, noisy children to teach and keep in order. Jane's need of her helped, for she, dared not give way to brooding when the child was near. Aunt Amy helped—perhaps most of all. She was a constant wonder to the girl, so cheerful was she, so thoughtful of others, so forgetful of herself. Her little fancies seemed to have ceased to fret her, there was a new peace in her faded eyes. Sometimes as she went about the house she would sing a little, in a high thready voice, bits from songs that were popular in her youth. "The Blue Alsatian Mountains" or "When You and I Were Young, Maggie" or "Darling Nellie Grey." She told Esther that it was because she felt "safe." "The blackness hardly ever comes now," she said. "I don't think 'They' will bother me any more."

"Why?" asked Esther, curious.

But Aunt Amy did not seem to know why—or if she knew she never told.

CHAPTER XXXVII

A robin hopped upon the window sill of School-house Number Fifteen and peered cautiously into the room. He had no business there during lesson hours and the arrival of Mary's little lamb could not have been more disturbing. The children whispered, fidgeted, shuffled their feet and banged their slates.

"Perhaps they do not know it is spring," thought the robin and ruffling his red breast and swelling his throat he began to tell them.

"It is spring! It is spring! It is spring!"

The effect was electrical. Even the tall young teacher turned from her rows of figures on the blackboard.

"Come out! come out! come out!" sang the robin.

The teacher tapped sharply for order and the robin flew away. But the mischief was done. It was useless to tell them, "Only ten minutes more." Ten minutes—as well say ten years. The little fat boy in the front seat began to cry. A long sigh passed over the room. Ten minutes? The teacher consulted her watch, hesitated, and was lost.

"Close books," she ordered. "Attention. Ready—March." The jostling lines scrambled in some kind of order to the door and then broke into joyous riot. It was spring—and school was out!

Their teacher followed more slowly, pausing on the steps to breathe long and deeply the sweet spring air. In a corner by the steps there was still a tiny heap of shrinking snow, but in the open, the grass was green as emerald, violets and wind flowers pushed through the tangle of last year's leaves. The trees seemed shrouded in a fairy mist of green. Robins were everywhere.

The girl upon the steps was herself a vision of spring—the embodiment of youth and beautiful life. Coombe folks admitted that Esther Coombe had "got back her looks." Had they been less cautious they might have said much more, for the subtle change which had come to Esther, the change which marks the birth of womanhood, had left her infinitely more lovely.

From the pocket of the light coat she wore she brought forth a handful of crumbs and scattered them for the saucy robins and then, unwilling to hasten, sat down upon the steps to watch their cheerful wrangling. Peeling for more crumbs she drew out a letter—a single sheet covered with the crabbed handwriting of Professor Willits. At sight of it a soft flush stole over her face. She forgot the crumbs and the robins for, although her letter was two days old and she knew exactly what it contained, the very sight of the written words was joy to her. Like all Willits' notes it was short and to the point.

"Our friend has gone," she read. "We wanted to keep him for a month yet, but the robins called too loudly. He left no word of his destination, only a strange note saying that at last he was up the hill and over. May he find happiness, dear lady, on the other side."

One thing I notice—this recovery of his is different from his former recovery. If I were not afraid of lapsing into sentiment, I should say that he has achieved a soul cure. The morbid spot which troubled him so long is healed. A psychologist might explain it, but you and I must accept the result and be thankful. It is as if his subconscious self had removed a barrier and signalled 'Line clear—go ahead.' It is more than I had ever dared to hope.

>   Your friend,
>   E.P. Willits.

"P.S.: Are you ready?"

Esther looked at the postscript and smiled—that slow smile which lifted the corner of her lips so deliciously.

"May we wait for you, Teacher?"

"Not to-day, dears."

The children moved regretfully away. Presently the school yard was deserted. The busy robins had finished quarrelling over their crumbs and were holding a caucus around the red pump. In the quietness could be heard the gurgle of the spring rivulets on the hill.

Was there another sound on the hill, too? A far off whistling mingled with the gurgling water and twittering birds? Esther's hand tightened upon the letter—she leaned forward, listening intently. How loud the birds were! How confusing the sound of water! But now she caught the whistling again—

"From Wimbleton to Wombleton is fifteen miles" —

The familiar words formed themselves upon the girl's lips before the message of the tune reached her brain and brought her, breathless, to her feet. He was coming—so soon!

Panic seized her. Her hand flew to her heart—she would hide in the school-room, anywhere! Then she remembered Willits' postscript, the postscript which she had thought so needless. Her hand fell to her side. The panic died. Next moment, head high and eyes smiling, she walked down to the gate.

He was coming along the road under the budding elms—hatless, carrying a knapsack. His tweeds were splashed with mud from the spring roads, his face was thin, his hair was almost grey. Yet he came on like a conqueror and there was nothing old or tired in the bound wherewith he leaped the gate he would not pause to open.

"Esther!"

She looked up into his eyes and found them shadowless. Her own eyes veiled themselves,

Neither found anything to say.

But overhead a robin burst into heavenly song.